Shadow Shinjuku

Shadow Shinjuku, Volume 1

Ryu Takeshi

Published by Purple Crow Press, 2021.

SHADOW SHINJUKU

First edition. July 22, 2021.

Written by Ryu Takeshi.

Also by Ryu Takeshi

Shadow Shinjuku
Shadow Shinjuku
Abalone

Watch for more at https://www.ryutakeshi.com.

To my wife, daughter and dog.

Hundred-yen coin

Every time I look at Tokyo's lights from above, loneliness engulfs me. I see life resisting darkness down there, but I can't feel it. It's too far away. Even the sounds are muffled, and an endless sea rumbles between me and the ground below. Sometimes, I can see it, its shallow waves steadily rising and falling, and no reflections escaping the murky surface.

That night was no different, and after a few seconds, I had to turn away from the window. I wanted to light up, but I couldn't. New rules. I clenched my fists, and I looked around. Everything was made of concrete. Grey and cold. Only the dark green of the carpet struggled against the emptiness of the space. There was no light, just what leaked in through the windows, and the pallid red of the "EXIT" sign at the end of the corridor.

My watch showed half-past midnight. I had been waiting for nearly half an hour to see the boss. He liked to make people wait. Uncertainty was his favorite weapon, or rather the fear it created, and he used it with everyone, in every possible way. Like the desolate corridors in front of his office.

Finally, the door swung open:

'Please, come in,' Kobayashi-san said.

I put my hands in my pockets and walked in. I had a hundred-yen coin in my right pocket. I took it between my thumb and index finger and rubbed it gently.

As I reached the door, I stopped to look at the nameplate. "Akira Yamaguchi". Most people knew the name, and most people feared it. Even Kobayashi-san. I was one of the few who didn't. I feared something else.

'Come in, please,' Kobayashi-san told me again.

I looked at Yamaguchi's aging assistant, and our eyes met. He was in his eighties, but still lively and full of energy. We stood with our gazes fixed on each other for a while. The only sound I heard was the whirring of the aircon somewhere in the depths of the darkness. I felt as if I had already experienced those same eyes staring at me, with those same feelings flowing around us, within us. It felt familiar.

'Be careful,' Kobayashi-san said, shaking his head. I didn't respond. I just put my hand on his shoulder, squeezed it a little, and entered the room. Kobayashi-san closed the door behind me.

The office was bigger than my studio apartment, yet it somehow seemed vacant. Not the way it was or wasn't furnished, but rather how it felt. Actually, there was nothing to feel, and this nothingness soaked the floor, the ceiling, the walls, even the boss himself.

Boss Yamaguchi liked the traditional and the old. He had never truly accepted the modern age and its "things", and this was something we shared. He drove a black, '71 Nissan Skyline GT-R, he used a not-so-smart cellphone with buttons, and he had never had a computer. Whenever he could, he'd flee the city and spend time in the mountains. His grandfather was of samurai descent, both in spirit and behavior, and everything the boss knew and stood for he had learned from his grandfather – martial arts, inner balance, distance from others, discipline. He hated mistakes of any kind, he despised waste, and he expected perfection in all things.

His office reflected his personality. On one wall he had a single scroll with a lonely kanji which meant "loyalty". Underneath it, a long sword and a short sword lay on a stand. The opposite wall was bare, and in front, an evergreen bonsai stood in the middle of a small, round table. Black pine, I think. The floor was covered with tatami, and in the back, a large window offered an imposing view of the Emperor's palace.

The boss was sitting behind his desk, facing the window. He was watching the city. He was watching it live and breathe and die each night, only to be reborn the next morning. I couldn't see him, only the smoke of his cigarette as it kept climbing higher and higher.

'Too much light down there,' he said in his raspy voice. 'It confuses me.'

'Confuses?' I asked.

'It hides the true face of this world.'

He turned around and looked me in the eye. His eyes were as stern as ever. I had never seen a sign of weakness in them.

'Take one,' he said, holding out a box of cigarettes. He smoked red Marlboros.

'Thanks,' I replied, shaking my head. I took a small, golden case from my pocket with cigarettes I had rolled myself. They were the only cigarettes I smoked. I had one left, and I put it in my mouth.

Yamaguchi flicked his lighter, and I leaned forward and let him light my cigarette.

I took a deep drag, closed my eyes, kept the smoke in my lungs for a long time, and let it out as slowly as I could.

'Thanks,' I said again.

'Let's sit down,' he replied.

I took two pillows from the corner of the office, put them on the tatami, and we sat down, facing each other. He always sat so that the two swords were right behind him. He put the ashtray on the floor between us.

'Won't the alarm go off?' I asked.

'I had it turned off,' he replied.

'I see.' We both took another drag.

Yamaguchi pulled out an envelope from the inner pocket of his suit, took out the letter inside it, and unfolded it. His eyes moved from one kanji to the next as if he were reading them for the first time. He took another drag, looked at me, let the smoke out into my face and read the letter aloud:

'I want to be your personal bodyguard. Sato.'

He looked at me again, and I stared back at him. I didn't blink. I was looking for something in his eyes. Some sort of clue or sign.

I didn't quite know what, I just sensed that there was something I needed to discover and understand. I often had this feeling. A sense that I know that there is a deeper layer of truth and meaning, and from time to time, it reveals itself in the form of an image coming seemingly out of nowhere or a dream I wake up from, not knowing whether it was really a dream, but as soon as I reach out to touch it, it evaporates into thin air. Not a single piece of information, only a strange feeling of emptiness.

We finished our cigarettes and put the stubs in the ashtray. Yamaguchi immediately lit another one.

'Why?' he asked as he exhaled the smoke from his first drag.

'Money,' I said.

'Bullshit.'

I just kept staring at him without saying a word.

'You're a bad liar. You should know better.'

I took my tobacco kit from the back pocket of my jeans and started to roll a cigarette.

'The thing I like the most about you is your honesty,' he said. 'You always give me a straight answer, no matter what. The other thing I appreciate is your total lack of interest in money. So, don't bullshit me. I know you better than anyone in this fucking world.'

I licked the paper of the cigarette, finished rolling it, and leaned forward so he could light it.

'I need this. I can't tell you why. I don't even know. It's just a feeling.'

'A feeling.'

'Yes, a feeling. I've had it for a while.'

'Hm.'

'Give me a chance,' I said.

He put his cigarette in the ashtray, turned around, took the long sword from the stand, and turned back towards me. He let the sword rest in his palms, and he let his gaze wander all over it. They glowed, and it seemed like dozens of stories of old were taking shape within his eyes.

The sword was beautiful. Its case had a dark, shimmering lacquer with an intricate engraving of a golden dragon whose tail coiled around the full length of the blade. The "tsuba" was golden as well, and it had several little cherry flowers on top, colored in black. The handle was a simple combination of black and gold again.

Yamaguchi pulled the sword halfway from its sheath, and the blade caught the light, blinding me for a moment.

He then slid the sword back into its sheath and put it on the tatami.

'Do you still have it?' he asked.

I nodded.

'Tomorrow evening, ten o'clock, Aoyama-cemetery. Bring it.'

I nodded again and then bowed so low my forehead almost touched the tatami.

'Remember what I taught you,' he said, as I was about to leave. We looked each other in the eye again.

'I will.'

***

I took the elevator to the ground floor, rubbing the hundred-yen coin between my fingers in my pocket all the while. It was a strange elevator, with mirrors on all six sides – on the door, on the back panel, to the right, to the left, on the ceiling and on the floor. Every time I was in it, I felt like all my other selves in the mirrors, the endless rows, were not really me in the here and now, but me somewhere else, in some other time, maybe a different dimension. As if the elevator made it possible for all of us, for all of me to come together and face ourselves, face how close we were to one another, and yet how distant at the same time. It always made me realize I was this tiny little particle of barely visible dust covering a completely negligible piece of an infinite universe. I was nothing, a half-scribble in a footnote in a never-ending story, and though I was surrounded by the totality of everything which existed, I was still alone.

The hundred-yen coin was my magic tool; my way of pulling myself back into a state of mind where I felt I was worth something. I remember well the day I received it.

***

It was the 4th of July 1993. On the other side of the globe, people were waking up to a day when they would go on to eat millions of hamburgers and drink gallons of Coke in the name of independence. "The Firm" was finally dethroning "Jurassic Park" in the cinemas; Janet Jackson's "That's the way love goes" topped the Billboard 100; and Pete Sampras won his first ever Wimbledon title, beating Jim Courier in the final round. It must have been a beautiful Sunday for many people. For me... For me, it was just another day on the streets of Tokyo, with nowhere to sleep. The rain kept falling, people kept walking by without even sparing a look, and my head hurt like hell. At least it made me forget how hungry I was.

It's not entirely true that I didn't have anywhere to sleep. I *did* have my cardboard box, like all the other homeless people in the vicinity of the Tokyo Metropolitan Building in Shinjuku. Mine was the average size, I would say, but as I was only ten, it looked like I had more living space than the others. You could say I was well off. It's all relative, right?

I was sitting in my box, the lid open, waiting for the rain to stop so that I could go look for some food. There was a broad road running above our heads, and it gave us protection from rain, snow, and all that stuff. I hated sitting in that box and waiting. I hated the uselessness of the moment, the time passing, going to waste forever. I felt robbed.

I was staring silently at nothing, letting my misery gradually crush my will to bother, when I suddenly heard footsteps behind me. Not the usual sound of footsteps that I heard all the time as people trundled past. They had depth. Each time the sole of the shoes touched the ground, I felt a wave of energy hit me, and a chill went down my spine. I was hesitant to turn and look, but my curiosity got the better of my fear.

I saw two men. One in his early forties, the other maybe some fifteen years older. They walked slowly, as if they had the time on their side, unlike me. The older man had a large, black umbrella, which he was holding above their heads. The younger man was walking next to him with his hands in his pockets, and I immediately knew that the footsteps I had heard belonged to him.

When they reached my box, I looked up at them, and suddenly I could hardly breathe. Time seemed to have stopped. Even the raindrops seemed suspended in the air as if attached to invisible strings; the wind had gone silent, staring at us with wide-open eyes; and the street, which a moment earlier, had been humming with the drone of a car or two, was empty.

Each of the two men was dressed in a black suit. Their perfectly ironed shirts were of the whitest of whites, a stark contrast with the grey of the gloomy day. The guy with the umbrella was wearing a striped, grey tie and a black waistcoat, while the other had the top button of his shirt undone. I could smell their fine leather shoes. Leather that has been soaked in rain has a distinctive scent, a scent I've always adored. It's raw and natural.

The younger man didn't even seem to notice me, and he probably would've continued walking, his universe never colliding with the one I was living in. His companion, however, stopped, turned his head, and looked me straight in the eyes. The look on his face is engraved in my memory. It penetrated all my defenses, into the inner depths of my soul, and it turned something on. Like a switch. Something which had been off for years, I didn't even know it had existed, and now it was on. Just like that.

At that moment, time started to flow again.

'A child,' the older man said in a gentle voice. The younger one stopped and turned his head to look at me. Several seconds passed, and strong gusts of wind kept slapping my cheek. He then took a step closer, and I felt a cold shiver run down my spine. The hairs on my forearms stood up like little needles.

'How old are you?' the man with the umbrella asked.

I struggled to find my voice. I wasn't used to being asked questions.

'It's ok, you can tell us.'

'Ten, I think,' I murmured.

The younger man narrowed his eyes. The older one looked at him and then turned back to me again:

'You think?'

'I'm not sure. No one ever told me.'

'Your parents never told you how old you are?'

'No one at the orphanage did.'

'What are you doing out here?' the younger man asked, but in a voice that seemed to belong to someone much older than him. It was a voice unlike any I had ever heard. Wise, firm, and deep. Like a mountain.

'I escaped.'

'So?'

'So what?' I asked back.

'You haven't answered my question.'

I was confused and didn't know what to say.

'You escaped what, a month ago? Maybe even a year, or two years ago? It doesn't matter. What matters is why you are sitting in a cardboard box doing nothing and wasting your time. Did you escape from the orphanage so you could sit around like some homeless kid without even a glint of determination in your eyes?'

He had me there. My heart was pounding.

'Do you like this?' he asked, pointing at all the boxes and homeless people around us.

I shook my head.

'Do you want to change it? To get out of here?'

I nodded.

'Then, do something,' he said.

I looked up. His eyes were sharp. As if he were holding a sword to my throat, and depending on how I reacted, my head would either roll off my shoulders or stay put, albeit with a scar to remind me of this moment forever. I chose the scar.

'Help me,' I whispered. 'Please.'

Even as a child, I thought of myself as someone who controlled his emotions rather well. Yet there I was, with tears in my eyes, scared and trembling. Like any ten-year-old when his little world has been shattered.

The man took another step closer, bent over, and looked straight into my eyes from point-blank range. I could feel his breath on my skin. It was calm and balanced. Not a trace of excitement.

I didn't know what to expect next. I had never experienced a hug, a kiss, a caressing hand on top of my head, or any other form of affection or love. I didn't know how a parent treated a child in such a situation. I only knew that whatever was coming, I craved it.

He slapped me as hard as he could.

I fell over, and for a few seconds I was lying in my little box like an abandoned puppy, but I pulled myself together, stood up, wiped my tears away, and looked him in the eye. My whole body was shaking.

'Finally,' he said. 'Now we can introduce ourselves. Akira Yamaguchi.'

I looked at the older man next.

'Kazu Kobayashi. Please, call me Kobayashi-san.'

'Sato,' I told them, and I bowed as low as possible. Kobayashi-san returned the bow, and as he was straightening up, I caught the slightest of smiles on his face. Yamaguchi only nodded.

'I'll give you an assignment,' Yamaguchi said. 'Kobayashi-san will buy you a meal now, so that you have energy for the task ahead, and I'll give you this hundred-yen coin as your first real money earned. It's not much, but it will remind you of this day.'

He extended his right arm and opened his palm, in which a hundred-yen coin lay. As I reached for it, he suddenly closed his fist again.

'It's on you now to do this right. This is the only chance you'll get from me. Kobayashi-san will give you the details.'

I nodded.

'The Fushimi brothers,' he said, turning to Kobayashi-san.

'I understand,' Kobayashi-san replied.

Yamaguchi opened his hand again. I took the coin and took a good look at it. It looked brand new, fresh out of the bank, or wherever Yamaguchi had gotten it from. All bright and shiny. I was certain no one had ever used it before. I can't say for sure, of course, but that's what I thought then, and it's what I think now too. It was the first time I had ever earned money and the first time I felt I had gotten something new. I put the coin in my pocket, but I didn't let go of it for at least another hour or so. I held it tight between my thumb and my index finger.

***

The strange, mirrored elevator finally got to the ground floor, and the doors opened. I walked out, still holding the coin between my fingers. The lobby area was almost as desolate as the upper floors, especially so late at night. The only difference being the presence of three men – two guards and a receptionist. All three heads turned in my direction.

I nodded. They nodded back.

We spoke little in this world of ours. Or rather, there were those who spoke little, and there were those who spoke all the time. No middle ground. You were in either one group or the other. I belonged to the silent group, of course. I barely ever spoke to my colleagues – only to a handful of people, at most, or when I needed to.

Some found me arrogant and thought I was being disrespectful with this silence of mine. Most, however, got used to it and accepted it. They were probably even glad not to have to talk to or have anything to do with me. The more distance from me, the better. I felt as if I were some lonely internal audit guy who did all the dirty work and, in exchange, was being hated and reviled. And I was fine with that.

The atmosphere grew tense, and I felt their eyes on me as I was leaving the building. I knew all three had short swords, and they were ready to draw them in an instant and cut me down if necessary. I also knew they would prefer not to. Not that it would have bothered them to hurt me. It wouldn't have. On the contrary. But they also feared me.

I reached the revolving door and stopped. They must have thought I would turn around and look at them one more time, but I didn't. I just stood there, looking at the door, breathing as slowly as possible.

Then, I closed my eyes.

***

Seven seconds passed, or eight, or maybe even nine. I felt as if I were in some no man's land. I always get this feeling when I'm about to enter or leave a building. It's like stepping out of one world to enter a different one. Like changing realities. There's the reality of the outside and the completely different reality of the inside, and they rarely mix. You can hear or see or smell the other reality through doors and windows, but you can seldom be part of both at the same time. Most people have no trouble making this transition from one reality to the other. It's like changing clothes or eating different food. Nothing in particular, just another layer of diversity in life. But for me, it's a process of change for which I need to prepare. Like a snake shedding its skin. I need my time. I need to leave behind what was and accept what will be. And in this moment of limbo, I feel vulnerable.

There's only one place where I'm able to escape both kinds of reality: the balcony. My favorite place. Wherever I live, I have to have a balcony. A covered one, so that I can spend time on it even if it's raining or snowing. It's one of the few places where I feel at peace. I often close my eyes in these moments of limbo, when I'm about to enter or leave a place, and I try picturing myself on a balcony. It helps me make this leap across the boundary between realities.

***

I opened my eyes again and stepped outside.

As soon as the fresh air hit me, everything that had happened inside the building instantly seemed as distant as the stars above Tokyo. I looked up and tried to find the star of the reality I had just left. I searched the sky, but the city lights made it impossible to see anything apart from the constant, shimmering glow. My recent reality was up there somewhere, like all the other ones, but I had to let go of it.

It was one o'clock. Most people were at home, sleeping, watching television, browsing the internet on their tablets and mobile phones, having sex. I could've been at home, too, like everyone else, but I wasn't. My place was on the streets, and the darker the night became, the more I felt at ease.

I parked my motorbike in front of the entrance. An old Kawasaki Zephyr 750. All black, with classic lines, fine curves, and the soul of a wild mustang. I called her Eleanor. Like the car in the Nicolas Cage movie.

I put my helmet on, sat on the bike, and turned her engine on. I revved her a couple of times, just to hear the sound. It was our way of greeting each other, I guess. She never failed to impress me.

I put her in first gear and headed off to Golden Gai.

Room fifty-five

I only visit Golden Gai once the sun has set. Otherwise, it's full of tourists taking pics and selfies and then going to a nearby Starbucks or whatever coffee shop they find, connecting to the free wi-fi, and posting the pics on Facebook or Instagram and tweeting something like "Golden Gai Rulez! #tokyounderground #yakuzaheaven #dreamcometrue".

I only go after midnight.

There is a secret to Golden Gai, you see.

Every night, exactly at midnight, a portal opens. It's hidden in a narrow alley between two small houses, and it resembles a large mirror. They say only those who can't see their reflection in it can enter. If you can, it's just a mirror, like any other mirror, and you can straighten your hair, check to see if there's anything between your teeth, and mourn over the wrinkles on your face. If you can't, you're like me. You go there, you see it's a mirror, but the only thing staring back at you is a dark, empty alley with a blinking neon light somewhere in the background. You're scared at first, borderline panicking, but then your curiosity prevails, and you touch it. It's fluid, or at least that's the best way to describe it. It's not wet, but it moves and swirls around your fingers, then your arms, then your legs, and your whole body as you enter.

It pulls you in.

***

I got there around half past one in the night. I would have gotten there sooner, but I had had to stop at a convenience store to grab something to eat.

I parked Eleanor near the entrance to Golden Gai, and I began to walk towards the portal. I took my time, as I was in no rush. This short walk was one of the few things I genuinely enjoyed. I don't know why. There was no particular reason. None that I was aware of, at least. I just had this feeling of completeness whenever I took those few steps. Nothing was missing, nothing was bothering me, nothing was weighed on my shoulders or my mind. It didn't matter if it was raining or if the winds were howling or if the heat was making me sweat like crazy. I wasn't even aware of the world around me. Or rather I was, but everything felt just right, just as it should in that particular moment.

On my way to the portal, I saw a drunk salaryman. He could hardly walk, and he was using his plastic umbrella in one hand and his bag in the other to keep his balance, though he seemed perpetually on the brink of falling over. He was this picture-perfect example of an average salaryman in his forties, in a cheap, striped, dark blue suit, one size larger than it should've been. He wore a pink tie with grey, white, and black stripes, and his shoes had yet to see a cleaner or even just a brush. His wristwatch looked like a very simple Citizen with a metal bracelet – it was obviously oversized as well, and the number plate hung on the inside of his wrist.

As we passed each other, he looked at me, and suddenly he started shouting:

'Idiot! You're an idiot! You-you-you-,' he kept pointing at me with his umbrella, but every time he lifted it, he almost stumbled. 'I hate you! I'll kill you! I really will!' He was spitting all over the place while berating me with every possible thing that came to his mind. 'Bastard! Son of a... lady of the night! Penis wanker! Disgusting... cucumber! Yes, cucumber! Cucumber with a huge nose! A carrot-nose! Yes, you ugly... you... you... crab-eating little mermaid!' Not that he was any good at cursing. 'I'll kill you! I'll... I'll... Aaaaa!'

He charged forward with the umbrella and took a wild swing. I moved back slightly, just a quick step to one side. He missed, spun around, and fell to his knees.

He then started to sob like a baby.

I stood there for a while, confused. Like a... well, a cucumber. Maybe this odd little man was right.

He cried for at least two minutes, then his tears slowly dried up and he began to mutter.

'I can't even curse. I'm a weak... pussy. I'm... I'm... useless.'

Another few sobs rose from his throat.

'Hey, come on,' I said, taking a step or two towards him. 'Come on, get up. Pull yourself together.' I grabbed his forearm and pulled him up. 'There you go.'

He wiped away his tears and blew his nose.

'Are you alright?' I asked.

He straightened his suit first and then his small, round glasses and then the little hair he had remaining, which he wiped from one side of his bald pate across to the other.

'Yes,' he replied.

'Are you sure?'

He nodded.

'What was that all about, by the way?'

He almost started to cry again, but I stopped him: 'Hey, hey, come on. Don't do that. Enough. You're a man, aren't you?'

He nodded.

'What just happened? A cucumber? With a carrot-nose? Really?'

'I'm sorry. I... I lost it. And I'm a little...'

'Drunk. I can see that.'

'I... I lost my job today. And my girlfriend. Yesterday.'

'Your girlfriend.'

'Yes. Yesterday. My girlfriend. My love. My one and only... Oh, I'm gonna cry again!'

And so he did. A little less than before, but he still managed to shed an impressive number of tears. It helped him sober up a little more. Again, I didn't really know what to do. I'm not good with people. From not having parents or friends when I was growing up, I guess. Later, it's like a curse. So, I just stood there and rolled a cigarette.

'Are you done?' I asked when he had run out of tears. 'Here,' I said, and I gave him the cigarette. 'It'll help you calm down a little.'

He wiped his eyes with the sleeve of his suit and took it.

'Thank you.'

I lit it for him and rolled another one.

'Look,' I said, after taking a puff, 'I don't know what's going, and I don't really care. It's none of my business.' I took another drag. 'But you should get your shit together. Crying won't help, cursing won't either. Beating other people up... It might, but only if you beat up the right ones.'

He looked at me and then turned his head to one side and continued smoking. His hands were shaking.

'We all have our demons,' I said. 'Believe me. So, do something about them. Whatever it takes.'

I put my hand on his shoulder.

'Good luck,' I said, and I left.

I don't remember him saying anything in reply.

As I continued my short stroll towards the portal, I suddenly felt strange. I think I was still processing what had happened somewhere in the back of my mind, and I didn't really know what to do with it, but for some reason, I felt excited. Gone was the calmness I usually experienced when walking that walk. I kept thinking of the odd little man. I even stopped for a moment and considered looking back.

But I didn't.

***

I soon reached the portal. The alley was as narrow and dark as ever, and it took the most trained pair of eyes to spot the mirror. Trained in seeing Tokyo's streets at night, I mean. Like mine. I'm convinced that people of the night have different eyes than people of the day. I don't know how people of the day see things, but we nightcrawlers can penetrate the darkness and see all the lines, shapes, and depths hiding in it. And the mirror was one such shape, one such depth.

I went as close as I could without touching it. I stood in front of it, then I closed my eyes for a few seconds. My heart began to beat faster, and my palms started to sweat. I had done this countless times before, always with the same outcome, yet I still hoped something would be different when I opened them again. I hoped I would see my long hair tied up in a knot, my big nose resembling a bird's beak, my dense beard with its patches of grey, the scar I had on my left cheek, my skinny but strong body, and my deep, dark eyes. But the hope would evaporate as soon as I opened my eyes just enough to see that the mirror was reflecting only an empty alley, nothing else.

It's strange to stand in front of a mirror and not see yourself. Like being a ghost. First, you wonder if it's real. Then, you wonder if *you're* real. "Does anyone see me? Do I exist? Am I here?" These kinds of questions.

So, I stood there, looking into the mirror, asking myself these same questions. It took me a couple of minutes. It used to take longer, but I guess it didn't surprise me as much anymore.

After I was done with my self-questioning, I raised my right arm and touched the surface of the mirror. It felt warm. It always did. Like putting a finger in a warm cup of milk. Silky and smooth. I loved the feeling.

As soon as my fingertips reached it, the strange, fluid surface began swirling around and gently pulling me in. Like a living creature looking to embrace another living thing. I felt as if I were being welcomed – a sensation I have only rarely experienced. So, I let it do it. I let it take me by my hand and lead me to the other side.

***

In the space beyond, you find yourself in a corridor. The carpet is red and old, the walls are yellowish, probably a permanent layer of dust. Light comes from fake, electric candles spread evenly both right and left, and between every two candles, there is a door. An endless number of doors, in a seemingly endless corridor.

The corridor probably has many different entrances. I'd always enter between doors number fifty-one to the right and fifty-two to the left. But the only door I'd open was fifty-five.

There's something about the number five that attracts me. It's like a perfectly shaped dancer, gracefully making a leap from the past into the future, yet the largest impact it makes is in the present. I like to think of it as a symbol of balance.

The first time that I found myself in the corridor, I knew I had to enter room fifty-five. The door was exactly like all the other doors, but the number fifty-five felt warmer than the rest. I had the sense that the other rooms were not meant for me, and I wasn't even allowed to enter them. So, I never really bothered. I always went straight to fifty-five.

***

I entered, and I closed the door behind me.

Soft music was playing, as usual. Low-key, instrumental electronic music. I went straight to the bar.

'The usual, Kei.'

'A scotch with a huuuge chunk of ice coming up! Yep, maaan!'

'Thanks, Kei.'

'Sure, maaan! Here you go!' The bartender poured me a glass and another one for himself. 'Cheers, maaan!'

'Cheers, Kei,' I said, and we both took a sip.

I liked Kei. He was strange, sure, especially the way he talked. But there was not even a trace of role-playing, of phoniness in anything he did. He was one hundred percent Kei, all natural and himself. A good listener, too. Most bartenders are, I guess. The good ones, at least. They make you want to talk. He definitely made *me* talk. Not necessarily a lot, but he made me talk about things worth talking about.

'You look great, Kei. As always.'

'Oh, thanks maaan! It's funky, yeah?! My first time wearing it,' he said, looking down at his pink shirt, which had colorful images of cats all over it. Funny, hand-drawn cats, like from a cartoon. 'Cats are coool, maaan!'

'Cool they are, Kei. Cool they are,' I said, and then I turned, resting my elbows on the bar.

I looked around. Kei's place was enormous. Lots of tables and chairs, several separate, quiet sections, even some rooms to relax. The main room had a single source of light – a huge chandelier right in the middle, with more than a hundred candles and even more crystals decorating it. The crystals had a cold, blue glint, and as they shimmered with the yellowish shine of the flames, they painted the whole bar in a tremulous green. The walls, the furniture, the glasses on the shelves all looked green. Even Kei looked green.

The walls were bare, with no windows, just a hole in one of them. A round hole the size of a large pumpkin. One of the shadows was standing there and looking through it.

'Is that a new one?' I asked.

'The one at the hooole, you mean? Yeah, maaan. A new one.'

'I see. How many of them are here right now?'

'One hundred.'

'So, a hundred shadows.'

'Not shadows, maaan. I keep telling you. It's peeeople.'

'I know, but you're the only one who can see them in their true form, as people. To me, they are only shadows. Formless lumps of darkness.'

'That's true. But they are still peeeople. I can see all of them. And I can talk to them.'

'How many of them are you talking to right now?' I asked.

'Oh, to aaall of them.'

'At the same time?'

'Yep!'

'But how does that work? I just can't imagine it. Not when my reality is you talking to me, and all these other shadows, all one hundred of them just silently hanging around like ghosts.'

'Well, realities overlap, maaan. But they don't necessarily penetrate one another. Mostly, they baaarely connect on the surface.'

'But you can see all of them.'

'Yep!'

'And you can be in all of them, at the same time, like here and now with me.'

'Yep!'

'You're crazy,' I said, shaking my head.

'Maybe I am, maaan. But so are you,' he replied, and he smiled.

I picked up my glass of scotch and walked around. Some of the shadows were moving, some were still, either sitting or standing. Whenever I got near one, I felt a strange mix of energy and emotions, and it was slightly different with each of them, both the sensation and the intensity. A few felt cold and made me sad, a few others felt warmer and brought a smile to my face. Some were distant and estranged, some I wanted to punch in the face, and some I just felt pity for.

I got to the hole in the wall. The new shadow standing in front of it immediately felt annoying, but at the same time, I somehow liked it. Like a little brother, I thought.

We kind of looked at each other, then he left. Or she. I couldn't tell. I think it kept staring at me and never really stopped. I stared back for a while, but then I turned away and looked through the hole.

'What do you see, maaan?' Kei asked from behind the counter.

'Just the usual.'

'Meeeaning?'

'I don't know,' I said, trying to find the right words. 'I see darkness, and within, several layers of thick, impenetrable clouds. They seem to be moving, but no opening appears. Not even a single crack where at least a tiny bit of light could shine through. Nothing. It's just darkness.'

'Hm. I see. That sucks, maaan.'

I turned around and looked at him.

'What?' he asked.

'Should I be seeing something else?'

'I don't know. Should you?' His eyes changed as soon as he asked me. His voice, too. He suddenly appeared more serious.

'Come on, Kei. Tell me,' I begged.

He just shook his head and sighed.

'I've told you already, maaan. I'm not here to give you aaanswers.'

'Then, why are you here?'

'Well, you tell me. Why am I here?' I looked him straight in the eyes, frustrated. 'Why are you here, Sato-kun? Hm?'

'Go to hell', I replied, and I finished my scotch. 'Pour me another one, will you?'

'That I can certainly do, maaan! Give me your glass!'

I put my glass on the bar.

'Sit down,' he said.

I took a deep breath, then I let it all out, like an old train releasing steam. I sat down.

'Tell me, what's bothering you, maaan?'

I looked at him, then I turned away and took a sip.

'There's fear in your eyes, maaan. I can tell.'

I took another sip.

'You in some kind of daaanger?'

'I'm not afraid of danger, Kei.'

'Then what is it, Sato-kun?'

'I don't know. Something else.'

'I see. It's always something else.'

We looked at each other and both took a sip.

'Can I roll one?' I asked.

'Oh, you can indeed roll it, maaan. Feel free.'

I took out my tobacco and started making a cigarette.

'But you're still not allowed to smoke in here, maaan.'

'Come on, Kei. Please.'

'Rules are rules, maaan,' he shrugged.

'You're cruel.'

'Am I?' he asked. 'And yooou? Are yooou not cruel?'

'Fuck you, Kei.'

'With pleasure, maaan,' he replied, bowing.

The moment he got up and I saw that funny smile on his funny face under that thin, Salvador Dali-like mustache, I started to laugh. He laughed back, of course, and soon we were both laughing hard, to the point where tears began to flow.

'Ha-ha-ha!'

'Ha-ha-ha-ha-ha, maaan!'

'I hate you, ha-ha-ha!'

'The same, maaan! Ha-ha-ha! The same!'

'Ah, anyway,' I said, wiping away the tears, and trying to calm myself down. 'I'll have this thing tomorrow evening.'

'You mean, tonight, right?'

'What?'

'It's waaay past midnight, maaan. It's already tomorrow.'

'Oh, yeah, right. Tonight. Whatever.'

'So, a "thing", Sato-kun?'

'Yeah, a "thing".'

'Will you have to do it? Agaaain?' he asked.

'I will,' I replied, putting my hand in my pocket to hold onto the hundred-yen coin.

'What for, Sato-kun?'

'I don't know, Kei. Not yet.'

I finished the second scotch and stood up.

'Are you leeeaving already?'

I nodded.

He took my empty glass to wash it.

'Next time, Sato-kun.'

'Next time, Kei.'

***

I found myself in the dark alley again. I glanced at my watch – only five minutes had gone by. Time passed differently in there.

I looked back. The mirror was still there, and my reflection still wasn't.

It's hard to describe my relationship with the mirror and everything beyond it. I think I both hate it and love it. Or, to be more precise, I'm drawn to it. No one was making me go there over and over again, and I could've easily stayed away from that strange little alley. I could've avoided seeing that I wasn't there to see, and I could've avoided all those complicated emotions I always felt when returning from that place.

But I didn't.

I guess darkness can be quite irresistible at times. When you're like me, when you've lived most of your life in the shadows of existence, far away from light, the darkness feels like home. And with it comes everything and everyone else living in the same darkness. The weird, the outcast, the forgotten. These things, these creatures become the only ones you can relate to. They were the only ones *I* could relate to.

After leaving the room, I'd always have this huge emptiness inside me. I'd imagine having a dry, seemingly bottomless well at the center of my heart, and from time to time, like when leaving the room, my heart would merge with the well. I'd *become* the well.

I looked at the mirror one more time, and then I left. I walked to the corner of the alley and turned right to go back to Eleanor. But after I had taken a few steps, I heard something, so I stopped. The sound had come from behind me. I knew someone was there. I was about to turn around when suddenly I felt something pressed against my spine.

I slowly raised my arms.

'Where were you?'

Killing a piglet

I immediately recognized the voice and turned around, lowering my arms.

'You again.'

'Where did you go?' the funny little man from earlier asked, pointing at the mirror with his plastic umbrella.

'None of your business,' I replied.

'There's... There's something strange going on! I can tell! There's definitely something strange going on!'

'What do you mean?'

'I... I saw you go in there! Yes! You walked in there, and... and you disappeared!'

I looked at the mirror, then at him again.

'I saw you! I saw the whole thing!'

'Did you?'

'Yes! Yes, I did! You won't fool me!'

'I see,' I sighed. 'Come with me, then' I told him.

'Where? What will you do to me?' he asked with fear in his voice.

'Just come, will you? I won't hurt you. I'm actually going out of my way here, so at least appreciate it.'

He gulped.

'Now, come,' I said, beckoning him forward.

We went back to the mirror and stood in front of it. We could see the whole alley in it – the graffiti on the walls, a sealed iron door, the dirty, red bricks, a neon sign, and even a dark piss stain. But we couldn't see ourselves. Not me, not him. We weren't there.

'What's this?' he asked, pointing at the mirror with his umbrella again.

'What does it look like to you?

'Well... a mirror?'

I nodded.

'A mirror?! But... but... I can't see myself! I can't see *you*! Where are you?! Where am I?! What the hell is this thing?!' He took a few steps back.

'A mirror, of sorts,' I replied. 'But don't worry, it won't harm you. Don't be scared.'

'Scared?! I'm freaking terrified! I'm gonna start screaming or crying! Or both!'

'Please don't cry, ok? I've heard enough of that for tonight. Come on, come closer.' I took his arm and pulled him next to me. 'Look,' I said, and I slowly raised my right index finger to touch, gently, the surface of the mirror.

It began to move and swirl like it usually did. It wrapped my finger in its grip and began pulling it in.

'Whoa! What's this?! I'm freaking out!' the man screamed, and as he took a few steps back, stumbled, and fell on his ass. 'Ouch!'

'It's ok. It's harmless. See?' I let it swallow my whole forearm.

'What the hell is this thing?!' he asked, standing up. He put his glasses back in place and stepped closer.

'I don't know, to be honest. I only know that some people see their reflection in it, and for them, it's just an ordinary mirror, but some people can't, like you and me, and for us, it works as some kind of gate. A portal.'

'A portal? So, you can go through it?'

'Exactly.'

'And where does it lead?'

'It's hard to tell, and hard to describe. You'd better see it for yourself.'

'Me? Go in there? Are you crazy?! No way!'

'Well, it's entirely up to you. I don't care, honestly. You asked, so I showed you. But you don't have to do it. You don't have to do anything. You're a free man, aren't you? No job, no woman, no kids, I guess. Not so bad! You can do whatever you want.'

He looked at me with a blank stare for a while. Then, he turned his head to look into the mirror.

'You're interested. I can tell. Otherwise, you wouldn't have stayed and asked questions and bothered me with your shit,' I told him.

He raised his umbrella and touched the mirror with it. As the mirror began pulling it in, he immediately took a step back.

'Leave the umbrella, and put down your bag. You don't need them,' I said. 'Try touching it with your fingers.'

He put his stuff on the ground. Both the umbrella and the bag at once appeared in the mirror, retrieving their reflection.

'Touch it,' I said.

He again went close, this time raising his empty right hand. He spread his fingers wide and let the surface of the mirror clasp them in its embrace.

'It feels warm,' he whispered.

'I know.'

'Like...'

'A warm cup of milk?' I asked.

'Like ash in a slumbering fire.'

'Very poetic,' I said.

He didn't reply. Instead, he let the mirror swallow his whole arm, and then, slowly, he followed it. As he was about to cross to the other side completely, I said: 'I'll wait for you here.' He probably didn't hear me.

While he was gone, I sat on the doorstep of one of the houses – the one with the sealed iron door. I rolled several cigarettes, lit one of them, and tucked the rest in my special little case. I was about to put the case into my shirt pocket when I stopped for some reason and took a good look at it.

The case was made of pure gold and had a crane engraved on top. Very Japanese. The crane was flying upwards, into the sky, its beak pointing towards the sun. Its head was missing, however. Only a small hole, or rather an indentation stood in its place, a bit more than a centimeter wide. I touched it with my thumb, and suddenly images of old emerged.

***

I remember waiting patiently the whole night, sitting behind a big tree. I held a handmade knife in my left hand, while with my right hand I fidgeted with the hundred-yen coin in my pocket. I was waiting for the light in the top right corner of the house to go out.

The room went dark around one o'clock. I waited for another half an hour, then I came out of hiding. I approached the sliding door with care and slowly opened it. Before entering, I closed my eyes and prepared to make another leap between realities. This turned out to be a particularly difficult leap, and I think I spent almost a minute just breathing in and out, trying to keep my emotions in check. I then opened my eyes again, went inside, and closed the door.

My eyes needed a little time to adjust to the darkness, but luckily the moon was shining through the windows and the thin rice paper covering the sliding door. The silence was overwhelming. I could hear the loud beating of my heart. My palms were sweating, and my breathing was heavy. I felt like a cornered, hunted animal, with nowhere to escape.

I had to go to the upper floor, but when I got to the stairs, I started to shake. There was a little table next to me, and I grabbed its edge. When I looked down, I saw a golden cigarette case next to my trembling hand. It, too, was shaking.

I picked it up and gave it a look. I instantly liked the crane and the way it left the ground to soar into the skies with resolve, and without the slightest sign of regret. It looked like it knew it was leaving one place for a much better place, and it couldn't care less what the world thought of its decision. It just flew away, and in doing so, found peace.

As I thought about this, I found a little peace myself, and my body stopped shaking. I took a few deep breaths, looked up, and slowly started to walk. I took the case with me and put it in my shirt pocket.

I climbed the stairs and looked around. The bedroom was to the left, and there was another small room in front of me. I went into the room in front of me.

I sat on the floor with my back against the wall separating the two rooms, I put the knife on the tatami, and I tried to relax.

After a couple of minutes had passed, I managed to loosen my muscles and calm my breathing. I used an exercise I had learned from Kobayashi-san. I focused my eyes on a single point somewhere in front of me, and I imagined the one place where I felt the most at ease. In my case, a balcony. As I let my imagination take over, the image of the balcony appeared from that single point. Then, it grew, slowly swallowing up my reality and eventually replacing the room I was sitting in.

My imaginary balcony was no particular balcony, nothing I had seen somewhere before, but rather a unique place hidden in the deepest of layers of my consciousness. I think we all have this unique, special place within us, and it's a place to which our souls can retreat. What makes it special is its ability to draw in all kinds of energies and, at the same time, protect our souls from them. It's a place from which we can observe the skies, the fields, the mountains, the seas, and all the lights and shadows, yet we remain sane and unhurt.

I spent several minutes on my inner balcony. I leaned against the railing and gazed at the stars. I tried counting them, from left to right, and I got to one hundred. Number one hundred and one would've been a particularly large and shiny star, but I wasn't able to count it. I kept staring at it with wide-open eyes, but somehow the words, the number wouldn't come. I had it on the tip of my tongue, but it stayed there.

The stars then slowly faded away, and the balcony turned back into the small room in which I was sitting.

I hadn't paid much attention to the room or its contents when I arrived, but as my mind returned from the balcony, I saw a desk in the corner and an old typewriter on top of it. I stood up and went to check it out.

I had never seen an actual typewriter before, only in old tv shows. I stood there for a while, mesmerized, and I let my eyes wander all over it. To me, it looked like a miniature piano, with its thick, black body, the many buttons, and the long typebars, which reminded me of strings. The small, round buttons were inviting me, whispering in my ear to sit down, rest my fingers on them, and let whatever was in me come out.

I allowed them to sway me, like a sailor giving in to a mermaid's song, so I sat down. A stack of white paper lay on the desk. I took one from the top, gently put it in the machine, and wound it.

It felt strange, sitting there at someone else's desk, in an unfamiliar house, staring at a blank sheet of paper in a typewriter. Yet it also felt familiar, like something I was meant to do. So, I put my fingers on the buttons. I just kept them there, without pressing anything.

I hesitated. Should I fill the page with letters or not? Perhaps I would do better to leave it pure and innocent instead of getting it mixed up with me and my world. I feared I would ruin something pure and leave a permanent stain. I didn't want that. I didn't want it to experience the pain I was experiencing. But the buttons kept telling me to use them. They kept telling me to let it all out, whatever it was. They encouraged me to write.

But I couldn't.

I took out the blank piece of paper, folded it, and put it in the back pocket of my jeans. I then went back into the hallway and closed the sliding door to the room.

I stopped to listen.

Nothing came from the bedroom. No snoring, no squeaking noise of a body tossing or turning in the bed, no sound of the pages of a book being turned.

I hoped I would hear something. Anything. The smallest of sounds would've made me turn around, go down the stairs, back to the garden, and disappear in the darkness of the night without a trace. And maybe, just maybe, it would've made me think things through one more time. I can't tell if it would've changed anything, but still, at least I would've had another chance.

But I didn't.

I heard no sounds coming from the room, so I went ahead. First, I opened the door a crack, as slowly and quietly as I could. Then, I peeked inside.

The room was sixteen tatamis big, and it had a pretty simple lay-out: a small drawer to the left with a white orchid on top, a mirror on the back wall, and a window to the right. Light came in just at the right angle to paint the middle of the room in a cold, blue color, separating it from the rest of the space. Like a stage light in a small theater. And on the stage, lying on his back, with his belly rising from the surface like the pitching mound of a baseball field, there he was. The Professor.

I took a deep, silent breath, held it in, and carefully entered the room. I don't know how much time it took me to open the door and walk inside, but the word eternity definitely comes to mind. It felt like someone could have written a book, published it, and become rich in the time it took me to make those few steps and end up a couple of feet away from the Professor, looking down on him.

He looked older in the pictures I had been given. I remembered gray hair and a goatee, but the man in front of me was cleanly shaven and had pitch-black hair. I took out a photo from the pocket of my jacket. I looked at the photo, then at the sleeping man, and again at the picture. The features were the same. There was no doubt. Fluffy, reddish cheeks, thinning eyebrows, and a disproportionately large, round nose which reminded me of a piglet. I knew everyone called him the Professor, and I also knew why, but as I was looking at him and preparing to do what I had been sent to do, my inner voice started calling him Mr. Piglet. "Mr. Piglet... I came for you, Mr. Piglet," I thought to myself, and as soon as I started thinking of him in this way, his body began to change from that of a rather fat man into an oversized piglet.

I think my mind played this little trick on me because it thought it would be easier to kill a piglet than a man. Especially since I was doing it for the first time.

But it wasn't.

I had seen pigs being slaughtered to process their meat, but now that I imagined myself slicing the throat of the piglet in front of me, my whole body felt numb, and I started trembling again. I imagined it squealing, I imagined tears flowing down its face, I imagined its piglet soul leaving its piglet body and hovering in the air frantically, not knowing what had hit it. I saw the blood shooting out the moment I made the slit, splashing the whole room with red splotches, including the orchid, which would have blood dripping from its leaves and petals.

I felt dizzy, so I closed my eyes for a few seconds and tried to shake it off. I hoped the darkness would wipe away the vision of piglet blood and all the other visions.

Then, from somewhere in that darkness, somewhere deep down, a loud bang made its way through to me. The sound seemed to come from very far away, but it reached me in an instant, and everything shook, like when an earthquake hits.

I opened my eyes. Mr. Piglet was pointing a gun at me. Smoke was coming from its barrel. I looked at my chest, then I looked up again and put my left hand over my heart.

Then, I fell to the ground.

I can't tell for sure how long I lay there motionless, my left hand pressed against my heart, my right hand still holding the knife. Everything went blank for a while. What I do remember is the moment I came to my senses. It happened when Mr. Piglet touched me a few times with his feet. I think he was checking to make sure I was dead.

I don't know why he didn't put more rounds in me. He must have been in a state of shock himself. Though he had a gun, I doubt he had ever used it before. Hitting me exactly in the heart with a single shot was pure luck. At least, that's what *he* must have thought.

I was careful not to make a single move, and I focused my hearing as much as I could. "I wish I were a dog," I told myself, but still, I was quite able to imagine what Mr. Piglet's position was and what he was doing based only on the few sounds he made.

I think he hesitated for a while, and he probably needed some time to process what had just happened. He breathed heavily and was pacing back and forth. I knew he still had the gun in his hand, as he kept slapping it against his other palm, each time making a clicking noise. It was a simple revolver with six bullets, like the ones the police used to have before they switched to automatics, so I presumed there were still five bullets left. I had to be careful.

My mind kept running through several possible scenarios, and I struggled to picture the perfect solution. It was bad. The one thing I knew for sure was that I needed to be patient. And that, at least, I was good at.

At that moment, I remembered something. An image, a fragment of a memory. I didn't know where it had come from, as it didn't feel real, rather like a small piece of a dream I might have had. Still, it came to me vividly, as vividly as only real experiences can. The ones which define one's personality, one's future, and leave an eternal mark on the soul. I saw a man. From behind. He stood firmly on his feet, panting, but composed, and perfectly aware of himself. He had a strong and frightening sense of intention oozing from every pore of his body, enveloping him in an impenetrable veil of darkness. The room itself was dark as well, but this veil, this barrier of energy of sorts which surrounded him, looked even darker. And in his hand, dangling next to his leg, a knife. Thick, fresh blood was dripping from its tip onto the floor, making a sound like when drops of water hit the bottom of the sink and disturb the silence of the night.

The last drop of blood to hit the floor felt much louder than the rest as if it had hit my very eardrum. I opened my eyes and jumped at Mr. Piglet from behind, and I started furiously stabbing him. I stabbed him again and again, in his side and his stomach, hitting several vital organs. Then, to finish him off, I stabbed him in the heart.

The blade went all the way in, as deep as possible. I held the knife handle in my right hand and clutched his neck tightly with my left arm, and we stayed like that for a while. I had nothing in my mind – no thoughts, no images, no words or sounds. Only emptiness. My head, my whole body was hollow, and they felt like they didn't belong to me. I was detached. I was there, yet I wasn't.

I looked up, still in the same position, and I saw a mirror on the wall. In it, I saw *us*. I saw this whole scene, this silent monument of violence, and I kept staring at it. I kept staring at myself, as I embraced the lifeless body of a person I had never met, covered in blood, with a knife in his heart. And then, something snapped. I heard it loud and clear. Like when a tight rubber rope breaks in two, and both its halves fly in opposite directions. And not only did I hear it, but I also felt it. Somewhere inside me, a strong quake tore up a mountain. A big piece of it fell into the ocean and slowly began drifting away to open waters. It set out to reach the horizon, all on its own.

I slowly pulled out the knife and let go of the Professor. The body fell to the floor with a thump. There was blood everywhere, and some was still gushing out of the wounds and holes I had made on him. But I didn't notice for a while. I just stood there, looking into the mirror, looking into the reflection of my own eyes in the hopes that I might see something. I don't know what I was looking for; a sign of some sort maybe, or a glimpse of light or the trace of emotion. Any emotion. But whatever it was, I didn't find it.

I touched my chest right above my heart. Where my shirt pocket was. Which now had a hole in it. And inside, the small, golden cigarette case with a crane engraved on its lid. And now the crane had a hole in it too. Or rather, a hole where its head should have been.

I wiped my face clean and looked at the body. I bent over to inspect it one last time – he wasn't breathing. "He dyed his hair black," I noticed. I pulled his photo from my jacket again, and I put it on his chest to cover the heart and the wound I had made. Then, I pulled his eyelids over his lifeless eyes.

As I was straightening up, I noticed a folded sheet of white paper in the pool of blood next to the Professor's body. I realized it was the paper I had taken from the other room, from the typewriter. It must had fallen out of my pocket during our tussle. I picked it up. It had blood all over it, but I didn't care. I put it back into the pocket of my jeans.

'Goodbye, Professor,' I said.

***

I was still sitting at the iron door and holding the golden case, looking at it, when the funny little man reemerged from the mirror. He looked bewildered.

'How was it?' I asked.

He gave no reply. He didn't even look at me.

'How was it in there?' I asked again, a little louder.

'Strange,' he replied, now looking me in the eye. 'Strange...'

'Which room did you try out?'

'S... Seventeen, I think. Yes, seventeen. It was the seventeen.'

'And what was there?'

'Well... Strange.'

'You told me that already,' I said. 'Anything more specific?'

He seemed to have gotten lost in his thoughts.

'Here, have one,' I said, and I gave him a cigarette.

'Thanks.'

'So?'

'So... It looked like a coffee house. A big one. And very old. It had this vintage, European furniture, and everything smelled like coffee. The tables, the chairs, the cupboards, the covers, everything. Like coffee. And... And there were these shadows. So many of them. Ambling around, sitting, just... being. So... Strange.'

'I see.'

'And...'

'And?'

'A barista. One person for the whole place. Serving coffee. Good coffee. Real good.'

'What was his name?' I asked.

'Her.'

'What?'

'Her name. You mean, her name.'

'So, it was a woman?'

'Yes, a woman. A beautiful woman.'

'Hm...'

'Eve. Her name was Eve.'

'Eve, I see.'

For some reason, I always thought Kei would be serving in the other rooms as well, so it surprised me to learn that it was someone else. On the other hand, it made sense. So, it was Eve. I kept repeating the name in my head, and as I did that, I realized I still didn't know the funny little man's name.

'I think we haven't introduced ourselves,' I said. 'My name is Sato. Just Sato.'

'Oh, you're right. I'm sorry for being so rude, Mr. Just Sato.'

'It's not Just Sato. It's just... It's Sato, all right? You can call me Sato.'

'Y-Yes, Sato-san. I understand. S-Sorry. My name is Kōnosuke Arawashi. Pleased to meet you,' he told me and bowed.

'Kōnosuke Arawashi,' I said, puffing out cigarette smoke. 'It's too long. I'll call you Kon, ok?'

'A-All right,' he replied, a little confused.

'Pleased to meet you, Kon,' I said and nodded.

The sound of pachinko

I met Kiki the next afternoon.

I'd see her once a month, always in a small coffee shop, halfway between Shibuya and Ebisu, close to the tracks of the Yamanote-line. The name of the place was Asylum Roasters. A favorite of mine, especially if I wanted to hide from the crowds of Tokyo or talk to someone in private. The owner, in his fifties, roasted his own coffee at the back of the shop, behind a glass wall. The smell always lay over the whole place like a warm blanket and made it cozy. All four tables were usually empty between two and four in the afternoon, and jazz playing from old vinyl records would fill the void with a soothing melancholy. I preferred to sit at the table in the street-front window.

Kiki arrived ten minutes after three. She opened the door forcefully and rushed inside.

'Good afternoon!'

'Good afternoon,' the young barista girl replied from behind the counter.

'Ah! I'm all wet! Look at my hair!' she complained, taking a seat at my table.

'Where's your umbrella?' I asked.

'You know I hate umbrellas!'

'Well, don't complain, then.'

She stuck her tongue out and grimaced.

'Happy to see you, too,' I said.

Her hair really was a mess. Even when dry. She had dyed it blonde a couple of months before, and she used all kinds of concoctions to make it look like a weird, furry monster living on top of her head. It was one of the many ways a seventeen-year-old could rebel against the world, I guess.

'What?' she asked, with apparent annoyance in her voice.

'Nothing,' I replied.

'Stop staring at me.'

'I'm not staring at you.'

'Yes, you are. It's my hair, right?'

'That, and your clothes, and your shoes, I guess.'

'What about them?'

'Nothing. I just... don't really understand you teenagers. Do the boys like it this way? All these colors and shapes?'

'I don't care if they like it or not. *I* like it, ok?'

'Ok, ok. Whatever you say. Just wear a slightly longer skirt next time, will you? I hate it when you show so much skin.'

'Why? You don't like my legs? Why should I hide them? I have nice legs.'

'That's precisely why you should hide them. There are men out there who might harass you. Especially in Shinjuku. And I know you spend a lot of time there.'

'Oh, god! You're such a pain in the ass, uncle! Don't worry so much! No one will harm me. And Masa-kun will protect me anyway.'

'You're still seeing that guy? I told you I didn't like him. You should stay away from him.'

'Oh, geez! Are we gonna talk about this again?'

'Only if you keep seeing him. Stay away from him, you hear me? He's trouble.'

'Oh, how would you know? You see me once a month and think you know everything. At least he's always there.'

'But he won't be. And then you'll scurry back to me crying and begging for help.'

'Oh, I swear...' she raised her hand, but the barista girl interrupted us.

'Excuse me, can I bring you something, Kiki-san?'

Kiki looked at her and suddenly softened up. Her body, her voice, her whole being. She went from furious to cute in an instant. It's just the way she was. She would experience wild emotions, and then just let them evaporate without a trace. Especially when she got angry. Her rage was frightening, but everyone knew it would never last more than a couple of minutes. It made her life easier, in a sense. The fact that she couldn't hold a grudge. But it also made her vulnerable. People took advantage of this trait of hers. They would harm her again and again because they knew she would forgive them each and every time.

'I'll have a chai-latte, Yumi-chan. Thank you so much,' she said, flashing her perfect, white teeth.

Her sudden transformations always made me smile. I just couldn't resist. Even though my facial muscles tug my lips into a smile, and often even resisted when I tried, they were helpless against the power of Kiki's kindness kicking her anger's butt.

'What?' she asked again, now with a shy smile.

'Nothing,' I replied, trying to hide my own smile. 'Anyhow... How's your mother?'

Kiki turned away.

'Tell me, Kiki.'

'She doesn't have much left. Six months, maybe less'

'I see.'

'She's in a lot of pain, so they put her on strong medication. She's just a shadow of her former self. An empty shell.' She looked me in the eye, then turned away again. 'I don't know...'

Her chai-latte arrived. 'Here it is, Kiki-san. Your chai-latte, the way you like it, with a lot of cinnamon on top. Please, enjoy,' the barista girl said.

'Thank you, Yumi-chan.'

'You're welcome.'

Kiki took the cup in both hands, using its heat to warm them. She then raised it to her mouth, gently blew some air to cool it down a little, and took three small sips.

'Mm, delicious.'

I looked into her eyes and tried to figure out what she was thinking, what was going on inside her. It wasn't easy. I always had the feeling she was hiding things. From me, from her mother, from the whole world.

***

Her mother was one of the people who constantly harmed her. The abuse was not physical, but psychological. She blamed others for her failures in life, and the blame often fell on Kiki. She was always the victim of something or someone, and Kiki was the one who had to find solutions to her problems. And Yuriko made sure Kiki would take all these issues upon herself. She made Kiki feel responsible for things Kiki never should've been responsible for.

Yuriko had lost her job as a post office clerk several years back, as they had caught her stealing money. Out of consideration for the fact that she was raising a child on her own, her former employer decided not to file a formal complaint with the police, so she avoided having a record or going to prison. They thought they'd at least give her a chance to find a decent job somewhere else.

But she never did.

For a while, she pretended that she was looking for work, and she even lied about going to job interviews, when in reality she was playing "pachinko". When Kiki found out, she went ballistic and shouted with her mother in a way a child should never shout with a parent. But she forgave her quickly, even felt sorry for her, and she thought she was at least partially responsible for the situation. And from then on, Yuriko didn't have to pretend or lie anymore – she openly stopped looking for a job and officially became a pachinko-addict. She knew Kiki would get angry from time to time, but she also knew Kiki would eventually forgive her and help her out again. And she was right.

They were lucky to inherit Kiki's late father's house. He and Yuriko had been living separately, though they had not divorced, with Kiki at her mother's, when he died. Kiki was only three. She didn't remember him at all. Not even a single image or memory. I was probably the closest to a father figure she ever had, and apart from the little money they got from social services, I was the one who covered their costs of living after Yuriko was fired.

I couldn't give her much, but it was enough for the two of them to get by. I never told her how to spend the money – she was smart and responsible, especially for her age. I only ever asked one thing from her: not to give it to her mother, and not to let her play.

But she couldn't resist.

I found out by chance, well over a year after I had started giving them money.

***

I was in Kabukichō, dropping in on one of our bars. We had had some trouble with the manager, as the boss suspected he was stealing money. He asked me to look around a little, so I spent the whole evening in and around the bar. I tried to be as casual as possible, pretending I was just enjoying my time. I chatted with some of the girls who worked there and whom I knew quite well, I had a few drinks with two or three regulars, and from time to time I went outside to walk a little and smoke a cigarette.

I decided to go home around two in the night. I grabbed my helmet, took my jacket, and left. Eleanor was waiting for me near the entrance. I sat on her, but I had to have one last cigarette before leaving, so I put the helmet on top of the tank and lit up.

The moment I exhaled the first puff of smoke, the doors to the pachinko parlor across the street opened, and along with the usual, loud noise of bleeping machines, metal balls, and annoying music came the wails of an almost hysterical woman. Two Korean security

guys were trying to make her leave, but she resisted and kept shouting: 'Let me play! I want to play! I need to play!'

'Get out, bitch,' one of them said, and he shoved her hard.

She fell on her knees, but she continued to yell at the guards: 'I
need to play! Please! I need to play! I'll win the next round! I know
it! I'm one hundred percent sure! Please, let me play!'

The guy who had shoved her spat at her and she suddenly went
silent.

'Fuck off, old hag,' he told her, then both guards turned around
and went back inside.

The woman stayed on her knees, facing the ground. A few bystanders had stopped to watch the drama unfold, but now that it was
over, they ambled off. One boy in his early twenties lingered for a
bit longer than the others. He had filmed everything using his smart-
phone, and he was now probably posting it somewhere. As soon as
the upload was complete, he tucked the phone in his pocket and
went to the bar where I had spent my evening. As he was about to
enter, I turned to him, still sitting on my bike and smoking.

'You leave her there, just like that?'

'What?' he asked, turning his head in my direction, his right
hand on the doorknob.

'Shouldn't you at least go over to her and ask if she needs help?
Especially after you filmed the whole thing.'

'Who are you? A know-it-all saint who spreads love across the
universe? She's just a stupid addict who spends all her time and money on stupid pachinko. Just look at her,' he said, and we both turned
in her direction. She was still kneeling in the middle of the crowded street, probably crying. 'Pathetic,' he continued. 'She got what
she deserved. I just hope she doesn't have any kids. If she does, you
should be worried about them, not this bitch. Oh, and go fuck yourself,' he told me, and then he turned and entered the bar.

I smoked the last bit of my cigarette, then stubbed it on the ground and stood up. I went over to the woman.

'Yuriko-san.'

My voice didn't reach her, so I tried one more time, a little louder: 'Yuriko-san!'

She raised her head and looked at me. Her eyes were all red, her make-up a mess, her hair like a bird's nest.

'It's me, Yuriko-san. Sato.'

'Sato-kun...'

'Come, let me help you,' I told her, then I helped her up. She reeked of alcohol.

'Thank you.'

'You've been drinking,' I said. 'And playing.'

She turned away.

I sighed and told her: 'Let's have a talk, the two of us. I'll buy you a coffee.' She nodded. 'But first, wait here for a little, will you? I have to take care of something. I'll be back in a minute.' She nodded again.

I went back to the bar. I looked around after I had entered, searching for the boy from before. I saw him at a table with two other boys his age and three girls, so I went over to them and stood next to their table with my arms crossed.

He looked up: 'You again? What do you want?'

I quickly grabbed the back of his hair and smashed his head against the table. His friends and the girls froze from shock, and everyone else in the bar looked in our direction. His nose was bleeding badly. I had probably broken it, but I didn't give him any chance to react, instead pulling him up and landing two hard punches in his stomach. He fell to the ground and I followed, kneeling on him and pressing my elbow against his throat.

I bent close to his ear and whispered: 'You never, ever leave a woman like that. Understood? Do you understand? Promise.

Promise you'll never be such a retarded idiot ever again.' I pressed his throat even harder. 'Say it.'

'I promise, I promise,' he stammered, almost choking.

'And ask for permission when you upload stuff about other people,' I said, and I gave him one final shove.

At that moment, someone came storming out of the staff-only room, screaming.

'What the hell's going on?! You!' a short, but visibly strong man said, pointing at me and rushing across the bar. 'What the fuck are you doing?! That's my nephew there! You'll pay for this, you bastard!'

I waited until he was about to grab me before raising my gaze. The moment he saw my face he stopped and didn't know what to say or what to do. Three of his henchmen were right behind him, gripping something under their coats.

'What's going on?' he asked in a more subdued tone.

I stood up, straightened my shirt and my jacket, tucked some loose hair behind my ears, and lit a cigarette.

'Is this your nephew, Aramaki?'

Aramaki managed several of our bars in Shinjuku. He was in his early fifties, but he had the strength and the physique of a thirty-something-year-old. He worked out twice every day in his private gym right below this particular bar, probably to compensate for his baldness. He was always angry at everyone, including himself, and he didn't mind using violence, and he often went overboard. The only thing I liked about him was his sense of style. Always trendy and immaculate.

'Yeah, he's my nephew,' Aramaki replied. 'What'd he do?'

'Teach him some respect,' I said. 'Although, I suppose you can't teach what you don't know.'

'You bastard,' he replied, clenching his fists. 'I'll rip you apart.'

I blew the cigarette smoke in his face and leaned closer.

'The boss knows,' I said. 'You're done here.'

As I took a step back, I saw his expression change. The corners of his mouth curled down and all the glossiness disappeared from his eyes. He couldn't blink.

I turned away and walked to the door. His men wanted to go after me, but he stopped them. 'Leave him,' he whispered. His left hand was shaking.

I closed my eyes before leaving. I had to prepare for my usual transition between the realities of the inside and the outside. I counted back from five, and as I got to one, the music playing in the background suddenly sounded like I had earbuds in my ears, the kinds which go deep inside and shut out all the external noise. It was an instrumental piece from a movie I had seen not long before. I couldn't remember though, so I let the music take over, and take me away.

I heard a piano with two voices: a high and a low one. Both started out gently, but with a certain strength, and as they went along, this strength increased. The alto sounded like an energetic and naughty little fox, playing and jumping around the deeper and calmer sound of a wolf. I imagined them come out of the woods to meet in the middle of a green, grassy field, and then play with each other, like two lovers. As the piano became faster, these two lovers embraced and rolled around in the grass. Suddenly, the music slowed down, almost grinding to a halt, and the animals just lay there, surrounded by vast greenness. The fox gently put her head on the wolf's chest, and they both breathed deeply, in synchrony, looking at the white clouds above them.

"Her," I remembered the movie, and I left the bar.

Yuriko was waiting for me outside, shivering a bit.

'It's cold,' I said. 'And you're sobering up.'

She nodded, without looking at me.

'Let's go,' I said. 'I know a place.'

One of the darker alleys of Kabukichō had a small bar I liked to visit late into the night. It was a dodgy little place with all kinds of weird guests, almost all of them regulars. Tourists and even local Japanese rarely visited, and if they did happen in, most would leave immediately after entering.

Yoshi-san ran the place – a distant relative of the boss. He was not part of our family, but we all treated him with respect. His place became a sort of a safe house, where anyone could speak freely, without having to fear anything would get out. It was a rule we all took seriously: what was said at Yoshi's stayed at Yoshi's. And he also served the best chocolate cocktail in the world.

The bar only had space for ten guests – ten bar stools around Yoshi's semicircular counter. He prepared the cocktails himself, and he had a single employee in a small kitchen in the back. He had spent a decade in New York, where he had learned his trade, and he had then come back to open his own little bar back in the nineties. He only played blues, or occasionally old-school rock. Jimi Hendrix was on when we entered.

'Hey, Yoshi-san.'

'Sato. Nice to see you. It's been a while.'

'Well, not really. I came in three nights ago.'

'Only three nights? Was it only three nights? Jeez, I'm getting old. I should retire.'

'Oh, you know you can't,' I told him. 'I'd hunt you down. I couldn't survive without your chocolate cocktail.'

'Yeah, I know,' he replied. 'I know you couldn't. And I know you'd hunt me down,' he said with a cheeky smile.

'So, make me one.'

'All right. And your partner? Miss, what would you like to drink?'

'I think I'll have the same,' Yuriko said.

'She'll have an espresso and a glass of tap water,' I intervened. 'Make it caffeine-free.'

'Y-Yes, Sato-kun is right. A coffee and some water, please.'

Yoshi-san looked at me, then nodded: 'Understood.'

We took a seat by the left corner of the counter, and we sat in silence until our order arrived. Yuriko immediately drank out her shot of espresso, and then she emptied the whole glass of water.

'Would you like another one?' I asked.

'No, thank you.'

'Ok.'

A few minutes of silence passed, and then I tried to break the ice. 'What happened, Yuriko?'

She kept staring at my cocktail without answering.

'Yuriko? What was that earlier?'

'They didn't let me play,' she finally answered. 'I... I would've won, but they didn't let me. Those idiots. They ruined everything.'

'They?'

'The thugs at the pachinko place. Those brainless muscle-heads. I hate people like that. They know only violence and how to intimidate others. And besides, what kind of job is that? Stand around all day, or worse, all night, and pester other people, decent people, normal people?'

'Like you?'

'Y-Yes, like me,' she replied hesitantly.

'So, you don't like their job?'

'I think they should be ashamed of themselves, that's what I think.'

'I see. And you? Have you found a job?'

She paused for a moment before giving me an answer.

'No, not yet. It's just... It's so difficult. There are no decent jobs, not even in a huge city like Tokyo. I know it's hard to believe, but I can tell you, there are no jobs for a woman like me.'

'A woman like you?' I asked.

'Yes. I mean, a woman in her forties, raising a child alone, divorced.'

'You're not divorced,' I said. 'My half-brother died before you could get divorced. You're a widow.'

'Oh, yeah, you're right. A widow. And now that you tell me, actually, I'd have a better shot at finding a job if I were divorced.'

'How so?'

'Well, getting a divorce and deciding to raise a child on your own shows strength. It shows character, right? People would say I was brave and tough and determined, and then they would give me a job, cause they'd think that if I was so brave in my private life, I'd be brave in the workplace too. But no. That stupid bastard had to die before we got divorced. He made me into a poor, good-for-nothing widow and took all my respect and self-esteem with him to the grave. He left me nothing.'

'He *did* leave you a house, didn't he? Quite a big one. You would be homeless by now if it wasn't for him.'

'Yeah, right. The house. It's more of a burden than anything, to be honest. There's always something to fix, it's expensive to heat in the winter, and that creaking sound the floor makes... Oh, how I hate that floor. Every step I take in that house, it laughs in my face and reminds me of how hopeless my life is. I hate it.'

'Then why don't you sell it? You could buy a flat and save up the rest for your daughter, to finance her studies.'

'Sell it? That house? Who would buy it? There's no way I'd get a halfway decent price for it. Especially with what's going on inside.'

'Why? What's going on inside?'

She suddenly went silent and turned her head away.

'What's happening in the house, Yuriko?' I asked.

'Nothing.'

'Yuriko,' I said, but she didn't say a word. Or even flinch. 'Yuriko!' I grabbed her hand and squeezed it, almost hurting her.

'There are... ghosts.'

'What?'

'Ghosts. You know what ghosts are.'

'Of course I know what ghosts are.'

'Ok, then why ask?'

'Because you're fucking mental, that's why,' I replied, almost losing my temper. 'So, what ghosts? What's happening exactly? I want to know.'

'Why?' she asked. 'Why do you want to know?'

'Because I care.'

'Yeah, right.'

'I care, Yuriko. I care about Kiki.'

'Kiki...' she repeated her daughter's name.

'Yes, Kiki. I want her safe,' I said, 'and I want her to have everything she needs in life.'

'Of course. Kiki should have everything. Kiki should have fun. Kiki should be happy. Kiki this, Kiki that, it's all about Kiki. Always her. Never me. Why, Sato-kun? Why? Why can't it be about me for once?'

She put her hand on mine and got a little closer, leaning in to give me a kiss. I could smell the cheap perfume she had probably stolen from somewhere, and its fake sweetness made her seem older than she was. But even the perfume couldn't hide the combination of alcohol and coffee coming from her mouth.

'Stop it,' I said, pushing her away.

She drew her hand back, then turned to Yoshi-san who had been watching us with one eye: 'Vodka. Clean.'

I was about to intervene, but she was quicker: 'Fuck you. I'm paying with my own money. Don't babysit me. I'm not your sweet little Kiki.'

I looked at Yoshi-san and nodded. He poured a small glass of Finlandia and put it in front of her. It was gone in the blink of an eye.

'Tell me, Yuriko. What's this ghost story of yours? I'm listening.'

She held the empty glass in both her hands and began to talk.

'I don't know, really. It happens from time to time, and more and more often. There are nights when I can't sleep, and I just stare at the ceiling from my futon. Then, from the depth of the darkness, I start hearing this strange squealing. Like a scared animal. The first time I heard it I thought it was coming from outside, and I waited until it stopped. But I kept hearing it night after night, so one time, I decided to take a look. I left my room, went to the living room, and listened. It got a bit louder, and it seemed like it was coming from above. From the upper floor, you know. One of the rooms up there.'

'So, you went upstairs?'

'Yes, but it took a while. I was scared as shit. I took a kitchen knife, just in case, and went upstairs slowly, really slowly.'

'Which room was it?' I asked.

'The one to the left. In the back. You know, the big one.' I nodded. 'So, I went to the door, trying not to make any noise. The squealing was definitely coming from the room. I peeked inside, and at that moment, a deafening scream shook the walls of the house. I dropped the knife and ran down as fast as I could. I almost shit in my pants right there, and I already imagined my new, pink, satin panties full of crap.'

I almost laughed.

'It's true,' she said. 'And I've been hearing it ever since. It's the same every time. I hear the squealing, then I go up, then something screams like crazy, but when I enter the room, there's nothing there.'

'Nothing,' I repeated.

'Nothing. No animal, no kids playing some prank, no recording of some animal being slaughtered. Nothing.'

'Strange,' I said.

'Strange indeed. Very strange.'

'And Kiki?' I asked.

'Nothing.'

'What nothing?'

'She never hears anything. She's a good sleeper, but still... Strange.'

'Hm.'

We spent the next few seconds in silence, and then Yoshi-san approached us: 'Anything else to drink?'

'No, thank you,' I said. 'The bill, please.'

Yuriko opened her wallet to give me money for the vodka, but I declined: 'Forget it. I'm paying.'

'Thank you,' she said, looking me in the eye.

'That money, that's not your money,' I replied. 'I gave it to Kiki so that she could take care of herself. But she's too kind and too forgiving. And she loves you, even though you do everything not to deserve it. I'm her uncle and I'll keep helping her. But if I catch you wasting her money again, wasting *my* money on games and booze, I swear, I'll hurt you.'

My words froze the air in Yoshi-san's bar. All the guests went silent for a second. Like ice sculptures at a snow festival. I left the money on the counter.

'I'll be watching you,' I told Yuriko. 'See you, Yoshi-san.'

***

I liked watching Kiki drink her favorite chai-latte. She looked so... innocent.

I rarely witnessed such innocence anywhere else. I had known the word since I was a child, but I never really understood its meaning until I first saw Kiki drink. It used to be hot cocoa milk when she was still a child, then she switched to chai-latte around age fifteen. But her expression stayed the same: closed eyes, the thin line of her mouth curving upwards on both ends, her cheeks turning red, her eyebrows rising as if they were saluting the new sun at dawn. There always seemed to be a certain glow around her in these moments; a soft light which made the lines of her body blur into its surroundings. This light felt warm and soothing. It made me understand the word "innocence" without any explanation. Innocence was on display in front of me, and I felt lucky to be in its presence. Even if only for a few moments.

At the same time, somewhere deep down, I also felt anger. Maybe even rage. I was angry at the world and all the adults in it, including myself, as we constantly failed to cherish, and even more importantly, to protect this innocence. And I saw this in Kiki's eyes. I saw the fear each time she opened them after finishing her cup of warm whatever she had been drinking. It floated across the surface of her eyes like a shadow – a shadow which kept whispering words of loss, words of pain, words of suffering. I felt ashamed each time, so I would turn my head away to look at the street from the window.

'What's wrong, uncle? You have this look on your face again.'

'It's nothing,' I replied. 'I just like watching the street. The traffic and the people. It calms me, I guess.'

'Why do you need calming every time I see you?' she asked. 'Is it because of me?'

I looked at her, then shook my head without saying anything.

'I see,' she said, lowering her look.

'Here, take this.' I gave her an envelope with two hundred and fifty thousand yen inside. 'For the next month.'

'Thanks,' she said, and she put it in her bag.

'Kiki.'

'Yes?'

'Please, use it wisely. It's not much, but it should be enough if you take good care of it. Soon, I might even be able to give you more. Just promise me you won't spend it on anything stupid.'

It was her turn to look out the window. She only nodded.

'Say it. I want you to say it.'

'I promise.' Her voice was deep but barely audible.

'I have to go now. I have some things to take care of.'

'When will I see you again?' she asked with a sudden change in her voice, with expectation and excitement.

'In a month. As usual, I guess.'

The excitement evaporated as instantly as it came. Like a shooting star streaking across the summer sky.

'Couldn't we go to movies or do something else together once in a while? We could visit the aquarium in Sky Tree, for example. My friends told me it was lovely, and they even have many-many cute little penguins. I looove penguins!'

'Maybe,' I said. 'But I can't promise. We'll see.'

'You always say that. Why can't you promise? You make *me* promise things, but you never promise me anything in return. Why, uncle Sato?' she asked, crossing her arms and smirking.

'I just can't. Believe me, I would if I could. But I can't.'

'But why?'

'Its... difficult. I can't tell you. Not yet. Maybe later. I will. Here, I promise I will tell you the reason when the time is right. Ok? I can promise that much.'

She grunted, then sighed, then loosened her arms again.

'Ok.'

'Ok,' I replied. 'I have to go now. See you. Be a good girl.'

'I will,' she said, flashing a faint smile.

***

I needed some practice, so I decided to go back home. My apartment was not far away, just across the train tracks, in Daikanyama. I rented a small studio from the boss. Our family had a ton of apartments for rent cheap, offered to family members, but mine was the private property of boss Yamaguchi. It cost me only forty thousand yen a month, so I was able to give money to Kiki since I spent very little on myself. Most of my money went into Eleanor and going to the movies.

The flat was on the top, the fourth floor of a relatively new building. It was small, but I liked it because it had a pretty high ceiling for Japanese standards, a small but covered balcony on the street front, and an empty rooftop to which only my apartment had direct access. None of the other residents used the roof, so I practically had it to myself. Apart from the occasional drying clothes in one corner, it really was empty, and it served as my little "dojo". I practiced a very traditional style of "kenjutsu", which I had learned from the boss and Kobayashi-san.

When I got home, I changed into my practice gear, picked up both the wooden and the real sword, and went to the rooftop. I wore a simple, black "hakama" which must have been some fifteen years old, and a dark blue upper coat typically used in kendo. My wooden sword, my "bokken" was even older – probably around a hundred years or so. I was the fourth generation to have it, and I had gotten it from the boss when I earned the first "dan" rank several years ago. It had belonged to his grandfather.

I did some stretching for a quarter of an hour or so, then I spent another fifteen minutes practicing just the basic cuts. I liked doing the basics, as it helped me settle in and forget about the outside world. It was the simplicity and the repetitive nature of the moves, I guess. A kind of meditation, really.

After the warm-up, I lay down the bokken and took the real sword in my hands. I hadn't used it for quite a while. I held it on top of my palms and had a look as if I were seeing it for the first time. It had this strange power almost to hypnotize people. I always wondered whether it was the pure, white color of the scabbard or the silver dragon engraved into it or the combination of the two.

Three white cherry flowers decorated its silver "tsuba", while the handle was again an elegant back-and-forth between the white and the silver. The sword was the exact opposite of boss Yamaguchi's, apart from the blade, of course. The blades were identical – like twins. A renowned swordsmith from a small village somewhere in the mountains of Gifu had forged them from the same piece of ore back in the eighteenth century. Yamaguchi's sword was called "Kuro" and mine was "Shiro". Black and white.

I put the sword on the inside of my belt, then I set up a rolled tatami rush mat as my practice target. I checked to make sure it was firm and straight, then I turned around and took a few steps back. I closed my eyes and concentrated on my breathing: through the lungs, into the center of my stomach, holding it for a bit, then back the same way, with a slow, elongated breath. I repeated the same routine exactly twenty times, and each time I felt my muscles loosen up a bit more, while the clouds hovering above my head slowly faded away. With number twenty came a clear, unblemished sky.

The moment the last bit of cloud evaporated, I opened my eyes, and at the same time, I quickly turned around, unsheathing the sword and landing a single, horizontal blow to the practice tatami. Its top half stood firm for a few seconds, then it began to slide down, like an iceberg when a quake cuts it in half. I stood motionless, watching, my right hand stretched out, with the sword as its natural continuation. I couldn't feel where my hand ended and the sword began. They felt as one.

The top part of the tatami finally slid down and was about to fall to the ground while turning over at the same time. But it didn't. It stayed there, hanging by a single, thin thread as if someone had reached out with a helping hand at the last moment. Someone didn't want it to fall just yet. Someone had kept it alive.

A purple-eyed bird

I took a shower after practice and then made a simple dinner. I had an omelet with three eggs, tofu, and green peppers. A typical dinner of mine – I would have it three or four times a week. Simple, light, tasty. And I liked the combination of colors. The yellow, the green, and the white went really well together. For a while, I had thought it was only me with this strange attraction to this particular set of colors, but then I learned that people over in Europe love preparing eggs with spinach and goat cheese. Of course, you prepare a dish because you want to eat something good, but it can't be good enough if it doesn't have the looks. Even before the tongue gets to decide whether the food is good or bad or somewhere in between the nose and the eyes give the first impression. And the first impression is crucial. It creates an idea of how the food will taste, and it's almost impossible to ignore. Like planting a seed inside the mind, for small veins to then grow out of it in the blink of an eye. These veins run wide, run deep, and attach themselves to all kinds of other veins from other seeds of other ideas. And it requires precision surgery to detach and untangle them. As I said, it's almost impossible. But there is a way. Kei once told me about a person who can fully remove one idea from the mind while leaving everything else intact. The "Cleaner", he called him.

According to Kei, artificially removing ideas is risky. When you remove them, they don't disappear, die, or self-destruct. No, they stay. More precisely, they go back to the "Sea of Thought" – the source of all ideas. The Sea of Thought is usually not visible to us humans. It resides in a different dimension. It's hard to describe, but a simple version would be to think of it as the outer layer of space. The one up there, with all the planets and stars. The infinite one. You take the space, then turn it inside out, like a sweater, and that's where you find the Sea of Thought.

The ideas, they all live in this sea, they form it, and we humans have more affinity to some and less to others. Essentially, we are more likely to get certain ideas. It's all fine when the process of getting a specific idea is natural and happens in a clear context. The troublesome part begins when we meddle with the process, and meddling happens when ideas are forcibly removed. Namely, when an idea becomes a part of us, a bond develops both at the physical and the metaphysical level. When someone removes an idea, the bond breaks in the physical, but it stays in the metaphysical. The more precisely an idea is removed, the weaker the bond becomes, but it can never disappear, not even when the Cleaner does it because the memory of the bond is engraved into the subconscious for eternity.

What the bond does is that it pulls back the removed idea to the mind from which it was removed. But this rebound typically occurs in the next life. And it happens uncontrollably, out of context, making it even more difficult for your next self to deal with it. So, you may think an idea was successfully eliminated by a psychologist, a guru, a healer, a medicine, or even the Cleaner himself, but it comes back to you. If the Cleaner does it, chances are the idea might only have a sniff at you in your next life, or just brush the surface of your mind and then leave. There are even accounts of ideas just watching from afar, but not returning to the mind for multiple lives. But they come back, eventually. And the longer it takes for the idea to return, the more violently it hits when it does.

***

I finished my dinner and soon left the apartment. It was roughly nine in the evening. I wore my favorite, dark-blue jeans with black motorcycle boots and a black leather jacket. I wrapped my sword, Shiro, in a white, cotton bag, and I carried it across my back as I rode away on Eleanor.

I got to Roppongi around quarter past nine. I left Eleanor near the National Art Center, under one of the cherry trees between the museum and the neighboring university. The trees had another couple of days before they would start to bloom. I loved them in this phase of their cycle – much more than with all the pink and white flowers covering their branches. I always felt the flowers were there as a mask, to hide their true nature. I don't really know why the trees wanted everyone to see them and love them with all that make-up on. Maybe they were just as insecure as anyone out there. But I was never really a fan of fake eyelashes, bright lipstick, or colorful nails. I prefer the bare, naked truth.

Watching these trees like this, just before they bloomed, felt like watching a nightclub dancer sit in her private room in the back of the bar, alone, in silence, preparing for the show. She would be sitting on a small chair in front of a large mirror with just her panties on. No paint on her face, no sexy lingerie, no glitter on her hair. She would lean closer and inspect herself in the mirror. A wrinkle on her forehead, small bags below her eyes, a slight paleness, and lips as thin as a thread. She would see herself the way she really was, and she'd see beauty. Beauty in how the wrinkles curved and curled, beauty in how the darkish bags supported her eyes from below, beauty in the innocence of her pale skin, and beauty in the perfect straightness of her mouth. But there would also be an undefinable something, residing in the depths of her eyes, making her even more beautiful. I'd see it even from the dark corner of the room I'd be watching her from. And she'd see it, too. Her true nature. Herself.

I left the trees and went to a nearby 7-Eleven. I bought a bar of simple Meiji milk chocolate. As I was leaving, I noticed a funny little man at the newspaper section near the entrance. He was looking at a soft-porn magazine – one which specialized in Japanese women with large breasts. He was turning the pages pretty fast, then he stopped at a double-pager in the middle of the magazine. He stared at the picture for several seconds, so I got a little closer to have a look myself. It was a girl in her thirties, probably a bit older than the rest of the models in the paper. She was sitting on a sofa in white stockings, with no panties or bra, just a fully transparent babydoll, also in white. Her breasts were big, but not as big as some of the others in the magazine. The room she was sitting in was bright, with a large window looking out on a typical Japanese garden. She was looking at the garden, or rather something specific in it. Her eyes were focused, and whatever or whoever she saw clearly made her anxious. It was written all over her face. She was scared.

'What are you looking at?' I asked.

'What? Who? Me?!' the man asked with apparent surprise and embarrassment, and he hastily closed the magazine.

'Hello, Kon.'

'Oh, hello! It's you! S-Sato-san! Hello!'

'What's up, Kon? Everything all right?'

'Oh, yes! Everything's perfect! I mean, it isn't! I mean... Oh, I don't know, Sato-san,' he replied, lowering his eyes to look at the cover of the magazine he was still holding. It pictured the same girl.

'You should be looking at job offerings, instead,' I said, pointing at the magazine. 'But you also lost your girlfriend, right?'

'Right.'

'I see. Well, if it helps... Come, I'll buy it for you,' I offered, and I grabbed the magazine.

'N-No, it's ok! Really! You don't need to!'

We looked each other in the eye, both holding the magazine in between us. We stood like that for a couple of seconds.

'It's all right,' I said, and he let go of it.

'Thanks.'

'You're welcome. But please don't cry,' I said as I saw tears in his eyes. 'You'll embarrass us both.'

'Ok, I won't,' he replied, wiping them away with his sleeve like the last time.

We left the convenience store together after I had paid for thirty-seven pairs of huge breasts, and outside I offered him one of my cigarettes.

'No, thank you. I'm fine,' he declined, glancing at the chocolate bar I was holding in my other hand.

'Oh, I see,' I said. 'You want some chocolate, right?'

He hesitated, then nodded.

'Let's split it, then.'

I opened the wrapping and broke the bar in two. I let him have the slightly bigger half.

'It's good, right?' I asked.

'Mm.' His mouth was full, and the chocolate disappeared from the face of the earth in less than five seconds. 'My favorite,' he mumbled, still enjoying the last crumbs.

'Yeah, mine too,' I said. 'It's the simple things that taste best. Anyway, I need to go now. It was good seeing you again. Take care,' I said, waving goodbye and turning around to leave.

'Wait! Sato-san! Please, wait!'

'Hm?'

'Where are you going, Sato-san? Are you in a hurry? I thought... I thought maybe we could... hang out a little,' he said in a voice as shy as that of a teenage boy asking out a girl for the first time in his life.

'Well, I'm in kind of a hurry. I've got something to take care of tonight. Sorry, Kon. Maybe next time. Ok?'

'O-Ok. By the way, what's that on your back, if I may ask?'

'It's nothing,' I replied, without turning back this time.

'Is it a sword, Sato-san?!' he shouted as I left. 'It is, isn't it?!'

I raised my hand and kept walking.

***

I went around the small university and the National Art Center and then crossed the street to head to the cemetery. On my way, I finished my half of the chocolate, savoring every little square of it. What distinguishes the Meiji milk chocolate from every other chocolate is the way it melts in your mouth. I just love the feeling. I wondered how someone could eat it as quickly as Kon did, without letting it reach its full potential, but then again, we're all different, aren't we.

Kon... A strange little man. And I kept running into him over the course of the past twenty-four hours. Here was a person I had never seen before, yet his face, his voice, his whole presence felt so familiar. It's funny how time plays tricks on your perceptions. I had a few people in my life whom I had known for years, but the fact that the experience with him was both recent and so out of the ordinary somehow made my mind put his image in front of everyone else's.

I got to the entrance of Aoyama-cemetery. It's a place I've always liked. Its grace, its silence, its magnificent cherry trees. Other people tend to avoid cemeteries, especially at night, but I find them peaceful, and a perfect place to retreat to. I would walk past the graves and imagine what lives, what experiences, what joys and tragedies all those people had gone through – in the recent past, in distant history, even in forgotten times.

I stepped inside and walked a couple of feet, and then I stopped at the grave of General Sōroku Kawakami to my right. He had been a prominent figure in the Japanese Imperial Army after the Meiji restoration and a brilliant military strategist of samurai descent. I knew a lot about him, especially his heroics in defending the besieged Kumamoto-castle during the rebellion against the Tokugawa shogunate. To Kobayashi-san, he was a role model of sorts, or a hero, if you like it, so he used to tell me stories about him when I was younger. People of his generation looked up to generals and martyrs of the past instead of the imaginary superheroes and fictional characters the youngsters of today hold dear.

I had another fifteen minutes until ten, so I lit a cigarette and sat on a nearby bench. I heard a car drive by and the bark of a dog, but then everything went silent as if the cemetery had gone into a state of slumber. Nothing came in from the street. I just sat there, smoking and fidgeting with the hundred-yen coin in my pocket.

Suddenly, the wind picked up a little, and as the branches of the cherry trees began to sway, a voice seemed to appear from somewhere, shooshing and whispering, like young lovers do in the back of a cinema.

I closed my eyes.

'Come inside, Sato-kun,' Kobayashi-san said.

I took off my shoes and stepped inside the dojo. Kobayashi-san and Yamaguchi had just finished practicing.

'You did well, little boy,' Yamaguchi said, putting his wooden practice sword away. 'The information you collected on the Fushimi brothers is very valuable and highly appreciated. Good work.'

'Thank you, sir,' I replied, lowering my gaze.

'I told you I'd give you a single chance. You remember?' Yamaguchi asked.

I nodded.

'You proved yourself worthy, so now it's my turn to provide,' he continued, taking off his sweat-soaked gear, and getting a little closer. He had perfect abs and big, strong hands. Especially for someone his age. 'You can live here, in the dojo. There is a room in the back,' he said, raising a finger, 'and you can use it as your own. It's not big, but way better than your cardboard box. You'll get breakfast, lunch, and dinner every day, and we'll provide you with clothes and other stuff you might need. In exchange, I ask four things of you,' he said, stepping even closer and looking me straight in the eye: 'you'll practice "kenjutsu" with me and Kobayashi-san, you'll keep this dojo clean, you'll do the tasks and jobs I assign to you, and most importantly, you'll be loyal to me and me only.'

I didn't know what to say or how to react. A couple of days earlier I had been a homeless kid living on the streets, begging for money, stealing stuff. There had been nothing in my life I could have been happy about, I could have held dear, I could cherish. I hadn't had anything to look forward to or aim for. I had been numb to anything this world had to offer. I had been a drifter.

And now, out of nowhere, I had been offered a life. Meaning and purpose. A home, even an everyday routine. And food. But more importantly, I now had other people in my life. People who weren't just passersby or bystanders on the edges of my world, but fully and properly involved. They didn't treat me like air, like filth, like a piece of shit. For the first time, other people saw value in me and trusted in me. For the first time, I felt like a proper human being.

'What's your answer, Sato?' asked Yamaguchi. 'Do you accept my terms?'

I nodded.

'Say it! I want to hear it! You have a voice, don't you?'

'Yes,' I replied.

'Yes, boss!' Yamaguchi corrected me. 'You'll call me boss, from now on.'

'Yes, boss!' I said, and I bowed.

The boss nodded and left the dojo. I stood motionless, looking at the sliding door he had just closed. His presence was still lingering in the air, like a dark, heavy cloud. He had this power to stay visible even long after he was gone. His subordinates would often say how they thought they had seen him in the corner of a room, on top of a bridge, or just walking next to them in the middle of the night, but when they looked again, they saw no one. Like a ghost. Or a god, as some of them put it.

'You're mesmerized, aren't you?' Kobayashi-san asked. 'He does this to you. Our boss. He has this impressive aura that draws you in and doesn't let go. You're seduced, but it never lets you know for sure if you should feel privileged or scared. It keeps you in a limbo between heaven and hell.'

Kobayashi-san walked over to me and put a hand on my shoulder. 'But you're impressive, too, kid. I sensed your potential the moment I saw you, but even I didn't expect you to get so much intel in such a short time. Well done, my boy!'

'It was easy,' I replied. 'I know my way around the city. Especially Shinjuku. It was easy to find them, and even easier to spy on them.'

'Well, if you say so... But just so you know, they are a nasty little bunch, the two of them. The Fushimi brothers.'

'Do you know them?'

'More or less,' Kobayashi-san replied. 'I know them well enough to know I don't like them.'

'So, what will the boss do with this information? What will happen to them?' I asked.

'Just let the boss decide on that. He'll know what to do.'

'Will he harm them?'

Kobayashi-san looked at me, then stared into the distance, far beyond the walls of the dojo. After a few seconds, he let go of my shoulder, he picked up a wooden practice sword from a large box full of practice gear and accessories and gave it to me.

'Have you heard of General Kawakami, Sato-kun?' he asked, changing the subject.

'No,' I replied, looking at the practice sword in my hands.

'He was a general for Emperor Meiji's imperial army about a hundred years ago. A very good general.' Kobayashi-san picked up a practice sword for himself, too, and he took a stance with his right leg in front and slightly bent, his left leg straight and serving as an anchor, the tip of his sword pointing straight at my face. 'But even before formally joining the military, he served our emperor during the rebellion against the shogunate. I think he was not even twenty when he fought in the all-important battle of Toba-Fushimi.'

'Fushimi?' I asked. 'Like the brothers?'

'Yes, like the brothers.'

Kobayashi-san got closer and showed me the proper grip. 'You hold it like this,' he said. 'Imagine squeezing a towel, but keep it a bit loose at the same time. You hold the handle mostly with your pinky and your ring finger on both hands. Maybe also the middle finger. But the thumb and the index finger are there only for support and feel.'

'I see.'

'And raise that tip a bit. It should point at the enemy's face. I'm your enemy now, so aim for my nose or my eyes.'

I did as Kobayashi-san had told me, and I tried imitating his stance.

'A bit wider. Keep a shoulder-length distance between your feet. That's right.' He then raised the sword above his head, 'And now, you strike down in a straight line, slicing your opponent in half, right down to his belly button. Like this.' And he swung.

I could hear the wooden blade cut through the air, and even though the strike was incredibly fast, the blade moved in a perfect vertical line and stopped in a similarly perfect horizontal position, as if reaching a flat surface full of instant glue and sticking to it the moment they connected.

'Come, give it a swing,' Kobayashi-san told me. 'Imagine being the young Kawakami in the middle of a huge battlefield, surrounded by thousands of enemy soldiers, out of which a single man, almost as young as you, steps in front of you, raises his sword, and starts screaming in your face. He wants to strike fear in your heart; he wants to show his strength, his bravery, his determination; he wants to kill you. Yes, you are scared, Kawakami is scared, but so is the young man rushing and yelling at you. All the twenty thousand men who faced off on those four days near Fushimi were scared. All of them. But that's no excuse. You can be scared and die, or you can be scared and live. It all depends on how you absorb the moment and your feelings within the moment. And then, on how you react.

'You summon all these emotions into a small, condensed sphere of energy inside your belly. You concentrate on the sphere, on your belly, and as you raise your sword, you channel the sphere through your body into the sword, you let it travel all the way to the top, then you let it leave the sword, right through the tip, and you imagine it hovering in the air, slightly behind your head, and slightly above it. Right here,' Kobayashi-san said, pointing at a spot a couple of feet behind and above me, while I was holding my sword raised. 'And now, strike!'

***

I opened my eyes again. The big handle of my vintage Seiko was approaching fifty-five minutes. It was almost ten. I kept looking at my watch, and I concentrated so that I could hear the sound of its movement. It was a mechanical Lord Marvel 36000 from 1972 – Seiko's first ever high-beat movement wristwatch, with thirty-six thousand vibrations of the balance wheel per hour. It wasn't a particularly rare or expensive piece – I had gotten it for as little as forty thousand yen –, but it was beautifully preserved, almost like new, and its minimalistic, simple elegance made it look like something special. I absolutely loved listening to its speedy movement.

I stood up and looked at general Kawakami's grave one more time. A few of the branches from a nearby cherry tree hung over it like dragon claws, and they looked as if they were either guarding it or eagerly waiting for the right moment to attack. As I was observing the branches, I noticed a big black bird on one of them. I was never good with birds, so I didn't know if it was a raven or a crow, but I had the feeling it was looking at me. Not like an animal would look at a human, but rather a person curiously inspecting another person. What made the whole thing even more confusing was that it or he or she felt familiar. I wasn't sure whether it was the *bird* I had seen before or the person behind the bird, but we most certainly knew each other.

It had purple eyes.

I nodded in the direction of the bird, and again in front of the general's grave, then I turned around and headed for the meeting point.

***

I had to go further into the cemetery along the main road and then turn left and walk for a little more. The others were already there when I arrived.

The boss and Kobayashi-san wore their traditional "kenjutsu" gear: a black hakama and an indigo blue upper coat. It's what they usually did on occasions like this – I had already seen it a few times. They had their long katana swords inside their belts, and they stood in silence, watching me approach.

A bit further away, Ryuji, the boss's current bodyguard, was sitting on one of the graves, inspecting his sword. He had chosen an immaculate navy-blue Ermenegildo Zegna suit for the event, wearing similarly colored Italian leather shoes and a very thin tie, again of the same color. His black shirt must have been freshly ironed. His face was clean-shaven. He was the silent type – the boss never used talkative people as bodyguards. I actually liked Ryuji, probably because we respected each other. We hardly ever spoke, only when necessary.

He raised his head the moment he heard my steps, and then he stood up without a trace of excitement. He was a tall, lean guy, who mostly relied on his speed, his flexibility, and his wit. He never pretended to be the strongest, but his confidence in his abilities and himself was high. He brushed some dust off his suit and straightened it and then put the sword back into its scabbard and lowered his arms, holding the katana in his left hand.

I stopped some fifteen to twenty feet away, took the white case off my back, and pulled out the sword. I, too, held it in my left hand, with my arms hanging next to my body.

'Ryuji,' the boss said. 'Sato here is challenging you for the position as my personal bodyguard. You know what that means, as you yourself challenged the guy who had had the post before.'

'Yes, boss,' Ryuji said.

'Good. And you, Sato, also know how this goes. You've witnessed it several times, right?'

'Right, boss.'

'Good. Any questions?'

We stood in silence, Ryuji and I, looking each other in the eye. We didn't have any questions for the boss or any words for each other. Ryuji had known this day would come the moment he had taken the position, and he also probably knew I was going to be the one who challenged him.

We bowed simultaneously, unsheathed our swords, threw the scabbards to the ground, and took a basic stance, holding our swords with both hands in front of us, right leg in front, the tip of each sword pointing at the face of the other foe.

For me, it was the first time dueling with someone in such a traditional way, with real swords. I had practiced one-on-one fights a lot with both Kobayashi-san and the boss and with some other guys who had trained with us. But fighting with wooden or bamboo weapons, often in protective gear, is completely different from fighting it out for real. It doesn't even compare. Of course, I had been involved in many situations where I had had to use my sword to hurt or kill other people, but that had been very different circumstances. Being an assassin for the family, in most of those cases, I had had the upper hand from the outset.

Ryuji had the advantage of having experienced a real duel with real swords when he had fought for the position. Also, as a bodyguard, he had been in several tight spots where he or the boss had been attacked by rival gangs – their henchmen or assassins like me. There was a rumor, an urban legend if you like, of him and the boss slaying ten men who had attacked them with swords and knives. According to some, the boss had dealt with two of them and Ryuji had fought off the other eight. It had happened shortly after Ryuji had become bodyguard, in a park near the Tokyo Metropolitan Building. Gossip was it had been a test – for both the boss and Ryuji. It never came to light whether the order had come from within or outside our family, but the next morning a homeless person living in the neighborhood had reported the whole incident to the police in the hope of getting a reward. He couldn't properly identify anyone, but his general description of the two men who had killed the other ten had fit the boss and Ryuji quite well. The police investigation got shut down pretty fast (probably the boss pulling some strings), but there had been a lot of talk in the news about the gruesomeness of the whole incident. The police had found the bodies (and body parts) piled up behind some bushes in a huge, thick pool of blood. Two bodies had had several dozen stab wounds, while the remaining eight had been cut up in bits and pieces and were missing hands, arms, legs, some even the head.

Looking at the man in front of me, it wasn't hard to imagine him killing eight men ruthlessly, all by himself. Yes, he was lean and thin and all polished, shiny, dandy, but behind the good looks lay a savage animal. I always thought of him as a wolf in disguise. It wasn't obvious, and you had to look deep into his eyes, way beyond the first few layers of his soul. But once you did, you saw the fangs of a big, black wolf, his eyes glowing in the womb of a dark cave.

Ryuji now raised his sword and held it high, to the right of his head, while putting his left foot in front, and leaning in a bit. I slid my right foot to the back in response, lowering my sword next to my right leg, the tip of the blade pointing to the ground.

We had total silence in the cemetery. Even the ghosts hushed their whispering. I could hear the beating of my heart, which was getting faster and faster by the second. Then, seemingly from nowhere, a big black bird flew in, and it settled on top of a gravestone somewhere halfway between me and Ryuji, opposite the spot where the boss and Kobayashi-san were standing. I turned my head slightly, just enough to see the bird while keeping most of my focus on my opponent.

The bird had purple eyes, but it didn't surprise me. What did was the girl standing next to the gravestone. I hadn't even realized she was there until that moment. "Where did she come from? Was she there all along? Who is she?"

A gust of wind swept across the cemetery, coming from where the girl was standing, and blowing right into my face. In that same instant, Ryuji threw himself at me, lightning-fast, slashing downwards diagonally with his sword. I stepped a bit to the left, lowering my whole stance, and striking upwards diagonally.

The wind kept blowing for a few more seconds, then it stopped.

I looked up at my sword, Shiro. It was pointing to the sky. All the lights of Roppongi tried relieving the blade of its pain, but they couldn't penetrate the dark, red blood dripping from it. Small drops kept splashing to the ground, breaking the silence with the sound of sorrow.

Ryuji's body thumped to the ground.

Kobayashi-san approached me with a piece of white cloth. I looked at him, then took the cloth and cleaned the blade. I picked up Shiro's white scabbard and sheathed the sword.

'Let me take it,' Kobayashi-san offered, extending his arms.

'It's ok,' I replied.

I looked at the boss. He nodded in silence, then turned and started walking away.

I looked in the direction of the girl. Her straight, long, black hair seemed to be of the same substance as the black feathers of the bird right next to her. But unlike the bird, she had green eyes.

The same gust of wind as before blew in my direction again, coming exactly from where she was standing. It brought her scent on its wings. A combination of musk, vanilla, and almonds.

I closed my eyes while inhaling the aroma. When I opened them again, she was leaving, back into the darkness of the cemetery where she had come from.

'Her name is Ren,' Kobayashi-san said.

The next moment the purple-eyed bird flew into the sky and departed in the direction of Roppongi, letting out a single, loud caw. I followed it with my gaze until it became one with the night.

'Ren,' I whispered.

Over the Rainbow-bridge

After the duel was over and everyone had gone, I felt as if I had been left standing alone on the shore of an infinite ocean. I saw no trees, no roads, no houses around me, nor were there any boats in the water or seagulls in the sky. There was only fine, white sand, and an ocean with no end.

I looked up, searching for the sun. I felt its heat and I saw brightness, but the sun itself was nowhere to be found. There were no clouds either, so it couldn't be hiding behind one, but I still couldn't see it. As if it had decided deliberately to conceal its face and never show it again. Out of disgust perhaps, or embarrassment, or even sadness. Its heat, however, became much stronger. Not necessarily on the outside, but the way it felt within my body. I had this burning sensation in the stomach, in the lungs, all around my heart, and every breath I took was feeding this inner fire.

It hurt. A lot.

I knew the only way I could ease the pain was to go into the ocean. So, I stepped inside, and I began walking in slowly, one step at a time. The water first covered my ankles, then my knees, then half of my body up to the hips. It felt like someone was gently washing me clean, with soft hands and a lot of care.

I went further in. I let the ocean embrace me and pull me into the deep. I let it touch every inch of my skin and hold me in its arms like a mother would hold her child. It took me deeper and deeper, into a realm of complete darkness, where I could see no more signs of life, no more traces of light, no more echoes of sound. It was still and silent down there.

When I finally stopped descending, a feeling I had never experienced before overwhelmed me. It seemed to have leaked out from a small hole in the bottom of my heart – a hole I hadn't been aware of until that moment. But the hole felt old, and the feeling which had come out if it also felt old. Very old. It's just that they had both been hidden. And now they had shown themselves. As if something had awakened them.

The feeling slowly penetrated every cell of my body, practically becoming one with me, or maybe even becoming me. And then it began to whisper to me. At first, I couldn't understand – as if it were still searching for the proper voice with which to talk to me. But gradually it found the right frequency, the right tone, the right color, and so the letters and the sound aligned:

'Again. Again. Again. Again...'

The feeling kept repeating this single word. Like a record that had gotten stuck.

'Again. Again. Again...'

I felt like I was standing in the middle of a crossing where past, present, and future, where different dimensions and realities, where life and death were intersecting. And the voice I heard somehow managed to transcend all of this, cut right through it, and find its way to me. This strange feeling and its strange voice finally reached me.

****

I went back to Eleanor. I put my helmet on, sat on her, and was ready to start her engine when someone called my name.

'Sato-san! S-Sato-san! Wait!'

I recognized the voice.

'Kon, it's you again.'

'Yes! Hello! It's me again! Hi!'

He was sweaty and panting, his heart about to jump from its tracks and run everything over.

'Hi, Kon,' I said. 'Calm down, will you? Just relax. You're making me nervous.'

'Oh. Ok. I will. Just a second.' He took a few deep breaths. 'But I can't! No! No way! How could I relax?! How possibly could I?! After this?! No, not after this!'

'What are you talking about, Kon?'

'Well, this!' he said, throwing his arms in all directions, and looking like he was doing a clumsy imitation of Luke Skywalker.

'You, and that guy in the suit, and the old geezers in even older robes, and swish and swoosh and cut-cut-cut! And the blood! Oh, my god, the blood!'

'You saw it.'

'Did I see it?! The blood?! My god! I've never seen so much blood!'

'Did you follow me?' I asked.

'So much blood! Sooo much blood!'

'Kon, did you follow me?' I asked again. 'Kon! Kon, listen to me!'

'Oh, my god! Is he dead?! He's dead! Oh, he's dead!'

'Kon!' I yelled, then I slapped him hard. He fell to the ground. 'Kon, listen to me, please. Calm down, get up, and listen to me, ok?'

He put his hand on his burning cheek. A single tear ran down his face.

'Don't cry, ok? Let's talk. We're men, aren't we? We can handle stuff and talk about stuff like men, right?'

He nodded.

'Look,' I said, 'you shouldn't have seen it. It was a mistake to follow me, and a mistake to hide wherever you hid and watch the whole thing. But we can't change that now, can we?'

He shook his head right and left a couple of times.

'Let me buy you a drink and let's talk, ok? You wanted to hang out with me, right? Let's do that now. Let's hang out.'

He looked up.

'Here,' I said, offering him my spare helmet. 'Put it on and we'll ride. Have you ever ridden on a bike at night? It's the best. We'll go to Odaiba. It's quiet there, no one will bother us.'

He stood up, took the helmet in his hands, and inspected it as if it were an old, valuable artifact.

'Hop on,' I told him. 'You're safe with me. I know what I'm doing.'

After several seconds of hesitation and thinking, Kon put the helmet on. It looked funny on him, as it was a bit too small for his large head, and it also had a scary-looking skull painted on both sides. Somehow it didn't quite fit with the rest of his outfit. I almost laughed, but I managed to keep it together.

'Let's go, Kon,' I said with a smile.

***

Eleanor hadn't had a guest rider on her back for quite some time, and I feared she would not react well. She didn't like change, and anything out of the ordinary, anything new or different made her have second thoughts. The only change she welcomed was riding on new, unknown roads.

Strangely, when Kon settled his rather large rear end on the back end of the seat and I turned the engine on, Eleanor awoke with an excited rumble resembling that of a young motorcycle ready to tear up any road and conquer any surface. It felt as if they had known each other for a long time.

We rode smoothly in the light, late-night traffic. Eleanor glided from corner to corner, from one traffic light to the next. I loved how at high speed all the signs, ads, and neon lights blended into a single stream of shapeless colors, pulsating or even dancing at the sound of Eleanor's engine.

We crossed the Rainbow-bridge around eleven in the evening to get to Odaiba.

Whenever I came to this artificial island, I felt at peace, especially when I came on my bike at night. As if I were at home. I don't know if it was the emptiness of the roads, the deep silence of the night, or the absence of Tokyo's otherwise omnipresent vividness, but Odaiba's darkness always welcomed and embraced me, like a gentle grandparent would do with a troubled grandchild. I would instantly feel the muscles around my heart loosen up, my breathing slow down, and the tension evaporate from my legs.

I parked Eleanor in front of a Daily Yamazaki convenience store, next to the large dormitory compound used by international students studying in Tokyo. We got off and went inside to buy some snacks. I got a latte from Hokkaido and a pack of dried squid. Kon got an amazake and two mooncakes filled with sweet red bean paste.

'Is that it?' I asked.

He nodded.

'Ok, I'll pay,' I said.

As I was standing in the line, I checked out the girl in front of me. She had long black hair, and her figure seemed familiar. Her wide shoulders, her straight neck and back, her long legs, like those of a dancer. Then, out of nowhere, that beautiful smell again. Vanilla, musk, and almonds. Creamy and silky at the same time. I could almost taste it with my tongue as if it were a piece of fine chocolate melting in my mouth.

I closed my eyes for a second, and as soon as I did, I had an erection. The blood just went crazy inside my body, rushing all over the place, my heart pounding heavily. I even started to sweat. I felt like a teenager who couldn't control his newly discovered sexual energy, or the thoughts it kindled inside him.

I had to open my eyes and look at something uninteresting, something ordinary. Like the fried curry-bread in the heated display box on top of the counter, or the four pieces of matcha-mochi lined up on a shelf next to me, or the instant noodle boxes a Chinese student was inspecting while counting the coins in his left hand. But the erection just wouldn't go away. If anything, I got even harder.

In the meantime, the girl in front of me had just paid for a pack of sweetened soy milk and a box of small Meiji chocolates. The clerk put them in a plastic bag. The girl took the bag, bowed just a little with her head without saying a word, and turned to her left to leave. As she was turning, for the tiniest fraction of a second, she looked in my direction. Straight into my eyes. The whole thing happened literally in the blink of an eye, but to me, it seemed like the longest moment ever. I saw everything in super slow-motion, one frame after another, with enough time to analyze and dissect each and every frame.

I probably would've been much better off seeing her face, her eyes, her lips in real-time, though. For just that tiny piece of a second. The pain of not seeing what I had been expecting or hoping for would've been the same, but at least it wouldn't have lasted so long. This way, however, I had to face the disappointment, then endure it, and endure it even more, and then some more.

I can't even describe the feeling when your body, your mind, and all your senses are prepared to witness a specific something, pushing you to the edge of the abyss of anticipation, and then that something never shows up, blowing everything that had been building up inside you into billions of small pieces of dust, to then disappear into thin air and give place to empty nothingness. Just like that.

It wasn't her. It was just a random young girl, living in one of the random studio apartments in this completely random building, probably studying some random bullshit at a random university to get a random degree, a random job, and have a completely random life.

I paid for our snacks, then turned to Kon. My erection was gone.

'Let's eat and drink by the water. There are some benches behind the naval museum across the road.'

'Ok,' Kon said.

We went behind the museum and sat on one of the benches. I opened my pack of dried squid and started to eat, and Kon made one of his two mooncakes disappear in a matter of seconds. I drank my Hokkaido latte, Kon his sweet amazake, and we just sat there for a while in silence, eating and drinking like two little kids.

It was peaceful out there. As if we weren't in Tokyo. We only saw the skyscrapers and lights on the opposite side of the bay, and the huge cranes working the night shifts in the shipyard, but none of the sounds reached us – no music, no cars humming, no construction sites buzzing or sea containers letting out metallic roars as they find their place on board a ship. I loved watching this scene, watching the big, bustling city, being so close to it, yet so distant at the same time. I was both on the inside and the outside, on the border between the two, and I felt protected by the sea separating Odaiba from mainland Tokyo. It was like the feeling I usually had on balconies. A feeling of being in my own space, free of any constraints, even free of the flow of time.

'Kon,' I said after having finished my latte.

'Hm?'

'What you saw... It's...'

I didn't know what to say or how to say it. I was struggling to find the right words.

'Kon... I'm... I'm sorry. Ok? I'm sorry that you had to see it.'

He looked at me, then at the mooncake he was holding in his hands. He slowly opened the wrapping, lifted the cake to his nose, and took a deep whiff. Then, without even exhaling, he stuffed it in his mouth and swallowed it whole.

'What the... How did you do that, Kon?'

'It's just that... I'm nervous, you know? I tend to do this when I'm nervous. I eat. A lot. And I just swallow the food as is. As if there were no tomorrow. It must be some kind of survival instinct,' he said, licking his fingers.

'You're weird, Kon,' I said with a smile.

'I know,' he replied and took a sip of amazake. 'I know.'

'So, about what you saw–'

'You killed a man, Sato-kun,' he interrupted me, suddenly changing the tone of his voice, and looking me in the eye.

'I did,' I said, turning away.

'It wasn't your first time, I guess.'

'No.'

'And probably not your last, right?'

'Probably not.'

'I see,' he said.

He stood up and walked to the edge of the shore. He leaned against the railing, sipping his amazake and looking into the distance. He might have had a million thoughts in his head, or none at all. I couldn't tell.

I rolled two cigarettes and walked over to him. I offered him one. He looked at me, then took it, and I lit both.

'I wonder how it feels to kill another person,' he said, exhaling the smoke. 'What goes on inside your head after you do it? How does your body react? Does it hurt? I mean, do the feelings you experience after a kill burn or scratch or do some other terrible thing to you from within? Do the thoughts start screaming so loud that you would rather shoot yourself in the head than to have to listen to them?'

I was looking at the murky water in front of us while Kon was asking these questions. The flow of the sea seemed so natural and evident as if it never ever had any doubts or uncertainties. Every particle of Hydrogen and Oxygen had its purpose, its meaning, and its course, and they lived a perfectly balanced, perfectly happy life. Happiness probably wasn't even a concept for them, as there was no reason for it to exist. They only had their "flow", and they let it take them wherever they had to go.

'You know,' Kon continued, 'I was just thinking if there was some kind of hidden door in the depths of a man's soul which stays hidden in the dark for a reason. It's there to protect us from something which we all have inside, something which is the complete opposite of where most of us would want to be. I don't know who put the door there, but she or he must've done it out of love. Yet, some of us, probably a lot of us still manage to find it, and even worse, open it. And I wonder... I wonder if this is somehow related to that mirror and the corridor and all those strange rooms with numbers?'

'Well... It might be,' I said. 'But you haven't killed anyone, right? Yet, you were still able to go through the mirror.'

'Right, but I don't think you necessarily have to kill someone to open that hidden door. There must be many different things a person can do to open it. Maybe even a thought, an idea is enough. I mean, who knows, right?'

'Mm,' I murmured.

'I... I... I think I've opened mine,' he said, looking at me. 'And... And... And it frightens me.'

The color of his eyes suddenly changed – from brown to thick black. They had no glow, no reflection, only this endless darkness, and it felt as if I were staring into an old, abandoned well.

'I've done things,' Kon said, 'and I'm still doing them, and I'm having these thoughts and feelings, and I just seem to let them swallow me, like a whirlpool in the middle of the open sea. I can't escape them, you know. I can't escape any of it. I...'

I put a hand on his shoulder. 'Wanna tell me?' I asked.

He shook his head. 'Maybe I will, and... and thanks for asking, but... not now.'

'Ok,' I replied. 'There's no hurry. I'm just saying. You can if you want. Anytime. Ok?'

He nodded. 'But the thing I asked. About killing. What does it feel like? Can you tell me?'

'Maybe,' I said. 'But not now.'

***

The next morning, I woke up early, around six o'clock. There was so much going on inside my head that I couldn't sleep. I wasn't thinking of anything in particular, rather, all kinds of images just kept popping up, jumping around, disappearing, then resurfacing. There seemed to be no order or logic to their content or the sequence in which they were appearing, so there wasn't anything I could hold onto and control. It felt like an experiment in which someone had attached a virtual reality device to my head and was playing random images. First, I saw a big tree with exactly a hundred and one branches, and each branch had a single leaf on it, except for one, which had a white flower. Then, I saw a black dragon and a white dragon swimming together in an emerald green lake surrounded by mountains. The dragons went back and forth, back and forth, then suddenly jumped, flew into the sky, and got entangled with each other, and I couldn't tell if they were fighting or making love. Next came a red sphere, which hovered in a dark, empty space, while something similar to blood kept dripping from its surface without leaving any stain or trace. An airplane dropping a bomb, lungs burning in fire, a giant wolf staring me in the face while showing his sharp teeth, a fox sniffing around in deep snow, a cigarette, a cup of coffee, and wings made of wind soaring higher and higher.

***

I decided to go see the boss. He was supposed to be practicing "kenjutsu" in the private dojo he had built in the garden of his house in Azabu. He still practiced every morning with Kobayashi-san.

I bought a custard croissant and a cappuccino-to-go when I got off the subway, and I took my time to walk to his house, enjoying my breakfast and the early morning April sun. I loved the neighborhood, with its huge, expensive houses, owned by some of the wealthiest people around, and the silence of all those thick walls. They all had eyes, the walls, and I felt their stare on my skin as I was passing by, but whenever I tried looking into any of them, they would turn away. They all held secrets inside – grave secrets –, but were not allowed to let anything out, so all they could do was to look at the outside world and wonder if there was anything or anyone innocent out there.

I arrived at the main gate around seven. I knew the pass code, so I typed it in, and the automatic door opened. Inside, I went straight to the dojo, crossing a small stone bridge that separated the garden into two distinct parts. One part had various trees and flowers, small artificial hills, and old stone lanterns, perfectly arranged and tended to by a professional gardener. The other part only had freshly trimmed green grass and the small dojo at the end of the path. Every time I crossed the bridge to get to the dojo, I felt like I was leaving this world and entering a completely different realm. I kept crossing paths with such borderline worlds again and again.

As soon as I crossed the bridge, my heart became heavier, as if it had been filled with some unknown substance from an unknown source. A substance that was solid one moment, then fluid the next.

I opened the sliding door and saw Kobayashi-san alone. He was wearing his usual practice gear and performing a very old kata called "Hōjō". I think he was doing the "Spring" part.

'Where's the boss?' I asked when he finished.

'Boss Yamaguchi left for the mountains,' Kobayashi-san replied, wiping the sweat from his forehead. 'He'll be away for three days.'

'I see,' I said. 'He didn't tell me anything.'

'You know he doesn't.'

'Yeah, but I thought he would, now that I've become his bodyguard.'

'Well... no. He always goes alone, and I'm the only person he tells. But you know that. You shouldn't be surprised.'

I turned and went to pick up a wooden sword from the storage box.

'What's the point of having a personal bodyguard, then?' I asked while taking a few practice swings.

'It's not that simple. Nothing is with the boss.'

I kept swinging the sword, each time a little harder.

'Being his bodyguard isn't really about being by his side every single moment to prevent some kind of attack,' Kobayashi-san continued. 'It's more about trust.'

'Trust?' I asked. 'He didn't trust me before?'

'Oh, he did. He did. In his own way, at least.'

'What way?' I asked.

'Well, there are several levels of trust which he establishes with people around him. He has his own criteria based on which he assesses each person, then categorizes them. It might sound rational and analytical, but it isn't. It happens subconsciously, I would say.'

'Hm. And you think my status changed? Does he see me differently now?'

'Definitely. He always felt special about you, but as of yesterday evening you're beginning to threaten even my position,' Kobayashi-san said with a smile, then suddenly he swung his wooden sword at me at full speed and with full force. I was barely able to dodge, jumping a little to the side and blocking with my own sword. He kept pressing his sword against mine, still exerting all the strength he had.

'But you're still his number one,' I replied with a faint smile of my own while trying to push him back. 'You're still the only person he tells about his past and about personal things he doesn't share with anyone else.'

Kobayashi-san was approaching his limit, and I was close to pushing him away completely.

'That's not entirely true,' he said, clenching his teeth. His arms were trembling. 'He does share a lot with me, but not everything. And there are things he only shares with you. And then...' His knees were about to crumble. 'There are things... things... which he only shares with... with Ren-chan.'

At that moment I completely lost my focus, my muscles lost all their tension, and my mind wandered off to some distant plains, far away from the dojo. Kobayashi-san pushed me back with ease, and I fell to the tatami.

'Ren?'

A White Russian, please!

I spent the next three days doing nothing in particular. I mostly wandered randomly on the streets of Tokyo – Ginza, Omotesando, Roppongi, Shibuya, Shinjuku, you name it. The usual, overcrowded neighborhoods, endless streams of people, a million shops selling everything from clothes to gadgets to musical instruments, and restaurants and coffee shops with more food than people in some countries could ever imagine.

It somehow felt good to disappear in the crowd and be a small drop in this huge ocean of people. It felt liberating. And it allowed my mind to entertain itself with all kinds of stuff that had nothing to do with all the complicated thoughts and feelings I had inside. Even when I wanted to have a coffee, or eat a meal, I chose the biggest, most crowded places: a Starbucks, a popular ramen shop, the food corner of a shopping mall, even a bakery where I had to stand in line for twenty minutes.

At night I didn't go home. Instead, I went to our nightclubs.

The first night, I visited "Lulu's", one of our new places, and I felt like spending time with one of the new girls. The one I chose was in her mid-thirties, a bit on the short side, but with beautiful, large breasts, and a lovely, round ass. I loved women like her, as they oozed sexuality and genuine lust. And I loved feeling their weight on me, holding the fullness of their round shapes in my hands, exploring and eventually adapting to the sensual movement of their body. It was easy to get lost in the moment and escape to a place of blinding intensity, which overwhelmed and engaged all my senses.

I didn't know the name of the girl I spent the night with, but I remember the feeling I had immediately after I had ejaculated. I felt... out of place.

I remember making her get off me, removing the condom, and going to the bathroom. I washed my penis in the shower, then wrapped a towel around my hips and drank exactly thirteen big gulps of cold water from the sink. I washed my face a little, then looked up, into the mirror. What I saw terrified me.

There was fire, burning with tall, sharp flames, fueled by a permanent, howling wind. It soon engulfed my face completely, and my skin began melting and peeling off. I saw blisters, I saw boiling blood, I saw my own flesh turn brown, then black. And I felt the pain of it.

I tried splashing water on my face, but it didn't help. If anything, the flames got stronger. I ran out of the bathroom, flinging the door wide open, went straight to the window, opened it, and let out a scream as loud as the cry of a thousand wolves. My breathing was heavy, with no rhythm at all. I just tried to gulp down as much air as possible.

When I turned, the girl was sitting on the bed, looking at me with an expressionless face. There was a strange shadow of understanding in her eyes. She gestured for me to come next to her.

I knelt in front of her in the middle of the bed. She made me lie down and rest my head in her lap. She then put her hand on the top of my head and started gently brushing my hair with her fingers. I fell asleep in a matter of seconds.

***

I spent the second night in a more familiar place – our oldest nightclub, the "Palm Tree". I was a regular there, but I always slept with the same woman. Her name was Julia. It wasn't her real name, of course, but everyone called her Julia. Like her favorite actress. And no, it wasn't Julia Roberts. It was Julia Ormond. Julia the whore had fallen in love with Julia the actress when she saw her in the movie First Knight, playing Guinevere alongside Richard Gere's Lancelot. That's her version, at least. I think she actually fell in love with Richard Gere. But she would never admit it.

Julia is almost fifteen years older than me, and she has been with us forever. We have a strange relationship, the two of us. After I began working for the boss and living with him, she quickly became like an older sister to me. And a mother. And when I grew up, a lover. In each stage of my life, she would assume the female role I was most in need of and treat me accordingly. It doesn't sound healthy, I know. But it is what it is. I didn't really have a choice. Except for the lover part, maybe. Then again, it felt good to have a woman in my life to care for me the way she did. It felt good to have a woman I could trust. I learned a lot from her, and I owe her more than I could ever give back.

As a lover, even at her age of almost fifty, she had no rival. Not as far as I was concerned, at least. She knew her own body well, she knew what she liked and how she liked it, and she knew how to make me understand it while we were having sex. She didn't need words or exaggerated moves, just the slightest, barely perceptible hints, a gentle touch here or there, or by applying force at the right time, in the right place.

I love it when a woman enjoys herself with me. I love giving pleasure and feeling all the vibrations and contortions of a woman's orgasming body. I suppose it gives me confidence. Especially if I can make her come two, three, or even more times. It makes me feel masculine. Of course, women like Julia know how to come several times with almost any man. It's more her knowing how to use her body than her partner being the next Casanova, but we men don't need to know that. We're perfectly fine with the experience of having made a woman come several times. And if it was the cock and not the tongue or the fingers doing it, even better.

All in all, Julia knew her way around under the sheets, and I enjoyed every moment of it. She also knew how to dress for me. Satin lingerie, stockings, preferably white. She was a pro. But even more importantly, she was one of the few women I was able to have sex with and not feel guilt or disgust immediately after. Most of the time I slept like a baby after the two or three hours we usually spent together, and when I couldn't sleep, we talked. Often until dawn.

'What's on your mind?' she asked after seeing I couldn't sleep, even though I had come twice within an hour, which was unusual for me.

I didn't give her a response, so she started to caress my chest and play with the hair I had on top of it.

'I know there's something,' she continued. 'I've known you since you were a kid. You can't hide your feelings from me. No way. And you know I'll keep asking until you talk.'

'I know,' I answered.

'So tell me. Better get it done with. Or you can leave, of course, but then don't come back tomorrow night with this depressed look on your face. You know I don't like being dragged down into pointless states of misery by other people. Unless it's you, of course, but my patience has its limits, even if it's my little Sato-kun we're talking about.'

'Don't call me your little Sato-kun. I hate it.'

'I know, my little Sato-kun. So, speak up. Come on, talk.'

I turned to my side and looked at her breasts. They were small, but she had beautiful, large nipples, which always made me hard. I started getting another erection, but then I shook it off and looked her in the eye.

'I don't know,' I said. 'It's not just one thing. It's several things at the same time.'

'Several things. Hm. That's new. I didn't know you could be bothered by multiple things at the same time. It seems I still have new things to learn about you.'

'Ha-ha. Very funny,' I said.

'So, tell me, then. What are these several things?'

'It's... difficult for me to put them into words. You know I'm not really good with words.'

'That I do, my dear. But try. For me. I might reward you afterward,' she said, sliding down her fingers all the way to my penis. She held it gently, pulling it back and forth with care.

I let her do it for a while, then I put my hand on hers and made her stop. 'Not now,' I said.

'Ok.'

'I became Yamaguchi's personal bodyguard.'

'I heard,' Julia said. 'It might do you good. You might be killing fewer people from now on. Or more. I don't know, actually. I hope it's the former.'

'I don't know, either,' I said. 'And that's the thing. I've had this strange feeling since this last kill. In fact, I've had it for a long time, somewhere deep down, but it seems like something changed two nights ago. As if it had been building up inside me, growing, filling all the empty spaces it could find, all the little caves, bends, narrow pathways in my body, and now it ran out of space and began eating me away from within.'

'I don't have to tell you what I think about all of this. The boss, and the work you do for him. I've been telling you to run away for as long as I can remember.'

'And I've been telling you I can't.'

'It's the same old conversation, my little Sato-kun. If they gave me a dollar – ok, ten dollars – each time I told you to forget about all of this, all of us, and just disappear somewhere, I'd be a rich whore by now.'

'Yeah, but it goes for you too.'

'No, it doesn't. You're a strong, young, healthy man. I'm an almost fifty-year-old woman. It's not the same, Sato-kun. It's not the same at all.'

'You weren't always fifty,' I said.

'But I've always been a woman, my dear.'

I stood up and walked to the cupboard in the corner of Julia's room. 'Is there something to drink?' I asked.

'Just a bottle of red wine I received as a gift from one of my regular clients.'

'That old fart who's in the stock trading business?'

'Yeah.'

'What did he bring you this time?'

'Something Italian, I think.'

I opened the cupboard and took out the bottle and two glasses. 'Primitivo di Puglia.'

'Is it any good?' she asked.

'Very.'

I opened it and poured some for both of us. 'Here you go. Cheers.'

'To a brighter future,' Julia said.

'Whatever that means,' I said, and we clinked glasses.

I walked to the window and opened it. The noise of Kabukichō came in like an uninvited guest who had had a bit too much to drink and didn't really care if he was welcomed or not. I took a sip of wine and looked at all the people still roaming the streets at such a late hour: businessmen who should have been sleeping in their beds next to their wives, young tourists thinking how they knew what Tokyo's hidden underworld was all about, a couple of our men chatting about the dropping levels of quality of the imported cocaine, a few escort girls returning from their dates with wealthy men twice their age, and a young couple kissing goodbye after what must have been their first night together in a love-hotel.

'There's this girl,' I said, still looking at the street. 'Ren.'

I turned around to look at Julia. She turned her head away.

'So, you've met,' she said.

'Not really. She was there two nights ago, watching the duel, but we didn't talk, we didn't get introduced or anything. We just saw each other.'

Julia stood up and put on a white, silky nightgown.

'Do you have a cigarette?' she asked, walking towards me at the window.

I looked at her breasts again. Her large, hard nipples almost pierced through the fine material of her dress. I had another erection.

She grabbed my penis and asked: 'Or shall I put *this* in my mouth?'

I pulled her closer and grabbed her face with my hand, pressing her cheeks. She stuck out her tongue and I started sucking it. She kept squeezing my penis. I then turned her around and fucked her hard from behind in the window. I came inside her and let out a huge cry into the night. Like a wolf howling on top of a hill.

'You're so predictable,' she said with a smile.

'Fuck you,' I said.

I went to the chair in the opposite corner of the room where I had left my pants and came back with two rolled cigarettes and a lighter.

'Thanks,' she said.

I lit both cigarettes and we leaned out the window, smoking, gazing at the street.

'Tell me about Ren,' I said.

She took a deep drag, inhaling as much smoke as possible, then let it all out as if hoping the smoke would bring out the words that she wasn't able to find on her own.

'There's not much I can tell. But you becoming the personal bodyguard certainly... complicates things.'

'What do you mean?'

'Did you honestly think the boss needed a bodyguard for himself? Our boss? The fearless Yamaguchi? He's too stubborn, overconfident, and proud to have someone guard him all the time. The body-guard is more for Ren than it is for him.'

'Ren?' I asked with surprise. 'And what does me becoming the bodyguard complicate exactly?'

'I can't tell you. And I won't. You can threaten me all you want, beat me up, torture me, but I won't say a word. I can't. And it's better for you this way. Trust me on this. I mean it.'

'I would never hurt you,' I said, stubbing my cigarette. 'You know that.'

'I know, my little Sato-kun,' Julia replied.

***

I left Palm Tree around three in the morning, although I prefer call-ing it night instead. Morning means brightness, it means a new be-ginning, it means hope, and I had none of those inside me when I covered Julia with a soft blanket, dressed up, quietly closed the door to her room, and went back to the street. I had my usual episode be-fore making the transition between the closed space and the outside world, but for whatever reason, I couldn't concentrate, and I didn't give myself enough time for the whole process. I knew I had made a mess of my routine as soon as I stepped outside, so I immediately put my right hand in my pocket to hold onto the hundred-yen coin. This backup plan of mine usually worked, but not this time. I tried scrubbing the coin, squeezing it, even rolling it between my fingers, but the more I did it, the worse I felt. My heart rate went up and cold sweat covered my forehead. I didn't know what it felt like to have a heart attack, but I thought I was having one.

"Fuck," I told myself, and I fell to my knees.

I closed my eyes and tried breathing slowly. I took several deep breaths and imagined I was on a balcony. Darkness surrounded me from all directions, and out of its depths a distant voice somehow found its way to me: 'Sato.' At first, I couldn't tell, but then I realized it was a young woman's voice. 'Sato-san.' It sounded familiar. 'Is that you?' It sounded concerned. 'Are you alright? Can I help you?'

I opened my eyes and saw Kiki reaching out to me. I grabbed her hand and let her pull me up.

'Thanks,' I said, still feeling dizzy and concentrating hard to stay firm on my feet.

'We've switched roles, it seems,' Kiki said. 'I never thought I'd be helping *you*, uncle.'

'Me neither,' I replied. 'Thanks again.'

'No worries.' She took a good look, then asked: 'What happened? You don't seem to be drunk.'

'I just... fainted a little, that's all. Nothing serious. Probably just lack of sleep and low levels of sugar. I haven't had chocolate for more than a day now.'

'I see.'

'And you?' I asked. 'What are *you* doing here so late at night? Shouldn't you be at home, in your bed, sleeping, like any other seventeen-year-old?'

Kiki looked away and didn't want to give me an answer.

'Tell me, Kiki. Enlighten me, please.'

'I... I just came out for a walk.'

'For a walk.'

'Yes.'

'At three in the night.'

'Yes.'

'In Kabukichō.'

'Aha.'

'Kiki,' I said, crossing my arms.

'I... I couldn't sleep. And I had this urge. To come here. To be here. To... smell the air of these streets. To hear the sounds. It's like... a magnet, you see. It seems to draw me. It... calls my name.'

She looked at the opening door of a nearby pachinko parlor. The noise coming from inside felt like someone was screaming directly into our faces. The door then closed again, and the noise disappeared.

'I guess... It's because of mom. I think something inside me wants to understand her. I want to know what it was that made her come here again and again and spend her money – our money! – on all of this, instead of the things a normal mother spends her money on. And all the time she spent here. I want to see for myself how it feels to be here. I wonder if it's... better than spending time with me,' she whispered in the end, her voice crumbling to pieces.

I sighed.

'I think she never really loved me, uncle Sato,' she said, and then a stream of tears began to flow down both of her cheeks. I pulled her closer, and I held her in my arms for some time.

As I was holding her, my shirt getting more and more soaked in her tears, I had this image in my head where I kissed her on the top of her head, then looked into her eyes and said, "Come, let's go home together. You can stay with me from now on. I'll take care of you."

But I never told her that.

'I have to go,' I said. 'And you better go home, too. Your mother might need your help. And it's late, anyway. You shouldn't be out here.'

I was about to walk away, but the moment I tried taking the first step, my knees crumbled a bit again, and I almost fell to the ground again. Kiki grabbed me by the arm.

'Uncle Sato!'

'It's ok,' I said. 'I'll be fine. I just... I just need you to help me a bit here. To get somewhere. It's not far. In Golden Gai. It'll take just a couple of minutes. Could you please walk me there?'

'Of course. No problem. Just tell me where, exactly.'

'I'll lean on you and we'll walk together, ok?'

'Ok,' Kiki said.

What should've taken us less than ten minutes took us almost twenty. I had a really hard time walking, but with each step, I regained a bit of my strength and felt more and more comfortable. Still, the whole experience felt weird. Not only the fact that Kiki was there with me in the middle of the night, but also this strange and sudden loss of power and dizziness. I just couldn't tell where it had come from. I was only certain that it wasn't physical. I knew it had come from within. And then I remembered the vision I had had after the duel. I remembered being deep in the ocean, a hole appearing at the bottom of my heart, and a strange feeling flowing out of it.

'It must be the hole,' I murmured to myself. 'It must be that feeling.'

'What's that?' Kiki asked.

'Nothing,' I said. 'We're here.'

We had arrived at the entrance to the small alley where the mirror stood.

'You can leave now,' I told Kiki. 'Thank you for bringing me here. I really appreciate it.'

'You're welcome.'

'And now, please go home. Please leave this place. Can you promise me that? Please,' I begged.

Kiki nodded.

'Look after your mother.'

She nodded again.

I waited for her to go back the way we had come. She went to the corner of the street, then stopped and turned in my direction. We looked each other in the eye as if trying to read the hidden thoughts which only the eyes can reveal. We stood like that for several seconds, then we each nodded, and she disappeared behind the corner.

I turned as well, and I went deeper into the alley, all the way to the mirror. I walked gingerly but was able to get there in one piece, without falling or anything.

As usual, I closed my eyes before looking into the mirror, and I opened them after a few moments. This time around, I wasn't really hoping to see anything. I knew my reflection would not be there. Instead, I was looking forward to entering the mirror, entering room number fifty-five, and talking to Kei.

I raised both my arms and touched the surface of the mirror. It seemed to form hands of its own, take mine, and gently pull me in. I felt warmth in my palms, which then traveled through my arms, and through my whole body as I was slowly entering the world beyond. It felt good. So good, that I decided not to turn back, even though I knew someone was watching me from behind. I didn't care. I just wanted to leave.

***

Taking those few steps in the corridor before I reached the door to room fifty-five, then entering the room and walking up to the counter of Kei's strange bar felt like returning home. It really did. And it was a feeling I hadn't experienced before. Not this clearly. I felt relieved to be there, and this scared me, in a way.

'Yo, Satooo! How are you?'

'Hey, Kei.'

'You look... weird, maaan.'

'What do you mean?'

'Hm. Let me see. You look... troubled, maaan. There's something cooomplicated going on inside. And you don't really understand. And you don't know who else to go to.'

'That about sums it up,' I said.

'But you know I can't really give you aaanswers, maaan.'

'I'm not looking for answers.'

'Oh, but yes, you aaare.'

I gave him the finger. 'Give me a drink,' I said.

'A White Russian with a twist of vanilla from Maaadagascar, coming up!'

'What the-'

Kei put a finger to his mouth to make me shut up. 'Just relaaax a bit, will you? Trust me, maaan. This will help. You don't always have to drink scotch.'

'I don't always drink scotch.'

'Maybe out there. But here you dooo.'

'Whatever,' I said and turned around.

The shadows were still there, doing what they usually did. I walked around while Kei was preparing my cocktail, but I was trying to avoid getting anywhere near any of the shadows. I wasn't in the mood to feel whatever each one of them made me feel. Even though there were so many of them, Kei's bar was so big, that I found it easy to evade the shadows. Of course, I couldn't avoid grazing at least the periphery of their aura, or whatever you want to call it, but that wasn't enough to evoke any strong emotions inside me. It just felt like the sounds of the street when I rode my motorcycle: they reached me, but they couldn't enter.

There were no shadows near the hole on the wall this time, so I went there. I looked through the hole, and I only saw the same, thick darkness with impenetrable clouds and not a single trace of light. I put my hand in the hole. I wanted the darkness to touch my skin. I wanted it to crawl up my arm, all the way to my face, to my ears, and tell me something. Or whisper. Or scream. I wanted to hear its voice. I *needed* to hear its voice.

Then, the same feeling that had escaped through the hole at the bottom of my heart suddenly appeared with full force and took me over. It felt like it tried to squeeze every single cell of my body while making my heart weigh twice, or even three times as much as it normally did. My stomach got wrenched completely, and my guts were on the verge of exploding. But a soft, soothing sensation followed, and a wave of early morning sun elevated me to heights I had never experienced before. I felt like I was dying and being reborn at the same time.

I turned around slowly, and there was a shadow standing right behind me.

'It's a neeew one,' Kei said from behind the counter. 'Number one hundred and one.'

The new shadow kept staring at me, while I remained stranded on the border between these two contrasting states of body and mind. Another ambiguous dimension on the edge of existence. As if God, or whoever was out there, was kicking me around like a ball with both his feet, unable to decide if he should stick with the right or the left.

'The White Russian is ready. Come back here, maaan' Kei said.

His voice seemed to pull me out from wherever I had gotten stuck, and the shadow slowly backed off. I took a few deep breaths, then walked back to Kei.

'Who's that?' I asked.

Kei just shook his head. 'Here, drink this,' he said, placing the glass in front of me. He prepared one for himself as well. He always drank whatever I was drinking.

'Where's your shirt with the cats?' I asked. 'I liked that one better. This one's too gloomy, with all the black crows and their purple eyes.'

'Oh, I just felt like glooomy, today,' Kei replied.

'I see.'

'Look, Sato-kun. It seems to me that you've reached the point where you can finally start faaacing yourself.'

'Facing myself?'

'Right. You know, like when you look into a mirror, and seee something, and realize that what you're seeing is not what you were expecting to see. And that's good. It's the first step. Many people don't even get to this point, maaan.'

'I hate mirrors,' I said and took a sip of the cocktail.

'Why?'

'Because I either don't see anything, or I see the living hell.'

'That's good, that's good, Sato-kun.'

'And what do *you* see, when you look into a mirror?' I asked.

'I see *you*, maaan.'

Mercedes-Benz

I woke up the next morning to the sound of my phone ringing. I couldn't bother to get it, so I waited until it stopped, then I rolled over and tried to get some more sleep. But it started ringing again. Someone was very eager to reach me. I rolled back over and grabbed it to see who was calling. It was Kobayashi-san.

'Hello,' I said.

'Good morning, Sato-kun.'

'What time is it?'

'It's ten in the morning,' he said.

'Already? Shit.'

'The boss wants to see you, Sato-kun.'

'He's back?'

'He is.'

'Ok, I'll be there in an hour.'

'Now, Sato-kun. I came to pick you up. I'm here in front of your apartment building.'

I stood up and walked to the window. A big, black Mercedes, probably from the late seventies or early eighties, was parked out front.

'Give me five minutes,' I said, and I hung up.

***

'Nice car,' I said after taking a seat next to Kobayashi-san.

'They finished renovating it a couple of days ago. I brought it home yesterday evening. It's beautiful, isn't it?'

The seats were fine, black leather, tailor-made for this car. It felt like sitting on a luxurious sofa. They used finely polished aluminum to make the interior more elegant but also to keep it rough, tough, and cold – just like the boss liked it. The car looked amazing, yet very simple and straightforward, both inside and out, but I knew it had one particular feature which overshadowed everything else.

'Turn the engine on,' I told Kobayashi-san, 'and please, rev it a bit. I want to hear it.'

Kobayashi-san obliged with a smile.

'Oh, wow,' I marveled, with a smile of my own. 'It's just... I don't even have words to describe it. It's like the old soul of a giant, black dog. You know, like those Newfoundland dogs. It's amazing.'

'I knew you'd love it. I can't wait to take the boss for a ride.'

'So, he still hasn't seen it?' I asked.

'No, he came in late last night, and we had our regular training session first thing in the morning, and then I came to get you.'

'I see. And how is the old bastard?'

'As usual, I would say. It's hard to tell with him. He doesn't give away that much.' Kobayashi-san put the car in first gear, and we started rolling. 'To be honest, there *is* something different about him. I can't really put it in words, but I noticed a slight change this morning during our practice. I saw a trace of something I haven't seen in him since his childhood. I think it was... fear. Yes, I think I saw fear in his eyes.'

We drove in silence for the next five minutes or so. I was looking out the window and watching the streets, the buildings, the people we passed, but nothing stuck with me. It could've been any city in the world, the most beautiful buildings ever built, the craziest looking people straight out of a Tim Burton movie, I still wouldn't have cared. The images of the outside world felt like clips from an old, grainy road movie played in a rundown arthouse cinema for an audience of one.

'Where are we headed?' I asked.

'A place you've never been.'

'How far?'

'With this traffic, I'd guess an hour or so.'

'I see.'

We stopped at a traffic light. I saw a mother carrying two babies – probably twins – in a stroller. The father was two steps behind them. They got to the middle of the crossing, then suddenly stopped. Both turned in our direction and began to stare at me. They stood motionless, like two statues. I became increasingly uncomfortable and tried looking away, but their gaze was so strong and hypnotic that I had to look into their eyes. As if they wanted me to see something that was hidden deep within and tell me a story I needed to know. I felt a cold shiver run across the surface of my skin.

Then, out of nowhere, both the mother and the father turned into two large, black birds. They hovered in the air, still staring at me. My muscles tightened up, and my heart felt like something was pressing on it from all directions. I wanted to move, but I couldn't. I wanted to breathe, but I couldn't.

The two birds flew up, high in the sky, then turned sharply, and came back straight at us with full force and speed. Like two hawks hunting their prey. I wanted to do something – move away, get out of the car, duck, whatever –, but I was completely paralyzed. I couldn't even close my eyes. They just kept coming, and as they were about to hit the windshield of our car, they suddenly turned into black ash, and the two babies started crying.

'Are you alright?' Kobayashi-san asked as the light turned green. 'You seem disturbed.'

'I'm ok,' I said. 'I just thought I saw something.'

'What?'

'Doesn't matter. Forget it.'

Kobayashi-san didn't look at me, but I still felt uncomfortable. I turned my head in the opposite direction and changed the subject.

'I'd like to know a bit more about the boss,' I said. 'You've known him since he was a child, right?'

'Right.'

'Tell me a bit about those times. I've heard bits and pieces, but I'm missing the big picture.'

'Why do you want to know?' Kobayashi-san asked.

'I don't know. Does there have to be a reason? I'm curious, that's all. He's my boss. And almost like a father to me, or the closest thing to a father I'll ever have.'

'Children often know very little about their fathers' past,' Kobayashi-san replied. 'I don't know if that's a good thing or a bad thing, but it's true. And there might be a reason for that.'

'Do you know of some such reason?'

'It's not for me to tell.'

'Well, *I* don't know of any such reason, and since we're stuck here, feel free to talk. Please.'

We had come to a stop in the traffic jam again, and Kobayashi-san had shifted into first gear, holding his foot on the brake. He clenched the steering wheel for a bit, but soon his hands loosened up again.

'I was eleven when the old Yamaguchi moved to Tsuruoka.'

'You mean the boss's grandfather?' I asked.

'That's right. It was in 1946, February, or maybe March. There was still some snow. He had bought an old house outside the city, at the foot of the three mountains of Dewa.

'Grandpa – as I called him – came alone. I first saw him a couple of days after he had moved in, when he came to town to buy some stuff for the house. I was living alone with my mother at the time, and we were selling homemade onigiri rice balls for a living. Our stand was next to the store he had come to visit. After he finished shopping, he stopped to buy a rice ball. At first, I didn't pay much attention to him, but when he reached out to take the rice ball my mother was giving him, I saw this huge scar on his right arm. It ran across his whole forearm, probably even further towards his shoulder, but the sleeve of his jacket covered his upper arm, so I couldn't see it. Still, it took me by surprise, and I stared at it for several seconds. When I realized how disrespectful I was being, I quickly lifted my gaze to look him in the eye. And *that* was the really scary part. I still remember the firmness of his stare, and the cold shiver it sent across my body. As if some sort of energy were pouring from him, and it paralyzed me for a moment. I froze.

'I think he scanned me with those eyes of his, both on the outside and the inside. Like in that movie, the Terminator. You remember? But grandpa was also capable of penetrating the depths of one's soul and having a clear understanding of the person he was facing. It's a trait our boss must have inherited from grandpa. It must be something that runs in their veins.

'After a couple of seconds, grandpa's eyes softened up a bit, and he asked if I could work for him. He said he'd pay me, and that he needed someone to help him out around the house. Some repair work, some maintenance, some cleaning, maybe some gardening. I looked at my mom, and she seemed as surprised as I was. "I don't know how to do that kind of stuff," I told him. "I'll teach you," he replied. My mom and I exchanged glances again, and then we both turned to him and nodded.'

'So, you started to work for him?' I asked.

'That's right,' Kobayashi-san replied. 'First thing the next day. The house he had moved into was big and old. It had once been a Buddhist temple, but the priests had abandoned it during the war. We never found out why, but the rumor was they had taken them to the battlefield. Anyhow, grandpa had bought the whole estate and decided to live there. It was obvious from the outset that he had money, but for some reason, he didn't want anyone else to help him renovate the house apart from me. We did everything ourselves. It took us a full year, and by the time we had finished, I knew every inch of the floor, every scratch on the walls, every little imperfection of the house – both those hidden from the eye and those in plain sight.

'After we were done with the renovation, he told me to come next morning at eight and to bring some light clothes that I could easily move in. He didn't tell me what we were going to do, but he sounded very serious, so I got all excited and couldn't sleep all night. I was out of bed at six, and after a quick breakfast, I went straight to the old man's house. Obviously, I arrived way too early.

'Everything was so quiet when I got there. No birds chirping, no dogs barking, no cars in the distance. Only the hollow talk of the wind as it moved gingerly among the branches of the trees. I stopped to listen to its voice in the hopes that I would be able to see its face. I imagined it to look like a huge bird, but with the gentle head of an intelligent and playful dog.

'A bird with the head of a dog?' I asked.

'Exactly. I've had this image of the wind ever since I was a little boy. I'm not sure anymore, but I think my late father used to tell me a story about a wind that looked like this, and everyone was afraid of it, even though it only wanted to play. A young boy found the courage to face the wind and understand it, so they became best friends in the end.

'Anyhow, I was standing in front of grandpa's house, and I tried following the movement of the plants to see which way the wind was headed.'

'And which way was it going?' I asked.

'It went behind the house and over the wall of the garden. I hesitated for a while, but then I heard something strange, like a voice talking to me from the other side of the wall, calling me. Actually, it was more like someone was singing, and I felt like I knew the song. I had heard it before. So, I climbed the wall and jumped down on the other side.

'It took me a few seconds to realize that I was in the only place of grandpa's estate to which I didn't have access. A small portion of his big garden which he worked on when I was not around. A sealed gate and tall bushes separated it from the rest of the garden, and the one time I had asked if I could enter, grandpa had grabbed me by the throat, looked me straight in the eye, and said, "Never ever go there. Understood? Never. If you do, I'll kill you. I swear."

'I believed he would, so I never went there. But now there I was, standing in the middle of this small piece of forbidden land, and I just knew I had to explore it. I just had to.'

'What did you find?'

'To my surprise, this part of the garden wasn't as orderly as the rest. It felt kind of... wild. You know what I'm saying? The grass was tall, some bushes were scattered around in no particular order, and tall bamboo trees occupied whatever free space there was. A short pathway of uneven, random stones led from the gate, across the middle of this little garden, to a small house of sorts at the back.

'I walked slowly, stepping from one stone to the next, observing the scenery along the way. It all felt surreal. Like being in a magic forest, the kind you would see in those Studio Ghibli animations. Do you remember those? We used to watch them together when you were younger.'

'Yeah, I remember. You always took me to that little cinema in Meguro, even when I wanted to go to one of the big ones in the shopping malls.'

'But even today, you only go to the small cinemas, right?' Kobayashi-san asked.

'I do,' I replied. 'They suit me better.'

'You see? I knew that even back then.'

I smiled without saying anything. I looked out the window and watched the streams of people walking the streets.

'So, this little garden looked like something out of a mystical story,' Kobayashi-san continued. 'I was mesmerized. Every moment I was expecting a magical little creature to peek out from behind a bush or a bamboo tree, a little "totoro" to cross my path, or a "mushi" to appear from below a stone. You know the "mushi"? The mostly in-visible beings that live in forests and waters and the air and the soil?'

'You watch too many cartoons, my friend,' I smiled, turning back to look at Kobayashi-san. He smiled back, with an inexplicable glow of youth in his elderly eyes. I liked looking at his face.

'I think it took me at least ten minutes to walk across the garden and get to the little house at the end of the path.'

'And what was it like?' I asked. 'The house, I mean.'

'Well, it was made of wood, to start with. It had an octagonal shape, with three stairs leading to a sliding door. I slid it open, took off my shoes, and stepped inside.

'The floor was covered with tatami, and seven of the eight walls had white rice paper on them, but no windows. I immediately knew the house was used for tea ceremonies, probably for only two people.

'The only fully wooden wall, the one opposite the entrance, had a scroll hanging on it, with a writing reading "faith". Below the scroll, on a wooden stand attached to the wall, lay two swords.'

'Let me guess,' I interrupted. 'Shiro and Kuro.'

'Right,' Kobayashi-san said. 'Shiro and Kuro. And beneath there was a small table, and on top of it another scroll. A really old one, rolled up and tied with a string.'

'And I guess you opened it.'

'Yes, I did. But I was too young at the time to be able to properly read and decipher everything that was written there. What struck me though was these two images, one at the top of the scroll, the other at the bottom. On top, a boy seemed to be planting seeds, and at the bottom, a girl was pulling fish from the sea with a net. Both images were simply drawn, yet they had this hypnotic strength. The boy had purple eyes, the girl had green eyes.'

Kobayashi-san paused for a moment as if allowing me to digest what he had just said. I imagined this little girl, in a small, wooden boat, out there alone at the sea, surrounded by deep blue vastness below and sky-blue infinity above. And I imagined the boy kneeling, the top of his head barely sticking out from the tall, green grass, and the same blue sky looking down on him. They both look up, the girl with her green eyes, the boy with his purple ones, and they see a big, black bird flying towards the sun, with its wings spread wide. And then a feeling throbs in both of their hearts. A mix of fullness and emptiness. Of love and loneliness.

'Then, I heard the wind again,' Kobayashi-san continued, 'as it swirled among the bamboo trees. It felt unsettled and tense, so I decided to go back the way I had come, following the wind along the stone path, over the wall, and back to the front gate of grandpa's house. When I got there, the gate was open, and grandpa was standing in the middle, with his arms crossed and a stern, cold look on his face. "Where've you been?" he asked, but I couldn't answer. Instead, I looked down, staring at the ground and a pair of red beetles attached to one another and moving together like a small train of two wagons. "Never mind," he said. "Come inside."

'We went straight to the dojo. He told me to get dressed. He gave me a wooden practice sword, and we immediately started practicing "kenjutsu", without him telling me anything in advance or explaining what we were doing. We practiced some basic stuff like grip, movement of the feet, a few basic cuts, and after an hour and a half he just stopped, told me to clean up the dojo, and then join him in the garden to help plant some new flowers. On his way out, with his big back turned to me, he said we'd be practicing like this every morning from then on.

'I clearly remember standing there motionless for the next five minutes or so. I wasn't sure I knew what was happening to me. It all felt like a dream. Just a year earlier I had been helping my mother sell rice balls to survive somehow, and a year before that we had learned of my father's death somewhere in the Pacific. We had never even buried him. And a year before that I had watched as my father was dragged from our house to fight in the war. It all seemed like a really bad dream which just went on and on, and now I was stuck in yet another dream, a much better one, where first I helped this mysterious man build a new home in a Buddhist temple and now I was learning ancient swordsmanship from him.

'I thought this world was crazy.'

'I agree,' I said. 'This world is definitely crazy.'

We stopped at yet another traffic light. I glanced at both sides of the pedestrian crossing. Dozens of people were just about to leave the safety of the sidewalk and cross the road. I always found it interesting how such points in time and space brought together people of different ages, colors, backgrounds to share one common experience, which was to overcome an obstacle (a road full of cars) so that they could continue following their different paths.

As the crosswalk light turned green, their orderly little formation broke up, and a colorful flow of people tore the stillness of the moment to pieces. I saw an old lady in a wheelchair with her stuffed, dead dog in her lap, a man in his late forties dressed as a teenage schoolgirl, a mother with three little boys struggling to make them pay attention, a businessman in a tight, black suit with wrinkles of worry on his forehead, a skateboarder in his twenties trying to get across first, a foreign couple holding hands and looking at their surroundings amazed, a policeman rushing back to his police booth, a father with his teenage girl doing his best to understand her, two young women with big Louis Vuitton bags over their shoulders and at least four or five shopping bags in their hands, and a homeless man in his fifties trying to avoid everyone else's gaze.

'I still remember the time I spent on the streets vividly. As if it were yesterday. Actually, all of this,' I said, pointing at the interior of the car and the two of us, 'feels like a dream. Just like you said. Or even worse, a lie. A big, fucking lie. That's what it is. It's a lie told by a world that doesn't really give a shit but pretends to. And it works. You believe it. We all fucking believe it.'

All the people disappeared, and our light turned green.

'What happened next? How did you get to know the boss?' I asked.

Kobayashi-san took a few moments to collect his thoughts and then went on with his story.

'In the May of 1950, on a rainy, gloomy Saturday afternoon, a big black car came to grandpa's house. I was inside, helping fix the leg of a wooden table when I heard the loud engine. I had had a fascination with cars since I was little, so I went straight to the window to take a look. It was a majestic Mercedes-Benz. I had never seen a car like that before.

'Grandpa went outside. He opened the rear door, and a woman in her forties stepped out, holding a baby in her arms. Grandpa took her suitcase from the trunk, and they both entered the house as the car left, with its engine rumbling with the same rage as it had on arrival.'

'So, they were bringing over the boss, right? He came as an infant with his mother?' I asked.

'He *did* come as an infant, but not with his mother.'

'Huh?'

'A nanny of sorts had brought him. Her name was Miyako-san.'

'Miyako-san...'

'Right. She practically raised him, together with grandpa, in that old Buddhist temple-turned-house. But she was much more than a nanny. She was a teacher, a mother, and a friend to him, however strange that might sound. The boss never went to school – grandpa and Miyako-san taught him everything at home. Grandpa was responsible for "kenjutsu", which we practiced together, and for... well... let's call it philosophy. He was shaping his view of the world. And

Miyako-san was responsible for everything else – math, history, literature, biology, geography, all that stuff.

'You know... Our boss grew up in a good environment. Very strict, but good. But... he grew up isolated. For most of his childhood, the only people he had proper relationships with were grandpa, Miyako-san, and me. I was something like a big brother to him initially, but as we grew older, it became more and more obvious that he was part of the family and I was not. I mean, I *was* part of the family, but not the same way he was. There were certain... privileges, that I didn't have access to. And I think grandpa raised him like that intentionally, to gradually put a bit of distance between us, and at the same time to put him more and more above me.'

'Didn't that bother you?' I asked.

'To be honest, it did. But it was normal. It was always meant to be that way, and I knew that from the beginning. I had been expecting it ever since he arrived as a baby, and in a way, when our current roles were finally established, I kind of felt relieved. On the other hand – and this is something I never really shared with anyone – I felt like I had lost someone. I still do today. I lost a brother. And I lost a friend. And... I think I lost a piece of my soul in the process.'

I looked out the window. We were already on the outskirts of Tokyo. There was a 7-Eleven convenience store on the corner, and I saw three young boys in their teens fooling around in the parking lot in front of the store. They had carefree smiles on their faces, and you could tell from their eyes that they were completely absorbed in the moment, blocking out both the past and the future.

Suddenly, a thrust of pain struck my heart, and with each breath I took, the pain seemed to increase. I stopped breathing for a few seconds in the hopes that the pain would go away. It had happened before, and not breathing for a while usually helped.

When I finally summoned the courage to breathe again, I took a deep one and then let it all out as slowly as possible. The pain was gone.

'I've never had a friend,' I murmured.

Kobayashi-san looked at me for a moment, then turned his gaze back to the road ahead.

'You *do* have a friend, you know.'

I looked at him, then I looked out the window again.

'Thanks,' I said.

'To lose someone you're attached to is difficult,' Kobayashi-san continued. 'It doesn't matter if it's a friend or a relative, a boss or a teacher. Those are just different names and forms of the same thing: a bond between two souls. And to lose doesn't necessarily mean not having that person in your life anymore; it also means a change in the nature of the bond. Often this change is even more difficult to accept, precisely because the other person is still present. Of course, change is inevitable, and it can be a good thing for both people, but it doesn't always work out. It just doesn't. Not for both of the people involved. I honestly hope you'll never have to experience anything like this.'

'Has the boss ever lost someone like that?' I asked.

Kobayashi-san didn't give me an immediate answer. He kept looking at the road, but it was obvious that a lot was going on inside his head.

'He has,' Kobayashi-san answered finally. 'But I can't talk about that right now.'

A grim look appeared on his face as if a cold wind from the north had suddenly blown away his serenity.

'It's all right, old man,' I replied. 'You don't have to. But you will. Ok? You'll talk about it when the time comes.'

'I will.'

'Promise me,' I asked.

He looked at me for a moment, then said: 'I promise.'

I nodded in return. Then, I asked him to talk about something else from their childhood. To tell me more about the boss and how they grew up.

'The boss used to be a shy, timid little boy,' Kobayashi-san told me. 'I know, it's hard to imagine, but that's the truth. He always seemed to be absorbed in his own little world. It's impossible to tell what this world of his might have been like, as he never spoke about it to the three of us, but I doubt it was – or is – a happy place. Even when he was with us, talking or doing whatever we were doing, part of him was in that world. He was only able to leave it entirely when he was practicing "kenjutsu" or hiking in the mountains.

'We often went into the woods. Sometimes with grandpa and Miyako-san, sometimes just us men, and sometimes just the two of us. I liked to watch him as we walked among the trees. His pupils widened, and he seemed to absorb everything like a sponge. He would often touch the trees, the bamboo, and other plants along the way. As if he wanted to feel them, and I tend to think he was somehow even communicating with them.

'When we reached a summit or a temple or a shrine, he would find a solitary rock, an empty bench, or a quiet corner, then sit down and stare for minutes on end without blinking. I wouldn't call it meditation; it was more like he was trying to grasp the world around him.'

'It sounds like he was a gentle, sensitive person back then,' I said.

'It does. And he was,' Kobayashi-san answered.

'So, what changed him?'

'What changed him? Well... It's complicated.'

'And you can't tell me yet, right?'

'Well... I can tell you this: when he was sixteen, he disappeared in the woods for seven days. By that time, he was already used to hiking alone, but he would always return by dusk. And all of us had complete faith in him, and we kind of took it for granted that nothing bad would or could happen to him. I mean, he knew those woods better than anyone. But that time he didn't return for a whole week.

'Miyako-san was worried as hell, and I think in those seven days she cried more than an average person cries during their whole life. As for grandpa, he didn't show much emotion, but I knew him well: inside he was both anxious and raging. I thought he could explode at any moment.

'Then, on the seventh day, a few moments after the sun had set, he came back. I remember the scene very well.

'It was raining outside, and lightning bolts were tearing across the dark sky. The three of us were eating a hot pot for dinner. I had already been a full-time employee of grandpa's for several years by then, and I was living with them. I had my small room in the northern corner of the house. I was just about to excuse myself and go back to my room when suddenly the front door opened. All three of us looked up.

'He was standing in the door, soaking wet, his clothes and hair a mess, with blood and mud all over him. He looked like a homeless person, and it took us a couple of seconds to recognize him. He slowly stepped inside and into the light. As his face and eyes became more visible, we all stopped breathing for a few moments. Time came to a standstill, and I heard a crack. It was a strange sound, completely out of place. It wasn't until much later that I realized it had been the sound of his, of our fate taking a turn and changing permanently. It was a crack in time and space.

'Miyako-san began to cry, not surprisingly. Grandpa, however, stood up, walked to him calmly, looked him in the eye, and then slapped him as hard as he could. The boss hardly budged an inch, and he never stopped staring grandpa in the eye. Grandpa then closed his eyes and hugged him. It was the first and the last time I saw grandpa show affection.

'As for me, I stayed where I was, frozen in place. I kept staring into his eyes, waiting for him to look at me. When he finally did, I saw something. I can't really say what it was exactly, but I know it scared me. It scared me... to death. There was something profoundly sad and at the same time vibrant and exciting in his eyes; as if agony and hope were fighting each other with bare fists, but agony seemed to be the stronger competitor. I sensed... inevitability. And it had a color.'

'Purple,' I said.

Kobayashi-san nodded. 'We're here' he said, stopping the car.

What are you thinking?

I got out of the car and closed the door. I saw two other cars parked in front of the house – boss Yamaguchi's old Nissan Skyline GT-R and a brand new BMW 7 series. Both black, of course.

Kobayashi-san opened the front gate and I followed. A short, marbled pathway led to the house through a well-kept Japanese garden. We got to the front door, where two men dressed in black suits and armed with short swords were standing guard. Kobayashi-san nodded to them, and they nodded back and opened the door for us. I just looked at them, without any salute.

We entered and took our shoes off. A long corridor led us further into the house, and I looked at the paintings on the walls as we walked. I didn't know much about art, but I liked what I saw. There were four paintings, each showing the sea in a different state, a different time of day, different weather. The calm, blue serenity of a summer morning; the small, playful waves created by a gentle breeze; the rough anger of a storm; and the lonely silence of the greatest of depths. All four paintings evoked strong emotions in me, and all kinds of different thoughts surfaced from the various corners and corridors of my mind.

Kobayashi-san turned around to see where I was. 'I'm coming,' I said.

Several doors led to several rooms from the corridor, and we entered the last one. It was a strange room with walls covered in blue velvet, and there was a glass door leading to a large garden behind the house. Boss Yamaguchi was sitting in a leather armchair in one corner. Two other guards were standing right next to him. In the middle of the room, I saw two people: a man in his fifties lying on the tatami with his eyes closed and a woman kneeling in "seiza" position next to him. The woman was bending over the man, and she had her hands pressed against his temples. She seemed to be concentrating hard, and I saw a faint, greenish light emanating from where her hands were touching him.

The green light intensified, and the man's body began to shake. I felt an oppressive tension in the air, and my throat dried up. The woman held his head firmly while doing whatever she was doing, and I could hear her murmur something indistinctly as if saying a prayer.

Suddenly, the shaking stopped, the light disappeared, and that stifling atmosphere just went away. The woman let go of the man's head, put her hands in her lap, and turned to the boss, saying: 'It's done.' Then, she collapsed.

***

'Are you all right?' I asked, removing a wet towel from her forehead.

Ren looked me in the eye. Her eyes were... intriguing. I could not figure them out. Maybe it was their green color, maybe something else. I don't know. There was a certain depth to them and a kind of mysteriousness. I felt like she was reading my mind, and it frustrated me that I couldn't read hers. I felt naked and vulnerable in front of her.

She grabbed me by my arm and tried sitting up.

'Take it easy,' I said.

'It's ok. I'm used to it. Just bring me a glass of water, please.'

I stood up and went to the kitchen. I poured tap water into a large glass, then I looked around to see if there was anything I could add. In the middle of the kitchen table stood a bowl full of fruit, with several lemons inside. I took one and sliced it up, then I squeezed some lemon juice into the glass. I also found some herbs in the window – basil, rosemary, mint, and some other spices I didn't recognize. I picked a few mint leaves and put them in the water. Finally, I added two cubes of ice.

When I returned to her, she was sitting in the armchair that the boss had been sitting in. I gave her the water.

'Thanks,' she said, and she took a couple of sips. 'Mm, it's nice. You're a very attentive man.'

'I don't know,' I replied. 'I just like it this way myself, so I thought you might like it, too. And it's healthy.'

'As I said, you're an attentive man,' she said with a faint smile.

'I guess so.'

She took a few more sips.

'So... shall we introduce ourselves? I'm Ren.'

'I'm Sato,' I replied. 'Pleased to meet you.'

'Pleased to meet you, Sato-san.'

'It's ok, just call me Sato. I don't like being formal.'

'I see. Then, it's just Ren for you, too.'

I nodded.

'Do you have a family name, Sato?'

I shook my head.

'How come?' she asked.

'I'm an orphan.'

'But orphans tend to have family names, too.'

'I don't.'

'I see. So, it really is just Sato.'

I nodded again.

'You're not very talkative, right?'

'It depends,' I replied.

'On what?'

'On the person I'm talking to,' I said.

'So... does that mean you don't like me?'

'No, I *do* like you,' I answered, but as soon as I spoke, my face turned red.

'So, you like me. That's good,' she said, smiling. 'I like you, too.'

'Anyhow, what's *your* family name?' I asked, trying to change the subject. 'You haven't told me yet.'

'Oh, right. How rude of me. Sorry. It's Yamaguchi. Ren Yamaguchi.'

'What?' I asked, surprised. 'Like the boss? Boss Yamaguchi?'

'So, that's what you call him? I see. Well, for me it's just dad. Or father. Or sometimes daddy.'

'What the...' I didn't finish the sentence. I was in shock, to say the least. I just couldn't believe it. 'You're his daughter?'

'Yep.'

'No way...'

'Well... sometimes I think the same thing myself,' she said, looking away.

'I need to sit down.'

I looked around, but there weren't any other chairs, so I just sat on the floor.

'I guess... you didn't know about me, right?' Ren asked.

I shook my head.

'That doesn't surprise me,' she said. 'Dad is very protective, you know.'

I looked her in the eye, but she turned away.

'How old are you?' I asked.

'You don't get to ask that first, my dear Sato! How old are *you*?'

'Thirty-seven,' I answered.

She took a good look, analyzing every wrinkle on my face, every grey hair, every inch of my body. She then looked away again and said: 'Me too.'

I sighed and rubbed my eyes with my palms.

We spent the next few minutes in silence. We must've looked like a tired, bored couple. I didn't really know what she was thinking, but I was just trying to find the right words, both for *our* conversation and for the one I was hoping to have with myself. It all felt so unreal.

Then, a small bird appeared in the window and began to sing. We both looked in its direction. I mean, you call it singing, but it sounded more like a monologue. Like it was trying to tell us something. The bird kept shifting its head as it spoke, looking at Ren one moment, at me the next. Ren and I looked at each other, and though we didn't say a word, we kind of had an internal dialogue between us, going something like this:

"Do you understand it?"

"No, do you?"

"No, me neither, but there's a feeling in the air, and it's slowly creeping under my skin."

"Yeah, I get you. I feel the same way."

"Maybe the bird brought it."

"Maybe."

"Or maybe you brought it."

"Maybe."

"And the bird is just a messenger."

"Or a catalyst."

"Or neither."

We looked at the bird again. It spoke its final words, then flew away.

But the feeling stayed.

'That was strange,' Ren said.

'Yeah, well, everything seems to be strange nowadays,' I replied.

'Including killing other people? Or is that not strange at all to you?'

'You mean the duel a few days ago?' I asked.

'For example. But somehow I have the feeling it wasn't your first time.'

'And probably won't be the last,' I said.

'Right.'

Ren stood up and went to the window. Her steps were a bit shaky and wobbly, but she had more or less recovered. She opened the window even more and let the morning breeze enter the room. It caught her hair and made it dance in the air, and her scent left the surface of her skin and slowly swayed across the room, all the way to my nostrils. I took a deep breath and held it inside as long as I could.

'We were close, you know,' she said, still looking out the window. 'I wouldn't call him a friend; more like a brother.'

'Ryuji, you mean?'

She didn't respond. Instead, she continued:

'I'm not a fool. I knew it would end like this sooner or later, and I tried to prepare myself as best I could. But when reality strikes, it's... painful. Nothing can prepare you for the feelings of loss, of solitude, of hopelessness. Nothing.'

I didn't see her eyes, but I knew tears had welled up in them. She wiped the tears away with her hand.

'I'm sorry,' I said.

'That doesn't change the fact that you killed him.'

'No, it doesn't.'

She sighed, then turned around to face me.

'Why did you challenge him?' she asked. 'He could've stayed my bodyguard, and you could've kept doing whatever you were doing until now.'

'I know,' I replied. 'But I had to do it.'

'Why?'

'Because I felt it. I had this feeling inside me telling me to do it, and I had no choice but to do it.'

Ren looked away, staring at the blue velvet wall.

'You always have a choice,' she whispered after a few seconds of silence.

'I'm not so sure about that,' I replied. 'I don't know much about life and its forces, but the feeling I most often get is that choice is just an illusion. Even the thoughts I have in my mind seem to be there deliberately.'

Ren looked me in the eye.

'So, you're saying you had no choice but to kill all those people you've killed so far because some higher force made you do it. Meaning, you're not responsible for your actions. Is that what you are saying?'

'I *am* responsible for my actions, because the moment I decide to do something, my mind thinks *it* made a conscious decision, making me live with that decision and its consequences for the rest of my life. It's just that at the subconscious level there's always something telling me things were happening to me because they were meant to happen. But I don't know, really. It's confusing,' I said, my voice becoming slightly agitated. 'Why? Are you telling me you're here in this house, doing whatever *you* are doing out of your own choice?'

Ren lowered her eyes, while I put my right hand in my pocket and began fidgeting with the hundred-yen coin.

'I don't know,' she replied. 'Maybe it's both. Maybe there is a narrative we are meant to be a part of, but we're also able to change its course. Wouldn't that make sense?'

'Maybe,' I said.

I walked to the window to stand next to her, and I looked outside. The garden in the back of the house was much larger than the one in front. It had a pond in the middle, with a stone bridge leading to a small hill, or rather a mound on the opposite side. On top of the mound stood a miniature version of a seven-story pagoda, made of stone and surrounded by bushes of various flowers. Behind the mound and on the perimeter of the garden tall bamboo protected the space from the outside world, and there was a tree on both sides of the pond. To the left stood an old black pine, with its branches stretching over the pond, as if trying to reach to the other side, where a gracious, young cherry tree was starting to bloom. There was a stone bench under the pine tree and a wooden one under the cherry tree, both facing the pond, facing each other.

'It's nice,' I said.

'It is,' Ren replied.

'Tell me, what were you doing to that man before you collapsed? And why am I here? Why do you need protection?'

Ren kept looking at the garden, without blinking.

'Let's go outside,' she said.

***

The garden had very particular energy, with a smooth, steady flow, like currents at sea. Its touch and presence felt liberating – like standing on the shore and looking at the blurred line of the horizon. Any feelings of tension I had had, evaporated.

We walked to the pond. The water was green, its surface completely still. I bent over to get a better look (probably to see if there were fish inside), but to my surprise, I couldn't see my own reflection. Everything else was there – the branches of the pine, the fluffy clouds, a couple of birds in the sky, but not my face. Or Ren's when she leaned over.

I looked at her, and she looked back at me. It felt like we were thinking the same thoughts, sharing the same memories of the same experiences. It felt like I understood her (or at least part of her), and I think she felt the same thing. It was a moment of mutual understanding – the kind of shared understanding accomplices would have, or friends, or siblings, or lovers.

I looked into the pond again, and I still saw no reflection of my face. I straightened up, turned around, and walked to the stone bench under the pine. Ren did the same thing, but going in the opposite direction, to where the cherry tree stood. We both sat down, facing each other, with the pond between us.

'So, tell me,' I said. 'Why am I here?'

'To protect me,' she said, looking into the distance.

'I know, but why? What were you doing to that man back in the house?'

'I was... removing things.'

'Removing? I don't get it.'

'What are you thinking right now?' Ren asked.

'What am I thinking?'

'Yeah, like, what thoughts do you have in your head? Close your eyes for a couple of seconds, and just tell me what you're thinking.'

I had a startled look on my face for a moment, but then I did as she had said and closed my eyes.

'So?' she asked after I had opened my eyes again. 'What's in there?'

'Well... lots of things. I mean, a few things. Yeah, a couple different things.'

'Like what?'

'I'm not sure I want to tell you the specifics. I don't even know you. I mean, I do, but... I don't. You get the point.'

'You don't have to be specific.'

'Hm... Well, there is a question in there. Actually, two questions. Or maybe three. And then, there are some images. Of people. And of places. A face. There's a face, too. And then... an idea. And a feeling. Yes, a feeling, but in a visual form.'

'Is that all?' she asked.

'Yeah. I think.'

'That's quite a lot,' Ren said. 'I mean, it's not unusual to have so much stuff in your head at once, but people, especially men, don't usually identify and distinguish all these different things. It's usually just a big, blended mash. Like a smoothie.'

'A smoothie?'

'Or a cocktail, if you like.'

'I don't usually drink either of those,' I said.

'Ok, whatever. You know what I mean.'

I nodded.

'Gosh, men...' she sighed, shaking her head. 'Anyhow. You have these thoughts in your head – ideas, questions, images, maybe even sounds. And they are always there, right? Not these particular ones of course, but something's always there. Even when you're asleep.'

'Unless you're a Buddhist monk practicing Zen meditation,' I said.

'Now, there you're wrong, my dear,' she said, raising her right index finger. 'No one can completely remove thoughts from the mind. Not even your enlightened Buddhist monk. The thoughts are always there in some form. You might make them invisible for shorter or longer periods of time, you might even make them withdraw, push them back, suppress them, but it's not up to us humans to do anything permanent to them. And besides, you're definitely not a Buddhist monk.'

'That I'm not.'

'But even if you were, you'd still have your thoughts, they'd be there, or if someone, somehow *did* manage to remove them, they'd return. In this life, or the next, or maybe even later. And they'd keep returning until you were truly ready to let them go.'

'I've heard about this before. The Cleaner.'

'The what?'

'The Cleaner,' I repeated. 'A... friend of mine once told me about the Sea of Thought, and our mind's connection to it, and this mysterious guy who can remove ideas and thoughts from people's minds like the most precise of surgeons, but the ideas would eventually return, and hit even harder. My friend called him the Cleaner.'

'Interesting,' Ren replied. 'You men always think of people with power as men.'

She had this piercing look in her eyes as if she were trying to stab me with them, but she looked away before her imaginary sword could reach me.

'Wait... No way... You...'

A big black bird let out a loud caw and flew up high in the sky from one of the pine tree's upper branches. Ren looked up, but I kept staring at her. In one moment, she could seem so... innocent, but then in the next, I would see her as this overwhelming, otherworldly presence. She was a creature of contrasts.

'You're the Cleaner,' I said.

She shrugged.

'What a strange name to use,' she remarked. 'I wonder where it came from. It sounds like a character from a superhero movie. Like Spiderman, Batman, the Joker, the Witcher. Does this make me a superhero? It must've been a man who gave me such a name.'

'You sound like you don't really like men. Or maybe you don't trust them.'

'Look, all my life I've been surrounded by men and men only. Literally. I grew up without a mother, without a sister, without a girlfriend. And I'm not saying there weren't men who treated me fairly. There were. There are. But most of the men I come in touch with are so... simple. Which can be good at times, but mostly it's painful and annoying. I can't stand simplicity. I can't stand shallow, narrow-minded people. I just can't. And maybe you're not one of them. Maybe you're different. I don't know. Based on my first impressions... I'd say I'd give you a chance. But I haven't decided yet.'

'So, I have a chance,' I said with a smile.

She nodded and smiled.

As I was looking at her smiling face and white teeth, I remembered something else Kei had told me. I didn't have the details or the full picture in front of me, only a fragment of a conversation we had had and a term he had used.

'What?' Ren asked. 'Why are you looking at me in such a strange way?'

'I'm not,' I said.

'Yes, you are.'

'It's nothing.'

'Oh, come on! I'm not stupid, you know. I'm the Cleaner, re-member?'

'It's just... Have you ever felt...? Have you ever felt that you were cursed?'

'Cursed?' she asked with apparent surprise.

I kept looking at her, without reacting.

'What do you mean by cursed?'

I shrugged.

'If you mean the life I've had so far or my superhero-like powers, then yes. It does feel like a fucking curse not being able to live a nor-mal life like any normal human being. On the other hand... I don't know. I kind of enjoy being able to do something no one else is capa-ble of. I feel... privileged. I feel chosen. It's like with this Jesus Christ guy.'

'Guy?' I asked with a smile.

'Yeah, I mean, he was crucified and all that, and he must have felt annoyed with God and the path he was more or less forced to walk, but on the other hand, I bet he also felt proud in those moments of agony, with those huge nails piercing his arms and legs. I can imagine him thinking "Fuck you all. I'm Jesus, and I'll be back."'

'That sounds more like the Terminator,' I said.

'Well, ok, not exactly like that, but you get the point. We all like to think of ourselves as special. We crave normality in our lives, but we ridicule it at the same time and strive to be different from every-body else. It's confusing. Jesus must've been confused. I'm confused.'

'And you're being used,' I added.

'What?'

'Used,' I repeated. 'Your father is using you.'

Ren suddenly went mute and looked away.

'You know he is,' I continued. 'He's using your abilities for his own goals, right? He makes you remove thoughts from the minds of his rivals, enemies, probably even business partners. He's manipulating everyone around him, including his own daughter.'

Ren didn't respond. She just kept staring at the pond between us.

'Will you remove something from my mind, too?' I asked. 'Did you do that to your previous bodyguards? What do you usually take away from them? The idea of fear so that they can protect you, no matter what? Or the idea of love, so that they don't fall in love with you? Or their sexual appetites, maybe? Is there even a limit to what you can remove?'

'Enough!' Ren said, agitated.

She was still looking at the water, and there were tears under her eyes. Her left hand was trembling a bit, and she tried holding it still with the other hand.

'Look,' I said, as I stood up and got a bit closer to her. 'I... really don't know what's happening here. This whole conversation with you today... I mean... First, I learn the boss has a beautiful daughter. Then, I learn she's the Cleaner and that it's not just an urban legend but a living, breathing human being. A young woman at that. And I learn how my boss, who's more like a father to me than a boss, is mistreating his own daughter, you, someone I barely know, but whom I've already grown to like. I'm just... I'm just trying to process everything right now. You, your father, this whole situation, and my role in all of this. I'm... as confused as you are. As Jesus Christ was,' I said with a faint smile.

She looked at me, her eyes filled with tears. Then, she stood up, walked over to me, and put her trembling left hand on my cheek. Her touch was soft and warm.

She leaned in close as if she was going to kiss me. I instinctively closed my eyes, but instead of feeling her lips on my lips, she suddenly pushed me hard with both hands, and I fell backward into the pond.

Only... there was no splash.

The black box

I found myself lying on my back in Kei's corridor of doors. I stood up and straightened my clothes a bit, then I looked at the door closest to me: "sixty-six."

I began walking down the corridor, back to my familiar number, the fifty-five. It was the first time I had entered the corridor through a different portal, and the first time I was walking in the opposite direction. The corridor was the same as usual, the doors were the same, but walking back from the higher numbers to the lower ones somehow felt different. It felt like... going back in time.

I got to fifty-five and grabbed the knob, but before turning it and entering, I stopped for a moment. Something felt different. The knob was warmer than usual, and there seemed to be a strong presence inside, its energy barely kept in check by the walls of Kei's bar. I could feel it trying to tear down everything around it.

I slowly opened the door and went in.

The energy which I had felt from the outside was swirling around the place like some mystical beast, caught in a cage and desperate to find its freedom. It emanated a dark green light, reminding me of the Aurora Borealis, which I had only seen on the internet. I watched it in awe.

'What's up, maaan?' came the question from a dark corner of the bar.

I looked to my right and saw Kei sitting on a sofa, his legs crossed, and a half-full glass of something strong in his hand. He took a small sip.

'Kei. Hello. You're not behind the counter,' I said.

'Nope. I'm here, sitting and watching. Enjoooying the view.'

'I see.'

I went to the counter, grabbed a bottle of an eighteen-year-old Nikka Taketsuru pure malt, and poured some into a glass. On the rocks, this time. I then went to Kei and took a seat in an old armchair next to him. We clinked glasses, and we both took a sip.

After a minute or so of silence, Kei whispered: 'Beauuutiful.'

I nodded and took another sip. Or maybe two.

'Something's happening, Kei,' I said, kind of expecting him to give me a full and clear explanation of everything I had been experiencing in the last week or so. But he just smiled and said: 'Yep.'

'I hate you,' I said, returning the smile.

'I know, maaan. I hate you, too.'

I finished my whisky, stood up, and looked around, with my right hand in my pocket, scrubbing the hundred-yen coin.

I scanned the whole bar, examining all the shadows, trying to find the source of the energy. It was hard to trace it, as it covered everything in its peculiar light, but then I noticed that the dark hole in the wall was not dark anymore.

I approached it.

A shadow was standing right in front of it, holding one arm inside the hole and the other one stretched out towards the bar. Soon, I realized the shadow was channeling this energy, this green light from the hole, through its body, and into the atmosphere of Kei's bar. What used to be a space full of empty darkness on the other side of the hole now was the source of something so strong and vivid that I was barely able to hold myself together. I felt overwhelmed, and I thought I would explode into the tiniest of particles of dust and dissolve into this light, becoming one with the energy. I even craved it. And the shadow was the conduit.

'That's number one hundred and one,' Kei said, walking up to me, holding his now empty glass.

'The one that appeared the last time I was here?'

'Yep, maaan.'

'I don't understand,' I said.

'What don't you understand?'

'Nothing, Kei. I don't understand a thing.'

'Well, you must understand something, right?'

'Like what?'

'Like the whisky you're drinking, for example. You must understand that it's whisky, that it was made in Japan, that you like it, that in general, you like to drink to relaaax, that this is a bar where a waiter named Kei serves damn good drinks, that you like coming here, and you like chatting with me. Right, maaan?'

'That's not what I meant, Kei. Try being serious for once.'

'Oh, but I *aaam* serious. I really am,' he said, looking at his empty glass. 'Why are you people so eager to understand all the seeecrets, all the truths of this world? Why can't you be content to understand just a fraction of life, and to understand that fraction *well*, instead of trying to grasp the whole of the universe in a single lifetime?'

'I don't follow, Kei.'

'Do you really think you human beings, in this human form of flesh and blood, are equipped and prepared to understand the totaaality of life? To accept it? To embrace it?'

'I don't know.'

'Well, of cooourse you don't! And that's ok. You don't need to. You're not meant to.'

Kei went back to the counter and poured some of the same whisky I was drinking into his glass.

'Don't dwell on things so much, don't contemplate everything so much,' he told me. 'Instead, try feeeling what you don't understand.'

We looked at each other.

'Do you know how to feeel?'

I looked away, without giving him a response. Kei sighed, then came back to me.

'Look,' he said. 'Lift your arm and try touching the light that is coming through this person's fingers. Then, close your eyes and relax.

Breathe slowly and loosen your muscles. Just let the light go through you the same way it goes through this person next to us.'

I did as Kei had said. After a while, he asked:

'What do you feeel? Tell me the words that come to your mind.'

I hesitated for a second.

'Don't think about it, just tell me the wooords.'

'Warm. Good. Light. Float. I feel... at ease. Blessed. It's... good. It really feels good,' I said.

'That's good, maaan. That's good.'

I opened my eyes again and lowered my arm.

'Do you understand this light, this person next to you, this whole bar, and me, and everything that surrounds you heeere?' Kei asked.

I shook my head.

'But you felt good, right? Even now, you feel good, right?'

I nodded.

'You seee? You don't need to understand everything, maaan. It's ok to not understand. It's ok, maaan,' he said, putting his hand on my shoulder.

***

After I had left Kei's bar, I used the same portal to return to the other side. I didn't know how these portals worked, but when out in the corridor of doors again, it seemed to be the only way out for me. I could've explored the corridor a bit more, I guess. I could've wandered a bit further down one side of it or the other, but I didn't feel like there was much point.

So, I went back to Ren's garden.

When I got there, she was gone.

I went into the house. I immediately noticed how quiet everything was, and how empty it felt. Not only was the space physically empty, but I also couldn't sense any kind of energy in the air. The only sound I heard was the slow dripping of water, coming from the kitchen. I went there, to the sink, and I closed the faucet. There was an empty glass in the sink, and it had a red stain on one side. I took the glass and had a good look. I smelled the stain, then I wiped it a bit with my right thumb. The lipstick was still wet. I licked it off my finger. It tasted like sour cherry.

I went to her bedroom next, but she wasn't there either. Just the same, heavy emptiness. As if it were glued to the walls.

I walked back to the entrance of the house. Outside, two of boss Yamaguchi's men were still standing guard, with bored looks on their faces.

'Guys, where did Ren go?' I asked them. 'Has she told you? Is anyone with her?'

They looked at each other, then at me, but they didn't answer.

'So? Where is she?' I insisted.

'She's... She's still in the house,' one of them answered finally.

'She might be asleep, in her bedroom,' the other one said, and the first guy nodded in agreement.

'She's not there. She's not in her bed,' I told them.

'How do you know?!' the second guard asked.

'Yes, how do you know?!' asked the first.

'Take a guess,' I said.

They looked at each other again, then at me, and they both shrugged.

'I went to her bedroom, dumbasses.'

'Her bedroom?!' they exclaimed together. 'That's forbidden!'

'So, you never go there?' I asked them.

'Never!' the first guard replied.

'Then how do you know she's there?'

'Well, this is the only way out, so if we didn't see her come through this door,' the second guard said, 'which we didn't!' the first guard added, 'then she must be somewhere inside the house, or in the garden. If you can't find her in the garden, or any other room, then she must be in her bedroom.'

'Or the bathroom,' the first guard said.

'But she's not,' I told them again. 'I checked both.'

'Even the bathroom?!'

'The door was wide open, and it was dark inside. So... no, she's not there either.'

'What the...' the second guard said. 'But there's no other way to leave the house.'

'Apparently, there is,' I replied. 'Stay here. I'll go back inside and check.'

I searched the house as thoroughly as possible, but I couldn't find anything. No secret door, no hint of where she might have gone. I ended up in the blue velvet room again, and I sat on the floor to take a break. I just stared through the glass door leading to the garden, and I watched the trees, the pond, the mound with the pagoda, and all the bamboo in the back.

'The bamboo...' I said to myself. 'Fuck!'

I rushed outside and went straight to the bamboo grove. It was dense, with the trees very close to each other, but there was enough room for someone slender to find a way through. I was thin enough myself, so I went in, and I crawled and climbed my way to the other side of the grove, all the way to the wall of the garden. As I got there, I immediately noticed that a section of the wall had a slightly different color. A bit darker than the rest. As if someone had painted over it. There was also a small black button on the wall. I pressed it, and the darker section opened like a door, revealing an empty street on the other side.

'Fuck.'

***

It was early afternoon and I was hungry. I asked the guards what the address of Ren's house was, and I called a cab to take me back to the city.

It took a while, but after almost an hour, I had arrived in Shinjuku. I went to a small restaurant in an alley close to the Tokyo Metropolitan Building, where Sakai-san was serving the best ramen in the town. I was a regular there.

The ramen shop only had four seats around the counter, and behind it, the old Sakai-san was cooking. He used a family recipe he had inherited from his grandmother. He had never revealed to anyone the secret ingredients that made his ramen taste richer and deeper than any other ramen in Tokyo. Unfortunately, he never married, and he didn't have any children, so he was bound to take his recipe with him to the grave.

'Good afternoon, Sakai-san,' I said when I entered the restaurant.

'Oh! Sato-kun! What a surprise! It's been a while! Come inside! Sit down, please!'

'Thank you.'

I took the seat closest to the entrance.

'The usual?'

'Yes, please.'

There was a strange, familiar smell in Sakai-san's restaurant. It was familiar not only because I came regularly, but also because it reminded me of something that I couldn't really picture or grasp. I had the same feeling every time I went there, and it would stay with me for at least a couple of hours after I had left. The smell was a combination of the food Sakai was preparing, the odor of the old man himself, the furniture, the walls, and probably the whole history of the place, which I felt I had some kind of connection to. What I would usually do is close my eyes until Sakai-san served me the ramen, and then I would try to imagine this history and my connection to it.

On some days, when I was in the right frame of mind, I would see the blurred lines of two people – a young man and a woman, sitting at the counter with their backs turned. I would also see the same green light which I had just seen at Kei's bar. The light would swirl around the two of them, creating a bond that made them appear as one entity instead of two.

I closed my eyes this time, too. I was hoping I would see these two figures again, and that I would somehow finally be able to get closer, to catch a glimpse of their faces. Just a fraction – a smile, a wrinkle, a look maybe – to get me a bit closer to understanding the feeling that I had inside. But what I saw was only the green light, overwhelming the little ramen shop. I sensed that the two figures were there somewhere, inside the light, but I couldn't see a thing. Then, I remembered Kei's words from our last conversation. I remembered him telling me to stop trying to understand.

'Your ramen, Sato-kun,' the old man said, putting the bowl in front of me. 'Are you alright? Is something bothering you?'

'Everything's fine,' I replied, wiping away a tear from my cheek. 'I'm ok.'

'You sure?'

'Yeah. Don't worry.'

'Ok. Well, whatever it is, this soup will help. My grandma knew how to soothe the soul with her ramen.'

'Yeah, she probably did,' I said.

'You know, she never told me, but I think she had experienced something bad, really bad, which had left a deep wound within her. I guess this was her way of coping, of closing the wound.'

'Yeah,' I said, slurping in some noodles. 'You might be right.'

We spent a couple of minutes in silence, me eating the ramen and the old man washing the dishes when I turned to him again:

'Sakai-san, can I ask you a question?'

'Of course! Ask away!'

'It might sound strange, but do you remember a couple, a young man and a woman coming to your restaurant regularly? I think it happened a long time ago. Probably decades ago.'

'Hmm. Well, I've been serving ramen in this little shop of mine for close to fifty years now. I've had many guests, and a lot of them regulars, like you. But I do remember one couple, a *strange* couple from many years ago. They used to come two or three times a week, for like at least two years, but maybe even more.'

'When was that exactly? Do you remember?'

'Let me see... I would say the early eighties. Yes, I think it was around then. The beginning of the decade. I remember them because they were peculiar in a way. They were somehow different than the rest of the people I would meet.'

'Different how?' I asked.

'Well, first of all, they were madly in love. They would kiss and touch each other all the time, and you could feel this energy and bond between them. People back then didn't show affection in public that much, so it was unusual to see them make out all the time. And there was something else.'

'What?'

'It's hard to put in words. As if there was an additional layer to their bond, something deeper and even more complicated than the typical love between a man and a woman. I could feel this thing between them, but I was never able to understand if it was good or bad, or what it really was. But it definitely made their relationship much more complex and complicated.'

'Hm.'

'And, you know, to be completely honest with you, I always felt tense in their presence. Don't get me wrong, I liked having them here, I really liked them as people, but whenever they were here, sitting on these very chairs, tension crept into the air and my body. I felt uneasy. As if something bad or unnatural could happen at any moment. Of course, nothing ever happened, but this tension was always there.'

'And do you remember seeing a strange, green light? The color of a jade stone, but metallic and flashy?'

'No, not really. Except for her eyes! Yes, her eyes had this very particular green color. Probably something like you just described.'

'I see. And what happened to them? Do you know anything?'

'I don't, unfortunately. They just stopped coming, and I haven't seen them since. I remember her being pregnant, though.'

'Pregnant?'

'Yes. I think she was expecting twins. She must have been in her eighth or even ninth month when I last saw them.'

'And you don't know anything about them or their kids.'

'No. This job of mine is like this, you know. I meet people, I get to know them, and with some, I even feel like we become friends. We talk about life, about personal stuff, and they share stories of themselves, of their friends, and their families. I mostly listen, but with those whom I let in close, I open up a bit myself, too. Like with you today. But our relationship always stays confined to these four walls, to this counter right here between us, and to the ramen I serve. Whenever these people move on in their lives, whether that means starting families or moving to a new home, or even leaving the city, they stop coming to my restaurant and our relationship abrupt-ly comes to an end. As if it had never existed. As if we were ghosts to each other, or imaginary friends like the ones children have, and then they leave them behind when they grow up.'

'I'll never forget you, Sakai-san. I promise.'

'Don't bother making promises like that, Sato-kun. Never make a promise you're not sure you can keep. I'm old, you know. I don't need things like that anymore. I've heard enough of that stuff in my life.'

I lowered my gaze and looked at the empty bowl in front of me.

'Now, if you'll excuse me for a second,' Sakai-san said, and he went to his small private room in the back.

I waited for several minutes for him to return, but he didn't, so I put the money on the counter and left.

***

I had to find Ren. But how do you find someone you barely know in a city of twenty million people? I could've stayed at her place and waited for her to return, of course, but I didn't know how long that would take. I mean, it could've been a habit of hers to disappear like that for days, and I could easily imagine her manipulating the minds of people around her so that no one would even notice her little Houdini act. I had to find her.

As I didn't really know where to start looking, I figured I had to find someone who knew something. I had no clue who might know her, but then I remembered the night I had spent with Julia a couple of days before, and I remembered her telling me that I would become Ren's bodyguard, not boss Yamaguchi's. And she was strangely secretive about Ren, too.

I decided to go to the Palm Tree and pay Julia a visit.

My complicated relationship with Julia meant that I couldn't just barge in and ask for her help without bringing something. Usually, I'd either bring her Godiva chocolate (for which she hated me) or buy her sexy, expensive lingerie that she would only use with me. At least that's what she always told me, though I wasn't so sure about being the only one who got her special treatment in the bodies, panties, and stockings I bought her.

We both had a favorite brand when it came to lingerie: Agent Provocateur. Although they didn't have an official store in Tokyo, a member of our family specialized in importing luxury clothing into Japan, including women's lingerie. He ran his shop in Roppongi, and it was a gorgeous one. From the outside, it looked like a perfect, black cube. It *had* windows, but only a few very narrow ones, like on a medieval fortress, and with really dark glass, so they were easy to miss.

Okabe, the owner, was a fashion freak with a very crazy style and a love of luxury. When I got to the black box, as I called it, I saw his red Maserati parked in front, together with two Audi Q7s. He typically had clients from the fashion and entertainment industries or gangster wives.

As I was about to enter Okabe's store, the thick sliding doors opened, and a group of eight people came out – four men in their forties and four fashion models. Two of the girls were of Asian origin and the other two were blondes, probably European. They were talking loudly and laughing, and the girls were carrying several huge shopping bags. At the same time, an older man, probably in his late fifties and apparently homeless, appeared out of nowhere, pushing a cart with all his life's belongings piled up in it. He just happened to pass the big Audis with his cart at the exact moment when the chatty group got to their cars. When they all met, with me standing just a bit further away, the air suddenly froze. The homeless man looked up at the man who was closest to him, and every single person in the group stared at him. Nobody moved, but as the seconds went by, the stillness of the moment gradually became more stifling, and the expression in everyone's eyes changed. I saw increasing emptiness in the eyes of the group and ever-deepening darkness in the eyes of the old man. I saw disgust on one side and shame on the other.

As soon as the homeless man lowered his gaze to look away, the man closest to him kicked his cart with full force, and all his stuff fell to the ground. There were cans of food rolling down the street, a broken yellow umbrella, a pair of old shoes without laces, several books, some pants, shirts, and underwear, and a small box. The old man immediately kneeled, took the box in his hands, and opened it. It looked as if he were checking if its contents were ok. He held the box for a while, then a single tear appeared under his left eye and rolled down his rugged cheek. The man who had kicked his cart burst out laughing.

Before I realized what I was doing, I was holding the man by his throat and hitting him hard in the stomach. I grabbed his head and banged it against the window of one of the Audis, smashing the glass. His face was bleeding all over the place. I was about to unsheathe my short sword and literally cut his head off when Okabe suddenly yelled from the door of his black box:

'Stop! Stop it right now! Don't you dare spill blood on my property and my beautiful car! And you, fucking morons! You mother fucking bastards and whores, pack up your shit and leave! Immediately! And never ever come back here, or I swear I won't stop Sato-san here from slicing you up into little pieces and feeding you to some disgusting, fat pigs up north in Hokkaido! Fuck off!'

The group left in a hurry, the men all silent, the girls sobbing and in shock. Okabe and I meanwhile collected the homeless man's things and put them back into the cart. He just kept kneeling the whole time, looking at his box. When we were done, I knelt next to him, but he immediately closed the box so that I wouldn't see what was inside. We then looked at each other.

'My memories,' he whispered.

I gave him a ten-thousand-yen bill, and Okabe gave him another one. We then went inside the black box.

'Shit, man,' Okabe said as the sliding doors closed behind us. 'This world's gone crazy. Like, fucking full-time, end of the fucking universe, shitstorm crazy.'

'Yeah, crazy,' I said.

'Luckily, we still have people around who are willing to take action in situations like this,' he said, patting me on the shoulder.

'Yeah, I guess,' I replied, but as soon as I did, my fingers began to tremble, and I immediately put my hands in my pockets, holding my coin firmly in my right hand. I kept seeing images meanwhile, or rather the looks on people's faces – those of Kon, Kiki, and Ren. They were upset with me, or maybe disappointed, or just plain angry. I just couldn't tell. And my fingers kept trembling.

'What are you interested in?' Okabe asked. 'The lingerie, again?'

'Mm,' I nodded.

'Let's go downstairs, then.'

The ground floor was nothing but a huge reception hall with black walls and a grey, concrete floor. There were no paintings on the walls, no decoration, no windows. Just a faint, yellowish light coming from a single, huge bulb; a stairway leading to the upper floor; and another one leading below the ground. Okabe had his office, a small meeting room, and a private room upstairs, and all the clothes were downstairs.

As we went down the stairs, I noticed black and white photographs on the walls of the corridor which hadn't been there before. They looked like a series of a single photoshoot showing a young girl from being dressed in a traditional kimono and sitting on a chair in the middle of a room to getting undressed and then tied to the chair with intricate knots and in a weird position. She had this mysterious, and frankly, intriguing look in her eyes, in which fear, subjugation, and immense sexual desire were all mixed together. Her pussy was visibly wet in the last photo.

'It's Araki,' Okabe said. 'I bought these at an auction last week. They're good, right? I especially like this last one. I just don't know if he helped her get so wet or it's just the situation and the ropes and everything. My only regret with these photos hanging on these walls is that I can't jerk off anymore while looking at them. Or I have to do it here,' he said, looking at me, then laughing out loud, clearly enjoying the stiffness on my face.

'Anyway, let's go,' he said, patting my shoulder again.

There were no other guests in the shop when we finally descended. I smelled a delicate scent in the air – like a mixture of white tea and jasmine. Okabe was a perfectionist when it came to style and appearances, and he had made sure that his precious black box was an immaculate exercise in high-end fashion. He didn't care how many customers or what kind of turnover he had, as he was subsidizing his little clothing venture with money from other businesses he ran for our family. This was his love project.

The dim lighting, the black walls, and the dark green tiles on the floor created an atmosphere in which I felt like I was in some treasure chamber, hidden beneath the dungeon of a secretive lord's castle. Okabe maintained an almost perfect balance between women's clothes and men's, and to be honest, the stuff he had for men was more extravagant than his women's collection. I saw an amazing leather jacket with a hood, stitched together from several pieces of recycled leather; pink pants with small diamond skulls all over them; and blue shoes made of a very unusual material.

'That's whale skin, my friend.'

I looked at him, then at the shoes again. 'Green Peace would kill you for this.'

'Fuck Green Peace. I'd fuck each one of them in the ass.'

'Even the boys?'

'The boys in particular!'

'You're an asshole,' I said.

'Yeah, I know. Luckily, there's an even bigger one standing right next to me,' he said. 'So, you're here for lingerie, right? Come.'

We went to a smaller second room. Everything was the same except for the scent, which contained more sexuality. Okabe had once told me he used musk to create this penetrating scent of sexual desire. It was the scent of a woman in her late thirties to early forties, with beautiful, long legs, an elegant waist, delicate fingers on her hands, short, black hair, and sensual lips covered in blooming red lipstick. I could almost see her standing there, going through the lingerie, touching every single piece to see how the silk, the satin, the latex, the leather, and the nylon felt on her skin.

'What're you looking for?' Okabe asked.

'I don't know. Something... special, I guess.'

'Everything is special here, my friend. Be more precise. Or you know what? I'll leave you here alone for a while. Just go through all this stuff, touch it, smell it, hell, you can even try things on if you want,' he said with a huge grin on his face, followed by a wink.

I looked at him with one of those famous stares of mine, and he instantly backed off, raising his arms apologetically: 'Ok, ok, I get it. None of my business.' He then turned around and left.

I did as he said. I touched and smelled all the lingerie around me. Of course, I didn't try anything on. I couldn't even picture myself doing it, but I did picture something else. I pictured long, straight legs in sheer, skin-colored nylon stockings. I also pictured white, French knickers made of pure silk, and... no bra. Just a white string connecting the knickers to a white collar around a long, thin neck.

After a couple of minutes, Okabe returned: 'You taking that?'

I nodded and reached for my wallet, but he stopped me: 'No need. Just take it. It's a gift.'

'I like you, Okabe, but you're not the one to give away presents just like that.'

'Consider it as a favor, then. You have... how shall I put it... useful skills. Yeah. So, in case I might need those skills of yours, I'll remind you of this little gift. Alright?' He patted me on the shoulder again.

I nodded.

'See you, then, Casanova!'

'Be good, Okabe.'

'Oh, I'm always good,' he replied with another one of his winks.

***

I took the Oedo-line to get to Shinjuku. The subway station in Rop-pongi was surprisingly empty. I saw only a few tourists and some young foreign students, probably from the nearby university. I think it was a small international university funded by the government, and they had all these South-East Asian, Central-Asian, African, even some European students here on a scholarship. I wondered how much they really saw and knew about the Tokyo in which *I* was liv-ing. They'd spend a year, maybe two or even three in this city and then go home and tell their friends and families how well they got to know Tokyo, how they felt it had become their new home. But did they really? Had it really? The Tokyo *I* knew had two very different personalities. One was living in the light, out on the surface, and the other was in complete darkness, crawling in the murky depths of exis-tence. You had to know both to know Tokyo properly and to be truly at home in Tokyo. And to be honest, I didn't really know both sides myself. Just the dark one. So, if I think of it this way, I was probably not at home in Tokyo either.

This feeling of not being at home, or being out of place, often arose when I took public transportation. I don't know if it was the trains, the buses, the subways, or the people taking them, or maybe the fleeting scenery when I'd look out the window, be it skyscrapers, old residential neighborhoods, mountains, forests, or just tubes and wires in dark tunnels. But it would usually become even stronger when I sat down. A big hole would appear in my stomach and slowly suck in everything around it, and I'd just keep sinking deeper and deeper into the seat. I'd have this strong desire to scream, to ask for help, to be saved, but a voice from within would always prevent me, whispering: "There's no point. They won't hear you. They won't care. Just look around. Look at them. They don't care."

When the subway finally reached Shinjuku, I quickly stood up and ran out, I ran to the top and out to the street, panting and breathing heavily. I even forgot to do my ritual of transition. At least I still had my hundred-yen coin to hold onto.

After I had regained my composure a bit, I went straight to Palm Tree to see Julia.

Drama at Lulu's

When I got to Palm Tree, the women working there seemed uneasy. The ones who were not with clients were all gathered around the main counter, looking at their phones, as if waiting for some news. The older ones were a bit calmer than the younger girls, but even they seemed a little off.

'What's up, girls?' I asked.

'Oh, Sato-san! It's good to see you. It always feels safe to have you around,' one of the girls said.

'Yeah, thanks. But you all seem a bit stressed out. What's going on? And where's Julia?'

'She's over at Lulu's,' another girl said.

'What's she doing there?'

'Tending to a situation,' a third girl replied.

'A *situation*?' I asked.

'Yeah, with a customer,' the first girl said.

'And one of the new girls,' the second girl added.

'What kind of situation?'

'A serious one,' the third girl replied.

'What situation could Julia possibly solve? They have muscles over there, too,' I said.

'Muscles are not enough,' the first girl replied. 'Julia knows how to talk to people. Especially the clients. We need her talking skills, or else...'

'What?' I asked.

'The new girl is in danger,' the first girl said. 'Maybe you should go, too, Sato-san.'

'Fuck.'

***

Lulu's was just a couple of blocks away, so I got there quickly. I entered the bar, but the reception area was empty, except for the old cleaning lady, Rukia-san, who was sitting on a chair, smoking a cigarette, her cleaning kit lying on the floor next to her. She was by far the oldest person working for our family. Hell, she had been old even when I had joined more than twenty-five years ago.

'They're all upstairs, Sato-kun,' she said in her barely understandable, thin voice, puffing out smoke like a chimney.

I nodded and ran up.

I saw seven or eight girls dressed in miniskirts and short tops. A couple of them didn't even have tops, only bras. Three of our muscle men were there, too, visibly annoyed and impatient, and then there was Julia, standing in front of one of the doors. She was wearing high heels and a black satin nightgown. As I approached her, I could smell men's perfume on her skin. It was strong and sweet. Probably Yves Saint-Laurent. She hadn't even had time to take a shower.

'What's going on?' I asked.

'Sato-kun. It's good that you came. We have a situation here,' Julia said, pointing at the door.

'What kind of situation?'

'A hostage situation.'

'A what? Hostage?'

'Yeah. There's a guy in there with one of the girls. A new girl. Her name is Yuki.'

'Yuki,' I repeated, searching my memory for some trace of a previous encounter.

'Her client took her hostage and doesn't want to let her go. He barricaded the door with furniture, and he's threatening to kill her if we break in.'

'What does he want?' I asked. 'What's his demand?'

'It's... well... It's time.'

'Time?'

'Yeah. He wants us to give him more time with her.'

'For sex?'

'I don't know. I don't think so. It's something else.'

'And Yuki-chan?'

'She's crying. You can hear if you lean closer.'

I put my ear to the door, and I heard a sob.

'I think he might be trying to get some information out of her. He wants to make her talk, but she doesn't want to. Or she can't,' Julia said.

'And who is he?' I asked. 'Do we know him? Is he a regular?'

'No. The girls told me they had never seen him before.'

'And what does he look like?'

'Girls?' Julia asked, turning to them.

'He's... odd,' one of the girls said.

'He's short and fat,' another one said, 'and he is almost completely bald.'

'He has this funny hair which he combs across his bald head from one side to the other,' a third girl added.

'Fuck,' I said, turning to the door. 'Kon! Is that you?! Kon!' I yelled, knocking hard on the door. 'Kon, it's me, Sato! Open up!'

I heard footsteps in the room, and someone approaching the door.

'Kon, is that you?' I asked.

A couple of seconds went by with no answer. Everyone was tense, and the possibility of a tragedy hung in the air.

'Kon,' I said, almost whispering the name, and resting my forehead against the door.

'Leave us alone, ok?' a crying voice replied from the room. 'Please.'

'I can't,' I said. 'Let me in, Kon. Let me help.'

'You can't help me!' Kon yelled. 'Just... just... give me time, ok? We need more time, that's all.'

'Kon, are you aware of your situation? You've practically taken a hostage. If I were to call the police now, you'd go to jail. Or get shot, maybe even killed. It's still not too late. We haven't told the police yet. I can still help you.'

Another moment of silence followed. I could almost feel Kon's anxiety pouring through the small cracks of the door.

'How? How can you help? You don't even know my situation. You don't know anything.'

'Well, tell me, then. Talk to me. Explain your situation, and I'll do my best to understand. But first, you have to let Yuki-chan go. I can hear her crying. Both of you are crying. That's not good, right? No one should be crying. Especially not the girl. She doesn't deserve it, right? Am I right, Kon?'

I heard more footsteps. He was probably pacing back and forth, trying to figure out what to do.

'Can I come in?' I asked.

'No, wait!' Kon yelled. 'Stop! Just give me a minute to think.'

'Ok, Kon. You'll get exactly a minute, not more,' I said.

I turned to the others: 'I need you all to go downstairs and leave me alone with Kon.'

I looked at Julia, and she saw in my eyes that I knew what I was doing, that she could trust me. She nodded and told the girls and the guards to do as I had said. She was the last one to leave, but I grabbed her by the arm before she started down the stairs: 'I need to talk to you. Wait for me at the Palm Tree.'

'I have clients, my dear,' she said.

'I'll be your client,' I replied. She nodded and smiled.

As Julia left, the corridor suddenly felt very lonely. As if the walls had somehow absorbed the feelings of all the people who were visiting or working at the place.

I turned to Kon again: 'Your time's up. Let me in or come outside. I'm fine either way. There's no one here. Everyone left. It's just us. You can trust me.'

After a few seconds, Kon removed the furniture from the door and opened it. He looked exhausted. And he was holding a gun.

I went in slowly, and I saw Yuki sitting on the bed. She was wearing nothing but her panties. When I saw her face, I remembered that she was the girl I had slept with a couple of nights ago when I had come to Lulu's. The one who had held my head in her lap when I lost it. She remembered me, too.

I looked at Kon, then I took away his gun. I immediately opened the magazine, but it was empty. I looked at him again, and I gave him a huge slap across the face. He flew sideways, hitting the door, then fell to the ground, weeping.

'Idiot,' I said.

I turned to Yuki.

'Did he rape you?'

She shook her head.

'Did he harm you in any way?'

She shook her head again, wiping away a tear or two.

'Ok, get dressed and you can leave,' I said, handing her over her clothes.

She quickly slipped them on and then began walking to the door, but she stopped halfway.

'Don't hurt him.'

I nodded, and she left.

I closed the door, found a chair, and sat down, holding the gun in my hand. Kon was still sitting on the floor, pressing his palm to his cheek and crying like a baby.

'I-I-I'm sorry, Sato-kun. I'm so sorry. I-I... I don't know... I'm... I'm really sorry,' he wept, tears flowing from his eyes and snot running from his nose.

'Clean yourself up,' I said, tossing him a pack of tissues. 'I hate it when men cry.'

Kon took it and looked at it as if it were the first pack of tissues he had ever laid eyes on. He examined it from every possible angle, then spent something like five minutes figuring out how to open it. He tried scratching it with his fingernails, tearing open the packaging, even biting it open with his teeth. I just stared at him, patting the gun against my palm and tapping the floor with my right foot. At least he had stopped his sniveling in the meantime.

'There's a small, red tape in the corner,' I said, pointing at it with my finger. 'Just pull it.'

He pulled the tape, and voilá: "Open Sesame".

He then took a single tissue from the pack and lifted it to his face, but he stopped and turned to me.

'There's nothing left to wipe.'

I buried my face in my hands.

'What happened, Kon?' I asked, raising my head again.

He turned away to look at the door.

'What was the gun for?'

'It's empty,' he replied.

'I know it's empty, but why do you have a gun in the first place? Hm?'

He shrugged.

'Kon, I'm serious. What the fuck is this thing doing here, and what the fuck were you thinking? Explain, please. Unless you want me to hurt you.'

Now he looked at me.

'Kon,' I said in a deeper, darker tone.

'I... I just want to protect her.'

'Protect?'

He nodded.

'By pointing a gun at her and taking her hostage?'

He shook his head, staring at the floor.

'Then how?' I asked.

He kept staring at the floor, his hands shaking a bit.

'How, Kon?'

'By killing the person who's responsible for all of this,' he said, looking me straight in the eye.

'Responsible for what?'

'This,' he repeated, drawing a semi-circle in the air with his right index finger. 'All of this.'

'Be more specific, Kon.'

'What else do you want me to say?! You know what's going on, no? Hell, you work for them, Sato-kun! Am I right? You work for these motherfuckers who-who-who make these poor girls do stuff! Stuff they shouldn't be doing! They're the real bastards here, not a fat salaryman with a bald head and an empty gun! They're the ones taking hostages! Fuck, slaves! Yes, these girls are slaves, Sato-kun! And you work for them! That makes you a... that makes you... you're a...'

'Come on, say it,' I said.

'You're...'

I kept hitting the gun against my palm.

'You're a swine! With... With a dick as small as my little pinky here,' he said, showing me his left pinky. 'I-I'll tear your heart out with my bare hands, grill it medium, no, medium-well-done, and eat it for breakfast with cucumbers! No, wait, for dinner with potatoes! Yeah! I'll eat your heart with baked potatoes and ketchup! Yeah!'

I stopped hitting my palm with the gun and looked at Kon with a stone-cold stare. He returned the stare, blinking with his small, fat eyes under his funny, round glasses. His forehead was sweating like crazy, but he didn't care. We stared at each other, motionless, for several seconds, and then I burst out laughing. I just couldn't hold myself back. I laughed as I had never laughed before. It was this genuine, liberating laughter that reached the heavens and back, but it didn't make me happy. I wasn't happy at all. No. I felt as if my soul were crying.

I stood up and went to the mirror. I saw my reflection, but it was faint and blurry, and almost transparent. Like a ghost. I saw the reflection of someone... hollow.

'Why do you want to protect her?' I asked, looking at him in the mirror. 'Why's she important to you?'

'She's my... love. I love her.'

'But she doesn't love you back, right?'

'That doesn't matter,' Kon replied. 'I don't care. Not anymore. I mean, it would be... It would be nice if she loved me. If we could... spend time together, and... and hold hands, and make love. But... But first, she needs to be free. She needs to leave this world of darkness.'

'When we first met, when you were drunk and you attacked me, you said you had lost your love. Did you mean her?'

Kon nodded. 'I... I know it's not ok, but... but I had been following her for months.'

'You mean, stalking her?'

Kon looked away.

'That evening, I finally summoned my courage, and I... I approached her. I confessed my love for her.'

'But she turned you down.'

'She told me to leave her the fuck alone, and she called me all kinds of names and stuff.'

'Well, I'm not surprised,' I said.

'But... I kept following her. Because... I love her. I'm...'

'You're obsessed.'

I went back to the chair and sat down.

'The magazine I bought you a couple of nights ago when we met – it was her, right? The girl with the big tits on the double-pager. It was Yuki-chan, right?'

Kon nodded again.

'What's the name of the magazine?' I asked.

'Tutti Frutti.'

It belonged to us. Captain Jack was running the business – one of boss Yamaguchi's direct subordinates. He was running everything related to the sex industry. And his son, Little Jack as we called him, was the "artistic and creative mind" behind all the porn mags. He chose the girls himself, he picked their lingerie, he took the photos, and he... raped them. All of them. Repeatedly.

We all knew it, of course, but everyone treated it as an unavoidable side effect – just part of the whole sex industry thing. Not that there weren't people in the family who didn't want to do something about it. I myself, for instance, dreamed of chopping off Little Jack's dick and stuffing it inside his disgusting mouth. But Captain Jack was too powerful, too important. You couldn't do anything to harm his one and only son and hope to escape unscathed. It would've taken a personal sacrifice to do something like that, and I guess no one was prepared to make such a sacrifice. The lives of these girls didn't matter as much as our own personal well-being.

'I-I like you, Sato-kun,' Kon told me, 'but if you belong to them, and if you knew what these girls were going through, if you knew what my poor little Yuki-chan was going through, and you didn't even try to do something about it, then you're just as filthy a piece of scum as they are. You're part of the problem.'

As I was listening to him, my heart rate went up. I felt my heart beating against my chest as if it wanted to jump out and run away, somewhere real far. I stuck my hand in my pocket and held the coin. I squeezed it hard and tried to calm my breathing. I felt this immense tension in every corner of my body, and it felt like all the veins in my brain were on the cusp of exploding. I pictured my head blowing up there in the room, with my blood covering all the walls and furniture in red, and chunks of my brain hanging from Kon's face and limbs.

'Can you help me, Sato-kun?' Kon asked, and when I heard these words, all the tension went away. 'Can you help Yuki-chan?'

I stood up and went back to the mirror. My reflection seemed to be a bit sharper and more colorful than it had been a couple of minutes earlier.

'It's not easy, what you're asking,' I replied. 'But first, tell me, what were you trying to accomplish through your little act here with Yuki-chan?'

'I... I just wanted some information from her. I wanted to make her talk and tell me everything about the bastards who are doing this to her. I-I need more clues to know who I'm looking for. I'm still more or less in the dark here.'

'They're my family, you know,' I said, looking at my own face in the mirror. 'The boss, he took me in off the streets, he gave me a job, a place to live, a purpose in life. And more than anything, he treated me like a human being, with respect.' I leaned closer to the mirror and looked myself in the eye. 'He's like a father to me.'

Kon stood up and came to stand next to me, looking at himself in the mirror: 'I don't know a thing about family, about respect, about right or wrong. I just know that Yuki-chan deserves a better life. Do you know of such people, Sato-kun?

'I do,' I said after a couple of seconds of hesitation, still holding my hundred-yen coin.

***

I went to the Palm Tree next, straight to Julia's room. She was expecting me. Her perfume filled the tiny space with dark and exquisite elegance. It aroused me every time.

'I brought you something,' I said, handing her a simple, black box with the logo of Okabe's luxurious store engraved on top in gold.

'Oh my, Sato-kun,' she said with a smile.

She opened the box carefully as if fearing she might damage what was inside. The smile stayed on her face throughout, and her eyes glowed with curiosity. I enjoyed watching her long, elegant fingers work at the box. She wore her fingernails bright red that evening.

'Oh, wow,' she said with an even bigger smile when she finally unwrapped my gift. 'Do you want me to wear it for you tonight?' she asked, looking at me. I instantly had an erection. 'I guess, you do.'

She stood up, kissed my left cheek, and whispered: 'I'll be back in a minute.'

I sat on her bed, crossed my arms, and after a moment, let myself flop on my back, and I lay there on the bed, looking at the ceiling.

The ceiling had cracks in it. Some were smaller, some bigger. Some were straight, some were not. I tried figuring out if any of the cracks or the patterns they made reminded me of anything. I was usually good at picturing all kinds of stuff in various stains and cracks I would see on the street, on walls, on ceilings. But I saw nothing here. None of the cracks reminded me of anything, nor did the patterns they made. Until... Until I looked at them as a whole.

"That's her," I said to myself. "Fuck."

I'm not sure if those cracks really formed her face on Julia's ceiling, but I clearly remember feeling her presence, feeling the piercing sharpness of her stare all over my skin. I felt overwhelmed by it.

I didn't even notice when Julia came back in, wearing the sheer nylons, the white, satin panties, and that white string connecting the panties to a white collar around her neck. She pulled my pants down, stroked my penis a couple of times, just to make sure it was hard enough, then she mounted me.

I closed my eyes. I saw the naked body parts of a young woman. Feet, thighs, hips, arms, shoulders, lips, neck. I saw them close up, almost as if I were able to put my lips on them and kiss them, lick them, bite them. I could almost feel their taste on my tongue, and I felt this immense craving and tension inside myself. Julia, meanwhile, kept riding on me more intensely by the second, and I kept squeezing her thighs harder and harder. The tension kept piling up in all my joints and muscles. I felt like I was a bow, and someone was drawing my string to the limit.

Then, instead of being released, my string broke. It just snapped.

Julia stopped, and after a couple of seconds, she lay down next to me. She caressed my chest for a while, gave me a few kisses, and rested her head on my shoulder.

'Who were you with just now?' she asked.

I didn't answer.

'Was it her?'

'Do you know where she is?' I asked.

'Why're you asking?'

'She escaped.'

'Oh, for Christ's sake,' she said, standing up, putting on her nightgown, and walking to the window. She opened it and lit a cigarette. 'Why do you men always think of women as your little pets or slaves? Fuck, Sato-kun. You, of all people, should know better.' Julia turned around to look at me. 'She probably just went for a walk, to do some shopping, or maybe to watch a movie. Who knows? And who cares? She should be free to do those kinds of things without the likes of you watching her every step.'

'I don't know where she is,' I replied. 'I have to find her.'

Julia sighed, then took a couple of drags.

'I know.' She finished up her cigarette and stubbed it in the ashtray. 'Try Yoshi's place.'

'Yoshi's?'

'Yeah, she goes there regularly.'

'But I've never seen her there.'

'You probably have, but you didn't know it. And she always wears a disguise. A wig.'

'A wig?'

'Yeah, a blue wig.'

Now that she mentioned it, I did remember a woman with a blue wig I would see here and there. She would always sit in the far-right corner of the bar, wearing dark sunglasses and slowly sipping a cocktail.

'I have to go,' I said, and I quickly got dressed.

'Don't hurry, Romeo,' Julia said. 'It's still too early. I'd go after midnight.'

I nodded and she nodded back.

'Be careful.'

'I will,' I said.

I looked at the ceiling one last time before leaving. There were no cracks in it.

Casablanca

Shinjuku is one of those places where you can just wander endlessly and get lost in your thoughts. Especially at night. It's full of people, stores, restaurants; you have neon signs all over the place; you hear all kinds of sounds and noises. But it also has some real dark, real quiet streets and allies, parks and skyscrapers, hidden corners, which cut through the fat body of the Shinjuku-craziness and allow you to glide through it unnoticed. I call it Shadow Shinjuku. It gives home to people and creatures you wouldn't typically see during the day, or even if you did, you'd just walk by without noticing or paying attention. And the residents of Shadow Shinjuku like it that way, or at least they pretend to.

I used to be a full-time resident myself, back in my homeless orphan days. It doesn't take long to become one, once you've spent some time on its streets. It is a remarkably welcoming and open place, and it is certainly easier to get in than to get out. You could say I was lucky to be able to escape it, although I'm sure there are many who would not trade places with me and would rather continue living in the namelessness of Shadow Shinjuku.

To be honest, even I had my moments of doubt. Often, just a matter of moments, but sometimes, it would drag out for hours or even days. I'd feel this longing for the anonymity and carefreeness of living in Shadow Shinjuku – being completely free of bonds to other people, of social structures with rules, of the wants and needs of this world. Yes, it is hard to get your hands on decent food, and it is difficult to protect yourself from rain and snow and heat and cold, but you learn to let it go, you adapt, and what remains at the end of the day is the realization that you can do whatever you want. You have all the time in the world, just for yourself.

I missed those days sometimes.

When that happened, I'd go for a walk in Shadow Shinjuku. I'd visit the places where I had spent my time either living in a cardboard box, looking for food or just strolling up and down aimlessly. I'd also visit my "viewing spots" – benches or stairs where I'd sit down to watch the people around me, or the buildings, or the cars going by. My favorite spot was the stairs of an office building in the vicinity of the Park Hyatt, where I'd spend hours and hours just sitting and watching life happen. And most of the time, I'd watch the windows of the coffee shop on the other side of the street: "Casablanca".

I'd carefully examine the people inside the coffee shop, and I'd see different emotions on their faces and interesting stories in their eyes. And that always made me wonder if my face would ever become home to such a variety of emotions and if I'd have my own stories to tell with my eyes.

Then, there was this family, which I loved observing. They'd start their day at the coffee shop with breakfast. The parents in their early forties and a girl around ten. They'd always sit in the window and have the same breakfast every morning. The father would eat an omelet and drink black coffee from a white mug. The mother would have a toast and a big glass of coffee with milk, while the daughter would have a croissant and tea. They'd arrive around seven o'clock and stay for forty-five minutes or so. The father would read the Yomiuri Shinbun, while his wife and his daughter would chit-chat and play around. The father rarely spoke or participated in the conversation, but when he did, the two girls seemed to absorb his words. Otherwise, he'd just read his newspaper and not even look at them, but I knew he paid attention to everything the other two were talking about, as I would often catch a smile or smirk on his face, and it was visibly a reaction to them rather than to the newspaper he was reading.

I tried (and enjoyed) creating and imagining their backstories and lives.

In the story I created for them, the father worked as a lawyer and was the manager at a small Tokyo-based law firm. He would never leave his job, as it provided a steady income for his family and allowed them to live in relative financial stability, but he hated it. He never spoke about it because he had been taught never to complain and always to put his family's interests in front of his own. But an observant eye could easily tell, as there was no passion in his eyes when it came to anything related to work. To cope, he developed a routine that helped him make the transition between home and work as smooth and painless as possible. The breakfast with his family was only one part of this routine – he'd spend exactly fifteen minutes in the shower early in the morning, the first five of which he used to masturbate. Then, he'd shave his face with Gillette blades; he'd carefully choose his clothes for the day and dress up in front of a large mirror, looking at the fat on his stomach throughout the process; he'd spend another couple of minutes winding up and adjusting his vintage Grand Seiko, which he had inherited from his father; and he'd polish his shoes until they glowed like new. But even after kissing his wife and daughter goodbyes and getting to his office using the subway, he'd first go to the bathroom and take a dump, and he'd continue to sit on the toilet for at least ten more minutes, counting the tiles on the wall. Then, he would finally start working.

The mother took their daughter to school after breakfast. She had a part-time job as an assistant at a travel agency in Asakusa, with work starting at eleven in the morning, so each day she had a bit of time between taking the girl to school and going to work. On Mondays and Fridays, she took private dance classes in this morning timeslot, while on the other three days, she just went for a walk somewhere – mostly to Ginza. She kept her dance classes a secret from her husband. Not that she had an affair with her teacher or anything, but she believed her husband wouldn't understand. They never really spoke about it, and she herself didn't know where this idea of her husband opposing it had come from, but whenever the thought of telling him came to her mind, she would feel uncomfortable. "There's no way he'll find out anyway," she would think. Of course, the husband knew. But he never brought it up. "For the sake of peace and harmony in the family," he would tell himself. In the afternoons, the wife would have lunch somewhere, then a coffee, and she would try to write. She had a passion for fantasy, so she would write short stories about knights who befriended dwarves, fought monsters, and fell in love with fairies and princesses. Unlike the dancing, this was not a secret between them, but they still didn't discuss it openly. The wife would instead read her stories to their daughter before bedtime, and then she'd go back to the living room, put her book or sheets of paper on the shelf, kiss her husband on the forehead, take a shower, and go to sleep. It was only after she had gone to bed that her husband turned off the television, took one of her stories, and read it. He never told her he did this, but she knew, and he knew that she knew, so her stories became their personal space, their way of communicating. She'd write her stories to share her thoughts with him, and her fears, her dreams, her feelings. She'd weave the threads of her soul into her fairytales. Reading them and deciphering them became her husband's favorite part of the day.

I had this detailed and vivid image of both the father and the mother, but the young girl remained a mystery to me. No matter how hard I tried, I just couldn't picture her life, her story. The only image I could see was her sitting at her desk in the classroom and staring out the window. The weather might change outside – from hot summers with clear skies to gloomy winter mornings –, but she'd still just sit there and watch. I had no access to her. Yet, for some reason, she was the one I felt most comfortable with. I enjoyed looking out that window with her.

***

One day, in my early twenties, when I went for one of these walks of mine in Shadow Shinjuku, I finally decided to go to "Casablanca". It was a random weekday afternoon, during the cherry blossom season, maybe around three o'clock. The weather was perfect, so people were outside looking at the flowers, and the coffee shop was almost empty. I performed my usual routine of transition before entering, and when I finally went in, I felt the old bartender's stare on my skin. He must had seen me standing in front of his door for several seconds, with closed eyes, and he was suspicious.

'What would you like to drink, young man?' he asked.

'Just a coffee.'

'What kind of coffee? We have short, long, single, double, with milk or without, from Africa or South America, roasted the Australian way or the Italian, hot or cold, just to name a few of the options.'

'Well... I don't know. What would you recommend?' I asked.

'Would you like to try something special?'

'O-Okay.'

'We have our very own specialty of the house, the "Humphrey Bogart". You won't find a better coffee in the neighborhood.'

'Okay, thank you. I'll take that.'

We both nodded, and I turned around to find a table for myself. I saw an elderly lady in the darkest corner of the coffee shop, drinking what looked like Turkish coffee and smoking an incredibly long and thin cigarette. She had a small black hat on her head, she was wearing a purple fur coat, and she had more make-up on her wrinkled face than a geisha. She wasn't Asian.

I kind of got scared for a moment, so I instinctively gravitated towards the light and the two tables in the two street-front windows. I saw a young girl sitting at one of the tables, but the other one was free, so I took a seat.

I looked around, and all I saw were black and white stills from the movie Casablanca on the walls. They had the entire movie out there. The old man was playing jazz from an old gramophone, and with the weird lady in the corner, the atmosphere in the coffee shop felt surreal. Like being on the set of a movie.

Soon, the old man came with my "Humphrey Bogart" and put it on the table: 'The best coffee in the neighborhood,' he said, winking.

'Thank you,' I said.

I stared at the coffee for some time. It felt... strange. The old man served it in a funny, green cup in the shape of a toad. He also put some weird yellow spice on top, which I later learned was turmeric. Frankly, it smelled odd. Like... old wool socks on an old man. I lifted the cup to my mouth, and the smell just hit me. It knocked me out completely, and my stomach went berserk even before I had tasted the coffee. But I saw from the corner of my eye that the girl was looking at me, and the old man was also staring, so I had to take a sip. It felt like a test or something.

I closed my eyes, stopped breathing, and took a sip.

It tasted like horseshit.

I had to summon all my internal strength to swallow that single sip of "Humphry Bogart" somehow. I almost puked. After putting the cup down and gently pushing it away, I looked at the girl. She was smiling. She knew all along.

I smiled back, and from there, a conversation began, and a couple of hours later we were having sex in her small apartment not far away. It came out of nowhere, and it not only surprised me, but it also made me feel proud. It was this very shallow, yet completely natural male-proudness, I guess – the feeling when you realize you are capable of seducing, conquering, and behaving like movies tell you a macho man should behave. I had never thought of myself as macho, but I really felt good about myself.

As we were lying on her bed, just looking at the ceiling and not speaking a word, she suddenly stood up and went to the window. She opened it, leaned out a bit, and stared at the street and the buildings across the way. I turned to my side and watched her for a while. She had an average body with average proportions, but her skin was smoother than anything I had ever touched before. It felt good just to think about touching it again.

A couple of minutes went by without any of us speaking a word, and then an image appeared in my mind. The image of the girl sitting in her classroom and staring out the window. The only image I could picture for the girl I had been observing at "Casablanca" more than a decade ago.

'I've seen you before,' I said.

She didn't reply.

'A long time ago. With your parents. You had breakfast at "Casablanca" every morning.'

She turned around and looked at me.

'I... Can I make a guess? It might sound weird, but wasn't your father a lawyer?' She nodded after a few seconds. 'And your mother worked at a travel agency, right?' She nodded again.

'How... How do you know?'

'It's just... something I saw,' I said.

'Saw? How?'

'I... don't really know. I just remember always trying to picture your lives as I was watching you from across the street, and...'

'Wait, you were watching us?'

'Yeah, but that's not the point.'

'Yes, it is! Why were you watching us?'

'I...'

'You?'

'I was homeless back then. I had escaped from the orphanage, and I lived in the neighborhood. And often, in the mornings, I'd sit and watch people in "Casablanca". Especially you. And your family. I... I tried picturing your lives, as I was saying. To... Maybe to create an image of a proper family in my mind, as I didn't have any images of my own. But... But I always felt that the image I had created for your family might actually have been the reality itself.'

She looked away and stared at a picture on the wall for a while. I realized it was the picture of her family, back from the days when she was a ten-year-old girl.

'And what did you picture for me?' she asked.

'Just a single image,' I replied. 'I saw you sitting in a classroom and staring out the window. Just like you did now. I couldn't come up with anything else.'

She looked away again.

'It feels like you're stuck somewhere. You're looking out the window, watching the seasons change, people come and go, but you're not moving anywhere.'

'My parents died,' she said. 'In an accident. When I was eleven.'

'I'm sorry,' I told her. 'I think I know how you might feel. Not exactly, of course, but I have a guess.' She looked at me again. 'I've been looking through the same window all my life.'

***

As I still had a lot of time before midnight and before going to Yoshi's bar hoping to find Ren there, I decided to go on a walk in Shadow Shinjuku and visit the place where "Casablanca" had once stood. It had closed some years ago. The old owner had died, and he had no relatives to inherit or continue the business. The real estate fell back to the municipality, and our family managed to buy it for a "very reasonable" price, as the boss liked to put it. We ran a secret VIP brothel there now, but we kept the name "Casablanca".

On my way to "Casablanca", I passed a row of ten, maybe twelve cardboard boxes for homeless people. They were all full. I saw mostly men in their forties and fifties, but there was also a teenager in one of the boxes and a woman in her thirties in another. Regardless of the so-called "freedom", they might have had, and all the time in the world, they just looked sad. I don't know. Maybe it's precisely this freedom that people find hardest to deal with. Most of them just don't seem to know what to do with it. They struggle to find motivation, to find purpose, and to focus on something that really matters to them. Most of them don't even know what matters anymore. I know, because I felt the same way. You just lose points of reference in life, and suddenly you're afloat in a vast ocean, with no land on the horizon.

I saw a convenience store on the corner, and I went inside to buy something for the homeless. I put fifteen onigiri rice balls in my basket and fifteen bottles of ice tea. The cashier had a strange look on her face, as if suspecting something out of the ordinary, something which might disrupt the world as she knew it, and I think she even thought of asking me something, but she quickly dismissed the idea and went about her business as usual. I paid around seven thousand yen, I think.

I returned to the place with the cardboard boxes, and I was just about to give the food and the drinks to the homeless people when I noticed another twenty or so boxes a bit further away. For whatever reason, I had been so absorbed in my thoughts when I first saw them that I had failed to notice these other ones. And now I panicked. What do I do? Do I give the food to the people I saw the first time around? Do I put it somewhere in the middle so everyone who wants a bit can take a bit? Or is it fairest not to give it away at all if there's a chance that someone might not get anything?

I froze and just stood there like an idiot for several seconds. An ignorant moron, really, who had thought he could change something in this world.

I remember looking at the sky and thinking something like: "Now what? If you hear me, if you even exist at all, then please help me out. Just this once, please. Do something. Please."

The next moment a small group of four youngsters, probably university students, appeared on the other side of the road, and they crossed to where I was standing. They were all carrying plastic bags with a supermarket's logo on them. As they reached me, all the ice that had kept me frozen just melted away. We looked each other in the eye, we all smiled, nodded to each other, and we began distributing the food to the people around us.

There was enough for everyone.

I saved the woman in her thirties for last. When I got to her, I had this warm feeling inside – a feeling of satisfaction. I approached her with a big smile on my face, and I gave her two rice balls and a bottle of ice tea. 'Please, take it,' I said.

She looked up from her box and straight into my eyes. 'Thank you,' she told me as she reached for the food. It was then that I realized I knew her. The girl from "Casablanca".

The smile instantly disappeared from my face and I took a step back. She kept staring at me, her hands stretched out and holding the food, and I saw a window in her eyes. The same window I had pictured her looking out of, the same "obstacle" she had been dealing with since her childhood.

'Thank you,' she said again, and she went back to the safety of her box, unpacking the rice ball and munching at it with much delight.

She hadn't recognized me.

After a couple of moments, I turned to the youngsters, nodded in their direction, and continued to "Casablanca". It was just a couple of blocks away, but it took me several minutes to get there, as the image of the "Casablanca" girl just kept swirling around in my mind, and it made each step I took feel like walking in waist-high water with heavy weights around my ankles.

When I finally got there, I went to the other side of the street, to my favorite stairs. I sat down as slowly as an old man would. Then, I leaned forward a bit and put my forearms on my knees. I stared at the windows of "Casablanca" for a while.

It wasn't the same as before. The windows were painted black with the logo of the bar in the middle – a golden butterfly. I couldn't watch the people inside anymore, and I couldn't imagine their lives. I just watched the occasional VIP guest arrive in a limousine and quickly enter the bar, or I saw a girl sneak out from time to time to smoke a cigarette.

I was just about to leave when another girl came out to get some fresh air. She was wearing lingerie and high heels, and she had a long coat on to keep her warm. She just stood there, looking up, as if searching for the moon and the stars.

"That's Kiki," I told myself. "Fuck."

I stood up and ran over to her.

'Kiki! What the fuck?! What are you doing here?!'

I caught her completely by surprise. She looked at me as if she were seeing a ghost, and she went pale.

'Kiki!'

'U-Uncle Sato? Why are you here?'

I grabbed her by the arm and pulled her closer: 'Kiki, what are you doing in "Casablanca"?'

It was probably the combination of the situation, her surprise, my tone, and the force with which I was holding her that made her break down and start to cry. I could feel her slim and fragile body lose all its power as she crumbled into my arms.

'Uncle Sato,' she whispered in a trembling voice, with tears flowing from her eyes like two rivers. She put her arms around my neck and buried her face in my chest.

It took me a while, but eventually, I wrapped my arms around her. I kissed the top of her head, and we stood like that for several minutes.

A security guy came out to check up on her, and he was about to say something and drag her away, but when he saw me, he immediately backed up. I looked him straight in the eye, and he went back inside.

'Kiki,' I said with as much tenderness as I was capable of when she finally stopped crying. 'What's going on? Tell me.'

'Uncle Sato... I... I don't know...'

She was still trembling.

'Ok. First, we go inside, you change back into your normal clothes, and we leave. Come on,' I said, and I took her by the arm and opened the door, and we went inside.

'But... I can't leave, uncle! I can't,' she told me, trying to resist.

'We're not having a debate, Kiki. You do as I say. We leave. Get your clothes, change, and we're out of here.'

'But... But... I... work here,' she said.

We looked at each other, and there was this window in her eyes, the same window I had seen in the "Casablanca" girl's eyes, and Kiki was looking out of it, into the distance, past the horizon.

'Go! Change! And we leave!' I said. 'Now!'

By the time I had finished my sentence the security guards had come, along with the manager.

'What's going on here?' the manager asked. 'What's this about, Sato-san?'

'What's this about?' I asked with anger. 'What's this about, you moron? What do you think this is about?'

'Hey! Watch your language! This is *my* place here!' he said, pointing his finger at me. His muscle-guys all tightened up.

'Do you even know what you're doing here, you fucking idiot? Do you know how old this girl is? Hm? Do you? Do you?!'

The manager didn't know what to say. He wasn't expecting this.

'She's seventeen you pig!'

He froze.

'She's a fucking high-schooler, you retarded fool! Shall I tell the boss? Hm?! Shall I tell him you're running minors and risking it big with the police?!'

Some of the security guards were clenching their fists, and the others had reached for their knives.

'Back off,' the manager told them.

'I'm taking her with me,' I said. 'Get dressed,' I told Kiki, and she immediately started changing clothes.

'You're making a big mistake, Sato-san,' the manager said. 'She's... special, you know.'

I looked him in the eye.

'She's... how shall I put this... one of Little Jack's favorites.'

As he spluttered out Little Jack's name, I took a huge swing and punched him hard in the face. He fell to the ground, his nose bleeding, probably broken. The guards wanted to jump me, but he stopped them: 'Don't! It's ok. Let him go. He'll get what he deserves.'

We looked at each other one more time. I grabbed Kiki by her arm again and said, 'Come on, we're leaving.'

I literally dragged her to Yoshi's bar. We didn't speak a word until we got there.

We were about to enter the bar when she suddenly freed herself from my grip and stopped.

'Let's go inside,' I said.

'I'm not going.'

'Yes, you are. Come on.'

'No.'

I frowned.

'Come on,' I beckoned with my hand. 'Let's go.'

'No.'

'Don't fuck with me, Kiki. I'm not one of your clients whom you can blow off with a fuck.'

'Fuck you,' she said, giving me the finger.

I tried to grab her again, but she evaded me.

'You're a fucking hypocrite!'

'Don't talk to me like that! And watch your language! You're not allowed to curse! And you're not allowed to work in a shithole like that, throwing away your dignity!'

'Who're you to tell me?! Huh?! You see me like what, once a month?! You give me money, ask a couple of questions, pretend you care, but I don't even know who you are! I've no clue who you are! Are you maybe suggesting you're a decent, law-abiding, responsible citizen or something?! Because I saw it! I heard it! Those guys know you! They know who you are! And they're afraid of you!'

I lowered my arm and stepped back, looking her in the eye.

'Who are you, uncle?'

'That's none of your concern.'

'Fuck that! It *is* my concern! You're my uncle, right?! And you're the only family I've got apart from my mother! And she'll be dead in a couple of weeks! Or maybe days! Or maybe she's already dead! And then...' Her eyes welled up. 'And then...And then you'll be my only family.'

She crumbled to her knees and started to cry.

I just stood there, not knowing what to say, not finding a single appropriate word. I felt... empty and... ashamed.

I knelt and put my hand on her face: 'Let's go inside, ok? It's cold out here. I'll tell you about myself, ok? I'll... talk, ok?'

She looked up, her eyes red and swollen.

'Let's go inside.' I repeated.

Kiki nodded, then stood up, and we entered the bar.

Yoshi was surprised when he saw me with a teenage girl, but he immediately knew she was important to me and that we had some serious talking to do, so he cleared the left corner of his counter, which he usually reserved for VIPs.

'What does the young lady drink?' he asked us both, looking first at Kiki, then at me.

She just shrugged.

'Give her the virgin version of your chocolate cocktail,' I said. 'And I'll have the full version, please.'

'Yes-yes!'

'Thanks.'

We sat in silence until our drinks arrived.

I looked around.

There were only two other guests in the bar: two businessmen, both in suits, drinking whisky. The bar was dimly lit, with only three faint spotlights throwing murky, yellowish light. Ian Siegal was on – a contemporary British blues musician. He sounded like he was the child of Howlin' Wolf and Tom Waits. He must had absorbed their music while still in his mother's womb. His raspy, yet melodic voice, along with the transcendent sound of his steel guitar electrified the air and elevated the atmosphere to a different level, into a different space compared to the outside world. It felt as if we were in the cabin of a flying ship high above the ground.

Yoshi had pictures of his favorite musicians on the wall. Mostly black and white, but some in color. Ian Siegal was there, of course, probably singing a Tom Waits song with half a bottle of whisky already inside him, and Tom Waits was right next to him, sitting on a chair with a loudspeaker in his hand. Jimi Hendrix had the prime spot in Yoshi's bar, standing on the Woodstock stage with a guitar, looking down on us guests from above Yoshi's head. I also saw some oldies whom I didn't recognize, probably from the forties and the fifties, and of course good old Neil Young "rocking in the free world".

'Your drinks,' Yoshi said, putting two glasses in front of us.

'Thanks,' I replied, and I looked at Kiki. 'Thank you,' she said.

'So?' Kiki asked after we had each taken a sip. I sensed that her anger had gone, and there she was with only her innocence left, and a pleading kind of curiosity.

'So, you'd like to know who I am, right?'

I heard the door to the bar open and close, but I didn't pay attention. Kiki just nodded.

'All right,' I said, and I took a long sip of the chocolate cocktail. 'First of all... I'm... not... your uncle.'

I looked her in the eye, but then immediately looked away and took another sip. My heart was racing.

'I know,' she said.

I don't know what kind of answer or reaction I was expecting, but this one took me by surprise. I almost lost my grip on the glass and spilled the cocktail in my lap.

'You knew?' I asked, looking at her.

'Of course,' she said. 'It's obvious.'

'How long have you known?' I asked.

'A while.'

'A while?'

'Couple of years.'

'Fuck,' I murmured, and I took another big gulp.

'But it doesn't matter!' Kiki rushed to calm me. 'I still think of you as my uncle, as my family.'

I looked at her: 'Why?'

'Because you're the only person who wants to help me.'

I felt deep pain when she said that. An innocent, young girl just shouldn't have to say words like that. It felt wrong and unfair.

'I knew your father,' I told her, making circles in the cocktail with the straw. 'I... didn't know him well, but... still... I felt I needed to take care of you and your mother after he had died. I owed him that much. I can't tell you why, but I felt and I still feel that you are my responsibility. I want to protect you. And I will continue protecting you.'

'I know,' Kiki said, putting her hand on top of mine.

'And... you were right. Those guys *did* know me. I work for the same organization. We are part of the same family. And that's precisely why I don't want you to be around them, to work for them, and I definitely don't want you to prostitute yourself. You're worth much more than that. Much more than any of us.'

Now Kiki looked away.

'I'll give you more money if you need it,' I said.

Her tears started to flow.

'It's not just the money. It's... I feel... I'm lost. And I'm looking for something. Or someone. I don't really know.'

'But what could you possibly find in a place like that?'

'I don't know,' she said, crying. 'Maybe the feeling of... belonging somewhere. Being... wanted. Desired. Treated nicely.'

I didn't know what to say.

'These men,' she continued, 'they too are looking for something, you know. Most of the time it's not about the sex. Most of the time, we just talk.'

'You can talk with me, Kiki.'

'No, I can't,' she replied, wiping away tears. 'I've tried. So many times. But I can't. *You* can't.'

I turned away. A wound opened on the surface of my heart, and it was growing, but Kiki kept her hand on top of mine, and it felt like she was trying to heal my wound. A tear ran down my cheek.

'Why are you with them, uncle Sato?'

'Because... I don't know any other way. And... they are my family.'

'But we can choose our family! Like you chose me, and I chose you! Let's run away, together! Let's live somewhere in peace, like a true family! Don't let these old bonds keep you chained!'

'And your mother?' I asked.

Now Kiki looked away.

'You can't just ignore these "old bonds", as you called them. It's not that simple,' I said. 'But I will protect you, no matter what. Ok? I'll be there for you. More than I have in the past. I promise. Ok? I promise, Kiki. Just leave this world and go back to school. Can you do that? Can you do that for me? And for your mother? Can you promise me that, Kiki?'

She didn't know what to say. She was confused. Her eyes welled up again, and I was about to wipe her tears away with my thumb, when I heard a roar, as several people tore the door wide open and broke into Yoshi's bar. Kiki went completely pale when she saw them. I was about to turn around, but I got hit in the back of my head with something hard, and I fell to the floor. I heard Kiki scream, and I saw two men grab her, but when I tried to get up and help her, someone landed another blow, and everything went black. Only the echo of Kiki's scream remained for a few more seconds, and then it, too, disappeared.

Talking to the moon

When I slowly opened my eyes again, the world around me looked blurred. And no, it wasn't some vision. The lines and the shapes of my surroundings had changed. Everything had gotten scrambled up somehow. People, objects, shapes, and colors had lost their boundaries, their firmness, their sharpness, to form an infinite flow. It felt like being in a Van Gogh painting, but I wasn't dizzy at all. No, I was part of this flow. And it's hard to tell if it felt good or bad. Probably neither. It was different. Like being in a different universe. And what appeared to surround this universe was an endless sea of sorts. A sea full of electricity, full of buzz, of sparks, of glow, of visions and images, of... thoughts.

There was a single constant, a single firm point of reference for me to cling to – a strange, floating blue object with two flashy, emerald-green lights. It hovered above me, in front of me, and as mysterious and strange as it was, it gave me peace of mind. I could've panicked and gone crazy with all this fluidity around me, but the blue shape with the green lights reassured me that I was in the right place.

'Sato,' I heard a distant voice calling my name. 'Sato, wake up, come back.'

The moment I heard the voice, the sea disappeared, and the world began to lose its fluidity, regaining its firmness and limitations. Along with it, the floating blue object slowly acquired shape and form – that of a woman's head. A head with... a wig. A blue wig. And green eyes as deep as the universe.

'Ren,' I whispered.

'Yes, it's me,' she said, holding my hand.

'Where am I? What happened?'

'You're still at Yoshi's place. He's here. I'm here.'

'Yoshi's... Kiki! Where's Kiki?!' I asked, pulling myself up and trying to stand.

'Slow down, Sato-san,' Yoshi said, holding me back, with his hand on my shoulder. 'You got hit in the head and you lost some blood. Take it easy, ok?'

Ren squeezed my hand a bit before letting it go, then she grabbed me by the arm. 'Come, I'll help you up,' she said.

Yoshi took my other arm and they helped me stand, then sit on a barstool.

'Thanks,' I said, pressing my hand against the back of my head.

'Does it hurt?' Ren asked.

'A bit.'

'Here,' Yoshi poured some more chocolate cocktail in my glass. 'I know this'll help you. I added an extra ingredient this time. You won't feel any difference in taste, but it'll help with your pain.'

'What did you put in it?' I asked, looking into the glass and trying to smell it.

'Oh, you know I never reveal my professional secrets,' Yoshi smiled.

I looked at him, and he nodded. Then I took a sip. And another one. And then two more.

'It tastes the same,' I said.

'I told you. The pain will be gone soon,' he said. 'My dear,' Yoshi turned to Ren, 'please take him home before the effect kicks in.'

She nodded, then smiled, and Yoshi smiled back.

'What?' I asked, looking at them both.

'Nothing,' Ren replied. 'Let's go, you.' She grabbed me by the arm again, and we slowly walked to the door. 'It looks like you're the one who needs bodyguarding.'

I looked at her, but I didn't say anything.

'Take care of him, Ren-chan,' Yoshi said.

'Don't worry old man, I will.'

'Thanks for everything,' I told Yoshi, and I waved goodbye. 'See you.'

***

I remember getting into a taxi with Ren, but what happened next is a blank. The next thing I know I'm waking up in her bed, and she's sitting next to me in a chair. She was asleep.

I sat up and looked at my watch. Eight o'clock. It was the day after. I looked out the window. It was dark outside. I had slept through the whole day.

The sky was clear, and a huge yellow moon was gazing down on Ren's garden. Its reflection was shimmering on the surface of the pond, and it seemed like it wanted to tell me something. The vibration of its voice caused turbulence in the water, and a mouth formed in the middle of the pond, in the middle of the moon's reflection. I was pretty good at lipreading, so I figured I'd give it a go.

"She tried. She went inside. I saw it."

"What the…" I said to myself.

"She broke in. I saw it," continued the moon.

"What the hell…?"

The next moment, Ren woke up.

'What are you seeing outside?' she asked.

'Nothing,' I said. 'Just the moon. In the pond.'

She turned around to look.

'It…'

'What?'

'Nothing.' I said.

Ren had a picture on the wall. A drawing by a child. A boy and a girl holding hands on top of a cloud and looking down on a body of water. The girl had green eyes, the boy purple.

'I drew that when I was little. I was five, maybe six years old,' she said.

'Cute.'

'I used to have a recurring dream back then, about a boy and a girl. I'd see them do things together. All kinds of things, like...'

'Like what?'

'Like fly among the stars, jump from one cloud to another, or swim in a vast ocean. And hold each other's hands. Always.'

'I see.'

'I drew this for my father, but he... didn't like it. When I gave it to him, I saw this immense anger in his eyes, and I got really scared. He just tore the drawing in two and yelled at me to go back to my room. I spent the next hour or so sitting crying on my bed, and then Kobayashi-san came to see me. He sat next to me, and he tried to calm me down. Then, he put the drawing in my lap. He had pieced it together, framed it, and he wanted me to have it, to hang it somewhere. He said: "Forgive your father. He's... not angry at you. He likes your drawing very much. It's just that... your drawing reminded him of something from the past, something of great pain to him. All his life he's been trying to erase the pain and to make it disappear forever. But you... You should keep the drawing. You should keep it as a reminder of your dreams."'

'I guess, you're the girl, right? With the green eyes,' I said. 'But, who's the boy?'

She looked at me, then at the drawing, then at me again: 'I don't know.'

I looked out the window again. The moon's reflection had already disappeared from the surface of the pond. We were surrounded by thick, black silence.

'Ren, did you go inside me? Were you...?'

She looked away.

'Ren?'

She just nodded.

'And did you...?'

She shook her head.

'So, you didn't...'

'No,' she said.

'How come?'

She looked at me, then out the window, searching the sky, as if looking for the moon.

'I couldn't,' she replied.

'You couldn't?'.

She shook her head again.

'I thought... I thought you had access to anyone's brain, anyone's thoughts.'

'I don't. I... You're the second person I couldn't enter.'

'Who's the other?' I asked.

'It was... my father.'

'The boss? I see...'

We were both searching the sky now.

'What would you have removed if you could?' I asked. 'I mean, now. From... me.'

She shrugged.

'Come on. I won't kill you or anything. I'm your bodyguard, remember?' I smiled.

'Yeah, but I'm the one protecting you,' she replied with a smile, too.

'Well... apparently.'

I liked her smile. It made her look innocent and down to earth. It was one of those smiles which allowed you to get away with almost anything. You just put it on and let it do its magic. She used it a lot. I guess it was easier than removing thoughts from people's minds.

'So?' I asked again. 'What would you have removed?'

'I don't know. Maybe... you knowing of my escape, of the secret door in my garden, of my appearances at Yoshi's in my blue wig. Maybe our meeting at the bar and me helping you.'

'That would've been a shame,' I said.

'Why?'

'Because... it felt good to see your face when I woke up. It felt... comforting.'

She kept staring out the window, but I saw her blush.

'Then I'm glad that I didn't remove anything,' she said.

'Is it tough?' I asked. 'I mean, on you. On your body. And your mind.'

She nodded. 'It hurts. And it drains me. I... I've been doing it for a long time now. Since I was a child, really. And every time I do it, it feels like a part of me disappears somewhere, never to come back again. This well opens in my heart, and a part of me just jumps into the well. I don't even hear it reach the bottom. It just... vanishes. And then I feel emptiness. And sadness. And I have to pull myself up, pull myself together to continue somehow. And it's getting harder every time.'

'I see.'

'And you?' she asked.

'What about me?'

'What would you make me remove from your mind if I could? Is there anything?'

'You mean is there anything I'd prefer not to remember? To forget?'

'Aha.'

'Hm... A good question.'

'It is, right?'

'I don't really know...'

'That's what everyone always says. And everyone knows perfectly well what they'd like to forget.'

'So, you do this? You remove people's memories at their request, and not just for the benefit of your father's shady dealings?'

'From time to time,' she shrugged. 'To earn some pocket money.'

'Pocket money?'

'Well, you know, a girl has her needs, and a girl typically requires money to satisfy these needs.'

'Yeah, I can imagine.'

'Anyway, that's not the point,' she said. 'I was asking what you'd make me erase. And don't bullshit me saying you don't know. I'm not buying that.'

'Honestly?'

'Of course! What other way would there be?'

'Well, look, why don't we make a deal then, you and me? I tell you one thing and you tell me one. Otherwise, I'd feel like I was in a therapy session or something with a psychiatrist, and I wouldn't like that. I don't want you to be my shrink.'

'Oh, then what *do* you want me to be?'

'Oh, no, we're not going there,' I said. 'You're quite manipulative, aren't you? You don't even need your psychic powers. You're worse than your father.'

'What?' she protested, opening her arms and raising them in the air.

'Let's stick to your original question, ok? And to our deal.'

'What deal? I didn't know we had a deal.'

'Don't we?' I asked.

She looked out the window again. 'Ok,' she finally said. 'Let's do it your way, you manipulator.'

'Me?'

'Yeah, you.'

I just smiled and shook my head.

'Ok, so, tell me. You go first,' she said.

'Ok, let me see.'

I really gave it proper thought, and indeed the problem wasn't that I didn't know, but rather that there were so many things that I couldn't choose.

'Do you remember the girl from the bar?' I asked.

'Of course.'

'Her name is Kiki. And... I killed her father.'

Ren's eyes opened wide.

'What?' I asked.

'You... You disgust me,' she said softly.

'Oh, so, now you're judging. First, you ask me to open up, and when I finally do, you make me feel like a piece of shit.'

'Well, maybe because you are.'

'Fuck you,' I said, turning away.

'Ok, you're right, I shouldn't be judging. Ok, ok. Tell me, then. Why did you kill him?'

'Well, guess. The same reason you're removing thoughts from people's minds. Your father. My boss.'

'He ordered it?'

I nodded. 'It was my first kill. I didn't know he had a child. When I realized, I... almost lost it.'

'So, you're saying it's ok to kill a person without a child, but not if he or she is a parent?'

'No, I, I mean... He was a scumbag, ok? But...'

'But the scumbag had a child. Yeah, I know, you just told me. So, if my father didn't have me, it'd be ok to kill him, because he is a scumbag, but since I'm here, it wouldn't be appropriate. Is that your logic?'

'It's... not! Ok?! There's... no logic here! I'm just saying that it made me feel bad, ok? The kill itself made me feel bad, too, but realizing that an innocent child was impacted as well made me feel even worse.'

'Well, just for your information, my dear bodyguard, there's *always* an innocent person impacted and involved. When you hurt someone, that someone either has a lover, a child, a parent, or a sibling, or just friends who care, and they suffer. They *all* suffer, you know?'

'And what about *my* suffering, hm?! I had been suffering my whole life before I met your father. I had lived on the streets, people had been treating me like shit, there had been no living person on this fucking planet to care about me, to care for me. And your father, as bad and vile as he may be, he gave me an existence, he gave me purpose, he gave me a life! So, the least I can do is repay him!'

'So, now you're saying it's ok to kill people if it's for your own benefit?'

'That's *not* what I'm saying!'

'Oh, but yes, you are, my dear. For the benefit of the life my father is providing, you're going around and killing people.'

'Oh, yeah?! And what about you, hm?! For the benefit of the life *your* father is providing, *you're* going around and fucking people's minds up!'

'I'm not doing this of my own free will! I'm a prisoner here!'

'Oh, are you now? So, what, you can escape from this place whenever you want, you can even make people forget about you escaping, you can make them forget about you completely, but you still keep coming back to this house. Why is that, my dear Ren? Hm? Explain that to me.'

'Well... It's not...'

'It's comfortable, this life of yours, isn't it?' I asked. 'You have a house with a beautiful garden, you have your daddy's money, you have protection, and even though you say you're a prisoner, you can actually come and go as you wish, you even make your fucking pocket money with your fucking magic, and you sip cocktails in Yoshi's bar wearing a blue wig and sunglasses. How is *that* not comfortable?'

I saw tears in her eyes, but I kept pressing her: 'You have all the power in the world to escape from here for good, to create a new life for yourself, to do something meaningful with your life, but you're not going anywhere. You're still your daddy's puppet. You're weak.'

'So are you, you idiot!' She stood up and burst into tears. 'The same goes for you! You're a fucking loser with no fucking life of his own who just goes around doing whatever he's being told to do! You're the same!' she yelled, and then she stormed out of the room.

'Yes, we *are* fucking same!' I yelled back.

***

I stayed in the bed for a while, just looking out the window. I was agitated. It felt like things were slowly slipping away from me. Kon had asked me to deal with Little Jack for him, they had taken Kiki away, and Ren was being a bigger pain in the ass than anything. And then there was this weird sensation that I had inside. This feeling of... confusion. Confusion over people who surrounded me, over my actions, over how I was living my life. I had always striven for some kind of balance, a state of harmony. And I'd typically achieve that through simplicity, through routine, and by minding my own business, with as little interaction with other people as possible. Just focusing on myself, on the tasks I needed to do, on training, on finding peace of mind in the little things that I did. But over the course of the last couple of weeks, my seemingly balanced life had somehow gone off track. It had gotten derailed. And it felt like I wasn't in control anymore.

I stood up and walked to the window. The moon was not visible in the pond anymore, but it was still up there, shining bright. I felt as if it were trying to talk to me again, so I focused and tried to listen. At first, I didn't know what it was saying, as its voice barely made it through the noises of our surroundings – the rattling of the branches in the wind, the siren of an ambulance on the street, the dripping of water somewhere in the distance. But I listened carefully, and soon it became louder, it became obvious: the moon was laughing. It was laughing hard. It was laughing at me.

"Fuck," I said to myself. "For fuck's fuck."

I clenched my fist and hit the window in front of me, shattering the glass. Blood ran down my hand in streams. I leaned into the hole in the window and yelled as loud as I could:

'Fuuuuuuuuuuuck!'

Purple eyes

I needed some sort of release, and I needed to talk, so I asked Kobayashi-san if he would do a training session with me. He told me to go to the dojo early next morning.

I got there around six-thirty, and the old man was already in his training gear, warming up. We nodded to each other, then I got changed and joined him for the warm-up. We did some basic techniques, and as the minutes went by, I started to feel that point of freedom where I began swinging the wooden sword with almost full force. It felt good just to whack the air and feel the pressure travel through my arms, run across the blade, and leave through the tip of the sword. I felt in control, I felt strong, and I felt like I was doing what I was supposed to be doing. I was ready to go on practicing at a hundred percent, maybe even cutting up some bamboo rolls with a proper sword, when suddenly Kobayashi-san told me to stop.

'Bring your "hōjō bokken",' he said.

"Oh, great," I said to myself. "Doing some heavy lifting and hard hitting with the big one. That's the way, old man."

I picked up this big, heavy wooden sword, which resembled the hilt of a huge ax, and I took a couple of practice swings.

'And now, we do the "Hōjō no kata",' Kobayashi-san said.

'The what?'

'Get ready.'

I wasn't expecting that. "Hōjō" is a very old and very traditional form, a "kata" with slow and measured moves. Very formal and very meditative. Like Zen, but with an enormous piece of wood. It has four parts, representing the four seasons. We always started with "Spring".

'Ok,' I murmured.

We got in position, and the old man signaled that he would be playing the master's role, or in other words, leading the dance. I nodded, and we began.

Doing the "Hōjō" felt strange at first. I hadn't practiced it for several months, maybe even a year, and I needed a little time to get used to the rhythm. But the old man was good at leading the way and getting me settled. He had this aura of calmness and reassurance around him, and I always felt in the right place when I was with him. By the time we finished "Summer", I had complete control over my breathing, my balance, and my movement. We went on to do "Fall" and then "Winter", and when we got to the end of the cycle, I let out a big sigh. The air leaving my lungs felt heavy, but it kept climbing higher and higher, finally leaving the dojo through the small cracks and spaces in the roof.

'Thank you,' I said as politely as I could, and I was about to approach the old man and have a word with him when he stopped me.

'Again,' he said.

I looked him in the eye, and I saw determination. Determination to go all the way, to guide me out of wherever I had gotten stuck.

'One more time,' he repeated.

I nodded, and we got back into our positions to do "Spring" again.

We performed another cycle of seasons, and then another one, and another after that. We went on to do exactly a hundred cycles, stopping only here and there to drink a little water and eat some bananas which he had brought. We finished around six in the evening.

When I finally put down my big, wooden sword, I felt empty. But it was the good kind of emptiness. The one which takes over right after you've cleansed your body, mind, and soul of the unnecessary stuff, and right before you fill it up again with fresh air, new feelings, and different kinds of stories and images. Like a clean slate. "Hōjō" does this to you.

'Let's have tea,' Kobayashi-san said.

I nodded, and we went to the tea-room in the back of the dojo, still wearing our practice gear.

It was a small and simple room, with just a scroll hanging from one wall, depicting two elegant cranes with their wings spread out, flying without a care in the world.

'We'll have matcha,' the old man said. I nodded again.

We sat down on the tatami, and he prepared our tea with great care while I was watching him in silence. He was always so focused on anything and everything he was doing. It was a pleasure to watch. Every little move he made felt simple and natural. It was everything the old man was about. I loved him. He was like a grandfather to me. It was moments like these when I realized.

'Here,' he said, sliding a small bowl of matcha in front of me.

'Thank you,' I replied.

'I don't have anything sweet,' he said, knowing that I liked eating "mochi" or a piece of chocolate with my tea.

'It's ok.'

We took our little bowls in our hands and spent a couple of seconds in silence, just looking at the bowls, at the tea, and then we drank it up.

'Thank you,' I said after we had both placed our bowls in front of us on the tatami.

'You're welcome.'

'I mean, not only the tea but...'

'I know,' he said. 'I'm glad you came.'

'Me too.'

'You have a lot on your mind,' Kobayashi-san said, looking at me.

'I do,' I replied.

'Do you want to talk about it?'

'I don't know. Maybe.'

'I'm listening.'

'I... I don't know. I'm... confused. So many... strange things are happening around me. I... You know me. I'm a loner, and that's the way I like it. Or at least I used to. Just tending to my own business, not really bothered by others, not depending on others. But now... there are people around me. Weird people. Annoying people. People I... care about. Things are happening to them. And to me. And this makes me feel a whole range of different emotions. It's... confusing.'

'It's normal, Sato-kun. To have people you care about, and to react with feelings to whatever is happening to them or between them and you.'

'Yeah, I know, but still. I mean, I care about you, too, and the boss, in a certain way, and Julia, but this... This is different. And... it's like they are questioning me, or making me question myself, and...'

'And you feel it's slowly changing you.'

'Well... I don't know. Maybe.'

'I'm happy for you, Sato-kun. I really am,' Kobayashi-san told me.

What he said surprised me. I must have had a strange look on my face. I didn't really know what to say.

'You know,' I continued, 'there's also this whole thing with Ren.'

'Her powers?'

'Yeah, and the boss, being her father and all. I mean, why didn't I know? And why is he treating her like that? And those powers... I mean, it just doesn't make sense.'

'It doesn't, right? To be honest with you, Sato-kun, I often catch myself struggling to believe the whole thing, even though I've been around, well, forever. I tried to understand her powers, understand their whole family, but it's difficult. It just frustrates me, that's what it does, so I figured I'd better just accept it as it is and try... I don't know... to go with the flow? Is that what you youngsters say?'

'No one says that old man,' I smiled.

'Whatever,' he waved. 'You get my point.'

I nodded.

'But, you know, I've been thinking, and... the boss... he's... bad, right?'

'What do you mean?' Kobayashi-san asked.

'I mean, the things he does or makes others do, they are... bad. *We* are bad. Like in the movies.'

'Well, Sato-kun, it's not that simple. It's never black and white. Some of the things he does, *we* do, you might call them bad from a certain perspective. But if you change the perspective, suddenly they might not look so bad at all. And what does "bad" even mean? What does it mean to you?'

'I don't know. Haven't really thought about that. It's just... an inner feeling that something is just... bad. You know? You see it happen, or you do it yourself, and then this... *knot* appears somewhere inside you, somewhere around the heart, just a fraction beneath it, and it sends weird kinds of signals to the brain.'

'Hm.'

'I mean, we do things that generate hundreds and hundreds of these little knots. Like... I don't know... dealing with drugs, running prostitutes, beating the shit out of people, killing them, or... removing stuff from their minds.'

'Hm.'

'Is that all you've got? Just "hm" and "hm"?' I asked with a little frustration in my voice.

'Do you think there would be no drugs on the streets if we were not selling them? Do you think no one else would seize the opportunity and step in if we just decided to pull out tomorrow?'

'Well...'

'And the prostitutes? Do you think they would disappear from society, along with the brothels, if we just stopped? And do you think those girls would get better, more respected, more lucrative jobs?'

'I...'

'Let me help you out: nothing would change. Maybe the names of the bars, yes, and the people earning money from all of this, of course, but the rest, *never*. We're not generating demand, my boy, we're satisfying it. Drugs and whores have been around since the beginning of civilization. Not just here, everywhere. We, humans, are frail. We have more weaknesses in our minds and our bodies than any other species on the planet. We need stuff, hell, we *crave* stuff to manage our fears somehow, our weaknesses, our fragility. And it's true for all of us. Look at yourself, for example. You need distance from other people, physically, and even more so emotionally, to control your insecurities somehow. And you practice traditional martial arts to manage your inner balance, otherwise, the anger that has been building up inside you since basically your birth, it would just burst and either make you kill yourself or go on a wild rampage causing chaos around you. And the killings you've been doing for the boss, for our family? They are your way of releasing some of that anger. Like when you release a little steam from a boiling pot. You should consider yourself lucky that the boss and I realized you had this inside of you, and that we found a way to control it, otherwise you'd probably be rotting in a jail somewhere, waiting to be executed. Not only that, but the people we made you kill weren't innocent bystanders or harmless citizens. They were as brutal and angry and ruthless as you or the boss or me.'

That was ruthless indeed. Those words. They hit me where it hurt the most. I didn't know what to say. Some of those knots I was talking about tightened up and I felt pressure in my chest. We sat in silence for a couple of minutes.

'Why are you with the boss?' I asked. 'Why are you so loyal to him?'

'Why are *you*, Sato-kun?'

'He... He is almost like a father to me. He took me in when I wasn't wanted by anyone, and he saw me when I was invisible.'

'And to me, Sato-kun, he is like a little brother. We grew up together.'

'I see,' I said. 'But... what happens if deep inside I... I start having doubts?'

'Well, I would say that it's always important to put things into perspective. And for you to be able to see as full a picture as possible, you should be able to put yourself in others' shoes. You should understand the people who surround you. But, most importantly, you should understand yourself.'

'Hm.'

'But, you know, ultimately we are all different. So, even though I know it doesn't help much, my best advice to you is that you should figure it out yourself. There are no magic tricks or wild cards here. Just... go and figure it out.'

As he spoke those words, my stomach began to produce weird sounds.

'I think I'm hungry as hell,' I said.

'Me too. Let's have dinner. I'll treat you to a hotpot. There's a nice place nearby.'

'Thanks,' I said. 'Let's go, then.'

***

The restaurant wasn't fancy at all. Most of the guests were simple salarymen. The waiters all seemed to know Kobayashi-san. They showed us to the upper floor where people were sitting and eating in booths. We got our own little booth and sat down.

I ordered an umeshu-soda, while Kobayashi-san only had sparkling water. We chose a Hokkaido-style hotpot with seafood for dinner, and we asked the waiter to bring us extra servings of rice, as we were both starving. As soon as the waiter had left, we continued our discussion.

'Old man.'

'Hm?'

'I'd like you to tell me more about the boss.'

Kobayashi-san scratched his head and frowned a little.

'Ok, let's do this. Where did I stop last time?'

'You told me about the time he had disappeared, and you said he had returned after almost a week as a completely different person.'

'Oh, yes. His disappearance. Well, what can I tell: he was definitely not the same anymore.'

'And... how was he different?'

'It's... complicated.'

'It doesn't matter. I want to know,' I insisted. 'We've got plenty of time.'

Kobayashi-san filled his lungs with as much air as he could and then let out a big sigh.

'Look, Sato-san. I don't even know where to begin...'

The old man paused for a moment, as the waiter had arrived with our drinks. We thanked him, and we both took several sips, as we were not only hungry but also thirsty.

My umeshu-soda was excellent.

'Boss Yamaguchi met someone during his disappearance,' the old man finally continued, putting his glass down. 'A girl.'

'A girl,' I repeated.

'Yes, a girl. Unfortunately, I don't know what exactly happened, as the boss never told me, but, apparently, they met in the woods, and they spent the next seven days together, falling in love in the process.'

'I... see. And... why is that complicated?'

'Well, the girl, Naoko, she was from here. I mean, she lived in Tokyo, but she escaped from home. She later told me that she had felt an urge to leave and go north. She switched two or three trains, and she hitched several rides, spending almost a whole day traveling, without any particular destination in her mind. She just had this feeling inside, and she let it guide her. I don't know if you've ever experienced anything like this, but I think we all have moments and situations in our lives when our instincts just keep pushing us forward, even though we don't know where we're headed. It must've been something like that for Naoko.'

'So, she came to the town where you were living, and she went straight into the woods?'

'Apparently.'

'And they met in the woods?'

'They did, I guess.'

'But you don't know how or exactly where they spent the next seven days.'

'No, neither of them told me. I only know that boss Yamaguchi was in love with her when he returned home. And... he had purple eyes.'

Our food arrived in the meantime, and we started to eat.

'This image,' I said, 'it keeps resurfacing.'

'What image?'

'The green eyes, the purple eyes. I keep stumbling across this image – either something I hear from someone or a vision in my head or... Ren herself, for that matter. And now the boss, too. I mean... something's odd here.'

The old man put his chopsticks down, crossed his arms, and looked me in the eye.

'Ren's power. It's just one side of the coin,' Kobayashi-san said.

'What do you mean?'

'She can remove thoughts from people's minds and put them back into the Sea of Thought, right?'

'I... guess?'

'But in life, there's always balance. There is a black to every white. Otherwise, things would just fall apart, and the world would turn into chaos.'

'So...'

'So, there is another power. A power to plant thoughts and ideas into people's minds. Directly from the Sea of Thought.'

'What the...' I began, but I didn't finish the sentence. 'So... what you're saying... the boss...'

'Not anymore,' Kobayashi-san said. 'He used to have this power, but he lost it.'

The old man saw the confusion on my face, so he continued:

'Grandpa Yamaguchi knew immediately when he saw those purple eyes. For the next couple of days, his mood kept changing from angry to desperate to sad. I had never seen him in such a state of uncertainty and disharmony. As if a great storm had arrived, which rattled and shook even the old oak tree.

'What followed was a complete change in how we lived our lives in grandpa's house and a complete change in our personal relationships. Grandpa and the boss spent more and more time away from Miyako-san and myself, and they became very secretive about what they were doing together. The two of them grew increasingly distant from the two of us, and the whole atmosphere of our home changed from warm and familiar to... well... I don't even have the right word for it. But I'd go with sad. It makes me sad to think about it even now, fifty or so years later.

'What do you think they were doing, the two of them?' I asked.

'Well, some time later it became obvious to me: grandpa was preparing his grandson for the role he's still playing today, the role of becoming the head of this family. He was also teaching him how to use his newly found powers.'

'Wait, are you saying, grandpa Yamaguchi had the same power, too?'

'Used to. When he began teaching our boss, not anymore. But he definitely knew how it worked.'

'Fuck. I... don't get this shit. This is just... crazy.'

'I know how you feel, my boy. I felt the same way when I learned about these things. Honestly, it's way beyond my comprehension. I mean, I've always believed in greater powers, in forces beyond those visible and known to us humans, but this... This is like giving god-like powers to simple human beings. On the surface, it might seem like something amazing, but in reality, especially if I look back at everything I've witnessed in the last fifty years, I'd say it was more of a curse.'

I leaned back, crossing my arms. My thoughts were all over the place, and I struggled to comprehend what all of this really meant. "Why did they get these abilities? Why them? Were there others with similar abilities? Or different kinds of abilities?" I ordered a double Jack Daniels on the rocks, just to help me relax a bit.

'What happened next?' I asked.

'As you've probably already realized,' Kobayashi-san continued, 'it turned out grandpa was the boss back in the day. Even though he was semi-retired and living in the countryside, he was still the head of the family. Neither his grandson nor I knew any of this, but after this whole incident had happened, we obviously both learned the truth. Me a little later, but that doesn't really matter.'

'And what happened with the girl the boss had fallen in love with?'

'Naoko? Well, it turned out, she was part of the wider family, too.'

'What?'

'Her father, the late Takuma-san, Takuma Suzuki, was the head of our Tokyo operations. Tokyo was obviously, and still is, the most important market for our family, and when grandpa decided to move to the countryside, he appointed Takuma-san to take care of Tokyo.

'Word spread quickly about Naoko escaping from home, and grandpa knew, so soon after both the boss and Naoko had returned to their respective homes, it became obvious that the two of them had met and spent time together. As they were both very young, full of energy and desire and whatnot, it was impossible to keep them apart. Both grandpa and Naoko's father knew that very well, so they didn't try to force the issue. Instead, they tried finding a way to contain the situation. To keep it under their control as much and for as long as they could.

'They agreed that the youngsters would see each other on weekends – one weekend in the countryside, one in Tokyo. In exchange, both the boss and Naoko promised that they would not escape, and they would become full and responsible members of our family.'

'So... is Naoko-san Ren's mother?' I asked.

The old man nodded.

'She died a long time ago, when Ren was born, actually, but I remember her well. She was an amazing person.'

'Tell me more,' I asked.

Kobayashi-san took another sip from his mineral water before continuing:

'I remember the time when she first came to visit us in grandpa's house, maybe a couple of weeks after the boss had resurfaced from his disappearance. It was a Friday evening. Grandpa, Miyako-san, the boss, and I were having dinner inside, and the boss was nervous. Nervous as hell. I had never seen him like that before and never have since. We tried involving him in our conversation, but he just wasn't there with us, mentally. He even lost his appetite and couldn't eat properly. At one point, I deliberately made fun of him, trying to provoke him, but he just smiled and did nothing. Even back then he hated being made fun of, but Naoko's arrival was apparently all he could think about. Nothing else made its way through to him.

'Then, at maybe around eight o'clock, we heard the engine of a car. The boss immediately stood up and went outside. I looked at Miyako-san, and I saw a smile on her face. I think she was happy for the boss. For both of them. But there was also concern on that face, hiding in the dark corridors of her wrinkles and the deepest of layers of her eyes. When I looked at grandpa, I saw the same concern. And I saw resignation. To the faith, maybe.

'I, too, stood up and went to the window. The same window I had been standing in when Miyako-san had arrived, carrying a baby in her arms. This moment, and the image of a car bringing someone new to our home, someone who would change the way we had been living until then – it felt like it was covered in a cloak of... inevitability. Things were changing, yes, but at the same time, things were also repeating themselves. The image I saw through the window felt like the modern retelling of an old tale. A tale that had been around far longer than any of us could even imagine.

'As the car stopped, Naoko opened the rear door and stepped outside. She was almost as tall as the boss, very lean, with beautiful long hair. I think I was mesmerized as much by her beauty and her presence as the boss was. He just stood there, a few steps away from the car, frozen in space and time, his heart probably ready to jump out and run around like a happy little puppy. Naoko on the other hand seemed very cool. She walked slowly towards the boss, and when she got there, they stood in front of each other for a while, looking into each other's eyes. It looked to me as if they were having a conversation in their heads.

'They then held hands and walked into the house. Both grandpa and Miyako-san went to the door to greet her. They all introduced themselves, and Naoko was very polite, but she kept her cool, even in front of grandpa, which I think made a big impression on him, as people tended to be intimidated by him.

'She then turned to me. I was still standing in the window, much less cool than she was. She came, told me her name was Naoko Suzuki, and she bowed. As she straightened up again, only then did I notice the color of her eyes. They were green.'

'Like Ren's,' I whispered.

'That's right,' Kobayashi-san said. 'The same green eyes. They glowed. I kept looking at them, at her, and I even forgot to tell her my name. I couldn't say a word. She waited for a bit, then smiled and turned away to walk back to the boss. The moment I lost sight of her eyes I regained my composure, and I quickly spilled out my name. She turned her head for a second and gave me another smile.'

'So... did Ren receive her ability from her mother?' I asked.

The old man nodded: 'The boss and Naoko stayed in their homes for the next two years or so, seeing each other on weekends, and learning and studying under the wings of grandpa and Takuma-san respectively on weekdays. They were the same age, sixteen when they first met, and when they both turned eighteen, grandpa decided to send the boss to Tokyo permanently. He asked me to go along and to take care of his grandson, to watch over him. I didn't even hesitate, of course.

'In Tokyo, the boss rose rapidly through the ranks of our family, and the two of them, the boss and Naoko, were seen as a real power-couple. People respected them, people feared them, people would do anything to stay out of their way. They both mastered their special abilities, and together, the two abilities combined, I mean... they seemed invincible.

'Everything looked perfect for the two of them. They were having the time of their lives, in control of great power, and in love with each other. They had a beautiful wedding up north in grandpa's house, and soon Naoko got pregnant.'

'With Ren,' I said.

'Right. With Ren. But then... tragedy struck.'

The old man's eyes welled up and he was visibly shaken.

'It hurts so much, just remembering everything,' he said. 'Even though it happened such a long time ago, for me, and I guess for our boss, too, it's as if it was yesterday. Naoko... Her smile, her eyes, her whole presence is so... vivid. And every time I see Ren...'

'You see Naoko.'

Kobayashi-san nodded.

'Was it the birth?' I asked.

The old man nodded again, and then tears began to flow from his eyes.

Father and daughter

'What's happening?' I asked Kei after entering his bar.

'Oh, Sato-kun, it's you, maaan!'

'What's going on here, Kei? What are the shadows up to?'

'You're becoming a frequent guest nowadays, maaan! Good to see you!'

'You're avoiding my question, Kei. Please, answer the question.'

'Oh, we can get to that later, Sato-kun. Please, have a seeeat, first. Have a drink, maaan.'

'I'm not in the mood, Kei. I've had enough drinks for tonight. I came for answers.'

Kei looked at me with a serious face. He put down the glass he was cleaning and poured himself some whisky.

'You might not need one, but *I* do,' he said, and he took a sip. 'So, tell me, what's bothering you, Sato-san?'

'Nothing's bothering me,' I said. 'I was just asking about the shadows.'

'About the shadows?'

'Yeah. Why are they all holding hands? And why are the three closest to the hole glowing and covered in light? I want answers, Kei.'

Kei took another sip of his whisky, then walked over to me, looking straight into my eyes. I could feel his breath on my cheeks.

'You know what, maaan?'

'What?'

'Hooonestly, I'd just punch you in the face right now, if I could. I really would, maaan.'

'So, why don't you?'

'I'm not allowed to. And that's both the beauty and the tragedy of this little place here. Of *yooour* place.'

'What do you mean, Kei? It's your place, not mine.'

'Are you reeeally such an idiot, Sato-kun? Do you honestly think this is mine? Do you think I neeed this, maaan? Do you think I'm here for fun? To amuuuse you?'

I kept looking Kei in the eye, but I didn't say a word.

'Why are you here, maaan? Why do you keep coming back?'

'I... I'm looking for answers.'

'Oh, right! Sato-kun is looking for answers! Oh, my! What shall we do? Shall we write everything down on a sheet of beauuutiful paper and hand it over to him in an elegant envelope? Or shall we send him a PowerPoint presentation with nice little chaaarts and pictures to make it easier for him to understand? No, wait! I know! Let's make a voice recording of everything he needs to know so that he can put his headphones on, sit back in a nice armchair, and just fucking relaaax!'

'You're not funny, Kei.'

'Well, I'm not meant to be, maaan.'

'Then what *are* you meant to be?' I asked.

'Oh, wow! Finally, an interesting question! Then, come on! Give it a try! What's the answer?'

'Fuck you, Kei.'

'Oh, is that all you have to say? Fuck you here, and fuck you there, and just fuck, fuck, fuck, and then some more fuck? I've heard you use this fucking word more than any other fucking word, maaan. You're a living, walking, talking fuckmaster, aren't you? At least you're consistent, maaan.'

'Fu-... Never mind,' I said, and I took a seat at the bar.

Kei poured me a glass of whisky, and he sat down next to me.

'Kei.'

'Hm?'

'Are you real?'

'Well, how do *you* feel about it, maaan?'

'You... look pretty real to me.'

'Then, I'm real.'

'And this place? The corridor, the doors, this bar? Is it real, too, or just something inside my head?'

'Does it matter?'

I looked at him.

'If something's happening inside your head,' Kei continued, 'does that make it less real?'

'Well…'

'What *is* reality, Sato-kun? Is it the things you can see with your eyes and touch with your fingers? If so, then you, being able to see me, or touch this glass of whisky and drink what's inside – does that make all of this reeeal?'

Kei paused for a second, giving me a chance to respond, but I didn't know what to say.

'And what if I'm just inside your head? What if this baaar and the shadows as you call them are only in your head, too? You can still feel this, right?' He asked as he gave me a little shove with his shoulder. 'How do you define what's real, then? And what about your feeel-ings? You can't see them, you can't touch them, you can't smell them. But you still feel, right? Are they *reeeal*?'

I stared into the glass I was holding.

'What I'm trying to say, Sato-kun, is that it doesn't really matter if all of this is happening inside your head or not. It also doesn't mat-ter if this really is a different dimension or a world between dimen-sions, or if I'm a human, or an angel, or a spirit, or an illusion, or something completely different.'

'What *does* matter, then?' I asked.

'*Yooou*, my friend,' he said, pointing at me with his finger. '*You* matter, maaan.'

Kei gave me a couple of moments for his words to sink in (and for both of us to drink some more whisky), and then he continued:

'Whatever's happening to you, whatever you are experiencing, maaan, it is all for you. Just – to borrow a phrase from someone I know – *fucking* embrace it, maaan, and do whatever *you* feel you should be doing.'

I stood up and started to walk around the bar. The shadows were all lined up, holding hands. They looked like one, gigantic serpent whose body occupied the whole place, bending and twisting through the various rooms and corridors of the bar. The serpent's head was the three glowing shadows near the hole in the wall, the last of whom was looking out the hole, looking into the sparkling green light that had been filling that outer space since my last visit to the bar.

I walked over to those three glowing shadows, with Kei right behind me. I reached out to touch them, and I felt such warmth that I broke into a sweat. This wave of heat just ran me over in a matter of seconds, and it opened my pores wide. It felt like my body was trying to get rid of as much filth and dirt as it possibly could.

***

I went home after the visit to Kei's bar. It was already way past midnight.

As I entered my apartment a weird smell hit me. A bad smell. It was a combination of dampness, stale air, and probably the garbage I had forgotten to take out. I couldn't even remember when I had last spent some quality time at home, just relaxing, maybe cleaning a bit, enjoying my own company and no one else's. If there ever had been such a time. Looking back, there probably hadn't. My apartment never felt like home, or to be more precise, it never helped me learn what the word "home" was supposed to mean. I could appreciate the fact that I had a place to sleep, a roof over my head, and a place to keep my stuff, but other than that, the apartment never gave me much more. If anything, whenever I was inside, in silence, alone with my thoughts, I'd have this sensation where all the little knots which had formed in my chest and around my heart would just gradually tighten up, until I felt like a wound-up toy, with an invisible hand holding the wind-up mechanism tightly, not letting it go, not letting me release my tension.

In those moments, I'd go to the wall separating my living room from the bathroom, I'd take down the picture hanging there, and I'd bang my head against the wall a couple of times. Then I'd put the picture back to cover the damage.

The last time I did this, I banged my head so hard that I finally managed to break through the wall and put a hole in it. Almost like the one in Kei's bar.

I still had a scar on my forehead. As I got home that night, the scar, or the wound behind it, began to pulsate, as if it were a living organism, and it made me remember the time when I had banged my head through the wall. It felt strange remembering it, remembering the details, and going through the mental images of all of it in my mind. It felt as if it hadn't even been me who had done it, but rather a stranger who had been living inside my body, and who'd appear from time to time, take control and just do stuff, without asking for my permission, without thinking of the consequences for me or my body, or the consequences for my mind.

I walked over to the wall and I looked at the picture. It was a photograph showing me and the boss practicing "kenjutsu" back when I was still a young boy. Kobayashi-san had taken the photo. He later framed it and gave it to me on my birthday. I didn't actually have a real birthday, as I didn't know the exact date of my birth, but Kobayashi-san decided that I should have one, so he chose a day for me: the 25th of April. He didn't tell me why he had chosen this specific day, but I didn't care much. I was just happy to have a birthday.

I really liked the picture. Apart from my sword and my motorcycle, it was probably the only material thing I really cherished. It made me feel I was... a living person and not just a ghost.

I leaned closer to examine the photo.

It was my second year with the family back then, and I was already progressing well in "kenjutsu". We were in the garden, and the boss was teaching me an "iai" kata, a sword-drawing form. I think it was the one with a backward movement, the "Urafune ushiro". I really liked that one. It was the one to provide the enemy with a false sense of security and confidence before you strike him down with no mercy. The boss liked it, too. He made me practice it every day for three months after that first lesson.

The photo itself captured the moment when I was drawing my wooden sword for the first time after the boss had shown me the first part of the form. We both had determined looks on our faces, and it was good to see, good to look at from time to time. As if there weren't anything else in the world, just the two of us and our swords. Those were good moments. Moments I liked to revisit.

As I was looking at the photo, I noticed something I had not seen before. In the corner, behind a bush, there appeared to be someone. A small head, peeking out, watching us practice. I leaned even closer to look. There was a peculiar glow in those little eyes. A vivid, green color.

'Ren.'

It felt strange to discover Ren in the photo, but at the same time, it made her whole being and her presence in my life even more familiar. As if the photo were evidence of her having been a part of my life for a very long time. Though I hadn't been aware of her, she was there, she knew about me, and we shared the same world.

I ran my fingers gently across the surface of the photo as if trying to caress the people on it, and then I removed it from the wall.

The hole was still there. A testament to how hard my head was, and a testament to my inner demons. Its edges were rough and gritty, and there were traces of my blood on and around it. It looked like a sacred place where you offered a blood sacrifice to gods in hope of salvation.

I kneeled, and I touched the edge of the hole at different points. I touched the bloodstains. I then lowered my head, and I carefully put it through the hole. It felt like my head was in a guillotine, awaiting the fatal blow. Strangely enough, it was a rather good feeling. A feeling of well-deserved punishment, of being in a situation where I could honestly ask for forgiveness and ask to be shown a path of redemption.

I had a large mirror in the bathroom, on the opposite wall. I was staring right into it. My head looked like a hunter's trophy – lifeless and with empty eyes.

One by one, tears began to flow down my cheeks, and I kept looking at my own face in the mirror. I felt a strong pain in my chest, with all the little knots inside it strangling my heart to a point where it couldn't pump blood anymore. Soon, the knots attacked my lungs, too, and I was struggling to breathe. And the tears just kept flowing.

And they kept flowing...

When I couldn't bear it anymore, I pulled my head out and fell to the floor. I sobbed loudly for several minutes, then silently for several more, and then I fell asleep, all curled up like an embryo.

***

I woke up to the sound of receiving a text message. I pulled my phone from the pocket of my jeans and checked it. It was from Kobayashi-san. He told me to go over to Ren's and escort her, as she needed to go somewhere important.

As I got up my shoulder felt sore, probably because I had been sleeping on it. I massaged it a little, and I went to open the window and let in some fresh air. Sounds and scents of spring gushed in, along with unusually strong sunlight. I must have looked like a caveman standing in the entrance of his dark cave, realizing there was a beautiful world out there. I filled my lungs with this fresh air, and it revitalized me.

I took a shower, shaved, and put on some clean clothes. I decided I wanted to use my bike, so I dressed accordingly: a pair of dark blue jeans reinforced with kevlar, motorcycle boots, a black shirt I liked to wear when riding, and my beloved "Dainese" leather jacket. I also wore a leg bag where I hid a medium-sized knife. I felt I might need the "wakizashi" short sword, too, so I took it with me. I had a special box attached to the side of my bike where I had room for both a short and a long sword. I had had it made specifically for this purpose by our family's mechanic.

It had been a while since I had last ridden Eleanor, so I spent a couple of minutes just looking at her, praising her a bit, caressing her. She was a proud lady, and easily offended, too, so I had to take good care of her to avoid any trouble on the road.

I then placed my short sword inside the box, sat in Eleanor's saddle, and turned her engine on. She sounded amazing, and the rumble of her motor put a big smile on my face. 'That's it, my girl,' I said, and we rode off.

***

I needed breakfast, so I decided to stop at a bakery in Meguro. It was a small shop with only two small tables inside and another two on the street. They also served specialty coffee. A young couple ran the place. Momoko and Ichiro. I liked them. They were always cheerful, always full of interesting stories and just pleasant people to be around.

I parked Eleanor close by and went straight to the bakery. The name was "Living Room". Momoko had once told me that she wanted all her guests to feel like they were spending time in her cozy living room and not just another random bakery or coffee shop. And the place really did feel like someone's home.

I took a good look at the fresh pastries, and I chose a croissant with almonds and chocolate filling. I also ordered a flat white, made from their own blend, and I took a seat at one of the outdoor tables.

The neighborhood was residential, so it was quiet and serene. I saw an old lady ride by on a bicycle, and a young, stylish man walking his French bulldog on a leash. The dog was funny, acting as if he were this mean, tough dog, all pumped up, but you could see in his eyes that underneath the act he was just a little puppy. He reminded me of Kon, actually, and the moment the image of my new friend emerged in my head, a small cloud appeared seemingly out of nowhere to cover the sun for a few seconds, sending a cold shiver down my spine.

Then, as the little cloud went away and we were bathing in the sunshine again, I saw a woman with a child on the corner of the street. They were holding hands, and they were approaching the bakery. The woman could've been anywhere between thirty and fifty – I just couldn't tell. She had a young face, youthful eyes, but she was dressed like a businesswoman, and she had this toughness and seriousness about her. The girl must have been somewhere between eight and ten. The woman had a wedding ring, so they must have been mother and daughter. It surprised me to see them, as school had already started and the girl should've been in class by then, but she wasn't even wearing a school uniform.

As I was watching them, I suddenly realized I had never thought of having a wife, a child, a family. In my childhood and my youth, I had spent countless hours imagining what it would be like to have real parents, maybe siblings, and my idea of family had always revolved around me being the child. I had somehow never thought of starting a family of my own. Maybe because I had never really had a role model. None of the adults I had around me were real parents – Kobayashi-san had no wife or kids, Julia had no husband or children either, and until recently, I had not even known about the boss being a husband and a father. But now, as the woman and her daughter passed by my table and entered the bakery, the thought took shape in my mind.

"But what actually makes a family?" I asked myself. "Is it a bond of blood? If so, does spilling our own and other people's blood for the sake of the family count? Or is it a bond of trust, which makes us both immensely strong and immensely vulnerable at the same time? Or maybe a bond based on feelings so deep most of us can't even comprehend them?"

The more I thought about this, the more I realized I had bonds to certain people that checked all the different categories I was able to come up with. The boss, Kobayashi-san, Julia. None of them was my real family, but I couldn't imagine a life without them. Yet, in recent days, or maybe weeks, I had slowly begun drifting away from them. I closed my eyes for a moment, and I saw this image of the three of them standing on a shore and looking at me, while I was rowing a small boat into the open sea. They didn't say a word, they didn't wave. They were just standing there, motionless, but I saw approval in their eyes. I think they understood me. Probably because the three of them knew me better than I knew myself.

My coffee and croissant arrived, and I opened my eyes again. Momoko brought them and put them on the table.

'Thanks,' I said.

'You're welcome, Sato-san.'

'Tell me, Momoko-san.'

'Yes?'

'You and Ichiro-san, you're married, right?'

'No, not yet,' she said with a smile, blushing. 'But hopefully soon.'

'I see. But you're like... like a family, right?'

'Well, I'd say we are, yes. Especially for him. I have a good relationship with my family, my parents and two sisters, but Ichiro, he doesn't. His mother... well, she's difficult. Very. And his father, he's been absent his entire life. And he has an older brother who's a real bully. He doesn't even speak to them if he doesn't have to.'

'I see.'

'It's strange, you know,' Momoko said, sitting at my table. 'We call his family a family, which they of course are, but they don't behave like a family. They don't live like one. So... I'm not sure if they deserve to be called a family. It's a disgrace to the meaning of the word "family". On the other hand, what Ichiro and I have got, it's special. At least that's how I see it. I hope he does, too,' she said, blushing and smiling again.

'I'd say he does,' I said, turning to look at Ichiro and then turning back again. 'To me, the two of you look like a family.'

'Thank you, Sato-san,' Momoko replied and then stood. 'You're a kind person. I can tell. Your family is lucky to have you.'

I looked at her without saying anything.

'Your breakfast is on the house,' she said, and she went back inside.

"My family is lucky to have me." I kept thinking about this sentence while I ate my breakfast, and later throughout my ride to Ren's house. It's a strange sentence to hear for someone like me, who's used to living a solitary life and who has based his entire existence on the notion that ultimately, he is on his own.

"Does this mean there were people who thought of me as family? And does this then mean that other people were searching for a family, too?"

Whenever I thought about my life and the way I was living it, I always thought of it from my own perspective. Never had I tried to put myself in others' shoes. But looking at our "family", looking at the people who were a part of it, and especially the people to whom I had the closest ties, we were probably in it for more or less the same reasons, whether we knew it or not. Kobayashi-san, Julia, but even the girls in the bars or the lowest level members of our organization, they were looking for a place where they felt they belonged. So is that all family is? A group of people who make us feel we belong?

***

I arrived at Ren's house and parked Eleanor out front. A caravan of several cars was already there, including a long, black limousine. It was a custom-built Mercedes, reinforced with bullet-proof materials all over.

A couple of our men were escorting Ren from her house the moment I arrived. We exchanged looks as she walked by me to go to the limousine, but I couldn't decipher anything from her green eyes. They were the usual mystery to me.

I left my helmet on the bike and took the short sword from the box. I then joined her in the car. The boss was sitting in the back, and Kobayashi-san was in the passenger seat. I took a seat next to Ren in the back.

'We can go,' Kobayashi-san told the driver.

The atmosphere was tense inside. No one said a word for several minutes.

I took the time to clean my sword, but in between all the wiping and oiling, I tried observing Ren's face and the boss's.

They really were father and daughter. They shared the same elegant but sharp and often tense features, and they had the same stubbornness – especially the way it showed on their faces. Their eyes were the same, too, apart from the color, of course.

I noticed that the boss was inspecting us. As if he wanted to say something, but he kept it to himself.

I put my sword away and looked at Ren. She was looking at the streets, the neighborhood. Her scent had such a strong presence that I felt it pulling me towards her, making me inch closer and closer. She was sitting with her legs crossed and her hands resting on her thighs. She was wearing a short skirt, so I could see most of her legs. As I was looking at her hands, her legs, I suddenly felt a strong urge to touch her, to feel her skin. It overwhelmed me, and I began to sweat. I opened the window on my side of the car and looked away, but her scent was still present, as was the image of her hands and her legs, and the image of me gently moving closer to her and resting my hand on top of hers. Then slowly moving my hand down her leg, then up again, and down again. I felt the warmth of her skin, and how soft it was. I got totally aroused, and I had to cross my legs to hide my erection. It was embarrassing.

"Fuck. You idiot," I thought to myself.

I could see out of the corner of my eye that Ren was looking at me. I didn't know if she had sensed something, but now I felt even more anxious, and I was literally a moment away from asking the driver to stop for a second and let me out.

But the boss intervened:

'Ren.'

'Yes, dad?'

'Are you prepared?'

'Don't insult me. Of course, I am.'

'I'm serious, Ren. This is important. He is a top politician.'

'I know.'

'This might be a longer session than usual,' the boss told her. 'There's a lot of stuff we want to remove.'

'Yeah, sure,' Ren replied nonchalantly.

'What's wrong with you?'

Ren looked at him with fake surprise, pretending she didn't know what he was referring to.

'You're acting strange today. You're not your usual self.'

'Oh, really? And how do you know what I'm usually like?'

'I'm your father, Ren. I know.'

'Oh, right, you're my father. I almost forgot. By the way, just so that I know, when will you start acting like a father? You know, just so I can be prepared. Especially if it's a longer session than usual.'

The boss leaned forward and gave Ren a huge slap. She fell into my lap. Everything happened so fast that I had no time to react. I looked at Kobayashi-san who was sitting in front, hoping I'd get some support from him, but he didn't even turn around. I knew he had heard everything, and he was completely aware of what was going on, but he didn't want to interfere. I was left alone with the two of them.

I saw anger in boss Yamaguchi's eyes, but I also saw remorse and pain. I didn't say anything, but the way I looked at him, he understood he should back off and cool down. He turned away, looking out the window.

Ren covered her face with her left hand. She didn't want us to see that she was crying, but I felt her tears drop on my pants. I gently put my hand on top of hers, and we stayed like that until we arrived.

***

We had come to an old farmhouse outside of Tokyo. It was probably ours, but I had never been to it or even heard of its existence. It looked like a random rural house, with a little garden, where any random person could've lived.

Our caravan of three cars stopped in front, and we got out of the limousine. The guards from the two escorting cars stayed outside, and Ren, the boss, Kobayashi-san, and I went in.

As usual, I needed to perform my little ritual of transition before entering, so I stopped in front of the entrance for a few seconds, and I closed my eyes. The boss and Kobayashi-san knew about my quirk, but for Ren, it was the first time seeing it. When I opened my eyes again, she had this weird look on her face, as if asking "What the fuck?", but there was also a smile, and I smiled back at her, saying: 'Sorry, it's just a thing I do. Don't worry about it.'

The whole situation felt a little embarrassing, but I was happy that she had seen it. It made me feel more comfortable around her.

Inside, two of our men were already waiting for us. They both bowed deep upon seeing the boss. One stayed behind and the other showed us the way upstairs.

At first, the house *did* seem like a simple, rural house, but now that I was inside, and the more time I spent in it, I sensed it had peculiar energy, which slowly but steadily crept under my skin. With every step I took, I was expecting something to happen – to hear a voice, or someone to appear maybe. But it wasn't spooky at all. I wasn't scared or anything. Rather, there was something familiar about the house.

I looked at Ren as we were walking up the stairs. She was inspecting the house with the same kind of curiosity and fascination. At one point, our eyes met, and it felt like we were both experiencing the same thing.

When I touched the railing as we were walking upstairs, I felt as if something had stung me, like a very small electric shock. It went through my fingers, then my arm, and all the way up to my brain. When it got there, blurry images appeared inside my mind. It was difficult to make any sense of them, but I clearly remember seeing a woman's face. She, too, had green eyes, like Ren.

Once upstairs, we went to one of the rooms. I saw two more guards and a man tied to a chair, his head covered with a bag. It was the politician the boss had been talking about in the car.

We all stood in silence while Ren approached the man. She removed the bag from his head. We could all see his eyes now, but his mouth was still covered with tape. He didn't even try to break loose or anything – it was pointless, and he knew it. Instead, he looked deep into Ren's eyes.

As the seconds went by, her eyes glowed stronger and stronger. It seemed like the man was not afraid. He apparently knew about Ren and her gift, and he knew what to expect. Or, at least, so he thought.

'Are you sure, then?' Ren asked her father.

The old man nodded.

'Oookay. Let's begin, then.'

A guard gave a small steel case to Ren. She thanked him, kneeled in "seiza" position, and opened it. I saw an average-sized syringe inside, and a small bottle with some kind of liquid. She put the needle inside and filled the syringe with the liquid. She then stood up again and leaned close to the politician.

'I'm sorry,' she said.

This was the first time a sign of fear appeared in the man's eyes.

'This isn't personal. At least not for me. But for my dad it apparently is. I don't know what you did to him, or what kind of threat you pose, but it seems to be serious. Otherwise, he wouldn't ask for such a huge intervention. Usually, it would be just one or two key ideas, and some collateral stuff. But this... Honestly, I don't know what'll happen to you after this. I've never done this before.'

The man began to shake, and tears appeared in his eyes.

'Don't worry,' she continued, 'it won't hurt. Also, I'm giving you this,' she raised the syringe to show him. 'You won't feel a thing. It's just that... well... I really don't know how this one will play out. But what I do know, is that your life as you know it is over. Oh, you'll live, don't worry about that. But the rest... The people you know, the people you love, all your amazing and not so amazing experiences, all your memories...' She paused for a moment as if thinking about her own life. 'I think you should just bid them farewell. There's nothing else you can do.'

The man was now shaking hard, and he tried to shout, to move, to break free, but to no avail. Two guards came to hold him down, and Ren stuck the needle in his neck and gave him the whole dose.

He shook for another few seconds, then he suddenly stopped, and his head fell. He was unconscious. And that was it. That was him saying goodbye to everything Ren was about to remove. His whole life up until then, really.

The guards helped Ren untie him and lay him on the ground. She put away her tools, went down in "seiza" again, and leaned over the man's motionless body. We all took a step back.

I saw her eyes glow even stronger than before, and she put her hands on his temples. Just like last time. She spent a minute or so concentrating, then the green light began to appear around the man's head.

The procedure took almost twenty minutes. There were moments I thought Ren would collapse, but she held herself together, even though it was apparent that both her body and her mind were going through quite an ordeal. From time to time, I'd look at the boss to see if I could spot anything on his face – a trace of an emotion, a hint of his feelings, a sign of concern, or maybe a bit of remorse. But nothing. I could see nothing. He didn't flinch. He just kept staring at Ren, not turning his head for a moment, not blinking.

When Ren was finally done, she collapsed. I took her to the neighboring room, where a soft bed was awaiting her. Boss Yamaguchi told a couple of his men to take care of the politician, while all the others were ordered to wait outside. He then joined me in the room where Ren was sleeping. There was a sofa and a chair in the room. I took the sofa this time, and he took the chair.

'She's a pretty girl, isn't she?' the boss asked.

I nodded.

'She reminds me a lot of her mother.'

I looked at him for a moment, and then my gaze returned to Ren.

'You know, you're like a son to me. Yet, I never told you about my daughter or my wife,' he said. I kept staring at Ren. 'And I don't really know why that is. It's just... difficult for me to talk about them.'

'Kobayashi-san told me a few things,' I said.

'I bet he did. He's a good man, Kobayashi-san. He's family. Like you are. Like Ren is,' the boss said, looking at her.

'Why do you make her do this?' I asked.

'Because... it's important.'

'For you?'

'For her,' the boss said. 'I want to create a world for her, and for the future generations of our family, where her power won't be needed anymore.'

'I see.'

I watched him as he was looking at Ren. For the first time since I was ten years old and since the first time I had seen this ruthless, hard man on that rainy day in Shinjuku, I saw deep feelings in his eyes.

'There's a curse in our family, you know. For generations and generations our family has been struggling with sad tales of power and love, and these strange, otherworldly abilities in the middle of it all. The misfortune is being passed down from parent to child, and the suffering just goes on and on. I want to break this vicious cycle. I plan to end it all.' He now looked at me: 'That's why I want you to protect her.'

I felt a cold shiver go down my spine as he spoke those words.

'Please, protect her, Sato. Do for her what I wasn't able to do for my wife,' he said, looking at Ren again. 'Naoko... My dear Naoko. She... She gave birth to Ren on this very bed. And she... lost her life doing so.'

A single tear ran down boss Yamaguchi's face.

Virgin chocolate cocktail

I dozed off on the sofa for a couple of hours. When I opened my eyes, Ren was still sleeping in the bed, in the same position I had left her in.

Her face looked innocent while asleep. It had no traces of the strange life she was leading. She was just another girl walking through mysterious fields of dreams.

I wondered if the thoughts and ideas which formed our dreams also came from the Sea of Thought. Or was there an island in the sea, the island of our dreams, which we only had access to when we were asleep? An island with pristine, sandy shores, with the sea gently embracing it from all sides. Various ideas and thoughts would swim out of the sea, slowly walk up the beach, leaving barely visible footprints in the white sand, to then enter an immense, thick jungle where other thoughts had already transformed into images of our dreams, to live among the tall trees.

From a distance, the jungle looked like a big mess, with no order or rules, but when one entered the jungle, it suddenly all made sense. Like when walking on a big field with uncut, tall grass, with an endless variety of flowers, and realizing the true order of nature was a complete lack of any order. What we would call disorderly chaos was actually the most natural state of things in this world. Maybe that's why our dreams seem so random and mysterious to our conscious, rational mind, and so natural and straightforward to our subconsciousness.

I myself am not good at dreaming. Or at least I seldom remember my dreams after I have woken up. Maybe just a glimpse here and there, but never the full story. It wasn't always like that – I used to have quite vivid dreams in my childhood. Before I began living on the streets. But almost nothing since then.

I often wondered what had caused my loss of dreams. Was it just a natural consequence of getting older? Or was there a triggering event, which somehow raised a barrier around my island of dreams, preventing me from swimming out, entering the jungle, and playing among the tall trees? Or was it a slow, degrading process caused by me living the life I was living, and making the jungle on the island slowly dry out? I'd sometimes see this image in my mind where all the dreams would open their wings, rise high in the sky, and fly away from the jungle, like birds leaving a burning forest. Maybe my dreams were waiting somewhere for the jungle to grow anew, for young and healthy trees to offer them shelter again.

I still remember one dream though, which I used to dream night after night when I was roughly eight years old. I'd find myself in a dark street, holding hands with a girl about my age. We'd stand in the middle of the street, surrounded by tall cypress trees on both sides, with dim streetlights throwing faint light, making it almost impossible to see anything. There were no houses, just the two of us, the trees, and the lights. And vast darkness. I'd slowly lean closer to the girl, raising my hand to clear her hair from her face, but before I could do so, a witch would appear right behind us, staring at us with wild, scary eyes. We'd run in the opposite direction, just straight down the street, as the darkness prevented us from going anywhere else. But the witch would follow. She'd fly behind us on a broom, like in fairy tales, and we'd just keep running as fast as we could, holding hands. After a while, we'd arrive to the end of the street, where we'd find a single house. With nowhere else to go, I'd open the door and we'd run inside to hide in a closet. We'd wait in the closet, breathing heavily and petrified, still holding hands. Then, after some time, the door to the house would slowly open, and I'd see the silhouette of the witch standing in its frame.

I'd always wake up at that point, never learning if the witch had found us or not.

I don't know why I remembered this dream while waiting for Ren to wake up, but these old, scary images sent a chill down my spine.

I stood and walked to the window.

Outside, I saw a small but pleasant garden. Someone must have been taking care of it on an almost daily basis. It had a small pond, a single black pine, a mound with a "jizo" statue, and a couple of stone lanterns covered in lush moss. One lantern was out in the open and visible, while the other was hiding in tall grass.

'Dad put that small "jizo" there a long time ago,' Ren said in a tired and soft voice. 'He burns incense next to it every year, on my birthday.'

'Do you know why?' I asked without turning to look at her.

'No. For many years I thought it was for my mother, but you don't plant a "jizo" for an adult. It's there to protect children.'

'I know,' I said. 'Maybe it's for you. Maybe that's his way of showing you love.'

'Maybe.'

I opened the window to let in some air, then I went to Ren and sat next to her on the bed.

'Thanks for taking care of me,' she whispered.

'It's my job,' I said. She looked away. 'But I'd do it even if it weren't.'

Now she looked me in the eye again, and her eyes were full of tears.

'I feel... empty,' she told me. 'These... eyes. This power. It's all... going to kill me, slowly. I can feel it.'

'I won't let anything kill you.'

She smiled and put her hand on top of mine: 'You're sweet. But... this is more than you can handle. More than either of us can handle. I've known since my childhood that one day it'll cost me my life, and it'll come sooner rather than later.'

'You shouldn't be saying stuff like that,' I said.

'I shouldn't, right?' she said with a soft smile. 'Then help me up, please.'

I let her grab my arm and she got up off the bed. She was visibly weak, but after a couple of seconds, she got her balance and walked back and forth a bit to get her body going.

'Could I ask you please to make me tea?'

'Of course,' I replied.

'And if you could find a snack or something, that would be great.'

'I'll check in the kitchen, downstairs.'

'Thanks.'

She came down ten minutes later, dressed up.

'Your tea is ready, and I found some cookies, too.'

'Thank you, Sato-kun.'

'Take a seat.'

'It's fine,' she said. 'I'd rather stand.'

'Ok. I'll stand, too.'

We spent the next fifteen or twenty minutes chatting about random stuff. It helped us relax a bit, I guess. The whole conversation was so light and carefree that she took me by complete surprise with her next question:

'So, Sato-kun, tell me.'

'Yeah?'

'What shall we do about the girl? It was Kiki, right?'

I needed a few moments to collect my thoughts on that one.

'What do you mean by "we"?' I asked.

'Let me help you.'

She saw on my face that I was hesitating, so she pressed on:

'I know what you're going to say: "It's too dangerous, stay out of this." Or, "I work alone, I don't need a partner." But that's precisely why you need my help – it's too dangerous and you're alone.'

I saw determination in her green eyes.

'You can't do this alone, Sato-kun. Let me help. I want to help. I, too, want to save Kiki.'

I put my right hand in my pocket and held the hundred-yen coin between my fingers, while letting out a loud, surrendering sigh.

'Ok, Ren. Let's do it. Together. Let's save her.'

She broke into a smile: 'Great! Let's go then! I'll call a cab.'

***

It took us a while to get back to the city. We were quite far out.

As we got into the taxi, we both fell silent for some time, just staring out the window, watching the rice fields, the old houses, billboards with ads for food, for mobile phone services, for cars, and those fluffy white clouds which look like huge flocks of sheep making their way to Tokyo.

The cab driver was playing chilled jazz on his stereo. A delicate piano, smooth drums, and a discrete bass. It was the sound of deep and long Scandinavian nights, performed by Peter Sandberg. I pictured myself sitting in a wooden house by a frozen lake, sipping red wine by the fire, with a lazy dog sleeping in the corner of the room and a cat purring in my lap. I also pictured Ren sitting next to me, drinking hot tea and reading a book. I think it was John Burdett's "Bangkok Tattoo". A philosophical crime novel about a half-Thai, half-American cop, torn between the East and the West, desperately trying to find a path for himself before he lost his mind completely.

I didn't know at the time why I had pictured Ren reading the story of detective Sonchai Jitpleecheep, but looking back, I'd say, to me, he was probably the ultimate symbol of a person misunderstood by everyone around him, and for some reason, I felt the same about both Ren and myself. I saw the two of us as two pieces of a puzzle that somehow didn't fit in the big picture. We were probably the missing pieces from a completely different set. Still, we were trying to find our place, somehow.

'Sato-kun.'

'Hm?'

'How do you want to go about this?'

'Saving Kiki, you mean?'

'Aha.'

'That's a good question.'

'You would be going against Little Jack, which means you would be going against Captain Jack, too.'

'We, you mean.'

'What?'

'*We* would be going against them.'

'Oh, yeah, right. We.'

'Hm... Let me think.'

I honestly didn't have a plan. I kept staring out the window of the car as if hoping there was an idea somewhere out there which I'd notice, and then I could open the window, and let the idea fly in and enter my mind through my nose. Or my ears. I wasn't sure about that part.

'I know!' Ren exclaimed.

'What?'

'I have an idea.'

'O-kay...'

'Look,' she began, 'obviously, the bad guy here is Little Jack. I mean, all of them are bad guys, don't get me wrong, but that little son of a bitch is the ultimate cockroach you'd just rather stomp on, right?'

'Y-es?'

'So, we have to take him out. I mean, for good. We have to... I don't know, get rid of him.'

'You mean, kill him?'

'No, not kill! Oh, my god, Sato! All you can think of is killing people. Gosh, try being more creative than that.'

'I don't follow.'

'Yeah, of course you don't,' she waved, rolling her eyes. 'Look, we'll use my powers, ok? We'll make him forget about our family, and everything about the things he has been doing to those poor girls.'

'And his father?' I asked.

'I'll remove any memory and thought he might have of his son. I'll erase Little Jack from his father's mind completely.'

'You're nuts,' I said.

'Why?! Do you have a better plan?'

I didn't. I looked at her, and she had this unwavering determination in her eyes. There was fire there, too. I found it... sexy. Yeah. She... had me there.

'If we made Captain Jack forget about his son,' she said, 'people would think the little cockroach had messed something up really bad, for which his father had banished him or something.'

'And what about Little Jack?'

'We'll figure something out. You'll... I don't know... take him to a remote village in Hokkaido or something. Just...make him disappear.'

'Hm... It might actually work,' I said.

'Of course, it will! Trust me! But we might need help.'

'I know. And I also know where to look for it.'

'Do you have someone in mind?'

'Yeah.'

'Well, great! Then, we have a plan!'

'Yeah, we have a plan,' I said. 'Sort of.'

***

It was early afternoon, and Yoshi's bar was closed at this time, but I had called him up and asked him to open it for us. I had also called Julia and Kon and asked them both to come to Yoshi's. We had agreed to meet at three o'clock.

When Ren and I got there, everyone was already inside, drinking virgin versions of Yoshi's signature chocolate cocktail. He poured some for the two of us as well, and we all took seats around the counter.

'Thanks for coming,' I said.

'What is this about, Sato-kun?' Kon asked with anxiety in his voice. 'Is there trouble? Are we in trouble? Is something bad going to happen?'

'Relax, meatball.'

The others chuckled.

'Hi everyone,' Ren said. 'My name is Ren. Julia and I know each other,' Julia nodded, 'and Yoshi-san has seen me a couple of times, but Kon, for us it's the first time, right?'

'R-Right! And it's a pleasure! My name is Ren! I mean, it's Kon! Sorry! It's Kon, of course!

Everyone laughed, while I just buried my face in my hands and shook my head.

'So, now that we all know each other, more or less,' I said, looking at the embarrassed Kon, 'let's begin.'

'Tell us, Sato, what's going on?' Julia asked.

'Look... You all know that our... family is not perfect. We... all do bad shit, but some are crossing certain lines.'

'You mean, Little Jack and his protective daddy?' Julia asked.

'Right,' I said.

'That mother-licking stupid piece of... dirty panties,' Kon swore, in his own funny way, clenching his fists, then knocking back his chocolate cocktail as if it were a glass of strong spirits.

'You want to go against them?' Yoshi-san asked. Ren and I nodded. Yoshi-san let out a big sigh and turned around to prepare some more chocolate cocktails. 'I knew it'd come to this sooner or later. I was hoping it wouldn't have to be you, but, honestly, I couldn't imagine anyone else doing it.'

'Fuck, Sato-kun,' was Julia's reaction. 'Yoshi! Put some damn liquor into that chocolate thing of yours! I don't care if it's three in the afternoon.'

'Yeah, give us some liquor, Yoshi!' Kon yelled, too.

'It's Yoshi-san, to you,' he replied to Kon.

'Oh, right, san, I mean, Yoshi-san, yes, I'm sorry, Yoshi-san! Could you please give us some liquor, Yoshi-san, please?'

We all laughed again, and this time I couldn't hide it either. Kon was just being... well, Kon.

'What kind of liquor would you like?' Yoshi-san asked, smiling.

'Whatever you recommend,' Kon said. 'I can drink anything. Everything.'

'All right, I'll figure something out, then,' Yoshi smiled again.

'Back to the Jacks,' I said. 'We decided to take care of them, especially Little Jack, and we need your help.'

'You can count on me, Sato-kun! You know that! And we will save Yuki-chan!'

'Oh, I remember now!' Julia said. 'You're the guy who held Yuki hostage over at Lulu's!'

'Well... y-yes, that was me, indeed, and... I'm really sorry for all the commotion,' Kon replied, lowering his head like a shy little puppy. 'I was just trying to protect her.'

'By pointing a gun at her?' Julia asked.

'N-No... by... by...'

'It's ok, you two,' I intervened. 'Julia, he's all right, I can vouch for him. Don't push him. Kon is a good man with a funny nature and odd habits, but... he's good.'

'Ok-ok,' Julia raised her hands in surrender.

'Thank you, Sato-kun,' Kon said.

'Ok. So, yes, we will save Yuki-chan and all the other girls from Little Jack. Including Kiki.'

'Who's Kiki?' Kon asked.

'His niece,' Julia told him. 'At least, that's what she thinks.'

'She doesn't, anymore,' I said.

'So, you told her, finally?' Julia asked.

I nodded.

'I see. But, wait! What does she have to do with Little Jack?! Don't tell me she's…'

It was my turn to lower my head like a puppy.

'Fuck… She's not even eighteen, right?' Julia asked.

'No.'

'How the hell did she end up there?'

'I don't know, but, I guess, it's partly my fault,' I said.

'You bet it is,' Julia scolded me. 'You should've taken better care of her.'

'It is what it is,' I said. 'Let's focus on making things right. Are you all in?'

'Of course, we are,' Julia said. Everyone else nodded.

'Ok, then. Thanks.'

'So, what's the plan?' Yoshi-san asked.

We discussed our little plan in detail. Kon was surprised to hear about Ren's ability, but Julia and Yoshi-san weren't. I wouldn't say they were all one hundred percent convinced and optimistic, but we couldn't come up with anything better. The plan was first to get Little Jack and take him to Yoshi's place, where Ren would remove from his mind everything related to our family and his dealings within the family. She'd also try to remove all the sexual deviances and perverted thoughts he might have in there. A friend of Yoshi's would then arrive to collect Little Jack and take him to a small village up north in Aomori. As Ren would need to rest up, we'd wait until the evening to get to Captain Jack. Ren would then remove all his memories of Little Jack, practically severing the bond between the two of them forever. The disappearance of Little Jack would create a commotion within the sex branch of our family, which we would then use to initiate reform. I planned to ask for Kobayashi-san's help in managing this reform internally.

The plan had several obstacles and difficulties down the road, but the biggest and most immediate ones were getting to Little Jack and then Captain Jack without raising any suspicion. They were both very cautious and well-guarded.

After we finished discussing our plan, Yoshi-san served us some sandwiches with tomato and mozzarella. They were good. Simple, light, but tasty. We were all starving, so we jumped at them, eating like happy little dogs.

After we finished eating, I looked at Julia, and our eyes met.

'Julia.'

'Yeah?'

'Let's have a cigarette outside.'

'I don't feel like smoking right now,' she said.

'Please,' I asked, suggesting with my eyes that I wanted to discuss something in private.

'Oh, right, ok.'

'Guys, please excuse us,' I told the rest of them. 'Julia and I will go outside for a smoke. We'll be back in a minute.'

The others nodded and continued discussing Yoshi-san's time and experiences over in the US.

'Let's go,' I told Julia.

We stood up and went outside. I offered Julia a cigarette and lit both hers and mine. We leaned against the railing of the stairs leading down to the street and filled our lungs with nicotine a few times before starting the conversation.

'Look,' I began, struggling a bit to find the right words. 'I really don't know how this whole thing will play out, and... you know me... I'm not that good of an uncle.'

Julia continued smoking, and she was staring at the street below us. We saw a dealer selling hashish to three young girls.

'So... what I'm trying to say...'

'...Is that you'd like me to take care of her, right?' Julia asked, puffing out smoke.

'Yes. Right.'

One of the girls down on the street gave the dealer some cash, and in return, he handed her a small plastic bag with the stuff. The other two girls were visibly on edge and impatient, but the one dealing with the dealer seemed confident and relaxed. All three were wearing school uniforms, and they looked like the uniforms from one of the more elite Tokyo high schools.

'There's an infinite number of moments that can derail someone's life,' Julia said, finishing off her cigarette and throwing it down to the street. 'And most of the time it's impossible to trace everything back and pinpoint that specific moment. It can be as subtle and harmless as witnessing something on the street, or hearing something from a friend, or seeing something on television. It can be anything, really. I don't know how parents cope with the responsibility. And the helplessness.'

'Maybe it's something they learn on the fly,' I said.

'Maybe. Or it's the feelings they have for their children.'

'That, too.'

I stubbed my cigarette and threw it over the railing, too. It fell close to the dealer, who looked up. He stared at us for a while, murmuring something, then walked away.

'Ok,' Julia said.

'Thanks.'

'And what about her mother?'

'She doesn't have much left. Probably days. If she's even alive.'

'I see,' Julia said. 'Let's go inside. It's a bit chilly today.'

The trenches of Gallipoli

We decided that our best chance at snatching Little Jack was during his morning walk with his dog. He owned a French bulldog named Hulk. After Hulk Hogan. It was a stupid dog, really. Just like Little Jack. He'd take Hulk for a walk every morning around seven, going up and down the streets of Azabu. Only his number-one bodyguard accompanied him for these walks. We agreed to strike as early as the next morning.

I spent the rest of the afternoon with Ren, helping with her shopping, and in the evening, she invited me to have dinner with her. We went to a small restaurant in Meguro, which served fusion dishes, mixing Japanese and French cuisine. Apparently, it was a famous restaurant and you had to book a table a month in advance. But Ren was a regular there, so she managed to get us a small table in the corner.

***

The only other time I had ever gone to a fancy restaurant was for my eighteenth birthday. Boss Yamaguchi took me to a sushi place somewhere in Roppongi, along with Kobayashi-san, and the three of us were the only guests there for the night. I remember feeling a bit awkward and tense about the whole thing as I was not used to spending so much money on food. Even if it wasn't me spending the money, I still felt strange about it. I think Kobayashi-san sensed it, so he told me something like: 'Relax, boy. Enjoy yourself. This is *your* evening.'

The boss just glanced at me out of the corner of his eye. Then, he went on to order a bottle of sake. I didn't yet know how to appreciate a drink, but when we toasted and took our first sips, I immediately noticed how different the sake was compared to all the rubbish sake

I had been drinking until then. Not that I was a big drinker or anything at that age, but I had had a sip, even a glass here and there. Even in my teens I somehow fancied strong drinks like whisky and cognac. Not that much for the alcohol in them, but rather the chilled and relaxed state of mind I felt after each sip. You can't just gulp down the entire glass in a matter of seconds – you have to take one step at a time with these drinks, and even then, they don't allow you to send them down your throat as quickly as possible. They make you savor them in your mouth for long seconds, and they engage all your senses. Otherwise, there's no point, and they all taste like rubbish.

So, when we had our first cup of sake, I sensed that the boss was inspecting me. He was looking at my facial expressions, my eyes, my mouth, my gestures. He was curious about my reactions. His eyes had their usual sharpness and intensity, but I also saw a small trace of tenderness somewhere deep down, and it surprised me.

'How do you like your drink?' he asked.

I swallowed the sake I had in my mouth and I told him: 'It's really good. I've had sake before, but this is different. It tastes a bit sweet but strong. And mature, I guess.'

The boss nodded, and Kobayashi-san allowed himself a barely visible smile.

'Good,' boss Yamaguchi said. 'You're not hopeless.'

Kobayashi-san nudged me a little, pointing at the bottle, so I took it and poured another round for all of us. Boss Yamaguchi raised his cup and said:

'Boy, you've become an adult. From now on, you shall take full responsibility for how you live your life. Be loyal to what you believe in, and trust only yourself. Kanpai!'

We raised our cups and drank the sake. I felt it a bit in my head, as I was not used to drinking, and my stomach was empty.

While I was fighting the effects of the alcohol, I also began having thoughts about boss Yamaguchi's words. They seemed perfectly normal and wise at first, like a typical message any adult would give to someone younger. What felt out of the ordinary was the fact that they had come from him. The big boss of a crime organization, where loyalty to the family and the senior members was way above anything else, and where very little room was allowed for any trace of individualism. Why would he say that I should be loyal to my own beliefs instead of his and those of the family? Why should I trust only myself instead of the members of our family?

I wanted to ask him these questions, and the sake had loosened me up enough to give me a bit of courage, but I still hesitated, and when I was just about to open my mouth, our food arrived.

'Oh, finally! Our dinner! Boy, you'll like this very much. This is the best sushi in town. Isn't that right, Nakata-san?' the boss asked the elderly owner and the chef of the small restaurant.

'I'm humbled to hear your words of praise, Yamaguchi-sensei,' Nakata-san said, bowing very deep.

'Oh, please, no need for such formalities. We're among friends tonight,' the boss told him. 'But, tell me, how are you doing, my old friend?'

'Very well, thank you. My health is still strong, and the restaurant is going fine as well. Although I have to admit, there is something, which has been bothering me for a while now.'

'What is it, Nakata-san?'

'It's my grandson. He's... lost, I would say. I feel he is in bad company, and he needs a strong hand to give him direction. Otherwise, he'll just stay as useless and lost and selfish as he is today,' Nakata-san told us. 'I apologize for using such strong words and bothering you with my problems.'

'No-no, not at all,' boss Yamaguchi told him.

'Yamaguchi-sensei, if I may, and I know this is too much to ask for, but... could you maybe take him in?' Nakata-san asked. 'Could he become a member of your family?'

Boss Yamaguchi's expression immediately took on its usual seriousness.

'Let me repeat, just to be sure I understand correctly: you would like your grandson to become a member of my family. Is that right?'

'Yes, sensei, that's right.'

'And you're saying this knowing very well there's no way back for him after that.'

Nakata-san nodded.

The boss looked at me, and I understood he wanted another drink. I filled his little cup with another round of sake, and he drank it.

'You know, people often think families are there to protect, to support, to give and provide, and they expect all of this, but they forget about contributing something themselves, too. Over the years, I've seen many young men join our ranks with enthusiasm and confidence, earn a name for themselves, even a position within the family, to then for whatever reason forget about their duties and obligations, about what is expected of them and where they've come from. I have a name for them: "shit". Pieces of shit. And like real shit, some are strong and firm in being a piece of shit, and they are more difficult to flush down, while others are soft and weak and easy to dispose of.'

The boss paused for a second, looking straight into old Nakata-san's eyes. The air froze around us.

'I'll give your grandson a chance. But be aware, mistakes are costly in our family, and I won't hesitate to punish him if that's what's best for the family.'

'I understand,' Nakata-san told him.

'All right, then. Send him over to Kobayashi-san. You two can discuss the details after dinner,' the boss said.

'Thank you, sensei.' Nakata-san bowed deep and stayed like that for a couple of seconds.

I never liked seeing old men bow so deep in front of younger men, and I never liked the formalities most people used in front of the boss. It always made me feel awkward. Grown-up, mature men were treating him like he was a god or something – they feared him, they put their lives in his hands. Why? Why would any person subjugate themselves to such a degree to another person? Being loyal is one thing, but to accept another person's complete authority over you and your life? Or to think you were somehow less than him?

I admit, the boss had this larger-than-life aura around him and immense charisma. Most of the time, it was enough for him to look at you, and you'd feel you had no other choice but to tuck your tail in between your legs and follow him blindly. But, looking at him from a distance, he was just like the rest of us. Another person, another human being. One out of seven billion.

'Now, let's eat this delicious food, shall we?' boss Yamaguchi said, putting a sushi roll in his mouth. 'Mmmm, amazing! It's so fresh!'

'The fish was still swimming two hours ago,' Nakata-san told us.

'Exquisite! This is how sushi should taste!'

I began to eat too, and it really was amazing. Most of the time, I just ate sushi from supermarkets or cheap restaurants in Shinjuku, so the new flavors felt like a whole new world.

We didn't talk that much during the dinner, but we enjoyed our food, and I'd say all three of us had a good time, each in his own way. Then, towards the end of the dinner, I finally asked what I had been wanting to ask since boss Yamaguchi's toast:

'Boss, can I ask you something?'

'Sure, go ahead,' he said.

'Earlier, you told me I should be loyal to what I believe in, and I should trust only myself.'

Kobayashi-san stopped eating and looked at me.

'Yes,' the boss said.

'What did you mean by that?' I asked.

'I meant what I said. Those are simple words, difficult to misunderstand.'

'Yes, I know, but still... I mean, shouldn't I be loyal to you and the family? Shouldn't I trust the members of our family?'

'Of course, you should,' he replied. 'That is, if you want to be a part of the family. That's what families are about. We trust each other. But we are not bound by blood. Our family is special because you're not born into it, but rather you choose to belong to it, and the family chooses to accept you. There is choice. But once you've chosen and you've been welcomed in, the only way this can work is through loyalty and trust.'

'So, does it mean I can leave the family if I choose so?'

'You're free to choose the life you want to live, boy. Your decisions are your own. And in making those decisions, as I said, you should be loyal to yourself and trust only yourself. Don't forget, though,' the boss raised his finger, 'every decision has its consequences. Never forget about the consequences.'

***

As Ren and I were waiting for our food to arrive, I remembered my eighteenth birthday and the dinner with the boss and Kobayashi-san. It felt as it had happened only a couple of days ago.

'What's on your mind?' Ren asked me.

'Nothing.'

'Come on, tell me,' she insisted. 'I know you well enough by now to know you're thinking about something.'

'I just... remembered a conversation I had with your father.'

'Oh, I see. So, what was it about?'

'About... choice, I guess.'

'Hm.'

'Yeah. That was my reaction too, back then. And might still be today.'

'Well, he never gave *me* any choice,' Ren said. I looked into her eyes, and she turned away. 'But, as you were saying a few days ago, I never really gave myself a choice either.'

'I didn't mean to offend you,' I said.

'You didn't. And sorry for yelling at you and being a bitch.'

'It's ok.'

'You were right. I could've escaped, I could've created a new life for myself, a new identity, a new everything. But I didn't.'

'Neither did I.'

'At least I'm not the only loser at the table,' she said with a smile.

'You're definitely not,' I smiled back.

'But, you know, fuck them.'

'Fuck who?'

'Everyone who throws wisdom at you, and life-coaching bullshit like it was candy you could just suck at or swallow.'

'Because life is not candy, right?'

'Right! Life is not candy! That's the wisest thing I've heard in years!'

'Maybe I should become a life-coach, then,' I smiled.

'A killer turned life-coach. I can already see the headlines. You'd be an instant Instagram star, Sato-kun.'

'What's Instagram?' I asked.

'Never mind,' she smiled with a dismissive wave of her hand.

Our eyes met for a second, and it felt as if there were an invisible string connecting her eyes to mine. I wanted the string to become shorter.

'You know... I'm glad you became my bodyguard,' she said, looking away.

'Me too.'

***

We were due to meet at six in the morning in Azabu. After our dinner, I escorted Ren back to her home, and I went to my apartment to get some rest. I took a shower and went to bed relatively early, but I couldn't sleep. There were too many thoughts racing through my mind. I kept staring at the ceiling and thinking about Ren, Kon, Julia, Kiki, the boss, Kobayashi-san, and then all kinds of images from my life, both from the distant past and as recent as an hour ago, got mixed in an endless stream of thought.

I wondered what the Sea of Thought might have looked like. And I wondered how it might have felt for Ren to connect to it. I closed my eyes and I saw an image of a fish, the color of Ren's green eyes, swimming against the current. The fish was full of determination, swimming towards something, a goal, but I wasn't sure the fish knew what the goal was. Yet, it didn't stop for a second to hesitate and just kept swimming. Small bubbles would form around its body, and each bubble would contain a word, a color, a scent, a feeling, or something else. But the fish didn't care much about any of the bubbles or what was inside them. It just continued speeding towards the undefined target.

I knew I had no chance of falling asleep, so I opened my eyes, dressed up, wrapped "Shiro" in a soft bag, hung it across my back, and went outside.

It was midnight, and the streets around my apartment were empty and quiet. A thick layer of clouds covered the sky, and with all the city lights reflecting back from the surface of the clouds, the night was unusually bright.

I had plenty of time, so I decided to walk from my apartment in Daikanyama, all the way to our meeting point in Azabu. It wasn't far. Maybe a bit more than an hour on foot. But it depends on how much one likes to walk. I like it a lot. Especially at night.

I like the steep, winding streets of Daikanyama, so I took my time getting down to Shibuya. I'd start going down one street, but then I'd see a small alley and change direction. There were always new corners, new places to explore, and it felt good just to wander, without any specific route in mind.

On one corner, I stopped and looked up. I saw a small balcony and, on it, a young woman leaning against the handrail. She was wearing a nightgown and was smoking a cigarette. She noticed me, and we looked at each other. We didn't exchange any words, gestures, or anything, and yet, we still connected. It was this moment of two people walking their own paths, never having seen each other, and probably never to meet again, but in this particular place, and in this particular moment in time our lives crossed, and in a single look which lasted only a few seconds, we kind of acknowledged each other's struggles, each other's dreams, each other's feelings. It was all happening somewhere deep down in our subconsciousness, but I could feel it, and I knew she felt it, too. And it was a good feeling. A feeling of reassurance, of comfort. A feeling telling me that I wasn't alone in this world. It's hard to say why such a strong feeling would come from such a mundane and trivial thing like meeting the gaze of a random person on a random night, but I didn't bother trying to understand it.

I continued my descent to Shibuya. The moment I had had with the stranger on the balcony had brought me peace of mind, so now I was walking with complete calmness. My feet felt light, and my body felt like all its pieces were in the right place and moving in full synch and coordination. Every step I took felt like a step in the right direction, and everything around me felt like it had its purpose, it was doing its job, and we all – the world and I – were doing just fine.

I was about to leave the silent streets of Daikanyama and turn onto a livelier street belonging to Shibuya when I saw a stray dog lingering around the entrance of a convenience store. It was rather small, but it didn't look like any particular breed of dog I knew. I went a bit closer. The dog was a male, and he had a rather young face, but he wasn't a puppy anymore. My guess was around two or three years old. He seemed shy, but he wasn't afraid. I bent down, and I extended my arm towards him. He took a few steps in my direction, trying to smell if there was food in my hand, but as soon as he realized I had none, he backed away. I wouldn't say he was malnourished, but he definitely needed food.

I went into the convenience store, and I bought a small can of dog food and a pack of dried beef jerky. When I went outside again, the dog was still there, waiting. He had a smart look in his eyes, and I knew that he knew I was going to give him food. He sat down and looked me straight in the eye. I kneeled, holding a strip of beef jerky in my right hand. I opened my hand, showing him the food. He came closer, sniffed around a bit, but again backed off. He was a bit scared after all, so I put the strip of jerky on the ground. I tried being motionless and not making gestures that might confuse him. He sniffed at the food again and finally took it. He immediately began wagging his tail, and he looked like the happiest dog ever. The strip of jerky was gone in a matter of seconds. I took another one from the pack and again tried feeding him from my hand. He came closer than he had before, but he still wouldn't take it straight from me. I put it on the ground again and let him have it on his own terms. I then put the pack away, and I opened the canned food. I used my finger to remove everything from the can and slide it onto the ground, and I left it there for him. I then took a couple of steps back and let him eat.

As I was watching him eat, I tried guessing what different breeds he was a mix of. I saw a little dachshund in him due to his rather lengthy body, but his legs were a bit longer and stronger. He had short, dark brown hair, but his feet were white, with small, light-brown dots resembling the looks of a pointer. His face, however, was that of a terrier. His ears were the funniest part. They reminded me of Yoda from Star Wars.

'Hey, Yoda. I'm leaving now, ok? I hope you'll get by somehow. Good luck, boy,' I told him, and I turned around and left.

In Shibuya, I didn't want to take the crowded streets, so I tried finding my way through the little alleys. I remembered there was an arthouse cinema close by, where I used to go a lot in the past, especially in my teens and my twenties. I decided I'd go and check it out, just out of curiosity and nostalgia.

When I got there, I saw a dozen young people on the street in front of the cinema, smoking and drinking beer. The gates to the place were open, and the lights were on. I went a bit closer to have a look. There was a large poster behind a glass window: "Nights of Mel. Watch Mel Gibson's greatest movies over three nights. Only in your favorite cinema, the Red Velvet."

I looked at the schedule. They had just finished screening the first Mad Max movie, and Gallipoli was up next. It was due to start at one in the morning. I checked my watch, and it showed twenty minutes to one.

I turned around and I saw two girls in their twenties standing right behind me and chatting. One of them had long, red hair and freckles on her cheeks and her nose. She looked like she was French or maybe from an English-speaking country.

'Excuse me,' I said to the red-haired girl, in English.

'Yes?'

'Is there a film festival in the cinema?'

'Yeah! They are showing Mel Gibson movies! Isn't that awesome?! Who would've thought that I'd be watching old Mel flicks in Tokyo in the middle of the night?!'

She was definitely not French. My guess was Australian, based on her accent.

'Yeah, Tokyo can surprise you if you let it,' I said with a smile.

'Yeah. It can, right? How sweet. I've been here only a couple of months, but I'm already in love with the city. It's the best place in the world.'

'Well, I've never been abroad, so I can't make comparisons, but I hear that a lot.'

'You do, right? Sweet! So, want to watch a movie? Gallipoli is next. Have you seen it?'

'No, I haven't. I've heard about it, but I never got to see it.'

'Well, now's the time, then! It's your lucky day! Or night, I suppose. Come, join us! You'll love it!'

'Have you seen it?

'Of course! Three or four times, I think. I'm Australian, you know,' she said with a smile, flashing her perfect, white teeth.

'Ok, I might then.'

'Great! Go, buy a ticket, and see you inside. There's no seating order, so you can sit with us.'

'Perfect, thanks.'

'No worries, mate. By the way, my name is Mary, and this is my friend, Aya. She's local.'

'Pleased to meet you,' Aya told me, bowing.

'Pleased to meet you, too,' I said. 'My name is Sato.'

'Sato! Great! Pleased to meet you, Sato. I hope you'll enjoy the movie.'

'Thanks. I'll go and buy a ticket, then.'

'See you inside.'

I bought a ticket and a Coke at the snack bar. I also got myself a Snickers chocolate bar. What an American way of spending time.

The girls caught up with me near the entrance to the screening room. We went inside and took seats near the center of the seventh row.

'You'd love it even more if you were a girl, Sato. Mel was gorgeous back then. You'd probably be in love with him. Although you might be anyway. You never know. I mean, boys can fall in love with Mel, too,' she said, smiling and sipping Coke.

'Yeah, well, I probably won't fall in love with him,' I said, smiling.

'Oh, cool. Is that because... you're already in love with someone?' she asked.

I saw her friend, Aya, blush as if the question had been addressed to her.

'I see you're not afraid to ask personal questions,' I said, still smiling.

'Well, I'm not Japanese, right? I'm Australian. We just ask stuff like that.'

'I see.'

'You haven't answered my question yet.'

'No, I haven't.'

'And will you? I mean, you don't have to. I don't want to press you, but... you know.'

'What?'

'Well, I'm just curious, that's all.'

'I see. Let's do the following, then. If I like the movie, irrespective of me falling in love with Mel or not, I'll tell you after the film. If the movie sucks, however, I'll keep it to myself.'

'Deal,' she said, and we shook hands. 'But no cheating, ok? You'll have to be honest.'

'I will,' I said. 'I promise.'

'Sweet.'

It had been more than a year since I had last gone to the cinema, and it was a great feeling. I didn't even realize how much I missed it. I settled in my seat, had a bite of my Snickers and a sip of Coke, and soon the lights went out and the movie began.

I watched the movie with Mary's question in the back of my head. It was there from the first moment, the first scene of the film, and it stayed with me until the end. For most of the time, it stayed tucked away and hidden, crawling out of the shadows here and there, gently touching the surface of my emotions. But on two occasions, the question burst out, trampling all over my soul, with no regard for my feelings. It was the two scenes of the movie where Jean Michel Jarre's Oxygene played in the background, with Mel running. First, across the desert, then, in the trenches. Both times my heart opened as if someone had sliced it open with a sword, and I felt this endless stream of hot blood gush out and form a huge, red sea within my body. My heart then slowly began to sink, drowning, asking for help, but to no avail; screaming, but to no avail. I felt this vast emptiness and solitude inside, like a desert, and I felt hopeless. Then, out of nowhere, a voice appeared, and an image, a face, with deep eyes, green eyes. And my heart swam up and exhaled.

After the final scene of the movie, I remained in my seat, motionless, staring but not looking at anything specific. I didn't even realize what was going on around me – I didn't see the end credits on the screen or the crowd leaving or the lights being turned on again. I just sat there.

At some point, I felt someone tapping my shoulder. I turned my head and I saw Mary.

'We have to leave. They're closing. Everyone's already left.' Her voice was soft and tender.

'I'm coming,' I said.

We walked out in silence. The street was empty, only Aya was there, waiting for Mary.

I turned to Mary:

'Your question...' I began, but I couldn't finish the sentence.

'It's ok,' she said, softly touching my left arm. 'I already know the answer.'

'Thank you for inviting me to watch the movie.'

She smiled and let go of my arm: 'Good luck.'

I watched them leave, and then I turned around to go in the opposite direction. I was just about to take the first step when I suddenly stopped.

'Yoda. You're here.'

Little Jack's little fingers

It felt good just to walk the dark and mostly empty streets of Tokyo alone after such a powerful movie like Gallipoli. I walked slowly, very slowly, avoiding people, avoiding the obvious route, trying to find streets and alleys I had never been down before. To make it even more melodramatic, I plugged my earbuds into my phone and listened to Dustin O'Halloran's soft piano music throughout my stroll.

I felt as if I were in a movie or a dream. I felt as if the buildings around me, the vending machines on the streets, the neon signs, and the parking cars were not real. I was not even sure *I* was real. I felt a bit like Joaquin Phoenix in the movie "Her" and a bit like Bill Murray in "Lost in translation". I remembered images from these films, and I remembered the last scene of Gallipoli. And then I remembered I had no parents, I remembered faces from the orphanages I had lived in, I remembered homeless people from my time on the streets, I remembered how it felt to be hungry, and how it felt to be cold at night, shivering, being afraid to fall asleep, or unable to fall asleep, and wishing I'd die.

It's easy to see the bad in people. To condemn their actions, to belittle them, to disapprove. And it's difficult to see beyond the surface. If I take the boss, for example, to most people, he'd be a mean and ruthless bully. The scum of the Earth. But to me, he was the family I'd never had. He had helped me forget about my wish to die, or at least he had helped me chase it away and make it hide in a deep, dark corner of my soul. I knew I'd never be able to eradicate the feelings and memories of my past completely, and that they'd resurface from time to time, like during my walk to Azabu, but I also knew I was safe. I knew they couldn't harm me anymore. Because I was stronger than them. And I had the boss to thank for that. And a couple of other people. People who were on the margins of society. People for whom there was no place in the daylight, only in the darkness of the night.

That's one of the reasons I never liked watching television, reading newspapers, or surfing the internet. People were constantly judging other people, explaining their motivations, dissecting their actions. "Based on what?" I'd ask myself. 'How can someone be so sure in judging another person?' I asked Yoda, turning around to look at him and raising my hands.

Yes, Yoda had been following me all along. He'd stay a bit further back, but whenever I turned around, he was there, looking at me with his innocent eyes and raising his Yoda-like ears.

'You're still here?' I asked him. 'So, what do you think, my friend? Why are we so judgmental? We judge you dogs, too, you know. We pretend to know why you're doing this or doing that, and we pretend to understand your nature. We start our relationship with you guys with the assumption of superiority and authority. It's fucked up, right? You don't even have a chance of equal treatment. You don't have a chance of living your life on your own terms. Unless you live on the streets as you do. But even then, if you're in a city, you depend on us humans – the waste we produce; the kindness we show; and in some cases, the brutality, the anger, the aggression, and all kinds of other stuff you really shouldn't have to deal with, yet you often end up suffering because of it all. How do you cope, boy?'

Yoda kept staring at me and waiting for me to do something.

'Ok, let's go,' I said.

We arrived in Azabu half an hour earlier than the agreed time, so I found a bench and sat down. Yoda sat on the ground, a couple of feet away.

Soon, Julia appeared, and she sat next to me.

'Hey, Sato. How's life?'

'I don't know. The usual, I guess.'

'I couldn't sleep,' she said.

'Me neither. I walked here. And I went to the cinema.'

'The cinema? In the night?'

'Yeah, crazy, right?'

'And what did you see?'

'An old Mel Gibson movie. Gallipoli.'

'Oh, I like that guy. He used to be quite a heartthrob back in the day. But I've never heard of that movie.'

'It's one of his early films. Beginning of the eighties, I think.'

'I see.'

'It's his eyes, you know,' I told her.

'What do you mean?'

'You girls fall for his eyes.'

'Those two sapphires?' she asked. 'I bet we do.'

'But you get it all wrong. It's not the color or the glow. It's not what's on the surface, but what's below.'

I looked at Yoda. He was lying on the ground and watching us.

'If you look deep into a person's eyes you can sometimes see behind the curtains. It depends, of course, how open you are, and how much those eyes are revealing, but it's possible.'

'So, did you manage to get a peek behind Mel's curtains?'

I nodded.

'And what did you see?'

'A vast, empty desert, and an infinite ocean licking its shores from all sides. There was a man in the middle of the desert, sitting on a rock, looking into the distance. He craved water, but he was hesitant. He didn't know whether to start walking or to wait for the rain to fall. So he kept sitting on the rock and waiting.'

'I can relate to that,' Julia said, lighting a cigarette.

I didn't say anything. I just kept looking at Yoda, looking into his eyes.

'Is that your dog?' Julia asked.

'I don't know.'

'What do you mean, you don't know?'

'He's been following me from Daikanyama.'

'He's your dog, then.'

I put my hand in my pocket and held the hundred-yen coin. 'I guess, he is,' I replied.

A few minutes later, Ren arrived, bringing us coffee and fresh pastries. Soon, Kon arrived too, driving a big, white van.

We all got into the back of the van and discussed our plan one more time while eating and drinking what Ren had brought us. Yoda stayed outside at first, but Julia kept insisting I open the door and let him in, which I did, in the end. He was hesitant at first, but then I remembered I still had some beef jerky in my pocket, so I lay a strip on the floor of the van. He came closer, had a few sniffs, then finally jumped in. I closed the door back while he was eating, but he wasn't scared. He looked at the door, then at all of us, but I gave him another strip of beef, and he seemed more than happy to stay with us.

'He's cute,' Ren said, leaning closer to caress him. He sniffed her hand, gave her a lick, then continued munching on the jerky.

Kon leaned closer too, raising his hand over Yoda's head, but the dog perceived it as a threat and let out a bark. It took Kon by surprise and he fell back.

We all laughed, and Julia told him: 'Watch out, Kon, he'll take a bite out of your juicy buttocks.'

'Th-That's no laughing matter, you all! This animal is dangerous! He might even kill us! Grab us by our throats and crush our aortas and turn this nice little breakfast into a bloodbath!'

'He's not a wolf, Kon,' Ren said, caressing Yoda and calming him down. 'Just don't raise your hand above his head. Try caressing him behind his ear. Like this,' she showed him.

Kon leaned closer again and tried imitating Ren. Yoda let him do it.

'I knew he was not a wolf,' Kon said after a while.

We all laughed again.

***

We first spotted Hulk, the French bulldog, sniffing around and trying to find a spot to pee. Little Jack followed a bit further behind, and his bodyguard still a bit further back. Ren and Yoda were right next to our van – Ren was kneeling and caressing him. Yoda was not part of our original plan, but he came in handy. When Hulk spotted Yoda, he immediately went over, and Ren seized the opportunity to caress Hulk and try to befriend him. At the same time, Julia approached Little Jack's bodyguard. She asked him for a cigarette, using her charm and sexual energy and successfully diverting his attention. A couple of seconds later, Little Jack approached Ren too, and he didn't recognize her, as she was wearing her blue wig and sunglasses. She waited for Little Jack to make a careless move, which he did when he kneeled to pat Yoda on his head. Ren seized the opportunity and stuck a syringe in his neck, injecting an extremely strong tranquilizer into his blood. He fell to the ground in an instant, and I quickly jumped out of the van to pick him up and put him in the back. Ren and Yoda jumped in, then I gave the sign to Kon and he drove away as fast as he could. When Julia saw us leave out of the corner of her eye, she politely thanked the bodyguard for the cigarette and left. The bodyguard and Hulk were left standing there in the empty, early morning street of Azabu, with no clue of what had just happened.

***

'So, what now? What happens next? What should I do?' Kon asked, walking up and down the room while biting off his fingernails and spitting them on the floor.

'Relax, Kon,' I told him. 'Just calm down, ok?'

'Ok-ok, I'm calm, I'm relaxed, see?' He shook his hands in the air. 'But what happens next? I want to know.'

'Ren happens next,' Julia told him. 'Have another drink and sit down, for Christ's sake. Here,' she said, offering him a glass of rum.

Kon took the glass, drank it in one shot, and sat on a chair. 'I hate rum,' he said.

'I bet you do,' Julia replied. 'You're welcome.'

'Ok, keep quiet, everyone,' Ren told us. 'I'm starting.'

Little Jack was lying on the floor, unconscious. Ren was kneeling next to him, and she slowly bent over his head and touched his temples with her fingers. Soon, a faint, green light appeared, and it gradually became stronger and more vivid.

I was standing, leaning against the door, with both my hands in my pockets. I held my hundred-yen coin between my fingers. I was squeezing it quite hard. My hands were sweating, and my breathing was much heavier than usual.

I looked at the others. Everyone was watching Ren as if she were a magician performing a magic trick. Kon was still biting his fingernails, Julia kept pouring herself drinks, and Yoshi just stood there motionless, with his arms crossed. There was heaviness in the air and a buzzing sound that I had not heard during previous extractions. It appeared to come from the green light around Little Jack's head. As if each thought, idea, and memory Ren was removing burned up and evaporated into thin air after coming into contact with the outside world. As if both the Sea of Thought and our minds were protected by an invisible forcefield, but once a thought was forced to cross this boundary, it disintegrated. And it seemed as if Ren were indeed making Little Jack's thoughts cross this boundary.

'A symphony of dying thoughts,' Yoshi said.

I looked at him, then at Ren and her green light. The buzzing went on and on. "A Symphony of dying thoughts," I repeated to myself. It *did* have a rhythm. And a flow. And it made me feel as if the world were losing shades of its color.

'They are not dying,' Julia said. 'She is just sending them back to the Sea of Thought.'

'I'm not so sure about that,' Yoshi replied. 'I think she's destroying them forever.'

'Is she even capable of such a thing?' Julia asked, turning to me.

I had no clue. I looked at her, then at Ren again, holding my coin even tighter.

'Fuck,' Julia said, covering her face with her hand.

***

When Ren was done with Little Jack and the green light had disappeared along with the weird sound, a heavy silence descended upon the room. Ren remained on her knees, with her hands resting in her lap. Her eyes were wide open and glowing green. She looked like she was looking far into the distance, way beyond the boundaries of our world. I approached her and kneeled next to her, putting one hand on her shoulder. She didn't react. I tried shaking her gently and squeezing her shoulder a bit, but she still didn't react.

I looked at the others and just showed them with my hands to take Little Jack away. Yoshi grabbed him under his arms, Julia and Kon took one leg each, and they carried him into the neighboring room. They were meant to tie him to a chair and let him come to his senses so that we could test to see if Ren had been successful.

'I'll be with you soon. Just give me a couple of minutes,' I told them.

I was left alone with Ren. I slid over to kneel in front of her, looking into her eyes. She was still not responsive.

We were in one of Yoshi's rooms, in his apartment. It was a small guest room with very little furniture. He had a couch in one corner, a small cupboard with an empty vase on top, and that was it. Not even a painting, a poster, or a photo on the walls.

I reached over and held Ren's hands for a while. They were warm. Almost burning. I wanted to say something, but nothing came to mind. I just kept staring at her face. She wouldn't even blink, and her eyes were still glowing green. The more time I spent analyzing and memorizing each and every detail of her face, the more I found her beautiful. Perfect. Yes, the word "perfect" crept into my mind, and I could feel it grow bigger and stronger as the seconds went by. The idea must have used the currents of the Sea of Thought to swim to me, and it seemed to have found a safe and cozy place inside my head to nest there permanently.

I used to hate the word "perfect". I had always felt it was meant to describe things, places, people, and moments that were out of my reach. I used to think it didn't belong in my world. Yet there it was now. Right in the middle of my world. And I didn't really know what to do with it.

I waved my hand in front of Ren's eyes, but she still didn't respond. But she was definitely looking at something, seeing something, and it intrigued me. I wanted to see the same things she was seeing. I wanted to know what had caught her attention, and how the world she was in looked. I wanted to be with her.

I turned around to try and follow her gaze. Her eyes were set at the window. She was looking right through it, so I did the same.

I saw a huge billboard on the building on the opposite side of the street. It was an ad with Beat Takeshi. He was staring right back at us, in black and white, holding a glass of whisky. Only the drink had color – a golden brown with a dash of deep, dark orange.

I knew Kitano "Beat" Takeshi a little, as he was a very good friend of boss Yamaguchi's. They shared a passion for sumo wrestling. Every two months, on the final day of the ongoing tournament, they'd close themselves up either at boss Yamaguchi's or Kitano-san's home to watch the action on television, and they'd bet some money throughout the day. Not much, really, just something to make the matches even more enjoyable. In their younger days, they had gone to see the fights live, especially when the tournament was held in Tokyo, and I'd sometimes accompany them. I guess, as they grew older, they had gotten less enthusiastic about the crowds. Nowadays, they had much more fun watching everything on a big screen, from the comfort of their sofas, with their favorite food and drinks. They'd usually order pizza or Mexican food, and they'd drink a bottle or two of wine. The food was always on the house, and whoever came as a guest had to bring the wine. Both made sure to find and bring the most amazing wine you can find in Tokyo. I'd sometimes run errands for the boss to collect his wine orders from various little wine shops around town. His favorite was a store in Odaiba which also functioned as a Spanish tapas bar. They always had an amazing selection in their makeshift faux cellar.

Anyhow, Beat Takeshi was now staring at us with a glass of whisky in his hand. I thought Ren was looking into his eyes, at first. Kitano-san had very interesting eyes. Most of the time, he'd close his curtains completely and no one could see inside him. But every now and then, when he was in the right mood, he'd let people have a peek. Only people he trusted, of course. And for some reason, I was one of them, even though we barely knew each other. Maybe it was just the trust he had in the boss, and the trust the boss had in me. But he'd let me have a look, from time to time. And what I'd find was a big, white room with a small, dark corner. And Kitano-san would always sit in the dark corner, calm, with his eyes closed, drinking tea. And he wouldn't move. Not even an inch.

But it wasn't this white room nor Kitano-san in its dark corner that Ren was looking at now. No, it was the glass of whisky he was holding on the billboard.

I focused on the whisky too. At first, I didn't notice anything out of the ordinary, but as I kept looking at it, I began to see movement. What was supposed to be a still picture of still liquid in a still glass, was actually not still at all. I saw currents and waves. I saw a constant flow of things. Like at sea or the ocean.

I let this flow draw me in. I didn't even need to move, as the waves left the safety of Kitano-san's glass, flooded the street, and entered Yoshi-san's apartment through the window. The tide pulled me in, and suddenly I found myself in the middle of an endless body of water, completely surrounded by it. Like in that movie the "Big Blue", when Jacques descends one last time, never to resurface.

What surprised me, apart from the fact that I was able to breathe, was the brightness that surrounded me. Unlike in the depths of the sea, there was a strong source of light, and warmth, too. I began to swim towards the light, and the water around me became increasingly warm. After a while, I also noticed that the water I was swimming in felt much denser than seawater would typically feel. But it wasn't salty, no, rather, it felt like I was swimming in a mix of all kinds of substances, flavors, colors. Also, I felt a strange, tickling sensation all over the surface of my skin, and this tickling translated into a very specific rhythm that I felt inside. As if music were playing in my mind and my body. Pulsating, fast music that took me over completely.

As I approached the source of the light, I saw a figure. A human figure. And as I got even closer, I saw the shape of a woman's body. She was naked, floating in the middle of this endless body of dense and colorful water, in a position similar to Jesus on the cross. Her long hair was floating weightlessly all around her, and her eyes were the source of the light.

'Ren', I whispered, and a small bubble formed, containing my voice pronouncing her name.

The bubble slowly floated to her right ear, then it burst, and my voice reached her.

She lowered her arms, and the light of her eyes became much weaker. There was barely enough light remaining for me to see her and not lose myself in complete and total darkness.

I reached for her hands and held them. They felt warm, but they were cooling down fast. I held them even tighter.

We spent a couple of moments like that, holding hands, then she too whispered something. Another bubble formed, and it slowly floated over to my left ear. As it reached me, I closed my eyes and the bubble burst:

'Don't let go.'

When I opened my eyes again, I was back in Yoshi-san's room, still facing the billboard with Beat Takeshi and his whisky. I also felt a weight on my shoulders and upper body. It was Ren. She gently fell on me, exhausted.

I stood up, took her in my arms, and carried her to the couch. I put a pillow under her head and gave her a gentle kiss on the forehead.

'I'm not letting go,' I whispered.

***

I went to the other room. The others had tied Little Jack to a chair, as agreed, and were waiting for me to show up.

'Finally,' Kon said, spitting out another piece of fingernail. 'What took you so long?'

I looked at him with such a stare that he backed off and immediately raised his hands in surrender.

'How is she?' Julia asked.

'She'll be fine,' I replied. 'She's strong.'

'That she is.'

I approached Little Jack. He was still unconscious.

'You tied him up well?' I asked, checking the tape around his hands and ankles.

'He won't move, don't worry,' Yoshi said. 'We're ok.'

'So, what's next?' Julia asked. 'Do we wake him up?'

'That's the plan,' I said.

'Here's the water,' Yoshi brought us a full bucket.

'That much water would wake up even an elephant,' Kon joked.

'But not you, right?' Julia threw his remark back at him. 'You'd just continue to snore and sleep like a baby, I imagine.'

'That depends!' Kon raised his finger.

'On what?' Julia asked him.

'On how much food I had eaten before. The more I eat, the better I sleep.'

'Well, looking at you, I'd say you sleep quite well,' Julia smiled.

'Ha-ha, very funny,' Kon replied, showing Julia his tongue, like a child. 'But... actually... now that I think of it, I do sleep very well.'

We all smiled.

'Ok, let's be serious here,' I said. 'Let's do this.'

I took the bucket and threw the water at Little Jack. He opened his eyes wide and gasped for air. He then began nodding his head up and down, turning it left and right frantically, trying to figure out where he was.

'What's this?! Where am I?! What's happening?!'

We stood back and watched. We wanted to see where he'd end up.

'What the fuck is going on here?!'

He tried breaking free, but Yoshi had done a good job with the tape, and he couldn't budge.

'Let me go! Do you hear me?! Let me go, you people!'

Julia and I looked at each other.

Little Jack gave it another go and tried to free himself, but he soon realized it was hopeless. He calmed down a bit, then scanned the room with his eyes. It was now that he saw us and took us all in, even Kon, who tried hiding in a dark corner of the room.

'Who are you people?' he asked.

'That doesn't matter now,' I replied.

'It matters to me,' he said.

'But it doesn't to us,' Julia told him.

'Anyhow, we'll let you go soon,' I said.

'When?' he asked.

'Soon,' I replied.

'But first, you'll have to answer some questions,' Julia added.

'What questions?'

'Just random questions,' she said. 'About yourself. Your life, your family. Stuff like that.'

'Why?'

'Because we say so,' she told him.

'And what if I refuse to answer?'

'Then we can't let you go,' she said.

'Meaning, you'll kill me?'

'Let's not get ahead of ourselves,' I intervened. 'The questions will be quite simple and painless. Just answer them as best you can, and everything will be fine. I promise.'

He looked away and sighed. 'Ok, let me hear these questions.'

'Ok, here we go,' I said. 'So, first, where do you live?'

He looked at me, then at Julia, then at me again. 'What do you mean?'

'Your home address,' I said. 'Where's your home?'

He stared at me for a while, then he looked away.

'So? What'll it be?' Julia asked, impatient. 'Answer us.'

Little Jack still wouldn't look at us.

'Come on, idiot!' Julia yelled. 'Give us a fucking answer!'

'I can't!' he yelled back, looking at Julia with a sign of despair in his eyes. 'I don't know! I... don't remember.'

'Yeah-yeah, bullshit,' Julia said with a dismissive wave of her hand, and then she took my sword and unsheathed it. 'Let's see if losing a finger will help you remember.'

She went behind Little Jack and put the blade against the fingers of his hands.

'So? Where do you live?' she asked again.

'I told you, crazy woman! I don't know! I really don't!'

'Oh, you don't? Then maybe we should ask your father. Or maybe we should cut his head off, bring it to you, and *then* you might remember something,' Julia threatened Little Jack.

'Do you remember your father?' I asked him.

Little Jack looked straight into my eyes, and I could see his despair growing.

'Your father!' Julia said in a firm voice. 'Or shall we ask all those poor girls? Do they know where you live?'

Little Jack shook his head and his eyes welled up with tears. 'I... don't know what you're talking about. I... don't know who my father is. I... the girls... I don't know which girls you're talking about. I swear.'

'Wow, what an actor you are!' Julia exclaimed. 'You should star in movies! You'd be famous!'

'You must miss your girls,' I told him. 'Or at least Hulk. You must miss Hulk.'

Little Jack just kept shaking his head, and now the tears began to stream down his cheeks. Julia looked at me, and I nodded.

'Ok, mother fucker, let's see if this'll make you talk.'

She raised my sword and swung it. A couple of Little Jack's fingers fell on the ground, and soon they were lying in a pool of blood. Little Jack kept screaming and screaming, and he lost all control. He tried moving, shaking, jumping until his struggle made him fall to the ground along with the chair he was still firmly tied to. His scream turned into a loud cry, and after a while, we couldn't tell if he had lost more blood or tears.

'Stop crying you piece of shit!' Julia yelled. 'You're a man, aren't you?! Behave like a man!'

'Where do you live? Who's your father? Who's Hulk?' I asked. 'Tell us, and we'll let you go.'

Little Jack kept sobbing on the ground, his pants soaking in his own blood. 'I don't know. I really don't know. I... I... don't even know who *I* am.'

***

A few hours later Yoshi knocked a few times and then entered the room where Ren was still resting. I was sitting on the floor, leaning against the wall.

'My friend just called me,' he said. 'Little Jack has been taken care of. We probably won't see him again.'

'Aomori?' I asked.

Yoshi nodded.

'Which village?'

'You don't need to know. Just rest up. We still have a lot of things to take care of.'

Of men and beasts

There are moments in life when chaos and turmoil reign supreme all around us, yet we manage to find peace and quiet. Like sitting on the porch of our house with our dog and a cup of warm coffee, looking at the mountains in the distance, while a war rages in the country, neighboring villages are in flames, and cities are being ravaged and left in ruins. We know we're not safe, there is fear and anxiety in the soul, the worst could happen at any moment, and the future is a mystery, yet calmness descends upon us, on gentle wings, with a touch as soft as a pillow of feathers. It might be God trying to say he wasn't completely gone, or just a thought deep down in the brain attempting to reassure us that everything will be fine.

Looking at Ren and waiting for her to wake up, I felt I was in a moment like that. Even if sounds were coming from the street, I could not hear them. Only her breathing. That was all I could hear. That was all I cared about.

After several hours had passed, she finally opened her eyes. Hours which felt like days, and I wanted these days to last forever. I wanted her breathing to stay as calm as it was, her face as gentle and innocent as it looked, her skin immaculate and scar-free. I wanted to continue looking at her, watching over her, knowing she was safe. I wanted the sun never to rise again, for us to hide in the darkness until there was no breath left to take.

'Come closer, please,' she said in a soft voice.

I sat next to the couch she was resting on.

She put her hand on my cheek and let it rest there for a while.

I let my head drop into her palm.

I closed my eyes.

'You didn't sleep much,' she whispered.

'Not really,' I said.

'You should.'

'I can't.'

'Me neither.'

'But you just did.'

'Not really.'

'Where were you?'

'Here with you, yet... somewhere far.'

'What was it like, this somewhere?'

'Quiet. Too quiet.'

'You're here now.'

'I am,' she said with a gentle smile.

We had to take care of Captain Jack next. A much tougher nut to crack than his son was. We had to do it quickly, before the rumors of Little Jack's disappearance spread, otherwise, we'd be in deep trouble.

Our plan seemed simple and straightforward enough. I had previously arranged for a personal meeting with the older Jack, telling him I'd bring along a "special" person for his pleasure. He was as bad or maybe even worse than his son when it came to women. Instead of spoiling himself with a whole harem of girls like the younger Jack did, he'd carefully choose a single woman to keep as his personal slave. A sex slave, mostly. He typically went for tall, thin girls with long legs, either in their late thirties or early forties. He liked them silent, obedient, with a lot of sexual experience. These women knew more or less what was waiting for them, but they'd go along, both for the money they had been promised and just out of some kind of strange sexual curiosity. Captain Jack would not choose just any woman, and he held thorough screenings. He'd meet the "candidates" several times, under various circumstances, to be sure he chose the right one, and she would then be his slave for anywhere between three to six months, but sometimes even longer.

As he once had told me, for him, the most important thing was to see it in their eyes. To see that they were scared and aroused at the same time. To see that they both hated and loved the whole experience. To see that to them, he was god and devil, heaven and hell.

I didn't know much about this whole thing of his, but I did hear that these girls would end up having miserable lives afterward, with some even committing suicide. They'd get a fat sum of money from him after he had gotten bored with them, but they would struggle to fit back into society. Mostly due to the difference in intensity. These women would get used to the extremes during their time with Captain Jack. The extremes in feelings, in impulses, in experiences and desires. After returning to "normal" life, all these extremes would suddenly vanish, and the mundane and the average would take over. The women could not bear the mundane and the average. They could not bear the absence of pain, abuse, lust, and the feeling of constantly being on the edge of a bottomless canyon.

We decided I'd bring Ren, in disguise, as a candidate, and she would make use of the situation and rob him of his memories of Little Jack. He held these candidate interviews in the absence of his personnel, all alone, and that was where we saw an opening.

***

We got to Captain Jack's house around ten in the evening on the same day we had taken care of his son. I had never visited his home before, and I was eager to see what it looked like.

He had had a mansion built on top of Daikanyama, very close to my apartment. He had this fascination with art deco and the architecture of New York from the twenties and thirties, so he had his home built in the same style. The house was huge, with enormous walls, pillars, windows, doors, and spaces, designed by a famous architect who specialized in art deco. I was not a huge fan myself, but it did impress me. It took me more than my usual time to make the transition from the outside world to the inside of Captain Jack's mansion, and when I finally entered his home, I felt overwhelmed.

This was a world different than the typical world of a typical indoor space, and I felt a strong current of energies inside. The energies were dark and cold and stark. There was very little trace of warmth. A shiver ran down my spine, and my body tensed up. The walls looked as if they had eyes, and the windows felt as if there were screams sealed within the glass. And there was melancholy in the air. Flailing around gingerly, like a bird's feather, left on its own, beaten by the rain and carried by the wind.

An assistant walked us to the room where Captain Jack was waiting for us. Ren and I entered, and the assistant closed the door, leaving us alone with our host.

The room was fairly simple compared to the lush extravagance of the rest of the house. Captain Jack was sitting in an armchair behind a desk, and he opened his arms to suggest we take a seat on the two chairs in front. We both sat down, and I looked around.

I saw two framed photographs on the wall behind Captain Jack. One was of him and his son when Little Jack was in his teens. They were on a beach, both in bermudas and with sunscreen all over their bodies. The other was of Captain Jack with the boss. They were dressed in suits, their sunglasses on, each holding a glass of whisky.

There was not much else in the room, only a plant in one of the corners and an average-sized window looking down on the garden behind the house.

'How do you like my home?' Captain Jack asked.

'It's nice,' Ren replied. 'I like big spaces, and you have plenty of those here.'

'I do, right? And how about you, Sato-kun? It's your first time here, isn't it?'

'It's a bit too much for me,' I said. 'I like small spaces. But, it's nice.'

'Oh, I like small spaces, too,' Captain Jack said. 'The big rooms are only for show. You know how it is in this crazy world of ours.

People measure your power and status by the number of things you possess, and by their magnitude. The bigger the better. Most of the people who work for me and respect me would not work for me or respect me if I didn't show off like this.'

'Maybe you're working with the wrong people,' Ren told him.

Captain Jack looked at her with a serious face, then he smiled: 'Maybe I am.'

He stood up and walked over to the window. He opened it and let in some fresh air.

'I look at this world, at life, at nature,' he said, 'and I see a lot of beauty out there. But it's all fleeting. It all changes and disappears so quickly. And it's all out of our hands. Out of *my* hands. I can get as rich and powerful as I want, and it would still be out of my hands. Whatever I build, it'll crumble someday. Maybe not today, not to-morrow, but someday. Or maybe today. Who knows? I don't. It's not in my hands, unfortunately.'

'Would you like it to be?' Ren asked him.

Captain Jack looked at her again.

'You like to have things under your control, am I right?' she asked.

He looked at her for a while, and then he walked slowly behind her. He had a strong presence, and the fact that we were seated made him even more intimidating. I felt cold in his shadow. He put his hands on Ren's shoulders and began massaging her. Although I was seated right next to her, it felt as if they were in their own space, and I was not a part of it. I felt relieved but also strangely out of place, and scared. For her. I was scared he'd do something to her, and I would not be able to protect her, not even from such a small distance. As I watched him massage Ren's shoulders, I felt powerless.

'And you, you like playing games, am I right?' Captain Jack asked her. His voice had a very different tone than before. Much deeper, much darker.

'Maybe I do,' she said.

'Oh, I know you do,' he replied.

He now stopped massaging her and began sliding his hands down her chest. Soon, he was holding her breasts in his palms, and he leaned in real close to her right ear and started licking it.

I tensed up. I felt this urge to just grab him, throw him to the ground and kick him as much and as hard as I could. I even imagined doing it, and I imagined him screaming in pain and bleeding all over the place. I imagined him smiling while I was doing it. I imagined him enjoying it – the pain, the humiliation, the taste of his own blood. And I imagined myself enjoying it, too.

I was about to snap and jump out of my chair when suddenly he pressed a knife against Ren's throat, and around ten men rushed into the room, all armed with short swords.

I had no time to react, and they tied me to the chair.

'My-my,' he said, smiling, and he lifted Ren's blue wig. 'Did you really think I was such a fool?'

"Shit." I thought.

'Bring him in!' Captain Jack ordered one of his men.

Both Ren and I turned our heads, and we saw Little Jack enter the room, holding a box. I could not believe my eyes.

'Come here, my son,' Captain Jack waved to him, and Little Jack obeyed. 'Put the box in Sato-kun's lap and open it for him.'

Little Jack seemed confused. He probably didn't really know what was happening, as Ren had removed so much of his memory.

'It's ok, just do it,' his father encouraged him.

'O-Ok,' he stuttered.

Little Jack placed the box in my lap. It was a nice, black, lacquered box, with images of clouds and cranes in gold. He opened it very slowly.

The moment its contents became visible, my eyes went wide open and I stopped breathing for a while. My heart began racing.

Ren leaned over to take a look, and when she saw what was inside, she let out a scream and started to cry.

I looked at Little Jack. His whole body was shaking, and he too was crying.

'Look at him,' Captain Jack pointed at his son in disgust. 'You turned him into a useless, stupid vegetable, you cursed witch.'

I looked at the box again. Yoshi-san's lips and cheeks had already lost their color. The blood from his neck had more or less dried up, and it left dark stains on the inner canvas of the box. His head didn't even look real, at first. It looked more like a prop from a horror movie set. Then, as I kept staring at it and examining every little detail of his face, it felt more and more real.

'This is big trouble for me, you know?' Captain Jack said. 'I'm very disappointed that you of all people put me in a situation where my only option is to kill boss Yamaguchi's only child and his favorite little pet. But I'm even more disappointed in this stupid fuck of a son, who got himself caught and got his memory all messed up. What a damn idiot.

'And what for? That stupid little bitch, Kiki? It's about her, isn't it? It's always about women. That's why I always keep mine on a leash or in handcuffs or closed in a secure room. The only woman I gave a chance was this idiot's mother, and it turned out to be the biggest mistake of my life. *Of course* she had to mess everything up. *Of course* that whore had to take her own life.'

'Don't you dare touch Kiki, or Julia, or Kon, or Ren. Don't you dare harm them.' I said, looking him in the eyes.

'Or what? You'll kill me?' Captain Jack asked with a huge grin on his face. 'Fuck you, orphan prick. If it wasn't for Yamaguchi's and Kobayashi's protection, I would have killed you a long time ago. Now I finally get to do it. I just need to make sure I erase every trace of your existence from the face of the Earth. That, of course, goes for you too, my darling,' he told Ren. 'But only after we've had some fun, the two of us.

'Take her to the cellar! I'll come soon,' Captain Jack ordered his men.

'What are you trying to do?' I asked, and I began moving around in the chair to try to loosen the ropes.

'Oh, don't worry, mister bodyguard. We'll just play around a little bit. Won't we, my darling?' he asked, holding Ren's face tight in his hands and squeezing her cheeks.

'Fuck you,' Ren cursed, spitting in his eyes.

Captain Jack wiped his face off and laughed hard for a couple of seconds.

'Oh, my! This'll be the time of my life! I can't wait to dip my dick into your sweet little pussy. And then your ass, and your mouth, down your throat. But don't worry, it won't hurt. Much. Or it might. It's all up to you. Some pain is inevitable, of course. Even necessary. Otherwise, it wouldn't be fun. But if you don't resist, and if you allow me to control the situation, you'll survive the pain, and I promise I'll then kill you in a nice and quick way. But if you *do* resist... Well, then, who knows, right?'

'You piece of shit,' I said.

'Oh, I know I am,' he replied. 'But so are you. Now, take her! Let this bastard listen in on how much fun we are having down there for a bit, and then kill him! We'll figure out how to dispose of their bodies later.'

Two men stayed with me, while another two grabbed Ren to take her away. She began kicking and screaming: 'Stop! Let go of me, you idiots! Do you know who I am? I'm the boss's daughter! You'll regret this! Stop!'

'Shut up, bitch,' one of the men told her, and he hit her hard in the head. Ren immediately fainted, and I saw blood dripping from her nose. At that point I lost it completely:

'Fuuuck! I'll kill you all! I swear I'll kill you all! Aaaaa!'

Then, I too received a strike in the head, and everything went dark.

***

When I opened my eyes again, I was lying on the ground, still tied to the chair. The two men guarding me were there, too. One of them saw me wake up.

'You're back with us, Sato-san. Good. We left the door open so that you can hear her screams. They are taking a break now. Your girl went unconscious. But they'll get back to it soon enough,' he said, smiling. 'We'll give you a taste of it, so that it's the last thing you hear in this world, and then we'll kill you.'

I looked in the direction of the door. It was wide open, but I could not yet hear anything. I moved my hands a little, and I realized the rope had loosened a bit, probably when I fell over. I immediately knew I would be able to free myself, but only if I managed to distract the guards somehow.

I looked around, then at the door again, and I saw Yoda. I don't know how the dog had found his way to Captain Jack's room, but there he was, standing in the doorway and staring at me.

I didn't say a word, nor did I give him any kind of signal, but he probably saw it in my eyes, and he rushed in barking.

'What the fuck,' one of the guards said, and they both turned around. Yoda bit the cursing one on his shin.

'Aaaa,' the guard screamed in pain, and he tried hitting the dog with his sword, but Yoda managed to jump away in time. He kept barking at them and threatening to bite, while the two men kept trying to slash him.

I quickly freed my hands and untied the rest of the rope, and I hit the one who was closer to me hard in the head. He immediately fell to the ground. I went for his sword, but the other guard saw me and attacked. I dodged the blow, rolling away, with the sword in my hand. At the same time, Yoda jumped on the guard, biting his already wounded leg again and sending him to his knees. I stood up quickly, and with a single blow, I cut his head off. It rolled all the way to the other guard, who was still on the ground, trying to collect himself. He panicked the moment he saw the head, and he looked in my direction with fear in his eyes. At that moment, I thrust the sword into his throat, and I slit him open to his crotch, spilling his guts on the floor.

I stood there for a few seconds, panting, eyes wide open. Complete silence. Suddenly, everything felt peaceful. Yoda came to my side, and he lay down, resting his head on his paws and looking innocent and harmless. I kneeled and patted him on the head: 'Thanks, boy. You saved me.'

The next moment, I heard a scream coming from the hallway.

'Ren. We need to go, Yoda! Come!'

I kept one of the short swords with me, and I ran out of the room. Yoda followed.

We were in a long corridor, with several doors both right and left, and a stairway on the opposite end leading to a level below. We stopped for a second, and then we heard another scream coming from the stairway. We immediately ran down the stairs.

When we made it down, we found ourselves facing two of Captain Jack's men, who were guarding a large secure door. They both drew their swords and attacked me. I parried the attack of the guy who was closer to me, while Yoda jumped high in the air and bit the other guy's arm, forcing him to drop his weapon. They were both visibly confused to see a dog with me, and I used this moment of hesitation to strike back. I cut my attacker's leg, making him fall on his knees, and then I cut off the other guard's arm. Yoda fell to the ground, still holding the severed arm in his mouth, staring at both men with eyes full of intensity and determination.

I was about to kill both men, but then I heard another scream from behind the door. Ren's voice conjured images inside my head – images of our conversation, of our argument several nights earlier. I pictured her face, sad at the sight of me killing other people, and I imagined the disgust she felt with me. I was filled with a feeling of shame.

I lowered my sword. Yoda felt the change in my energy, and he let go of the arm and backed off.

'Let's go, boy. Let's save Ren,' I told him.

I opened the door and we entered.

We found ourselves in yet another corridor. The darkness was thick, with only a few candles showing us where to go. Each step we took felt like we were descending deeper and deeper into the belly of a monster from hell. My heart was in my throat, and my hands were sweating. Every now and then, we would hear Ren scream in pain, and each scream felt like a dagger being thrust into my stomach. I wanted to hurry and get to her as soon as possible, but I was unable to. My legs felt like two enormous stones, and I needed all my force and will to drag them forward. Not that I was afraid of Captain Jack or that I feared getting killed, but rather the whole atmosphere of the place and the situation. And most of all, I was scared I'd see Ren suffer, be violated, raped, and left broken into so many pieces that not even time could make her wounds heal. I feared I'd see the darkest side of humanity with my own eyes.

At the end of the corridor, Yoda and I reached another door. With large candles on both sides, it was the brightest spot in the basement. The door was carved out of wood, and it had intricate engravings of clouds and ocean waves on its surface. I leaned closer and ran the tips of my fingers over it. It felt smooth. As if I were touching the contours of a human ear. A woman's ear.

'Aaa!' another scream came from the other side of the door.

I kicked it in.

It's probably the most difficult thing I've ever had to put into words. What I saw still makes me feel sick and empty whenever I remember the images.

The room was not that big. The only source of light was a long neon lamp that ran across the ceiling horizontally. One of the walls was dedicated entirely to all kinds of tools. Sexual tools and tools for torture. There were so many, I could not even count them. Another wall had photos all over it. Some were black and white, and some in color. Pictures of Captain Jack's slaves. All the girls he had used and then thrown away like useless pieces of garbage. You could see it on their bodies and in their eyes. You could see that they didn't believe they were humans anymore. He had fucked up their bodies, and in the process, he had fucked up their minds, too. I felt a deep wound open on the surface of my heart just from looking at them.

The third wall, the one opposite the door through which I had entered, had an iron grid across its whole surface. I saw hooks of various sizes, handcuffs in various colors, and several whips. And I saw Ren.

Her hands and feet were tied to the grid, her legs spread wide open. She was bare naked. She had a large tattoo on her back – two black birds, one with green eyes, the other with purple. Her back was also covered in fresh blood coming from the wounds from who knows how many lashes with a whip. I saw streams of blood flowing down both her legs, all the way to the floor, forming a thick, red pool around her feet.

Captain Jack was standing right behind her, holding a whip. It had small thorns all over it, like those of a rose. A "rose whip". He was wearing female stockings with garters, red high heels, and a satin babydoll. His penis sticking straight up, and it was dripping wet.

I leaped across the room. He only had time to look in my eyes and see the fury in them. With a single blow I cut his penis off, and I looked on as his face and his whole body began to writhe in agony.

Captain Jack's screams echoed through the dark basement like shrieks from hell. He was lying on the ground, all curled up like a fetus. I grabbed him and pushed him against the grid, right next to Ren. Then, I tied him up.

Ren slowly turned her head in Captain Jack's direction to look at him, and he looked at her. They both had red, swollen eyes.

I thrust my sword into his stomach very slowly. He opened his eyes even more, and blood began to flow from his mouth. I then slowly turned the sword upwards, still deep inside his body, and I cut up to his chest. He let out a final scream, then, still looking at Ren, his lips turned into a smile, and his head dropped. Ren looked at him for a while. Then, she closed her eyes, and her head dropped, too.

I was about to untie her when I heard a sob. I turned towards one of the dark corners of the room, and there I saw Little Jack. He was sitting with his arms around his knees, his face buried between his two legs. Captain Jack had made him watch everything.

I took out the sword from Captain Jack's body and walked over to Little Jack. He looked up at me.

'Kill me,' he pleaded, with tears streaming from his eyes. 'Please!'

'Fuck you,' I said, throwing the sword to the ground. 'Do it yourself, you piece of shit.'

Burning down the house

I was confused. I was enraged. I was sad. I didn't know where to go or what to do next, so I went to the only place where I felt safe – Kei's bar.

I entered the corridor with all those numbered doors through the mirror in Golden Gai. I was carrying Ren in my arms.

When I entered, Kei was waiting for me in the middle of the corridor, in front of door fifty-five. I had never seen him outside the bar before. He had a serious look on his face.

'Sato-kun.'

I nodded.

'Come with me,' he said.

We went past door fifty-five and then past many other doors, and we got to a section of the corridor where, instead of numbers, the doors had colored tiles on them. Kei led us to a door with white tiles, and he opened it for us.

'Please, enter,' he said.

I carried Ren into the room. Kon and Julia were already there. So were Kiki and Yuki. They were all sitting on a large couch. Kon and Yuki were holding hands. Kiki was half asleep, her head resting on Julia's shoulder.

There was another, empty couch in the room, where I put Ren.

A woman I had not seen before approached me with a blanket. I thanked her, then I covered Ren and sat down next to her, holding her hand.

We all stayed like that for a while, in silence.

The walls of the room were white, covered with the same tiles as the door. The floor was made of light-brown wood, and there was a big, standing lamp in one of the corners. The light it was producing felt like natural sunlight coming from a window.

I looked at Kei, then at the woman who had given me the blanket.

'My name is Eve,' she introduced herself. 'Pleased to meet you.'

'Eve. You're from Kon's room, right? The European coffee shop.'

'That's right.'

'I see. My name is Sato. Pleased to meet you, too.'

'Kon brought the women here,' Eve said, 'so I put them all here, in this room, as they are not allowed to enter Kon's space. Only he is.'

I looked at the others. Kon was shaking, and so was Yuki. Julia's face was covered in darkness, and Kiki... still looked innocent.

'What happened, Kon?' I asked him.

Kon raised his head, and he had this look in his eyes. The look of fear.

'They... They... came for us. And they... they were chasing us. They wanted to kill us. They knew. They knew everything. And... Yoshi-san... they got Yoshi-san. We need to save Yoshi-san. We... We need to get him, Sato.'

Julia and I exchanged glances, then she looked away.

'He's gone,' Julia said. 'There's nothing we can do, Kon.'

'But-but, there might be! We could still try! We saved Yuki-san! And Kiki-chan! Maybe we could-'

'You don't understand, Kon,' Julia interrupted him. 'Yoshi-san is dead. He's... gone for good.' A tear ran down her face.

'Oh...,' Kon said, and he lowered his head again. 'Oh.'

'How is she?' Julia asked me, looking at Ren. 'What happened to you?'

'She's... I hope she'll be fine,' I said. 'I don't know. She... This shouldn't have happened. This...,' I couldn't finish the sentence. My eyes welled up, and it felt like something or someone was holding my heart and squeezing it. Images of Ren being hurt and beaten appeared in front of me, and they wouldn't go away. I heard her screams all over again, and I felt the pain she must have felt.

I bent forward, buried my face in my hands, and started crying.

I don't know exactly when Kiki had woken up and how much she had heard, but she came over and kneeled in front of me, caressing the top of my head.

'It's ok, uncle Sato. Everything will be fine. We'll be fine. Don't you worry.'

I raised my head and looked at her. She must have had some kind of magic power to eliminate any trace of a rough life from her face. As if she had never been through all that stuff with Little Jack and the work she had been doing for him.

I put my hand on her face. 'Come here,' I said, and I hugged her. I don't think I have ever hugged anyone with such intensity. It felt good.

'We'll be fine,' I repeated her words.

'I'm sorry to interrupt,' Kei said, 'but you can't stay here looong. We have strict ruuules here, and you'll have to leave soon. You could all go to your respective rooms, of course, but I'd adviiise against it. It's never a wiiise idea to spend too much time here.'

'I understand,' I replied. 'Thanks, Kei.'

'Where do we go?' Kon asked. 'This-, I-, we-, I mean... we're in trouble. In deep, deep, deep, deep, super deep trouble.'

'Not necessarily,' I said. 'I killed Captain Jack.'

Everyone looked at me. They didn't seem surprised.

'He got what he deserved, the bastard,' Julia said.

'He probably did, but you're wrong, Sato-kun. This doesn't make you safe. Not at all.'

I looked up, and I saw Kobayashi-san standing in the door.

'Old man? What are you doing here?'

'Your friend here let me in,' he pointed at Kei.

'You can access the corridor?'

Kobayashi-san nodded. 'I've been coming here for decades.'

'Which room?'

'It's not far. Pretty close to yours, actually.'

'I see.'

'But that's not the point. The point is that you've become an outcast now.'

I kept staring at him.

'So have Julia and Ren. And Yuki-san and Kiki-chan.'

'But Yuki and Kiki were never part of the family,' I argued.

'Not the way you were, of course, but they were in a way, and you know that perfectly well. I shouldn't have to explain it to you.'

'He's right, Sato-kun,' Julia said. 'We're outcasts now.'

'Even the daughter of the big boss himself?' Kon asked.

'Even the daughter of the big boss,' Kobayashi-san replied.

'And what happens to outcasts?' Kon went on.

'For an incident like this…,' Kobayashi-san began.

'…mostly, they get killed,' I finished his sentence.

'Even if it's family?' Kon asked.

'Everyone is family,' Kobayashi-san replied.

'Fuuuck. This is a real fucked up family, then,' Kon said.

'It's fucked up, all right,' Julia agreed.

I looked at Ren. She was still unconscious. The makeshift bandages I had covered her in were soaking in blood and falling apart.

'We need a place where we can rest for a while,' I said. 'Ren needs to heal. And we need time to think about what to do next.'

'We'll go to the old house in Tsuruoka,' Kobayashi-san said.

'Boss Yamaguchi's old house? Are you crazy?' I asked.

'That's the safest place you could be right now. No one would be looking for you there. Not even the boss.'

'I don't know,' I said. A thousand thoughts were swirling in my mind.

'Trust me,' Kobayashi-san said.

I looked at the others, but they were at a total loss. They were not in the right frame of mind to think about options and possibilities.

'All right,' I sighed. 'Take us to the old house, then.'

Kobayashi-san nodded.

'Kei, please let everyone stay here just a bit longer. I have to take care of something, but I'll be back soon.'

'We don't have time, Sato-kun,' Kobayashi-san said.

'I know. I'll be back in an hour. I promise. You arrange for our transport until then. And Julia, please take care of Ren. Her wounds need proper treatment.'

'I'll help,' Eve told us. 'We can wash her and bandage her up properly.'

'I'll help, too,' Kiki added.

'Thanks, girls,' Julia said. 'Let's do this.'

'Thank you, everyone,' I said. 'Kei, I'd like to talk to you in private. Let's go to the bar.'

'As you wish,' he replied, bowing.

***

When we entered the bar in room fifty-five, I saw something I had never seen before. The shadows had separated themselves into two distinct groups. The large majority was sitting on the ground, grouped tightly in a dark corner of the bar. They all seemed motionless, and I could sense no particular energy coming from them. As if they had gone into hibernation. Or distanced themselves from me. Or maybe it was me who had distanced myself from them.

The other group only had seven shadows. They were all holding hands, forming a semi-circle around the hole in the wall. That strange, green light was still shining through the hole and into the bar. But now the light seemed more focused than before. As if it were slowly finding its purpose. And among the shadows, even though they were holding hands, I could feel tension. It was a semi-circle of conflicting emotions.

'What's up, my friend?' Kei asked. 'You seem to be having a rough tiiime.'

'Yeah, you could say so.'

'You need a drink?'

'Yeah. Something...'

'Strong?'

'Sure.'

He poured drinks for both of us.

'I... think everything is falling apart,' I said.

'What is?' Kei asked.

'Well... everything.'

'I don't know what everything meeeans, Sato-kun. I must have slept through the class when they were teaching us this word. I haven't heard it before.'

'You're a prick.'

'Now, *that* word I do know! I was definitely awake for thaaat one!'

'You joke around even in the most difficult situations, Kei. Sometimes it's fun, but not now. Not today, Kei.'

'Why? Would it be better if I were cryyying? Or nodding in silence to your bullshit whining?'

'Stop it, Kei!'

'Oh, I will, don't you worry about that. You just tell me what you meant by "everything". What is this "everything", Sato-kun?'

'Well, everything! This whole stupid world, and this fucking stupid life, and all the things I've lived for since I was ten!'

'I see. In other words, if I may translate, you've been living a stupid life in a stupid world, right? Oh, sorry! A fuuucking stupid life!'

We looked at each other, and we both took a sip.

'Well... I guess.'

'So, if it was sooo fucking stupid, maybe it's not such a bad thing that it's falling apart, right?'

'I don't know. I just want these people to be safe. Ren to be safe. I don't really care about anything else.'

'Well, if I may, in my humble opinion, this is quite a lot to caaare about. I mean, we're talking about peeeople, here. I could hardly imagine a greater thing to care about.'

I looked at Kei, then at the seven shadows around the green light.

'I'm afraid I won't be able to protect them all. I'm afraid I'll fail them.'

'Well, that's quite an amazing feeling, isn't it? I'd say you've come a looong way, Sato-kun. A long way indeeed.'

***

I went to Yoshi's apartment next. It was just a few blocks away from Golden Gai, right above his bar.

When I got there, the door was ajar. I wanted to go straight in, but when I grabbed the door handle, I felt electricity run through my whole body. And this electricity created images in my head. Images of pain, of blood, of fear. And images of pride, of determination, of strength, too. And I saw Yoshi. His face. A gentle smile, and peace in his eyes.

I slowly opened the door and entered. The window was open, and a breeze was blowing the aromas from a nearby restaurant into the apartment. It smelled of grilled meat.

The only source of light was a streetlamp in front of the building, and it was enough for me. I didn't need more light than that. I didn't want more.

I walked to the center of the room. The chair we had tied Little Jack to was still there, with ropes on it. It was standing in a pool of blood. Yoshi's was still fresh, and Little Jack's was already dry. They must have tied Yoshi to the chair, too.

I sat on the chair. On the wall in front of me hung a framed photo of Yoshi, probably in his forties, hugging a woman and smiling.

They were in New York, in Central Park, in late autumn, with the trees and the ground covered in yellow leaves. They both had a gleam in their eyes. The kind you rarely see, and the kind you wish you saw more often.

I've heard only bits and pieces about his life in the US. He himself once told me he had moved there to get some fresh air and distance himself from the "shackles of living in Japan as a Japanese", as he put it. He wanted to experience a different life, and to try himself out in a new environment. Test himself. And improve himself.

New York's Greenwich Village was his choice, and he spent nearly a decade in its bars and jazz clubs, honing his cocktail skills. And along the way, he learned English, he met new people, and he absorbed the diversity only New York can offer.

One of the people he met would become his wife. A local girl with Irish origins. A girl with long, curly red hair, freckles, and eyes the color of green olives. I heard they had made a beautiful couple. A couple pleasant to look at, and funny to be around. A couple full of warmth, of kindness, of joy.

Unfortunately, she passed away. Cancer took her, along with that sparkling glow from Yoshi's eyes. He moved back to Tokyo after her death, he opened his little bar, and he spent the rest of his days serving the best damn cocktails in the city. His drinks had a unique flavor – something impossible to identify properly, but something that was always there, to penetrate beyond the basic senses of taste and smell, and to create a feeling of longing. As if he had imbued his drinks with his own memories, and the feelings attached to these memories, and he wanted them to live on in all the people he served his cocktails to.

Looking at the picture on the wall of him and his wife hugging each other, I understood what those memories were, and where those feelings had come from. And I appreciated his cocktails even more, and the way he carried himself behind the counter of his bar in Shinjuku.

'I'll miss you, old friend,' I whispered, looking at the photo.

Shiro was lying on the ground right beneath the picture. I bent down and picked it up. The blade was covered in blood, and I saw small pieces of flesh all over its edge. Probably Yoshi's flesh.

I went to the bathroom and washed the sword. I need a bit of time to remove all the stains. I then cleaned it dry with a towel. I didn't have any oil with me, but I found Yoshi's beard oil in one of the drawers in the bathroom, so I applied that to the blade. It smelled nice. The scent of wood and spices. A strong, manly scent. I liked it a lot, so I put some on my beard, too. Shiro had never felt so fresh before. Neither had my beard.

On my way out, I stopped in front of Yoshi's photo again. I had a good look, then I took it down. I removed the frame, folded the photo, and put it in the pocket of my jeans.

While going downstairs, I passed the door of Yoshi's bar. The "closed" sign was on. I stopped for a second, waiting to see if anyone would open the door and leave the bar. Or invite me inside. I wished I could experience its atmosphere one last time. I wanted to sit at the corner of the counter, sipping my chocolate cocktail and listening to Tom Waits. I wanted to see Ren come in wearing her blue wig, remove her sunglasses, and wink at me. I wanted to see Yoshi out of the corner of my eye as he shook his head and smiled at us. I wished Kiki would be there too, smiling and sipping a chai latte with a kilo of cinnamon on top, and Julia and Kon quarreling and holding a drinking contest. With Julia winning, of course. And Kon falling off his stool and all of us laughing.

But the "closed" sign wouldn't budge. Neither would the door.

***

I took a cab and went back to my apartment. When I entered, I was greeted by nothing but dampness and stale air. I turned the light on, but I still felt as if I were surrounded by darkness.

I paced back and forth in the living room for a while, just touching stuff – the sofa, the dining table, cupboards and shelves, books, and vinyls. I was trying to feel something. I was trying to remember what all these things meant to me. I had this image in my mind of me entering my apartment, turning the light on, sitting on the couch, and feeling relaxed. Relieved. At home. I had been holding onto this vision for a very long time, but I never managed to experience it. And now, touching all this stuff, *my* stuff, didn't make me feel anything.

I went to the bedroom and opened the top drawer of my nightstand. I took out a small piece of paper. It was the paper from the Professor's house, the one covered in his blood. The blood I had spilled. The *first* blood I had spilled.

I went back to the living room. I put the bloody paper in the middle of the dining table, and I put Yoshi's picture on top of it. I lit a cigarette, and I tossed the burning match onto the photo and the paper. Both caught fire.

I stood back and watched the flames. They swallowed the paper and the photo, and then they started licking at the cloth covering the table. I saw immense hunger in the flames, and the more they ate, the hungrier they got. Like all these people I had been surrounded by for so many years. It was never enough. Never enough money, enough power, enough pleasure, enough lust. And soon the table began to burn, too.

I took one last drag, and I tossed the cigarette into the fire. I took Shiro and my helmet, and I went downstairs.

Eleanor was waiting for me, ready to go. I started her engine and revved her a bit. Her rumbling overpowered the sound of the fire inside my apartment. The flames were already licking the door of the balcony and eating up whatever came their way.

I took off on my bike without looking back.

***

When I arrived at the dark alleys of Golden Gai, Kobayashi-san and the others were already inside a big black van and an accompanying car. Yoda was there too, sitting next to Ren.

'Are you ready?' Kobayashi-san asked me.

I nodded.

'Where's your stuff?'

'I've got everything I need,' I replied.

'I see. Let's go then.'

'How is she?'

'She needs time. But she'll be fine. She's tough. Julia and Kiki are with her. And your dog.'

I nodded again. 'Go ahead. I'll follow.'

Kobayashi-san nodded and entered the smaller car.

I looked back at the mirror leading to the corridor with the numbered doors. I saw a pair of eyes looking at me, then they vanished. And then I saw Eleanor in the mirror. And sitting on her, I saw the faint contours of a person.

Garden of stones

We drove all night and arrived at the old house in Tsuruoka early in the morning. A dirt road led up to it, as it was nestled deep in the mountains surrounding the city.

A thick mist covered the whole mountain in a white blanket as if trying to hide the house from unwanted visitors. As our convoy slowly approached it, we could only see the tip of the main building's roof peeking out. I knew the boss wasn't there, but it still felt like he was watching us from that rooftop, and I felt my stomach twitch.

We parked in front of the main gate and turned the engines off. I removed my helmet but stayed seated on Eleanor. Kiki opened the door of the van and came out first. Yoda followed, and he ran straight to me. Kon and Yuki appeared too, holding hands.

No one said a word for a while. We were all looking at the big gate, at the patches of the house we could see through the cracks and windows appearing on the wall of mist, and at the immense trees surrounding us from all directions.

The silence was all-encompassing. A bird broke it for a moment, but only to yield to an even more penetrating silence as its voice was swallowed by the forest. There was no wind to rattle the leaves, and no animals were hiding in the bushes. Or if they were, they must have been observing us without taking a breath.

I petted Yoda on the head and got off the bike. I turned to face the gate. More and more walls, tiles, and windows appeared as the mist began to ascend. As if the house were greeting us. As if it were an ancient dragon who had been sleeping in its cave for thousands of years, and now it was slowly waking from its slumber. And then I *did* see a dragon. A black one, with green eyes, painted on the main gate. And then another one, right next to it, on the other half of the gate. A white dragon with purple eyes. They were staring at me.

Kobayashi-san opened the door of his car and came out. He left the door open. I heard a song coming from the car. It was "Again" from one of my favorite bands, "Archive". The song was just about to pick up tempo and intensity after a gentle, soothing intro. The electric guitar was about to get louder, to get rough, to get all dirty. It was about to destroy the purity of the moment with the roughness of reality.

'We're here,' Kobayashi-san said, stepping next to me.

'I didn't know you listened to that kind of music,' I said.

'Oh, it's the driver. It's his music.'

'I see.'

'Shall we go inside?'

I looked at him, and I nodded.

I walked to the van, with Yoda following me. I looked inside, and I saw Julia wiping Ren's forehead with a towel.

'She's got a fever,' Julia said.

'Is that good or bad?' I asked.

'It's good. It means her body is fighting. She's still got quite a road ahead, but she'll get there.'

Ren opened her eyes and looked at me for the first time since we had left Captain Jack's house. She didn't say a word, nor did she show me a smile or anything, but there was something in those eyes. Something strong. Something I had not seen before. Their green color seemed to be a much deeper green than it used to be.

'Let's take her inside,' I said.

Julia helped me get Ren into my arms, and we began to walk to the front gate. Kon, Yuki, Kiki, Julia, Kobayashi-san, and me, holding Ren. And Yoda, of course. What a strange bunch.

When we got to the gate, it suddenly began to open on its own. For a moment, I was frightened, and I imagined seeing the boss on the other side, in the company of a dozen crazy, wild men, ready to cut us down. But then I saw the gentle face of an old lady.

'Welcome all,' she greeted us with a smile.

Her voice was deep, but it felt soothing. And kind.

'This is Amaya Hara-san. She takes care of the house,' Kobayashi-san introduced her.

'Pleased to meet you, everyone. Please, call me by my first name. I don't like formalities. I may look old, but I'm a young girl at heart,' she said with a big smile, and she bowed just a little.

'Very pleased to meet you, Amaya-san. My name is Julia.'

'And I'm Kiki!'

'Kon. Pleased to meet you.'

'I'm Yumi.'

'And you must be Sato-kun and Ren-chan, right?' The old lady asked me.

'That's right,' I replied. 'Pleased to meet you. And thank you for having us.'

'Oh, but of course. Don't you worry about anything, my dear. Everything will be fine. And you'll love it here.'

'Thank you,' I said.

'Now, come inside, please. And let's take care of Ren-chan.'

'Uncle! You forgot to introduce the dog,' Kiki said.

'Oh, right. The dog. This is Yoda. Hopefully, he'll behave. He kind of just started following me a few days ago, and it seems he's here to stay.'

'Well, aren't you a cute little puppy?' Amaya-san bent forward and petted Yoda behind his ear. He loved it and licked her hand several times. 'We'll take care of you too, my little furry friend.'

We entered through the main gate, then Amaya-san closed it.

What had once been a temple courtyard was now an immaculate garden in the traditional Japanese style. It had all the typical features: a small pond with a stone bridge, mounds with lush, green grass, several pine trees in different shapes, and all kinds of other bushes and plants I wasn't terribly familiar with. A pebbled pathway led to both the main building and another two, smaller houses on the property, one of which was the dojo where Kobayashi-san, boss Yamaguchi, and the old grandpa Yamaguchi used to practice "kenjutsu". Kobayashi-san saw me looking at the dojo, but he didn't say anything.

We entered the house, and Amaya-san immediately led me to a room with a bed where I put Ren to rest. Amaya-san and Julia changed Ren into new clothes, which the old lady had brought. The clothes fitted her perfectly.

'They used to be her mother's,' Amaya-san told us. 'Naoko-chan left some clothes here, as she used to come often to visit the boss when they were young.'

'Did you work for the boss back then?' I asked.

'Not for the current boss, but the previous one. Grandpa Yamaguchi. I was even younger then than I am now,' she chuckled. 'When I began to work for the family, boss Yamaguchi and Naoko-chan were already a couple.'

'I see. And... What was she like?' I asked.

'Naoko-chan? She was an amazing girl, and she grew into an amazing woman. She was a pillar of strength in this household, but also the voice of empathy. She had this charisma, and she'd touch people in a way very few people could. She was a bit younger than I, but she definitely felt more mature,' Amaya-san chuckled again. 'I looked up to her, in a way. And I still do. She still lives on inside me, and inside all of us, I guess.'

'As Ren does,' I said, looking at Ren.

'Probably. I don't know, I haven't seen her for a very long time.'

'The boss didn't bring her here?'

'He used to, very often, when she was a child. But she hasn't been back here for more than thirty years now.'

'Why?'

'Who knows,' Amaya-san shrugged. 'The memories of Naoko-chan, maybe? I think he uses this house to escape from... well, everything. Including his own daughter.'

'You're probably right,' I said. 'When do you think he'll come again?'

'The last time he was here, a couple of weeks ago, he said he'll come back in the summer. When it gets humid in the big city. Probably after the rainy season.'

'That gives us a few months, then,' I said.

Amaya-san nodded. 'And what do you plan to do after that?' she asked.

'I don't know yet. We'll figure it out, I guess. We'll have to.'

***

Three weeks later we were still in the house. It was mid-May, and the weather was beautiful. It was still a bit cold in the mornings, but the days were full of sunshine and gentle warmth. The kind you can bathe in for hours and hours and just lose yourself looking at the blue sky, watching the branches of the trees flail left and right, listening to the birds hiding behind the green robes of the forest.

One morning, I woke up earlier than usual. I was using the dojo as my bedroom. Probably my childhood memories and instincts. My body must have remembered the times when I had lived in boss Yamaguchi's "dojo" back when he took me in. As if nothing had changed. I was living and sleeping in his dojo again. And it felt good. It felt like the old days when my only care in the world had been to practice "kenjutsu", clean the dojo, run some errands for the boss, and eat and sleep. I had been happy to have a home, to have a hot meal every day, to have a job, to be welcomed and accepted. The happiest days of my life.

I changed into my practice gear and began to practice. I just felt like it. And I practiced with a real sword instead of a wooden one.

With Shiro. It felt good to hold its hilt, to feel the weight of the steel in my hands, and to hear the swishing sound it made after each swing. I liked cutting the air like this. I'd always imagine I was cutting up reality and opening doors into other dimensions with it. And I'd imagine all kinds of beings appearing through these portals – some good, some bad, and some really bad. Fairies, talking animals, ogres, and demons. Gods and goddesses. And I'd spare the good ones, smiling at them, and kill the bad ones, smiling at them, too. Like a child. Like twenty-something years ago, when I first trained with the boss and Kobayashi-san.

'I like your smile.'

I stopped and looked towards the entrance to the dojo.

'You're good at hiding it,' Ren said.

She had gotten out of bed for the first time since we had arrived in Tsuruoka.

I lowered my sword and slowly walked towards her, looking into her eyes all the way.

'I also like seeing you with a sword in your hand. Even though I hate when you use it. But still, it looks good on you.'

'It's good to see you on your feet again.'

'I know. It feels good.'

'Would you... like to take a walk in the garden?'

'Yeah, sure. I'd like that.'

'Let's go, then,' I said, and I put away the sword.

The sun had just come out from behind the mountains, and its early morning rays made the whole garden glow. There was some mist too, and it created an atmosphere of serenity. And otherworldliness. It felt as if we were walking in heaven's backyard.

'I like these brief moments of transition,' Ren said. 'When the world is waking up again after a long, dark night.'

'I never had a good relationship with mornings,' I said. 'For me, it was a sign to hide. A symbol of a world I didn't belong to.'

'I see.'

'But here... It feels different. For the first time in... thirty years or so, I've been able to sleep at night and enjoy the days.'

'It's nice here, isn't it?' Ren asked.

I nodded.

'I remember my father bringing me here when I was little. I also remember his mood and his face. He'd have this aura around him, where he'd feel as if he were not in the same reality as me. His eyes felt much deeper than usual, and I'd always think he was looking far into the distance. Looking at something, or someone, only he was able to see. And sometimes I'd catch him mumbling to himself.'

'But he never brought you here again.'

'Never. I think I was five the last time we came here. And that was the first time I used my powers. It happened here.'

We walked in silence for a couple of minutes.

'She... doesn't know, but it was on Amaya-san,' Ren said after a while. 'She used to be married, and she also had a child. A girl my age. We'd play together from time to time, whenever Amaya-san brought her here. But then, one day, the police came to our house. This house. Amaya-san was here with us, cleaning, taking care of the house, or whatever it was she was doing. It was Kobayashi-san who spoke to the police. And then he spoke to Amaya-san, too. She... just collapsed.'

'What happened?'

'A car accident.

'Amaya-san spent the next several hours lying on a couch, unconscious. Or maybe she was conscious, and she just didn't want to open her eyes and get up. I remember sitting in the corner and just looking at her for a long time. Kobayashi-san would come over every now and then to try and talk to me, or to make me eat something, or just make me leave Amaya-san be and go to another room, but I wouldn't budge. I kept staring at Amaya-san. And I kept thinking about her daughter. The concept of death was still very new to me, and I had to wrap my own head around the fact that I wouldn't see her again. It was so strange.

'Then, at one point, Amaya-san began to talk. Or rather mumble. She said all kinds of stuff out of context, and often her sentences didn't make any sense. As if her mind were making her go through scenes from her life and different images of her family. And she'd address her daughter. A lot. Telling her how pretty she was, or telling her to be careful when playing, or showing her how to hold chopsticks and eat properly.

'Even if I was only five, I felt so sad for Amaya-san. I could feel her pain. And tears began to flow from my eyes.

'I stood up and walked over to her. I sat on the couch, and I put my hand on top of hers. She held it tight and thought I was her daughter: "My sweet little baby. Hinata-chan. My darling. I love you, Hinata. I'll never let you go. I'll hold you tight, here by my side, and we'll be together forever. You and me. My baby."

'Tears flowed from her eyes, too. She wouldn't let go of my hand, and she kept talking to me as if I were Hinata-chan. I was scared, and I felt powerless. I wanted to escape, but I also wanted Amaya-san to get better, and I wanted everything to just go away. All that sorrow. I wanted it to leave us. And then... I wished Amaya-san could forget about everything. That she could just leave everything behind and not remember all the things which made her so sad. And I placed my other hand on her temple. I closed my eyes, and I kept wishing these wishes of mine. I imagined Hinata-chan sitting in a small boat, next to her father, and both of them waving goodbye to us. I imagined the boat slowly drifting away from the shore, their two figures gradually becoming smaller and disappearing on the horizon.

'When I opened my eyes again, it was my father who was holding my other hand instead of Amaya-san. I looked him in the eye, and I could see the reflection of my own in them. They were glowing.

'Kobayashi-san was there, too. My father let go of my hand, and said, "It's time." He then left the room, while the three of us stayed. Kobayashi-san came closer and gently caressed my hair.'

Ren stopped walking, and she looked in the direction of the dojo. 'Have you been behind it?' she asked.

'You mean, behind the dojo?'

'Yes.'

'Well, I have, but there isn't much to see. Just an old, sealed gate overgrown with grass and bushes.'

'Precisely,' she said, and she grabbed my hand. 'Let's go!'

We went behind the dojo and to the gate. It was small and rusty, with a lock holding together a heavy chain.

'Where does it lead?' I asked. 'Is there something on the other side?'

'You can't see now, because it's so overgrown, but there is a small house in the back. Like a teahouse.'

As she mentioned the teahouse, I remembered my conversation with Kobayashi-san, and the story from his childhood, when he had snuck into the garden.

'Have you been there before?' I asked.

'Never. Dad wouldn't let me. Nor would Kobayashi-san. I only saw it from behind this gate. But there's something else in this little garden,' she said, looking at me. 'The graves of Amaya-san's husband and daughter.'

'What?'

'When I used my power for the first time, it was like releasing a wild animal from a cage. It went on a rampage, enjoying its freedom, and I couldn't control it properly. I... erased all Amaya-san's memory of her family. She didn't remember a single image or experience afterward. As if they had never existed.'

I stood next to Ren, looking into those bewildering green eyes, and my heart suddenly sank.

'Even though I released so much power, my body back then dealt with it easily. I didn't faint, I didn't feel tired or weak. But I did feel empty. Like never before. I mean, at the age of five, you don't define it as emptiness, of course, but looking back, that's definitely what it was.'

'And the graves?'

'Well, as Amaya-san had no connection to her family anymore, dad and Kobayashi-san had to take care of them. A couple of days later, they asked Amaya-san not to come to work, and then someone came to our house, bringing two small urns. Kobayashi-san buried them here, and he erected small memorials to both, without names or signs or anything. Just two stones. A large one for Amaya-san's husband, and a small stone for Hinata-chan.'

'How do you know?' I asked.

'I watched him do it. I snuck out and hid behind a bush.'

I looked at the small garden behind the gate. It seemed so wild and natural. The exact opposite of the rest of the estate.

'Let's go inside,' Ren said.

'Why?'

'Why not?'

'Because it's forbidden. You said so yourself.'

'Well, for me, that's a reason to enter. You should know me better by now,' she smiled. 'Come.'

'But we need a key.'

'You mean, this key?' she asked, pulling a key from her pocket.

'Where did you get it?'

'I borrowed it from Kobayashi-san.'

'Borrowed?'

'Well, sort of,' she shrugged.

'So, you've been planning this all along?'

Ren just smiled again. It felt good to see her smile. She looked like a child, eager to explore secrets and find forbidden treasure.

There was a glow of excitement in her eyes. And it probably helped her momentarily forget about the horrors she had experienced at Captain Jack's.

'Ok, open the gate,' I said. 'Let's see what's inside.'

Ren opened the gate, and we entered.

The grass was very tall, and the whole garden appeared disorderly. But in a good way. In a natural way. It was clear that no one had been taking care of it, and it felt refreshing to be in such a wild environment, free of human intervention and planning.

We found a narrow path through the tall grass, and we took it. Someone must have been coming regularly. We saw footprints, too.

Now that we were inside the garden, I could see the small teahouse Ren had mentioned. It was tucked away at the back, surrounded by bamboo. I felt like we were characters in a scene of a Miyazaki animated movie. Just like Kobayashi-san had told me.

Halfway to the teahouse, Ren stopped and pointed to the left.

'There,' she said. 'The graves.'

I saw a large stone peeking out from the tall grass. We couldn't see the smaller stone, so we went closer and removed some of the grass. It was there, all right. Like a child hiding in its father's shadow and holding his hand.

'Hinata-chan...' Ren whispered. She then put her hands together and prayed.

'Amaya-san still doesn't know, right?' I asked.

'No, she doesn't. And she never will. There's no point in telling her.'

'But if one could bring back some of her thoughts and memories from the Sea of Thought, and then plant some other, new thoughts as well...'

'Like what thoughts?'

'I don't know. Something like her husband having died a couple of years ago peacefully after a long and happy life with his family, and

Hinata-chan being married to a rich American businessman, living in New York.'

'That's a stupid idea. I wouldn't mess with someone's head like that. Creating new thoughts seems even more dangerous than removing existing ones. And anyhow, it's impossible. I can only remove thoughts. I can't bring them back, and I can't plant new ones.'

'Yes, but if there was someone who could? Someone else with such a power?'

'Like, who?'

'Like, your father, for example.'

'No, that's impossible,' Ren said, waving me away. 'I'd know about that.'

'He might not have it anymore, but he definitely used to.'

'What are you talking about?'

'Hasn't he told you? Or Kobayashi-san? Has neither of them told you?'

'Told me what?'

'That your father used to have this power. He used to be able to plant thoughts inside people's minds.'

'What the hell are you talking about? Who told you that?'

'Kobayashi-san. He said your father had gotten the power around the time he had fallen in love with your mother. And his grandfather, your great grandfather, the old grandpa Yamaguchi had also had this power.'

'No one has ever told me about this,' Ren said. 'I only knew about my mother, and that I basically inherited my power from her. But this...'

'So, you're saying, he definitely doesn't have any kind of power now,' I said.

'Right. I'd feel that. I'd know it.'

'Then, he must have lost it somehow.'

'Maybe. I don't know. I don't know anything, anymore.'

Ren was visibly shaken. Thoughts must have been racing inside her head. But I don't think she was that surprised. It was rather the fact that it was now out in the open.

'Wouldn't you want to give back Amaya-san what's hers?' I asked.

Ren looked at me. 'I don't know. I really don't. Would you?'

I looked at the gravestones. They seemed so peaceful.

'I don't know, either,' I replied.

Ren took my hand again, and we walked to the teahouse. She opened the door, and we entered.

The teahouse had an octagonal shape, with seven walls of white rice paper. On the single wooden one hung a scroll reading "faith", just like Kobayashi-san had told me.

We went closer. Beneath the scroll, we found an empty stand for swords.

'This was made for Shiro and Kuro,' I said, touching it.

'You mean, the swords?'

'Yes. Grandpa Yamaguchi held them here.'

'And what's this?' Ren asked, finding the rolled-up scroll on the small table below.

'An old scroll, but Kobayashi-san didn't tell me much about it. Only that it had pictures of a girl and a boy, and some writing he couldn't comprehend back then when he was a child.'

'Let's open it,' Ren said, removing the string that held it together.

We saw the two images: a boy with purple eyes planting seeds on the top, and a girl with green eyes fishing on the bottom.

'These images just keep repeating themselves,' I said.

'What do you mean?'

'They come in pairs, and they have these strange eyes. Crows, dragons, boys, and girls. I see them everywhere. Even on your back,' I said, looking into Ren's eyes.

'You've seen it?' she asked, and then she must have remembered the scene and experience from Captain Jack's house. 'Oh...'

I put my hand on her cheek.

'It's ok. We're here now. You're with me now.'

She shed a single tear and it fell on the scroll. We both looked at it and began to read in silence.

'This is difficult,' I said after a while.

'This is a very old language, with very old kanji. The scroll must be several hundred years old,' Ren said.

'Can you read it?'

'I can. Dad made me learn it when I was young.'

'What does it say?'

'I'll read it out loud:

***

"One seed, two faces.

They grow separately – one in darkness, one in light,

riding the waves of the Sea of Thought,

seeking each other in acts of might,

never finding what they truly sought.

Love shall keep them together.

Death shall keep them apart.

Forever."

Something's glowing at the bottom of the ocean

'It's a poem,' Ren said. 'It's beautiful.'

'It's about you, my dear,' said a voice behind us, and we both turned around, to see Kobayashi-san.

'And it's about your parents, and your grandparents, and your great grandparents, and so on,' he continued.

'What is this, old man?' Ren asked, showing him the scroll.

'It's the story of your family. It has been for more than a thousand years now.'

'I don't get it,' Ren replied.

'Come, sit down. I'll make us tea, and I'll explain everything.'

We sat on the tatami, and Kobayashi-san began preparing matcha for all three of us.

'It's been a while since I last had tea here,' he said. 'The boss has been coming here alone for many years now.'

'You used to come here often?' I asked.

'Well, initially, as I have already told you, I was not allowed to enter this small garden at all. Only grandpa Yamaguchi came here. Not even the boss or Naoko-chan were allowed in.'

Kobayashi-san put two scoops of powdered green tea in each of the three cups he had prepared, and he poured hot water over it.

'Several years later, when I was already living in Tokyo with the boss and Naoko-chan, grandpa Yamaguchi asked me to come here alone.'

He now took the bamboo brush, and he stirred the tea with quick yet elegant strokes, creating a perfect coating of barely visible, tiny bubbles.

'Here,' he said. 'Please, take it.'

'Thank you,' both of us said.

We drank the tea and put the cups back on the tatami, in front of us.

'Grandpa Yamaguchi was dying, and he wanted to pass on the family's secret to someone he could trust,' Kobayashi-san continued. 'He had cancer, and he didn't have much time left.

'He brought me to this garden, to the teahouse, and he prepared tea, just like I did now. Everything looked the same, apart from the sword stand. Shiro and Kuro were still here back then.

'Grandpa opened the scroll, and he read it to me. I, too, thought it was a beautiful poem.'

'But it isn't, right?' Ren asked.

'It's a curse,' Kobayashi-san replied.

We heard the wind rattle the bamboo outside, and then it entered the teahouse through its small cracks and openings. I could feel the cold on my skin.

'The story goes back to the eighth century. And it goes back to a couple, a boy and a girl, who were in love with each other.

'The emperor of Japan at the time was emperor Kōnin. He had several wives and children, but unofficially, he also had twins from a lover who had died giving birth to them. The children initially lived together with the royal family, but they never really formed bonds with the other children, or with anyone within the court apart from their mother's best friend, an aide who had promised to take care of them.

'The twins were inseparable even as they grew older, and in their late teens, their relationship changed. They fell in love with each other.

'The others in the imperial court had looked down on them even before they had become lovers, but after their new relationship came to light, they were increasingly isolated within the court. More and more people found their intimacy and even their existence shameful, a stain on the emperor's image, and the voices against them grew louder.

'The emperor was a gentle man, and quite timid too, so he didn't really know how to deal with the whole situation. He decided to put it in the hands of one of his chief counselors, who was only interested in results and wasn't hesitant to resort to any means available.

'The twins were soon removed from the court and banished to a small village, somewhere around here, not far from today's Tsuruoka. Their surrogate mother went with them, and for a time, through her connections within the court, she was able to protect them. But the threat was always there, as many people wanted them dead.

'Then, one night, assassins came to their house. They murdered the twins' surrogate mother, but they failed to kill the twins themselves. The boy was a skilled swordsman, and he managed to stave off the attack, and they fled into the woods. Into *these* woods. They hid from the assassins, and they spent several months in a cave not far from here.'

'You told me how the boss and Naoko had met and spent a week together in these woods,' I said. 'Were they in the same cave?'

'I don't know,' Kobayashi-san said. 'Maybe they were. The boss never told me. Nor did Naoko-chan.'

'And what happened next?' Ren asked.

'You probably know that Shintoism was thriving in those days. But the Shintoism of today is not what it was a thousand years ago.

'Those who practiced Shintoism were connected to nature and the Earth's forces in a much deeper way than any of us are today. It was a *real* connection, not just a superficial thing. They were able to communicate properly with these forces and even tap into them.

'Now, the cave was not an ordinary cave. It was home to a shrine, and a hermit had been living in it for many years. He gave the boy and the girl shelter, he fed them, and he gave them time to recover from what had befallen them, both physically and emotionally.

'As time passed, the boy and the girl realized the hermit was a Shinto mystic with a strong connection to the universe – with great power if you like. The power you have now, Ren-chan, and the power your father and your grandfather used to have – the hermit had them both.'

'So, you're saying, they got it from him?' I asked.

'Exactly. They asked him to teach them.

'He resisted at first, telling them that great power always went hand in hand with great sacrifices, but they pleaded with him, saying that they were willing to do anything, to sacrifice anything, in order to protect themselves. So, in the end, the hermit went along, and he passed his knowledge on to them.

'But nature is smart, and it knew the boy and the girl were linked by a deep bond, so the only way it would grant them access to this power was to divide it between them, giving the boy the power to plant thoughts and the girl the power to remove them.

'The sacrifice, too, had to be a reflection of sorts of the person making it. It's not the same for everyone. We don't know what kind of sacrifice the hermit had had to make, but the boy and the girl had to commit to an endless cycle of love and death. Their descendants would inherit their powers, but they would always be born as twins, then fall in love with each other only to be separated prematurely by death.

'The scroll you are holding is a testimony to that. It's like a contract of sorts. The boy and the girl received it from the hermit before leaving the cave and returning to the outside world.'

Ren kept staring at the scroll. I watched her eyes, and they were moving up and down, reading the text over and over again.

'So, you're saying it's a cycle,' she finally said.

Kobayashi-san nodded.

'And... My father and my mother were actually... twins.'

'Right.'

'Then, why am I alone? Why don't I have a brother?'

'You did,' Kobayashi-san said in a soft voice. 'But he died during birth. He was stillborn.'

Ren's eyes went wide open.

'Then, the "jizo" statue I saw in the garden of the old house...' I said.

'It's for boss Yamaguchi's son. Ren's stillborn twin brother,' Kobayashi-san replied, looking at Ren.

We spent the next several minutes in silence. All three of us were buried in our thoughts. We made not the slightest movement. We must have looked like a painting, or a puppet installation.

'The cycle,' Ren said. 'It broke.'

'It broke,' Kobayashi-san confirmed.

'Why?' Ren asked him.

'I don't know. But, that's a good thing. It means that your children, when you have them, won't have to suffer. Hopefully, they won't inherit any power, and they won't have to experience what you have experienced.'

'But, the scroll, it says "forever". There, at the end. It says this cycle will continue forever. Why would it then end so abruptly? There must be a reason,' Ren insisted.

'And there probably is,' Kobayashi-san said. 'But why must one know the reason? Isn't the fact that your family won't suffer anymore enough?'

I looked at Ren. Her eyes glowed.

'My mother and brother are dead,' she said. 'That's more than enough reason for me to want to know.'

***

We spent the rest of the day separately. Ren went to the city, to Tsuruoka, while I headed for the woods, bringing along only Yoda.

Walking among these tall, old trees made me realize I had never really been outside of the world of the city before. I had never even left Tokyo and its outskirts. And I couldn't really say why. I mean, I had had so many opportunities to just hop into Eleanor's saddle and ride away or buy a train ticket or take a plane, but I never had. For some reason, I couldn't leave the dirty streets of Tokyo behind and discover new places. Something wouldn't let me do it. A feeling inside me. A feeling binding me to those streets as if I owed them something. As if I owed them my entire life, and if I left them, even if temporarily, they'd feel betrayed. And, in a way, they'd be right.

But I finally left, because I was forced to. And I'm happy I was forced to, because otherwise, I might never have experienced what it felt like to walk in a forest, among trees, all alone. Or with a dog. Or with anyone, really. And when I thought about this, I thought about Ren. I thought about the two of us, or rather the three of us with Yoda, walking in the forest together, breathing the fresh air together, hearing birds and seeing squirrels together, ringing bells to chase away bears together, praying at small shrines together, talking to old trees together, believing they were spirits, protectors of the forest, of the whole mountain, and grantors of wishes, wishes about happiness, about family, about peace, about random stuff, really. Like normal people. Like anyone.

***

That evening all of us gathered together in the house for dinner. It was the first time we were all sitting around the same table, as Ren had been confined to her bed until then.

I was the last to arrive. The table was round, like in King Arthur's Camelot, and only one chair was empty, so I took it. Amaya-san prepared a simple but delicious meal: "tonkatsu curry". One of my favorites. I hadn't had it for a while, so I was really looking forward to it, especially as I had spent the whole day in the woods. I was starving.

It felt surprisingly good to eat with such a large group. I wasn't used to it. I had mostly eaten alone, avoiding other people, protecting the sanctity of my time with my meals, protecting my solitude in those moments. But here I was eating dinner at a table with seven other people and a dog. And I was having a good time.

Kon was being his usual self, making us smile and laugh. Especially when he and Julia would get into a word fight. She'd pick on him all the time, and his reactions were a treasure trove.

I spent quite a lot of time observing Yuki and her strange relationship with Kon. She seemed shy and quiet, but she'd laugh together with us, and she had this serene look on her face, which was telling me she was in a good place. It was weird to see, knowing how not so long before, Kon had practically taken her hostage with a gun, trying to get information on Little Jack, but it somehow made sense. Here was a woman who had probably been mistreated by men all her life, her body used and misused, even violated, and now a man, however quirky and clumsy, was willing to sacrifice everything to protect her. I almost laughed when, for a moment, I pictured Kon enter Little Jack's mansion, rip his shirt wide open to show the Superman sign, and tell Yuki something like: "I came to save you, baby. Let's fly away into the sunset and make babies together. A lot of babies." But even if it was just him showing up, grabbing her hand, and telling her Little Jack had been taken care of and he'd protect her from what's to come, I could see the appeal, and I could understand Yuki. And just the fact that she wasn't alone anymore, that she was now a part of a group of people – of outcasts admittedly, but still, people –, must have made her feel safe. Much safer than ever before.

It made *me* feel safe, too. Not that I was afraid of the boss or his goons, or that I was afraid to face them, to fight them, but the presence of the others definitely helped me relax. There was warmth around our round table, and there were smiles and laughs, even though we all knew how difficult a situation it was. I felt like we were a family, but also friends. It was more than both. A mix of the two. I don't even have a word for it. But I distinctly remember the feeling. I still have it inside. And I don't think it'll ever go away.

At one point during the dinner, I saw Julia and Kiki whisper to each other and flash cheeky smiles. They looked like a mother and her daughter.

'What are you two girls talking about?' I asked them.

'Just girl-stuff. It's none of your business,' Julia shrugged, smiling at me.

'Is it about me?'

'Maybe. Maybe not. Who knows, right Kiki?'

'Who knows,' Kiki smiled, too.

'It must be about me,' I shook my head.

They both smiled.

'Is it true, uncle Sato, that you were once beaten up by a girl younger than you?' Kiki asked.

I looked at Julia, then at Ren.

'Is it true, uncle Sato?' Ren asked, too, smiling.

'What are you all talking about?'

'Don't you remember, my dear?' Julia asked.

'Remember what?'

'When you had a crush on that sweet little girl from the neighborhood, and you kept following her, and then you made your move, and tried kissing her, and ended up getting a huge slap that sent you to the ground,' Julia reminded me.

'How do you know about that?' I asked.

'Why the surprise, Sato-kun? I was practically your mother when you were a child. Mothers know that kind of stuff,' she said.

The moment she said the word "mother", Kiki's smile vanished. I looked around the table, and everyone's expression had changed.

Everyone seemed to have a story and a history with their own mothers, stories which evoked deep feelings. Or in my case, and that of Ren, an empty void.

'I haven't spoken to my mother in years,' Yuki suddenly told us, after not having said a word throughout the dinner. 'I don't even know if she's well.'

'Why is that?' Amaya-san asked her.

'I... don't know. Lots of things, I suppose.'

'Like?' Amaya-san insisted.

'Like my job. And the fact that I dropped out of the university. I've wasted my life and the chances I had been given, and that didn't go down well with my mother, who had practically raised me alone, trying to give me everything she possibly could.'

'Maybe even too much, right?' Amaya-san asked. 'It's easy for a parent, especially a single parent with a single child, to give too much, and by doing so to create expectations which become a burden. A weight too big for a child or even a young adult to carry.'

'Maybe,' Yuki replied, looking at her empty plate.

'Have you ever thought of reconciling with her? Reaching out?' Amaya-san asked.

'Many times. All the time. But I don't have the courage.'

'Why not? What could possibly happen to make the situation worse than it is?'

'I think... there is a part of me that feels she might still love me, miss me, think about me, and it gives me strength in difficult moments. If I spoke to her, and if it turned out I was wrong, that part of me would die. And I don't know if I could live with that,' Yuki explained.

'I see,' Amaya-san said, folding her arms.

'I also don't know if my mother is well,' Kiki said, and we all turned to look at her. 'She's been ill for a while. And I... I haven't been there for her. I'm not there *now*.'

'But you have, Kiki,' I said. 'You've been there for her all her life. All *your* life. She's the one who hasn't been there for *you*. And you know that very well. We've talked about it many times.'

'I know, but...'

'There's no "but", Kiki. There's only the fact that you had to become an adult way too early, and that she's been using you and manipulating you since you were a child. She doesn't deserve your care,' I said.

'How can you say such a thing?' Ren intervened. 'How can a mother not deserve her child's care?'

'Do you know her mother? Do you know how she's been treating Kiki?' I asked.

'No, but she's still her mother.'

'And what about your father?' I asked. 'Are you caring for him? Are you there for him?'

'Of course, I am. He's my father.'

'Oh, really? Being treated the way you were treated by him throughout your life? And now hiding from him? Here in the middle of nowhere, fearing for our lives, uncertain of... well, everything?'

'He's not perfect, sure, but he's my father. My only family.'

'He might be, but he's not behaving like family would,' I said. 'If he were, he wouldn't have allowed this to happen to you. It never would have come to this. And on top of that, he's been holding stuff back from you. Keeping secrets, not telling you the truth. Is that how a parent should act? Is that someone worthy of your love?'

'Why the fuck are you so against our parents, hm?!' Ren erupted. 'Can't we love our parents even if they are flawed? Or are you just being a bitch because you never had parents, and you want us to be as frustrated and miserable as you are? Is that it? Are you venting your frustrations?'

'Fuck off,' I told her.

'Fuck you, too!'

'Children,' Kobayashi-san tried calming us down. 'Don't do this. Don't be like this with each other.'

'Yeah, Sato-kun, man. Be nice to the lady,' Kon said.

'And you be nice to Sato, Ren-chan,' Julia added.

'Why is everything so complicated?' Ren asked, looking away. 'I just... wish I were normal. With a normal family. A normal life.'

'I think we all wish that, my dear,' Julia said, leaning forward. 'But I don't think any of us really knows what "normal" means. And I'm not sure we'd appreciate or even recognize this "normal" if we were to experience it. And maybe nobody would. I've been working as a whore for as long as I can remember, and I've seen my fair share of "normal" men, "normal" husbands with "normal" wives and "normal" families, living "normal" lives. And if I remember correctly, and I think I do, none of them was happy.'

'What I'm trying to say is that happiness isn't necessarily connected to an idealistic vision of normality or family or job or friends or any combination of those things, but maybe something else.'

'What kind of else?' Ren asked, with tears in her eyes.

'I don't know, dear. It's not necessarily for me to tell you. It's a cliché, I know, but you'll have to figure it out yourself. But, if I look around this table, I see a lot of good things and good people. And, to be honest with you all, even though we're practically on the run, the last few weeks have been the happiest I've had in a long time. So... I don't know. Maybe *this* is my "normal". Maybe *you* are my "normal".'

The next moment Ren burst into tears and ran away.

'Go after her, my dear,' Julia told me.

***

Ren's room was empty, but I still went inside. Her scent filled the air, and it pulled me in. Vanilla, almonds, and musk. I inhaled deeply, and I felt tension in the muscles of my heart. I felt the weight of my heart, and I felt like that little spot inside my body, the upper-left corner of my torso was the center of the universe. All the important things, anything and everything that mattered were happening there. And the more I inhaled Ren's scent, the more evident it became.

Some of her clothes were on a chair. I went closer, and I took her sweater in my hands. It felt soft. But not sweater-like soft. Rather, skin-like soft. Ren's skin.

I raised the sweater, and I buried my face in it. I took a deep breath, and I stayed like that for a while, pressing the sweater against my cheeks, against my nose, holding her scent inside as long as I possibly could.

I had an erection.

I put the sweater back, and I went to the window. I saw the dojo, and I saw the entrance to the forbidden garden behind it. The small gate was open. There were no lights, but the moon shone brightly.

I climbed through the window and walked to the gate. I saw a big black bird on top of it, staring me down. And then another black bird flew over and sat next to it. Both were looking at me as if they were trying to say something.

I entered the forbidden garden and closed the gate. The moonlight illuminated the path to the teahouse, so I was able to find my way through the tall and overgrown vegetation easily. I passed the tombstones of Amaya-san's family, and I saw the two black birds fly over to the stones and perch on them. They were still watching me. Their presence could've made me anxious or tense, but it didn't. If anything, they made my tension go away.

When I got to the teahouse I stopped for a moment. The door was slightly open, but before entering, I had to perform my usual ritual of transition. I held the hundred-yen coin in my hand, and I closed my eyes.

While counting to nine or maybe ten, I had a strange vision. I saw Ren's back and her tattoo of the two black birds with green and purple eyes. I then saw them gain physical shape and slowly leave her skin, then fly up in the air, and go their separate ways. I looked up to the dark, evening sky, and I saw these two bright lights, a green and a purple spot, flying in opposite directions, leaving a trace of light behind them, moving along an imaginary circle. They drew a perfect circle in the sky, with one half green and the other purple, and when they met again on top of the circle, the two lights became one, changing their color and that of the whole circle into bright white. When I opened my eyes again and entered the teahouse, it felt as if I were entering through this circle.

Ren was sitting on the tatami, holding the scroll. Her eyes were red and tired, and I saw a couple of teardrops on the scroll.

She looked up as I entered.

I closed the door and sat on the floor in front of her.

We stared into each other's eyes for several minutes, without saying a word. We were surrounded by silence and that scent of hers. I tried breathing evenly and staying calm, but the scent just kept overpowering me and making me inhale it deeper and deeper. My lungs were so full of it that they couldn't contain it anymore. I felt the vanilla enter my bloodstream, I felt the almonds inside my mouth, and the musk seemed to wrap every cell of my body in a soft, warm, coating.

My breathing intensified.

My palms began to sweat.

Ren's eyes had dried up in the meantime, and she was breathing heavily, too.

I looked at her breasts, and I watched them move up and down, up and down, each time with a little more weight, with a little more intensity.

I knew that she knew I was looking at her breasts, but I didn't care. I kept staring at them. I didn't blink. I didn't think of anything. I didn't care about anything. I just watched her breasts move up and down. And I visualized the flow of the air. In through her nose, all the way to the lungs, lifting her breasts, holding them, holding them a bit more, and a bit more, and then slowly letting go of them and leaving her body forever.

I then imagined breathing in the air she had breathed out. But in my case, it wouldn't stop at the lungs. It would go all the way down, to my penis, gradually lifting it.

I knew she was looking at it just the way I was looking at her breasts, and I still didn't care. I let my penis grow, and I let her watch it.

Suddenly, we heard a loud caw. Probably one of the big black birds.

We looked into each other's eyes again. Hers were glowing. Her pupils opened. There was so much depth in them. I felt as if I were standing on the edge of an abyss.

She blinked, for the first time after several long minutes, and I slowly moved forward. She stayed in the exact same position.

I put both my hands on her shoulders, holding the edges of her silk kimono. I then slowly pulled it down along her arms, revealing her breasts.

Her breathing intensified further.

I watched her breasts for a while again, now without any clothes to hide them, and I felt my erection become even stiffer.

I leaned in, and I gently made her lie on her back. I then pulled her panties off, and she spread her legs. She was wet.

I then pulled my pants down, and I went in.

The moment I was inside her, our eyes locked, and I jumped into this abyss of hers. This endless void within her eyes.

I kept falling. I was a stone, released into the ocean, cutting through an endless body of water, leaving behind all sounds, all colors, all light, descending into deep, thick darkness.

And where most people would be frightened and probably turn around and go back into the light, I just kept going down. Instead of tension, I felt comfort. Instead of cold, I felt warmth. Instead of fear, I felt pleasure.

And at the bottom of the ocean, where one would expect ulti-mate, all-encompassing darkness, I found light. Brighter and whiter than anything I had ever seen.

Cavemen

I woke up to her touch. I felt the softness of her fingers on my back.

'I didn't know you also had a tattoo,' she said.

'Because I never told you,' I replied.

'Is it a wolf or a dog?'

'A wolf.'

'It's a gentle wolf, then.'

She kissed my back, touching her lips to the wolf's mouth.

'Let me see yours,' I said, turning around to face her.

She hesitated for a second, but then she showed me her back.

The early morning light entered the teahouse with soft steps, crossing the thin rice paper of the walls as if it were swimming across a serene lake. It fell on Ren's back like a warm blanket and allowed me to see every little detail of her skin.

The scars had barely healed. There were so many of them. One, in particular, was larger than the rest, and it ran across both black birds tattooed on her back. As if cutting them in half.

I ran the fingers of my right hand over the scar several times. Ren tensed up a bit the first time I did it, but then she relaxed again and let me do it. I didn't see her face, but I knew she had tears in her eyes.

'I like your tattoo,' I said.

'It's ruined.'

'No, it isn't. I like it better this way than without the scars.'

'Why?'

'It's... not perfect anymore, and that makes it more beautiful. And... these birds... look more alive than they ever were.'

'You think so?'

'I really do,' I said, kissing the big scar.

She now turned around and looked me in the eyes. She put her hand on my face, and it felt warm.

I also put my hand on her face.

We held each other like that for a few moments. I enjoyed every bit of it. I felt calm. I felt like a lot of small pieces that needed to align had finally aligned.

Ren kissed me, and she began getting dressed.

'Let's go back,' she said with a soft smile. 'I'm hungry.'

***

We went back to the house holding hands. It wasn't something we had thought through but rather was instinctive. And for me, it was the first time I had ever held a girl's hand like that.

We kept holding hands even when we entered the house, probably also because deep down we knew that everyone had already been aware for a while. When I opened the door, I had already imagined the various reactions, with Kon telling us how he had known it all along, Julia telling Kon he was lying, Kiki applauding and cheering, and the two oldies just flashing their smiles.

So, I opened that door quite prepared, even looking forward to these reactions, but when we stepped inside, both Ren and I froze.

'Dad,' she said, squeezing my hand to a point where it hurt.

Boss Yamaguchi had roughly ten men with him, all with their swords drawn.

'I see,' he said to us. 'Why am I not surprised?'

Boss Yamaguchi's men gathered everyone in a corner, making them sit on the ground, and pointing swords at them.

'Come, sit down. Both of you,' the boss told us, pointing at two chairs he and his men had prepared for us. He sat on a third chair facing the other two.

Ren and I walked to the chairs, still holding hands, and we sat. She was still squeezing my hand quite a bit. The situation was eerily similar to the one we had experienced at Captain Jack's house, and it must have made Ren even more anxious.

'So... what do we do with you all? Hm?' the boss asked.

No one replied.

'You've put me in a very difficult situation. Not in my wildest dreams could I have imagined something like this. Especially not from you, of all people,' he said, looking at us, then at Kobayashi-san and Amaya-san. 'But the biggest betrayals and disappointments always come from those who are closest to you, don't they?'

'No one betrayed you, father,' Ren said, still not letting go of my hand. 'If anything, we helped you get rid of two pieces of junk who had been tainting the reputation of our family for years.'

'You know it doesn't work like that!' Boss Yamaguchi shouted, sending shivers down our spines. There were few more terrifying experiences than hearing the boss shout. 'The functioning, the success, and the sheer existence of this family are built upon two things: loyalty and authority! If either is compromised, even in the slightest way, everything crumbles! And in this family, you all should be loyal to *me*, because *I* am the authority and no one else! Period!'

Ren stared into her father's eyes, and he stared back at her.

'Do you understand?' he asked. He then stood up and leaned over Ren, grabbing and holding her face, pulling it close to his own. 'Do you understand?!'

'Leave her alone,' I told him.

Boss Yamaguchi turned his head to look at me, still holding Ren's face:

'You pathetic little piece of shit,' he said. 'I gave you everything. I gave you your life. You'd be nothing without me, maybe even dead by now. The only thing I asked from you was to respect my authority and be loyal. And your only job was to take care of and look after this stupid daughter of mine. And you failed. You failed at everything, miserably.'

'Maybe I did, and if so, then go on, punish me. Do whatever you want with me. But leave Ren alone. She's got nothing to do with this. It was my idea, my plan, and my responsibility. Let the others go.'

'You don't understand, do you?' boss Yamaguchi said, shaking his head. 'You've always lived in your fucking little bubble.'

He let go of Ren's face and sat on his chair again, leaning forward and letting out a loud sigh.

'Our family is a delicate and complex structure. We have many strengths, which we have been building upon for many centuries now, but we also have weaknesses. Like any structure, like any family. My responsibility as the head of the family is to protect the structure from these weaknesses because my responsibility is also to protect each and every member of our family, both on a professional level and a personal level. Without prejudice. Without discrimination.

'Individual, unauthorized actions like the one you have undertaken, acts of rebellion, if you like, are something I cannot tolerate. I cannot allow it. Otherwise, I'd set a precedent that would eventually lead to a total collapse of this delicate structure of ours. There'd be no more family, no more members to protect.

'Can you even imagine what it would mean if suddenly all these people were forced to go back and assimilate into the so-called "normal" society? Do you think it would even be possible? Just look at yourself, Sato. Where would you be today without our family? And where would the rest of us be?

'We provide jobs. We provide livelihood and safety. We provide services. We are an integral part of this society. Why do you think politicians and armed forces tolerate us? Even support us? It's not just about money and power. It's also about our contribution to the health and balance of our economy and society. You might say we are criminals. And yes, we *are* criminals. At least in the eyes of the law. But what about all those fuckers out there who only think of themselves? Who only want to earn money for themselves, seek pleasure for themselves, and take care of only their own shit and nothing else? We are *more* than that. We give back. We take care of our family, and of this stupid fucking society of ours, which never thanks us, never acknowledges us, and we still do it. And we will continue doing it, at least as long as I'm the head of this family. And that I still *am*.'

'You're a hypocrite,' Ren said softly.

'What did you just say?' her father asked.

'I said you were a hypocrite!' she now shouted in his face. 'You preach authority and loyalty, but you're not loyal to the laws of this country, or any country, and you don't respect the authorities! You say our family gives back to society, but at what cost?! At the cost of selling drugs, guns, and sex?! At the cost of violence that we use and spread, and the cost of all the lives we have taken?! It's all bullshit! You're just trying to soothe your conscience! Do you even hear yourself?! You're fucking defending crime, defending killing, and defending all those monsters like Captain Jack and his fucking piece of a shit son! If it weren't for our family, people like that wouldn't have the power they have, they wouldn't have the resources, and they wouldn't have the respect they don't even fucking deserve! A person like Captain Jack would've been rotting in a fucking jail instead of enslaving people, raping people, killing people!'

I had never heard so much power in Ren's voice. She exploded. All the emotions she had been holding back – feelings towards her father, but also herself –, everything came out.

'You provide refuge to monsters! You give jobs and money and protection to monsters! You fucking *create* monsters! And you, you're the biggest monster of them all! Fuck, you even made your only child into a fucking freakshow of a monster! Do you see this?!' she asked, removing her kimono to stand in front of us completely naked, showing her back with all the scars and injuries. 'Do you fucking see this?! That's your daughter's back there! Your own daughter's skin! Abused and ruined by those fucking monsters you so much care about and protect!' She now turned around and continued to shout in her father's face: 'That's *your* fucking doing! *You're* responsible for this! *You* did this to me! *You* did this to your own daughter! And you didn't protect me! You neglected me! You've been neglecting and mistreating and abusing me my entire life! You're the biggest fucking piece of shit on this fucking planet, and you know what's really sad?' she asked, her voice slowly losing its strength, and tears flowing down her cheeks. 'The saddest thing is that I still love you, dad. Even though you don't deserve it. I still think of you as my father. And you're the only family I've got. My only family. Abusing me. Slowly... killing me.'

Ren fell on her knees and began to weep. For a couple of seconds, no one moved, no one said a word. We just stared at her, all of us, and we didn't do anything. We *couldn't* do anything. It felt like the whole universe was crying.

I then took her kimono and covered her back. I helped her get up, and I walked her to the corner where the others were being held captive. I made her sit between Amaya-san and Kobayashi-san, and when I let go of her, the old man and I exchanged glances. We understood each other perfectly, and he just nodded a little.

In the next moment, I spun around, and I kicked one of Yamaguchi's men in his balls. I quickly took away his sword and cut his head off.

Apart from Kobayashi-san, it took everyone by surprise. As they watched the headless body fall over and the head roll on the ground, I shouted: 'Run!'

The next few minutes were chaos. I don't have all the details, as everything happened so fast, but I remember that Kobayashi-san somehow managed to take away the sword from one of the men, and he joined me in cutting a path for us to escape from the house. Yoda helped, too, in his own way.

I remember seeing out of the corner of my eye Ren being helped by Julia and Amaya-san. Kon, Yuki, and Kiki were a bit faster and they ran ahead. When we all got out of the house and into the garden, I shouted: 'Kon! Make sure that the girls and Amaya-san all get to the van! Take it and leave! Go somewhere! Anywhere! Just drive away!'

'Ok, Sato! U-Understood!'

'Kobayashi-san and I will hold these fuckers back for you! Don't wait for us! Go!'

Boss Yamaguchi and his men followed us into the garden. Luckily, because of the layout, they weren't able to go around us that easily. We tried blocking their way the best we could. I kept looking behind my back to see if the others had managed to reach the main gate and get to the van. Meanwhile, boss Yamaguchi drew his sword, too. Kuro looked menacing in his hand.

When I saw Kon reach the main gate and open it, for a moment, I felt relief, but Kon then suddenly stopped and closed the gate again, sealing it from the inside.

'What's the matter, Kon?!' I shouted.

'It's no good! They... They're everywhere! These potato-heads, these-these... knife-wielding punks are outside, too! There are too many of them! We can't get to the car, Sato!'

'Amaya-san! Do you have the keys to the small garden behind the dojo?!' Kobayashi-san shouted.

'I do!'

'Then take everyone there! Now!'

'What are you doing?' I asked Kobayashi-san.

'There is a section of the wall we can easily climb. We need to escape into the woods. That's our only chance,' he said.

'I see.'

'Let's hold these idiots back. They're no good with these swords of theirs.'

'Ok, let's do this,' I said. 'Kon! Bring my sword from the dojo when you get there! Shiro is in there! You'll see it!'

'Ok, Sato!'

The old man and I held our ground, while the others ran to the dojo and then behind it. We were right behind them. For some reason, the boss looked on, but he didn't get involved. As if he were hesitating. I saw Kon run into the dojo, and soon, he returned holding Shiro in his hand.

'Here, Sato! Your sword!'

He waited for Kobayashi-san and me to get to the dojo, then I took it from him.

'Thanks. Here, hold this,' I said, giving him the sword I had been using until then.

'But-but, I don't know how to use this?!' he panicked.

'Just wave it in front of you if anyone gets near,' I said. 'Protect our girls at any cost. You can do that, right? Can I count on you?'

'Y-Yes, you can! I will protect the girls! Kon will cut these crazy cucumbers down!'

'Let's go, Kon! Let's catch up with the others! Hurry!'

We ran to the small garden, entering through the gate.

'Close it, Amaya-san!' Kobayashi-san shouted the moment we were in. 'Quickly!'

Amaya-san sealed the small gate, and we ran to the middle of the garden, through the tall grass.

'There, behind the gravestones of Amaya-san's family,' Kobayashi-san said. 'We can climb the wall there.'

Ren and I looked at each other, then we both looked at Kobayashi-san.

'What?' he asked.

All three of us then looked at Amaya-san. She had a puzzled look on her face.

'Oh, shit,' Kobayashi-san murmured.

The air froze around us for a moment, but Julia kept her cool: 'We don't have the time now. Let's go, everyone! We need to hurry.'

We ran to the wall, and indeed, it was missing a part at the top, and its surface allowed for an easy climb. Kiki went first, then Yuki, followed by Ren, Julia, Amaya-san, Kobayashi-san, and finally, Kon. I had to push Kon's fat ass a bit from below, as he struggled to pull himself up, and with the final push he let out a loud, stinging fart, right in my face.

'Fuuuck, Kon! What the hell?! Did you really have to?'

'S-Sorry, Sato-kun! I didn't want to, but I couldn't hold it back. So sorry!'

'No worries,' I said, shaking my head and gasping for fresh air. 'Stay up on the wall, will you? I'll lift Yoda up. Take him and give him to Julia on the other side.'

'Ok!'

We lifted Yoda over the wall, and it was my turn to go. I gave Shiro to Kon, who jumped down holding it, then I grabbed two outstanding stones to climb. I was about to pull myself up, but then I stopped for a moment, and I turned around to look at the gate.

Boss Yamaguchi was standing on the other side, looking at me, holding Kuro in his hand. His men were not with him anymore, so I guessed he had already sent them to go around the property. We stared into each other's eyes for a couple of seconds, not saying a word. He had this look on his face. It seemed like doubt had crept into his mind, and he didn't really know what to do with it. As if he couldn't fully commit to hunting us down, but he also couldn't hold his men back. Like a general, completely losing control over a battle, just watching it from high grounds, from a safe distance, and wondering if anything made any sense anymore.

I turned and climbed the wall as fast as I could. When I jumped down, I saw some of Yamaguchi's men in the distance.

'We have to go,' I said. 'Let's hurry.'

The forest was dense, which helped, but I knew we were much slower than our pursuers, especially with Amaya-san and Kobayashi-san in our group, so I told the others:

'We'll split here. You all go to the city, I'll go in the opposite direction, deeper into the woods. Kobayashi-san, lead the way. You know this place better than anyone, and I'll make all kinds of noises to lure them in my direction. You just try staying silent and find your way to the city.'

'I'm going with you,' Ren said immediately. 'Don't even try to resist, it won't work.'

I smiled and shook my head. 'I know.'

'Ok, Sato-kun, I'll take the others back to the city, and we'll find a way either to hide or to escape,' Kobayashi-san said.

'Better escape,' I told him. 'You'd get caught if you tried hiding there. I know.'

'Ok,' Kobayashi-san nodded.

'Let's go, then.'

'Wait! Uncle!' Kiki jumped in. 'What'll happen to you?!'

'Don't worry, Kiki. We'll be all right. Yoda will protect us, right boy?' I asked, patting the dog on his head.

'Be careful,' Julia said.

I nodded.

'No, but seriously. Be careful, all right? I still need to teach you how to behave properly with a fine lady like our dear Ren here. You can't just go on being an annoying little punk now that you have others to think of, too, not just yourself.'

'I know, mom,' I smiled. 'You'll get to teach me, don't worry.'

I saw tears in Julia's eyes, but she turned away. 'Come, everyone,' she waved. 'We need to hurry. These fuckers will catch up.'

'Take care,' I told Kon, squeezing his shoulder, and I nodded to everyone else. I then grabbed Ren's hand, and we began running up the hill, deeper into the forest, with Yoda following us.

'Come on, let's go! Follow me, everyone, let's hurry!' I kept shouting, hoping that boss Yamaguchi and his men would follow us instead of the others. 'Come on! Deeper into the woods! Stay with me!'

***

For a while, we just ran. I held Ren's hand tightly, and Yoda was right behind us. I made sure to make enough noise for the men to follow us, and from time to time, we stopped to check and see if they were indeed coming in our direction. Then, at some point, I felt we had distanced ourselves enough from the others, and it was time for us to lose Yamaguchi's men.

The forest felt like an endless maze. I tried to memorize our surroundings, to later be able to make our way back, but after a while I let it go. I also tried to figure out if we were heading west or north or east, but the dense shroud blocked the sun, so I had no idea.

Running among those tall trees, and being surrounded by so many of them, felt intimidating at first. As if we were intruders. And with the three of us moving, while the trees just stood their ground and watched us in silence, I also felt as if we were stupid little kids, ruining the peace and calmness the forest had been building and preserving for thousands of years. I felt a little ashamed.

But then, from one moment to the next, and for no particular reason, this feeling of being completely out of place changed into a feeling of liberation. The deeper we ran into the forest, the lighter my steps became. The tension gradually disappeared from my legs and my shoulders, and every time I took a breath, my lungs seemed to grow bigger. I saw shades of colors I had not seen earlier – colors of the trees, their leaves, other plants, the ground. And I heard little sounds – the sounds of small animals, branches swaying in the wind, and whispers of some sort. I didn't know if those were voices inside my head or were spirits of the forest or maybe just the trees talking among themselves, but the whispers seemed to be slightly ahead of us as if trying to show us a path.

I looked at Ren, and this image of the two of us holding hands, running among tall trees, having no idea of where we were heading, somehow felt familiar. And it felt good. There were literally no thoughts in my mind. I didn't dwell on the past, I didn't think about Kiki, Julia, or the others, and I didn't think about the future either. I was completely in the moment. And it felt amazing not to think about stuff. As if all these thoughts I'd usually have were some kind of distraction, and now that they had gone into hiding, I was finally able to breathe properly and see clearly. And seeing clearly didn't mean understanding life or my purpose or anything like that. No, it literally meant that I saw things, even the smallest of details, and I appreciated them. Everything.

I looked at Ren again, and I saw that she was getting tired. She was breathing heavily, and she struggled to keep up the pace.

'Let's stop for a little,' I said. 'Let's rest.'

'Ok,' she said, panting.

We sat on a tree trunk, and Yoda lay down on the ground next to us. We sat in silence for a few moments, taking deep breaths. Now that we were not running anymore, the tranquility of the forest became even more absorbing. Like gentle piano music, slowly penetrating the soul.

'I don't know if I can continue like this,' Ren said. 'My wounds hurt, and some of the cuts might be bleeding again.'

'Let me see.'

She only had her kimono on. I drew it down a bit, and indeed, the large scar running across her back had opened.

'My feet hurt, too.'

'Ok, let me think,' I said.

I stood up and looked around.

'Stay here with Yoda. I'll just have a look. I'll be back in a second,' I told her.

'Ok, but hurry, please.'

'I will. Yoda, stay here,' I told him, raising my index finger.

'Come here, boy. You look after me,' Ren patted him.

I climbed a bit further up the hill. I didn't even know what I was looking for, but I hoped I'd find something. Anything.

Then, between two enormous trees, I spotted the entrance to a cave. I went closer, but I feared there might be a bear in it, so I made some noise.

Nothing came out.

I made more noise, and I also sang, but still, nothing came out.

'Ren!' I shouted. 'Come up here! There's a cave we can hide in!'

'I'm coming!'

Ren and Yoda soon joined me, and now all three of us were standing at the entrance.

I had my matches with me, and I lit one to make some light. I took a couple of steps forward, and Ren and Yoda followed. Soon, I had to light another match, and then another. We took baby steps. It was too dark inside just to rush in.

Then, I noticed torches on both sides of the cave wall.

'There were people here. Look, torches,' I said.

I couldn't light the first torch, but I managed to light the second one. I then took it and used it to light the other torches we found in the cave. When we lit almost all of them, we realized how big the cave was, and that it had several other rooms. Also, we found a wooden "torii" inside, and behind it, a small Shinto shrine,

Ren approached the shrine, passing under the "torii", and touching the pillars of the gate with her fingers along the way. Yoda and I stood back and watched. Ren then touched the shrine, too, removing some of the dust.

'It's the shrine from Kobayashi-san's story,' she said. 'This is the cave in which my ancestors took shelter. Where they got their powers.'

'And probably where your father and mother spent time, too, when they first met,' I added.

'That's right,' said a voice from a dark corner, from one of the chambers of the cave that we still hadn't explored.

'Father,' Ren whispered.

Boss Yamaguchi came out into the light, holding his sword, Kuro.

Family

After my first kill, when I took out the Professor, Kiki's father, I felt hollow inside. Not just my soul, but my mind, too. My whole being. I felt like an empty shell at the bottom of the ocean.

After I had made the kill, I spent a week or so either curled up in my bed or wandering the streets of Tokyo. I couldn't eat properly, and I couldn't look at people's faces. I was afraid if they saw my eyes, they'd be frightened and run away. I was afraid they'd see a monster inside me. Still, I craved large crowds whenever I was in the city. Probably because I wanted to hide. From the world, from God – who knows. And the best way to hide was to do it in plain sight, where there were distractions, such as thoughts and the sins of others.

One night, while I was sleeping in my small room at the dojo, or rather trying to fall asleep, I heard a swishing sound.

I turned my head and listened.

It was still there.

The sound had a precise rhythm to it, and it felt elegant but strong.

I got up from my bed, and I put on some clothes. I also took my wooden practice sword, just in case.

I carefully opened the sliding door to my room, and I saw a figure in the middle of the dojo, standing in one place and taking practice swings with a sword. Swing after swing, each time with the exact same motion, on the exact same line, like a machine.

A bit of light entered through the window, and it reflected off the blade, which made me realize it was a real sword.

I moved very slowly in the direction of the switch to turn on the light, but the man stopped me just as I was about to raise my hand.

'Don't. We don't need more light. We have enough,' he said. I recognized boss Yamaguchi's voice.

'Is that you, boss?' I asked.

He continued making those perfect practice swings without saying anything.

I moved a bit closer to him, but I remained alert and focused.

'Boss? Sir?'

I took another step forward, and then, as he was at the top of his swing, boss Yamaguchi took a sudden step forward and swung his sword at me with full force, as if trying to split my head wide open. I parried with my bokken, raising it and making his blade slide along the side of my wooden sword, but he immediately countered with another attack to my left armpit from below. I stepped to the side and blocked the attack with another parry, holding the bokken vertically, along the side of my torso. I then quickly jumped back into a defensive stance.

'What's going on, boss?!'

He still wouldn't answer, and after taking a couple of deep, loud breaths, he let out a big roar and began attacking me with full force. He now made a series of diagonal blows towards my head, alternating the right and left sides. I parried by raising the tip of my bokken and turning it slightly always to face the direction of the incoming attack. I had to take five steps back, blocking the same number of attacks.

After the fifth attack, I saw a small opening, probably because he had gotten a little tired, and his motion slowed down just a fraction. It was literally an instant, but the years and years of practice helped me see the opportunity. The minute I blocked the fifth attack, I took a quick and low step to the side, landing a horizontal blow to his stomach. His arms dropped, and I immediately followed up with a vertical strike to his hands, making him drop the sword to the ground. I then quickly grabbed his sword, threw away my bokken, and stood in front of him, holding the tip of the blade to his throat.

We stared at each other, and we both panted heavily.

Though it was still quite dark in the dojo, I could see his eyes clearly. And in them, I saw satisfaction.

'Well done,' he said, raising his arms in surrender.

He took a step back and bowed slightly. I did the same.

I then reached out holding the sword to give it back to him, but he refused:

'No, Sato. I'm not taking it back. It's yours.'

'But...'

'It's yours,' he said again.

Boss Yamaguchi turned around and went to the corner of the dojo. He picked up another sword and unsheathed it. He then came back to me, holding the sword in his right hand.

'My sword is called Kuro, and yours is Shiro. They once belonged to my late grandfather. Please, accept this sword from me.'

I looked at the sword in my hand, and its beauty mesmerized me. It felt like I was holding a living being, with a soul, and not just a weapon of steel.

'Will you do me the honor of performing a Hōjō-no-kata with me, with these two sacred swords?' boss Yamaguchi asked.

I looked at him, and after a couple of seconds, I nodded.

We took our starting positions, and we performed all four seasons of this old kata. He was the master, and I was the apprentice.

While following his lead and doing all these traditional and stylized moves, I kept thinking about boss Yamaguchi – how much he had done for me, and what this whole ritual might have meant. He wasn't a man of words, and he definitely wasn't a man of emotions – at least not in front of me or anyone else I knew. But it was obvious that this meant a lot to him, and that he was showing me respect and appreciation that very few people had received from him.

When we finished the kata and bowed, I wanted to ask him "why". Why me? And why *with* me?

I had the questions on the tip of my tongue, and he might even have answered them, but I never asked in the end. And looking back, I think I should have. And I also think he had wanted me to ask them. He would've liked to have had a conversation with me and tell me things he only could tell *me* and no one else.

I put away the sword, thanked him for it, and I returned to my room.

That night I didn't sleep at all. I spent several hours just holding the sword and looking at it, and then I spent some more hours looking out the window of my small room, looking at boss Yamaguchi's big house, and thinking about him.

The whole experience filled my empty shell with new thoughts and new feelings, and it allowed me to move on.

***

'You were already here, waiting for us,' I said, holding Ren's hand, and Shiro in my other hand.

'I knew my daughter would eventually find her way here. It's in her blood,' boss Yamaguchi answered.

Yoda growled, but I told him to stop.

'It doesn't have to be like this,' I said. 'We can work this out.'

The boss didn't say anything, and he kept staring at us for a while. Then, he walked to the small shrine and touched it, as if greeting it.

'I haven't been here for a long time,' he said.

'You met mom here, right?' Ren asked him.

The boss didn't reply immediately, but after a few seconds, without turning to face us, he said: 'More or less. But it was a long time ago.'

'Tell me,' Ren said. 'I'd like to know.'

'We... met in these woods. I was hiking, alone, and I was about to head back to the house as it was getting dark, but then I heard a sound.'

'What kind of sound?' Ren asked.

'I thought it was an animal, running, maybe a boar. I was a little frightened, so I hid behind a tree and watched. The sound got louder and louder, and I knew it was heading in my direction. My heart was pumping fast.

'Soon, the sound was there, in my vicinity, and I was expecting to see this animal jump out of a bush and run past the tree I was hiding behind. And when it finally did, I saw a girl, instead of a boar.'

'Mom,' Ren said.

'Yes, your mother.

'She was breathing heavily, her clothes were torn, and she stumbled and fell to the ground when she jumped out from behind that bush. I reacted on instinct and hurried to help her up. When she saw me, she panicked for a moment, then she jumped at me, kicking and screaming. I had to hold her back and calm her, telling her not to be scared and that I wouldn't hurt her. We struggled for a little, but soon, she realized I was telling the truth, so she stopped resisting.

'I asked her what she was running from and why she was scared, but she just told me there wasn't time and we needed to hurry. When I asked again, suddenly I heard sounds and noises of several men running in our direction. I asked who they were, but she still wouldn't say anything. She grabbed my hand, and we ran. I was confused, and I couldn't think clearly, so I just followed her.

'We ran for several minutes, but the sun had almost disappeared behind the mountain, and it was getting quite dark in the forest. She said we needed to hide, and because we had strayed from the path I knew, and I wasn't sure we'd be able to find our way to the house, I agreed. We searched the area, and that's when we stumbled upon this cave.'

'So, you hid here from those men, right?' Ren asked.

'Right.'

'And who were they?'

'Naoko told me she had run away from home because she had had a feeling inside – a voice, telling her to come here. An instinct, if you like.

'While wandering in the forest, she came across this group of bandits. She didn't know they were bandits, of course, so she approached them to ask for water, but they caught her and wanted to rape her. She managed to escape from them somehow, but you know how wild animals are: when they smell their prey, they hunt it down. The hunt itself becomes a source of pleasure.

'But you managed to escape from them in the end, right?'

'We did, but it wasn't easy.'

'What do you mean?' Ren asked.

'They stayed in the area and searched for us. For her, I mean. They didn't know I was with her. They split up, and one of them found the cave and came inside. I... I hit him in the head with a stone and knocked him unconscious. Naoko then used her power to remove a part of his memory.

'I didn't know what the hell was going on, and I was quite scared, frankly. I just saw this green light in her eyes, and around that man's head, and then she passed out, too. Luckily, she woke up before him, and she told me about her power. I didn't believe her at first, but then the guy came to, and he wasn't the same man, anymore. The way he acted, the way he talked, the way he looked at us. He just wasn't the same person. I knew that immediately.'

'And what did you do with him?'

'We let him go. He wasn't a threat, anymore. He had no more memories of the other men.'

'I see,' Ren said.

'I stayed by Naoko's side. I watched over her as she was recovering. I had some food and water in my backpack, so we were ok.

'I... You know... I fell for your mother immediately. It's hard to describe. I just... I had this feeling inside, this strong attraction, and a sense of a bond transcending both our lives. And I knew she felt the same. We both knew.

'We spent the following seven days together, wandering the forest during the day, and staying in the cave at night. We just... felt like we had found this... bubble, on the border of my life and hers, where we were able to escape both and be in our own little space and time, not caring about anything else in the world.

'We talked a lot. And we also spent a lot of time in silence. Both made us learn so much about each other and ourselves.

'I believe most people have situations in their lives, where they face life-changing experiences, going through a huge and deep change in a very short amount of time. This was such a situation for both of us, but especially for me. I had basically lived in an extremely protected environment until then, and Naoko brought the whole world to me. So much so that it awakened my power.'

'You mean, the power to plant thoughts inside minds?' Ren asked.

The boss nodded.

'Why have you never talked about it?'

'To protect you.'

'From what? The truth? My heritage? My destiny? Who I really was? Who my parents really were?'

'It's not that simple,' the boss said.

'Oh, but it was simple to teach me how to use my power and then use it, use *me* to your own benefit!' Ren erupted.

'It was *not* for my benefit!'

'Oh, really?! For whose, then?'

'For yours, of course!' We all stood in silence for a few seconds, then boss Yamaguchi added: 'I wanted to break this fucking curse, to break this fucking cycle once and forever!'

'But it's already been broken,' Ren said. 'When my twin brother died.'

'It hasn't.'

'What makes you think so?'

'I... began having dreams, having visions around the time Sato joined our family,' he said, looking at me.

'What kind of visions?' Ren asked.

'Visions of you... giving birth to twins and dying in the process. Just like your mother. Just like every woman in our lineage, going back more than a thousand years.'

'I was around ten, when Sato joined, right?'

'That's right.'

'And you began making me use my power around the same time, too.'

'Yes. On the Fushimi brothers. They were the first.'

'So, why did you do it? What was your grand plan for breaking the curse?'

'I had spent countless hours studying the text on that scroll in grandpa's teahouse and thinking about the origins of it all. And I figured, maybe the key to ending it all was to eliminate what had caused it in the first place. To eliminate the source.'

'I don't understand,' Ren told him.

'What caused it?' boss Yamaguchi asked her. 'What do you think was the source?'

'I... don't know. They... wanted to protect themselves?'

'Protect from what?'

'From... people in the imperial court?'

'From the abuse and discrimination coming from people in power. From the thoughts in their minds which made them behave like that.

'Our ancestors tried breaking the curse for centuries, mainly by trying to separate the newly born twins. But they would always end up finding each other and falling in love. It was the same for your mother and me. We were twins. Her father was my father, too. Grandpa was *our* grandpa.'

We didn't know what to say. Everything felt so surreal.

'I first tried doing the same thing,' the boss continued, 'and for a while, I thought I was more successful than my ancestors. But then I began having the visions.'

'Why did you think you were more successful? I don't under-stand. My brother-'

'Your brother wasn't stillborn,' boss Yamaguchi interrupted her. 'I... ordered him killed.'

Ren and I couldn't believe what we were hearing.

'You what?!' Ren asked, in complete shock.

'I ordered the only person I trusted to kill my baby boy so that I could break the cycle.'

'Kobayashi-san,' I said. 'It was Kobayashi-san.'

The boss nodded.

'You, fucking piece of-,' Ren said with tearful eyes, ready to jump at her father and start hitting him with her fists.

'Stop it, Ren! Don't!' I held her back. 'Don't.'

'It's ok,' the boss said. 'Let her. She has all the right to do it. I'd do the same if I were her.'

Ren clenched her fists and her tears just kept pouring.

'It's a big burden, you know,' the boss continued. 'This whole... thing. The curse. The weight of our family's history. And the endless cycle of pain it brings. I only truly began to feel this unimaginable weight when Naoko died. It doesn't really sink until then. But once you experience the pain of such a loss, the loss of... the other half of your soul – it becomes unbearable.

'I... acted on instinct. Oh, I had thought about it, don't get me wrong. But knowing what I knew about our family's destiny, I prob-ably felt I had to do something radical. And not a day has gone by since that I haven't thought of my baby boy. Of how he might have lived his life, of how much joy we could have had together, of what he could have become. Not a single day. Believe me. It's been a lifetime of sorrow and pain for me since that moment. These past thirty-odd years. Almost forty. And then to start having those visions, and realize I had probably not succeeded in changing the course of destiny... I really don't wish anyone ever to have to experience such pain.'

'So, what was your plan for eliminating the source of the problem?' I asked.

'You know, the thoughts we have in our minds, they are not just there in isolation, existing in one single mind, to then go back to the Sea of Thought after death. No, they spread. And they get passed down. Like a virus. It's been like that forever. Since the beginning of civilization. Those in power have always looked down on other people, have always felt privileged and entitled. Entitled to decide what's right and what's wrong, entitled to decide over other people's lives.

'So, my plan was to try and change the minds of those in power. And I've been using Ren to that end. I've been using my might and influence to achieve this.'

'And have you?' I asked him.

'What do you think?' he asked back.

'I think you're just like them,' Ren said, with resentment in her voice. 'You became a man of power who thinks he can decide what others should think. You disgust me.'

'There you have it,' the boss said. 'At least, I have a smart daughter.

'My... visions, they went away for a while, but then they returned. And in the last couple of months, they intensified. Especially in the past few weeks. Since this whole incident happened, and you all came here. I've been having them not only at night but during the day, too. I'd see Ren in a hospital, lying on a bed, and the doctors pulling out one, and then another baby. I'd then look into her eyes, and I'd see them slowly lose their beautiful green color, fading away into cold, hollow darkness. They would never blink again, never have love in them again, never send warmth again to those who had the luck to see them. And then I'd hear the babies start to cry. Both, at the same time. And what should be a moment of joy would turn into a moment of terrible pain. The cry of those babies would not feel like the announcement of a happy life ahead, but rather a sad song of tears and misery to come.

'I don't want to see any more children brought into this world to go through the same hell as I have. It's... enough.'

Boss Yamaguchi lowered his head, and there was a real sense of pain in his words. The man known for his ruthlessness and unwavering resolve was now standing in front of us, looking... broken.

I didn't know how to feel about the whole situation. There was love, there was hate. There was anger and contempt and pity. There were all the things he had done for me, and all the things he had done to Ren and his family. He was a big part of who I was and how my life had unfolded.

I looked at Ren, and in her eyes, I read the same doubts, the same conflicting emotions. She was in pain.

I wanted to say something, but I couldn't. I just held her hand tightly.

'I... I'm really sorry,' boss Yamaguchi said, stepping a bit closer. 'My whole adult life I believed I had an answer. I believed I could... change things. Change destiny. But I failed. And now I realize, there's only one way to end this all. There's only one thing left for me to do.'

With the speed of someone much younger than *he* was, boss Yamaguchi leaped forward, thrusting his sword towards Ren's stomach.

I jumped in front of her, and Kuro's blade pierced the lower-left side of my torso. At the same time, I thrust Shiro into boss Yamaguchi's heart.

The two of us stared into each other's eyes. His were dark, and getting darker by the second. As I kept looking into them, another color began to appear. A hue of sorts. And then it grew stronger, it grew brighter. It grew into a light of a... purple shade. And then I realized it was the reflection of my own eyes.

'My-,' he began to say, with eyes wide open, but only a stream of blood left his mouth, and his head dropped.

We fell to the ground, with our swords holding us together.

Epilogue

I felt the softness of her skin on my hand. It was warm, and it made me open my eyes.

She was sitting on the bed, next to me. Seeing her face made my blood flow again. She smiled, and I smiled back.

I tried sitting up, but she wouldn't let me: 'Don't. You need to rest. You're still weak.'

'How long has it been?' I asked.

'Three days.'

'I see,' I said. 'Where am I?'

'In grandpa's old house. Everyone's here.'

'And your father?'

Ren shook her head.

'I see.'

'Here, have some water,' she said, handing me a glass.

'Thanks.'

'Rest up, ok? I'll come back a bit later. I'll bring you some hot soup.'

'Ok,' I said, and I fell back asleep.

***

I woke up again a couple of hours later. I looked to the side, and I saw a small bowl of soup on the nightstand. I got up slowly, but I didn't have an appetite. What I needed was fresh air.

It took me a while to stand up, but I managed. The wound hurt a lot. I pressed my hand against it while I walked to the window.

I was about to open it, but then I saw my own reflection in the glass. My eyes were purple, and they glowed.

I heard the door open behind my back, and in the glass, I saw Kobayashi-san enter the room. He wore his business attire.

'You never carried out those orders from thirty-seven years ago,' I said, looking at his reflection in the window.

'Welcome home, boss Yamaguchi.'

***

THE END

Don't miss out!

Visit the website below and you can sign up to receive emails whenever Ryu Takeshi publishes a new book. There's no charge and no obligation.

https://books2read.com/r/B-A-AOFN-RMDQB

BOOKS2READ

Connecting independent readers to independent writers.

Also by Ryu Takeshi

Shadow Shinjuku
Shadow Shinjuku
Abalone

Watch for more at https://www.ryutakeshi.com.

About the Author

Ryu loves to write. It's a way for him to find and explore new worlds, both inner ones and those way outside. And this process is spontaneous and instinctive, his stories born out of a single image, following a path Ryu himself never fully understands - not its origin, nor its end -, immersed in the magic of the moment, and the magic of everything that sorrounds us, the visible and the invisible. Ryu is a daydreamer, a believer in the magic of humanity, a friend to all the mystical creatures of the night, and a sucker for the visual beauty of anime. But above all else, Ryu is just a human being, like yourself.

Read more at https://www.ryutakeshi.com.

About the Publisher

Purple Crow Press is all about the weird, the magical, the gritty, the emotional, the visual, the beautiful. We publish what we love, and we love what we publish. The world of magical realism is our home, the streets of Tokyo are our own, and we dream of books that can transport us to amazing new worlds, and make us feel the essence of who we all really are.

9 786150 122472